ABOUT

MELISSA SCRIVNER LOVE was born to a police-officer father and a court stenographer mother. After earning a master's degree in English literature from New York University, Melissa moved to Los Angeles, where she has lived for over a decade. She is an Edgar Award–nominated screenwriter who has written for television shows, including *Life*, *CSI: Miami*, and *Person of Interest*. She and her husband welcomed their daughter in 2014. *Lola* is her first novel.

PRAISE FOR *LOLA*

'Stunning....This powerful read is at once an intelligently crafted mystery, a reflection on the cycles of violence and addiction, and a timely mediation on the double standard facing women in authority. Love's writing is artful and evocative, her story's sense of place and culture are strong, and in Lola, love has created a fully fleshed-out and uniquely compelling antihero who commands fear, respect, and adoration in equal measure.'

Publishers Weekly

'...ove fleshes out Lola's character to perfection....A gritty, fast-paced thriller rife with gangland intrigue layered over a moving story of absolution.'

Booklist

'What I loved most of all was Lola, and the way Melissa Love has made her vulnerable and powerful all at once. It's a long time since I've felt so connected to a character's emotions and motivations in a novel.'

Gilly Macmillan,
New York Times-bestselling author of *What She Knew*

'Intense, gritty and breathlessly paced, *Lola* is a thriller that's been elevated by exquisite writing and deep character development...Melissa Scrivner Love's exceptional debut brought me to deep empathy and cracked my heart in all the best ways. I fell hard for Lola in all her fierce and broken beauty, her reckless and necessary hardness, her bottomless capacity for loyalty. Don't miss this ride.'

Joshilyn Jackson,
New York Times-bestselling author of *The Opposite of Everyone*

'A glorious invention, the Latina daughter of Lisbeth Salander and Walter White, on a lifelong tear of revenge after being pimped by her mother for drugs and then living with the double invisibility of her gender and her race.'

Kirkus

'An art book, a lens, a page turner, a provocative examination of the many cities that are one city, Los Angeles, as well as the woman who drives the story, the woman who sees, notices, processes, relentlessly, our Lola. But also as important, Lola's vulnerability, as concrete as her authority. The constant interplay between the two is enthralling. My phone is chock full of screenshots of paragraphs of beautiful, purposeful prose. An unforgettable book about a smart woman, the way her mind works, her heart too.'

Caroline Kepnes,
author of *You*

LO
LA

MELISSA SCRIVNER LOVE

POINT
BLANK

A Point Blank Book

First published in Great Britain and Australia by Point Blank,
an imprint of Oneworld Publications, 2017

ISBN 978-1-78607-086-9
ISBN 978-1-78607-087-6 (eBook)

Printed and bound in Great Britain by Clays Ltd, St Ives plc

Oneworld Publications
10 Bloomsbury Street
London WC1B 3SR
England

For David, Leah, and Clementine

LOLA

ONE

HEAT

Lola stands across the craggy square of backyard she shares with Garcia. He mans the grill, rusted tongs and Corona with lime in hand, making the center of a cluster of men, their biceps bare and beaded with sweat, Crenshaw Six tattoos evident in their standard uniform of wife-beaters and torn cargo pants. If Lola were alone with Garcia, she would take her turn over the smoking meat, too, but as afternoon transforms Huntington Park from light to shadow, Lola stays away from the heat. Her place now is at the center of a cluster of women, their necks craning toward any high-pitched squeak that might be gossip, each one standing with a single hip cocked, as if at any second someone might place a sleeping child there for comfort.

Kim speaks loudest, her voice loose change clinking on delicate glass.

"Chicas gotta be buzzin' around, like we don't know what game they runnin'. I were you, Lola, I'd tell that bitch to stay the fuck away from my man."

Lola's eyes find a younger girl, no more than seventeen, weaving too close to the men, Garcia in particular. Lola can't blame her. The entire neighborhood is aware of Garcia's chosen profession.

In Huntington Park, a ghetto suburb of Los Angeles just east of

South Central, a legit man has two choices: landscaping for off-the-books Westside white cash, or sweating through twelve-hour shifts at a factory in Vernon. The lucky factory bodies get Sara Lee; the unlucky are stuck with the fat-rendering plants, where they operate gleaming metal machines that dissolve flesh and bone to liquid.

Garcia does not make his living either way, because he is not a legit man. He is the leader of the Crenshaw Six. Everyone at this barbecue could recite the corners the gang controls, from the retirement home off Gage and State to the middle-school crossing at Marconi. Despite this knowledge, no one is willing to risk a good rack of ribs and a cold Corona over a few moral scruples. Drugs are an understandable, if not respectable, way to make a living in the ghettos of Los Angeles, and the Crenshaw Six members have their own rules—no selling to kids, no soliciting to old folks unless they're in pain. The gang's code keeps the community appeased, and everyone, those who make their living legally and those who rely on committing felonies to survive, coexists. Everyone likes ribs, Lola had told Garcia when she first brought up the idea of throwing a party.

Garcia didn't want to host this barbecue. He was tired from work, business being good, though neither one of them would ever use that expression for fear of the inevitable fall from success. Their tiny nugget of South Central Los Angeles—or so they consider it, even though they've just missed the eastern border—with its strip mall Laundromats, grease-slicked taquerias, and glass-fronted bail bond offices, is no Wall Street. There are no second chances, no getting back on one's feet. Nobody here has enough time for a comeback. Instead of minimum sentences at white-collar resorts, people here get bullets to the head, either victims of circumstance or mere collateral damage. The success stories are few and far between, and they never last.

Still, Lola had told Garcia they should spend a little of their extra cash, show their neighbors a good time. Like normal people who've had some good fortune—dole out free food and beer, generate some goodwill and community spirit. She had won what never became an argument, Garcia shrugging and saying, "I'll buy the meat."

Now, watching the younger girl scout her man, Lola feels a surge of something she can't name. Someone wants what she, Lola, has. Garcia, aside from a passing glance at tits and ass, ignores the girl. The other men follow suit, sizing her up, approving her, then continuing to talk what Lola assumes is business, although she can't hear over her circle of women, squawking about who's packed on pounds and which neighborhood nail salons overcharge.

Lola nods agreement—she'll never go back to Oasis Nails—then continues to watch the men. Jorge, a round-faced banger in baggy jeans, his ball cap turned backward, texts on one of the Crenshaw Six's jailbroken iPhones. Because the phones don't connect to any mainstream network, Jorge is free to say what he wants. Marcos, a wiry, hardened man with sunken black eyes, sneaks an under-cooked rib from the grill and tears into it with pointy teeth. At his feet, Valentine, the pit bull Lola stole from a fighting ring a year ago, waits for a stray piece of flesh. The dog, Lola's baby girl, is the sole female allowed around the grill. Valentine must have recognized an outsider in Marcos, the only member of the Crenshaw Six to have done time, six years in federal max when he was arrested on his eighteenth birthday. Marcos has been out over three years. Still, he eats when there is food, sleeps when there is a chair, fucks when a girl presents herself, as this girl is doing now. Lola guesses Marcos is eating first because he, like the other men, knows the girl will be there whenever he decides to acknowledge her. The ribs, however, will disappear into hungry neighborhood mouths as soon as Garcia transfers them from grill to platter.

Lola wants to pull the prowling girl aside, tell her if she wants to try to screw one of these bangers, fine, but stalking back and forth like a wannabe ghetto runway model is not the way.

"Girl knows to go after the leader," Kim interrupts, catching Lola staring.

"She's nothing," Lola says.

"He's been got before, is all," Kim says, because before Garcia was Lola's, he belonged to Kim. "Bet if Carlos were here, she'd be after him, too. Women like that, they always want the man in charge."

The women around them freeze, knowing Kim's words are meant to wound Lola, who has dated two gang leaders in quick succession. But all Lola feels is a quick drop of her heart, thinking of Carlos, Kim's older brother, who was the leader of the Crenshaw Six before he was murdered three years ago. Back then Carlos was Lola's man, and Garcia was Kim's. The Crenshaw Six was the Crenshaw Four, with only Carlos, Garcia, Jorge, and Marcos as members. Under Carlos's reign, the gang didn't control any corners, instead relying on sticking up other gangs over shitty coffee tables used to cut coke and heroin. It should have surprised no one that Carlos wound up shot in the face, dumped in the Angeles National Forest along with countless other bodies not expected to be missed.

Kim misses Carlos, though, calling the cops once a month for updates on his as-of-yet unsolved case. Lola feels for Kim. Carlos was charismatic, buoyant, beloved by the neighborhood, Lola included. Yet Kim is the only one who doesn't seem to realize the cops aren't going to do shit to find out who killed some brown ghetto Robin Hood.

"Carlos were here, he'd have burned the meat 'cause he'd be off talking to everyone," Lola says now, diffusing the tension and scattering titters of laughter through the ladies of the neighborhood.

"Or eating my chocolate cake." Kim puffs up, never missing a chance to bring up the one recipe she has that's renowned in their twenty square blocks of Los Angeles.

"You bring some of that today, Kim?" a neighborhood woman asks.

"Damn right I did," Kim says to a resounding chorus of "that's rights" and "shit yeahs." Kim discusses the dessert she brought to the barbecue with the same intensity she used when discussing the girl trolling Garcia. "Not as good as Lola's," Kim adds, as if making the best chocolate cake in the neighborhood is all Lola needs to keep her happy in her little backyard of barrio heaven.

Lola hears awkward murmurs from the other women, each of them split somewhere between protests and agreement. They don't want to insult Kim or Lola, but they know Kim makes a better cake.

"I always use your recipe," Lola says to Kim, smoothing over the moment.

"Oh." Kim blushes, or maybe she's just wearing too much makeup. "Well, you got better things to do, don't you? College and all."

Lola attended two night classes at East Los Angeles Community College before Carlos died. This fact has somehow cemented her as a college girl, despite her dropping out after her former boyfriend's murder, and the term is not necessarily a compliment. Here in Huntington Park, "college girl" means Lola dared to want more. She knows none of these women has a clue what she does all day. Lola doesn't mind. She prefers the periphery, where she can move without notice.

"Must be why you haven't gotten around to pulling the weeds around the flower bed," Kim continues, gesturing with her bloodred press-on nails to a patch of dirt Lola has never bothered to tend.

"That was Carlos's thing," Lola says, because when he was alive, the backyard of this rental house used to burst with sunflowers. Garcia doesn't know how to plant, and Lola doesn't know how to tend, so together they keep the grass clipped and, for the most part, stay on the concrete that borders the back of the house.

"Yeah," Kim agrees. "Garcia got one of those black thumbs, kills every green thing he touches," she explains to the other women, reminding them she once shared a home with Lola's man.

Lola steals another glance at Garcia now, only to find him looking back at her. They smile at each other—a simple, shy smile, even after three years together. She wonders if tragedy would change her feelings toward him. She wonders when they will be tested, if the day will come when they look at each other and think, *Who the fuck is that person I thought I knew?*

"What's up?" Lola hears the unmistakable half grin in the voice of her baby brother, Hector, who has emerged from her kitchen with a can of salt and a bag of limes. Either item could be for the meat or for the beer, but his question is, without a doubt, directed at the ghetto girl.

"Nothing. Hungry," the girl purrs.

The other men give Hector smacking pats on the back and grunts of approval. He is one of them, a fact Lola had to make peace with years ago. Hector has been her baby brother since she was eight years old, and Maria Vasquez ended up queasy and pregnant from one of the nameless men who rotated out of their house every couple of weeks. No one knows Hector's father's identity, which is fine with Lola. He is her brother, even if they don't share a father. Lola knows her own father's first name—Enrique—but since he left two months after her birth, she tells herself she doesn't care enough to remember his last.

Now, Lola feels a glimmer of hope that eighteen-year-old Hector might settle down with someone from the neighborhood, someone close to his age, someone who would keep him near her, Lola. Then Lola sees the look her baby brother shoots at her, wanting to make sure his sister is watching, and she realizes his flirting is all for show. Hector has a girl in the wrong part of town, and he knows Lola doesn't approve of her. In his own way, Hector is trying to console Lola by flirting with this neighborhood skank. The realization both angers and touches Lola.

"Your brother's puttin' on a show," Kim remarks.

Lola is fine with Kim crying over Carlos's flower bed and reminding the neighborhood Lola's man used to fuck her. Kim is not allowed to comment on Lola's baby brother, Lola decides now, her face flushing. She needs an escape.

She spots the Amaros ducking through the chain-link fence, the husband and wife pair moving with bowed heads. They are middle-aged, which here means early forties, with crinkled potato chip skin and eyes sunk too deep in their faces. They are old before their time, people outside South Central would say, but here they just are.

"Gonna say hi to the Amaros," Lola gives her excuse to Kim and the other women.

"Tacos," Juan Amaro says in greeting, and, on cue, his wife,

Juanita, holds up a large foil pan. The Amaros are the only guests to have brought a disposable dish. They own a combination bodega and taco stand, getting all their supplies below cost from a shady distant cousin. Everyone else will have to wait while Lola soaks their respective glass dishes in warm, soapy water and gives them back, streaked with residual cheese scabs from their neighbors' casseroles and potluck enchiladas, but the Amaros can make a quick escape.

Lola reaches for the tacos as she smiles her welcome.

"Chicken, beef, and pork. There wasn't any good fish today," Juanita Amaro says, an apology present in her soft voice.

"Don't need it, with all this," Lola says.

"Told her not to worry about it," Juan mutters, and Juanita bows her head deeper, eyes on her feet. They're only a few miles from the Pacific, but it might as well be a world—all the good stuff goes to the Westside, where celebrity chefs in Venice, Santa Monica, and Malibu pluck the finest from the day's catch.

"I'll take these to the kitchen," Lola says. She sees a shadow at the corner of Juanita Amaro's skirt. Big brown eyes emerge from behind the cotton, and there is the Amaros' granddaughter. Lola has only seen the girl, whose name she can't remember now, once or twice before, perched on a corner stool in her grandparents' bodega, punching numbers into an old dead adding machine.

"Lucy, greet your hostess." Juanita nudges her granddaughter forward, but Lucy clings to the woman's cotton skirt.

Lucy. That's the girl's name. Lucy belongs to the Amaros' junkie daughter, Rosie, who appeared in Huntington Park last month, Lucy in tow, after years in Bakersfield doing God knows what to score her fix.

A sticky sheen that could be sweat or old milk or remnants of today's lunch coats Lucy's cheeks and forehead. Someone has taken the trouble to give the little girl's face a cursory wipe, but the job was so poorly executed it has served only to smear an even layer of the sticky substance over Lucy's cheeks and tiny button nose.

"Hola, Lucy," Lola tries. She doesn't know if Lucy prefers English or Spanish.

Lucy stares up at Lola.

"Lucy, what do you say?" Juanita prods her granddaughter, a weathered hand, bony fingered, tightening on Lucy's shoulder.

Lola doesn't like to see Juanita Amaro's claw sinking into her granddaughter's shoulder, prodding Lucy to give attention or affection, so she throws her head in the direction of the house. "Wanna help me in the kitchen?"

Lucy looks up at her grandmother, unsure of how to answer.

"Yes, she does," Juanita says, her claw of a finger poking Lucy forward, toward Lola.

"Yes," Lucy repeats, too loud, but the noise of the party doesn't stop as the little girl follows Lola, picking her way through trodden grass and weeds sprouting from dry drought dirt, the yard of a family with no landscaper, even though there are plenty who live in the neighborhood.

In the kitchen, more women—older than the ones gathered outside with their vodka cranberries and bloodred press-on nails—bustle. In here, the women are thicker from ass to earring. They speak only Spanish, as if it's some secret code Lola and the younger ones don't understand.

"No, it was his ex-girlfriend's mother's cousin—" Lola catches from one of the women.

"Lottie's girl?"

"No, Lottie was dead by then. You remember her husband? The one with the hammer toe?"

"Ohhhhh. . . ." A chorus of collective remembrance fills the tiny kitchen, where maternal bodies touch hip to hip. Their symphony is composed of deeper voices than that of the younger women outside. In here, it's a cacophony of decades-old cigarettes and fucking and family—followed by the clapping of Lola's rusting oven door as one of the thick women opens it. Something steaming hot and smelling of melted queso emerges, encased in a glass dish Lola recognizes as her own. The women ignore Lola, even though it is her kitchen. They have co-opted it for themselves, with no explanation, and they never asked permission to use either her appliances or her dishes.

Lola knows it is because they believe they know better than her how to use them. They are right.

"Lola," another one coos. Veronica, her mother's oldest friend, approaches with a wet paper towel.

"What's that for?" Lola asks.

"Lipstick," Veronica explains.

"What lipstick?"

Veronica kisses Lola with hot pink lips, then dabs at the stain she's left on Lola's cheek. The women laugh, shrill ringing that fills the room, heating it up more than the open oven alone.

"Veronica," Lola says, soft, but the other women catch the chiding tone in her voice and turn on her. Lola is not supposed to speak this way to Veronica, her elder.

She changes the subject. "Where's Kim's chocolate cake? People're asking for it."

"Kim made the cake?" Veronica asks. "I thought you were going to."

The room is so quiet Lola can hear the drippy faucet Garcia promised to fix. The hippy-ass women all face her, waiting.

"Other stuff to do." Lola shrugs. "But the guys want it."

The room snaps back into motion, ringed and bare fingers wringing, all with a task—find Kim's cake, where is Kim's cake, the men want it. Lola can't hear the words, just the voices, low hums and hems and questions. She weaves through the warm bodies to Lucy, catching the little girl yawning in the stifling oven heat.

"Are you tired?" she asks the little girl.

Lucy tries to stifle a second yawn as she shakes her head. Lola catches the little girl's fleeting glance outside, to the circle of men surrounding the smoldering grill.

Lola thinks of her own junkie mother, of the men she introduced Lola to, of the things Lola had to do for these men at night so that Maria Vasquez could score her own fix. Lola thinks of all the sleep she lost losing her innocence.

Now, Lola lowers herself to Lucy's level and speaks so only the two of them can hear. "Are you scared of the men out there?"

Lucy hesitates, and Lola keeps her distance, not touching the girl, but staying down here with her. After a few seconds, Lucy nods.

"I understand," Lola says. "Would you like a safe place to sleep?" Lucy stares at Lola, licking her lips, wanting to say yes.

"I can show you how to lock the door," Lola says. "You can follow me if you like, or you can stay here. Either way, I won't be upset."

Lola rises, slow, so as not to frighten Lucy. She leaves the kitchen and heads down the narrow hallway where three doors creak open to bedrooms.

The room Lola enters is plain white—white walls, white ceiling fan, buzzing white air conditioner percolating in the window, white bars outside it. Lola doesn't know who it's for—guests? But no one ever comes to stay with her and Garcia. The room belongs in an institution, one where patients need their minds wiped clean. Maybe it is perfect for Lucy, who looks like she didn't sleep last night. Lola wishes it were just Lucy hearing her mother shoot up in the next room keeping the little girl awake, but Lucy's look outside to the men hints at something more sinister.

Lola stops these thoughts. There is no point. She is not Lucy's mother. There is nothing she can do to save this child.

She hears a floorboard creak and turns to find Lucy, staring at the lock on the white door.

"Here," Lola says. "Let me show you."

Lola helps Lucy practice with the lock. "Righty-tighty, lefty-loosey," Lola repeats as Lucy locks to the right, unlocks to the left. She can't remember where she learned the saying, but she likes sharing it with Lucy now. She may not be able to save this child, but she can give Lucy an hour's reprieve in this white room, so that is what she does. She lowers the dusty blinds. Lola turns out the lights, even though outside the sinking sun is still too bright, the shadow-streaked sky still too blue. Lucy needs dull—grays and whites. Lola wishes she had a teddy bear for the little girl to squeeze. If Lucy is dealing with what Lola thinks, though, a locked bedroom door will give her more comfort than any teddy bear.

Lola shuts the bedroom door behind her and waits in the hallway until she hears the padding of little feet, then the click of the lock. The walls are so thin she can hear Lucy sigh as she sinks into clean sheets.

Lola will wait outside the door until the little girl has had enough time to fall asleep. The women's voices in the kitchen dull to a buzz. The changing light outside shifts the shadows in the house. No one will look for her here.

The sharp knock at the front door interrupts Lola's respite. The women's kitchen chatter silences quick as a blaring television switched off.

The only people who knock on front doors in this neighborhood are cops who've exchanged their battering rams for bad news.

From the hallway, Lola can see through the master bedroom's small square of window to the backyard. Garcia is still charring meat, sporting the same smile he wore half an hour ago. No one outside heard the knock. They are still living in a party.

When Lola opens the door, her breath catches in her tiny cavern of a chest. The man standing there is not a cop. He is Mexican, not Mexican American, like everyone else here. He wears a tailored suit and steel-toed boots. Lola searches his face for a bead of sweat but comes up empty. She has never met him, but she knows his name. Everyone in this neighborhood does. They call him El Coleccionista, the Collector.

"Hola," she says, tucking an ankle behind a calf and tilting her chin down, playing dumb. Luckily, Lola spent the first twenty-three years of her life, until she met Garcia, figuring out how to make sure men didn't feel threatened by her. It is a skill that has served her better than any chocolate cake recipe ever will.

"Garcia," El Coleccionista says.

"Out back," Lola responds, planning to dart ahead, pretending a tour of the house, ending with the master bedroom, so she can signal to her man.

But El Coleccionista doesn't wait for an invitation. He steps forward, and Lola steps to the side, losing the game of chicken her guest wasn't playing.

Lola follows him into the kitchen, where the now-silent older women are not so good at playing dumb. They, too, know this man's identity, and they are too stunned to see him here, in the chipping yellow paint and burnt-out fluorescence of Lola's kitchen, to hide that knowledge. Lola hears only the vent over the stove blowing its constant neutral air and the click of Garcia's boss's boots on her linoleum, which is gleaming clean but bent up at the corners.

The man on her heels, his breath so close she can smell his most recent mint, once led the cartel crew that invaded a small Mexican town, taking out dozens of civilians in under twenty minutes—doctors, lawyers, cops, housewives, children, criminals—all because one citizen was harboring a witness against the Los Liones cartel. That guy, the witness, El Coleccionista spared, only to draw and quarter him with four Honda Civics the next day. Even that small car could tear a man limb from limb in less time than it took the cartel to mow down dozens of the would-be witness's innocent neighbors. But El Coleccionista made sure his death took over half an hour, and he recorded the man's screams.

El Coleccionista gave a copy of the death to Garcia the day they started working together—a preemptive warning. The Crenshaw Six were allowed to work their six corners in Huntington Park with cartel shit, and the cartel would even throw in a few extra corners for good measure, but the Crenshaw Six better cut them in on the profits. And they better not fuck it up.

Lola needs to warn Garcia. El Coleccionista's boots move in a calm one, two rhythm across her kitchen floor. Lola takes off, ducking between padded female bodies that reek of perfume and grease, taking the long way outside, through the laundry room, where Garcia's boxers thunk and click in the dryer. She rounds the house, breathless, and Garcia sees her face. *He's here,* she mouths, and Garcia is the only one who sees her.

Everyone else has turned to watch El Coleccionista taking the cement steps down from the kitchen door, never breaking the rhythm of his stride. One, two, one, two.

The entire yard quiets, the neighborhood stills. Somewhere in the distance, a bird tweets, and then the neighbor from two streets over starts his shitty car to a booming backfire. No one jumps. They are all staring at El Coleccionista. Everyone has only seen his picture, or they know him from his clothes. No one here dresses like that.

"Garcia," El Coleccionista says. Lola can't be sure if he has an accent, since this is the only word she's heard him say.

Garcia hands his beer to Lola, who has migrated to the spot behind his right shoulder. It's her place. An automatic safe zone. The beer is sweating—Garcia wasn't drinking it. He doesn't drink much, and beer has never been his choice. He has only been pretending at playing house this whole time. So has she.

She hopes Garcia's boss isn't here to kill them all. Still, Lola doesn't feel fear. This Mexican thug wants the little lady scared, and she plays it that way. She holds Garcia's beer and makes sure not to look directly at his boss. But she knows his secret—El Coleccionista is middle management.

She wishes only that Los Liones had sent someone higher up. El Coleccionista doles out messages and punishments. He doesn't call the shots.

"Inside," El Coleccionista says. Slight accent. Lola has no accent in English or Spanish. The thought comforts her as Garcia follows the man into the house. She can hear the scatter of thick older women on her aging linoleum, then they all break into the backyard, hands still wringing, hens running out of a fox-invaded coop.

After Carlos's murder three years ago, the Crenshaw Six transitioned from stickup crew with no turf to call their own to bona fide gang with six corners no one else would touch because of their proximity to schools and police stations and nursing homes. The cartel has probably always supplied the product the Crenshaw Six peddles, but until recently, the gang was too low in the pecking order to know more than the identity of their loser tweaker of a middleman, Benny, who carried an empty pistol and an eye twitch everywhere he went.

Then, two months ago, El Coleccionista sought out Garcia, the small-time South Central dealer, because the LAPD had seized one of Darrel King's warehouses. The cartel wanted to keep product flowing to its dedicated customers, and they couldn't do that when Darrel, their largest dealer, was out of commission. Would Garcia be willing to do his part and take on a few more corners to keep his neighborhood flush with quality smack?

It was the break the Crenshaw Six needed. Perhaps El Coleccionista has stopped in this evening to give Garcia a friendly employee evaluation. Lola knows that isn't it, though. Garcia has stuck to the cartel's terms, allowing Crenshaw Six soldiers to sell the cartel's product only on the additional corners Los Liones gave them. Even with the added turf, the Crenshaw Six controls only a molecular sliver of Los Liones's middleman Darrel's fifty-one point zero eight square miles of South Central pie. Garcia has followed the Crenshaw Six's own principles, including never selling to kids, as well as the cartel's only declaration—turn a profit. He hasn't tried for a power grab. He has worked hard and humble, and the thought makes Lola swell with what she imagines is pride.

As the guests cluck and spit and swig more alcohol, faces paling, voices silent, Lola is sure she knows why El Coleccionista is here.

TWO

BREAK

Lola hears the rumble of men's voices on the other side of the flimsy wooden door. Their words run together, but she can pick out certain fragments from El Coleccionista. He emphasizes the last word of each sentence.

"Warehouse . . . emptied . . . heat. . . ."

Lola finds her hand turning the fake gold doorknob before she thinks to stop herself. For once, she, the woman, is not supposed to be in the laundry room.

She finds the men leaning against her appliances, El Coleccionista closest to her, his arms crossed, his hip touching her ancient mustard yellow Maytag. Garcia stands straighter against the mismatched bright white dryer. Lola recognizes her man's attempt to show respect. Or maybe she caught him surprised to see her. Her boldness has surprised her, too, and the saying about curiosity killing the cat flits through her mind. Her need to know what the men are discussing isn't mere curiosity, though.

"Can I get you anything? Coffee? Cake?" Lola asks.

"Coffee," El Coleccionista says without looking at her.

Good. She has a way back in the room, where she can blend with the peeling floral wallpaper and absorb the reason behind El Coleccionista's visit to her home.

When she returns with a steaming mug and some almond cookies one of the older gossips left on a tray in Lola's kitchen, El Coleccionista is still talking.

"Darrel King emptied his warehouse before the police raided it. Unfortunately, he can no longer move our product. There's too much heat there. That's why we sought you out in the first place."

"And the Crenshaw Six is grateful for the opportunity," Garcia says.

El Coleccionista gives an impatient nod and sucks the coffee Lola brought him through his teeth. His subsequent gulp and lip smack turns Lola's stomach. She sneaks one of the almond cookies from the plate she brought, but the action draws Garcia's boss's attention.

"May I have one of those cookies?"

He knows the answer. Lola holds out the plate to him, not stepping any closer. He likes her for her timidity, and after he chomps the cookie in a single bite, he takes two more. The sugar must make him forget Lola's presence, because his next statement is a cartel secret.

"Problem is, Darrel went and found himself another supplier."

"Shit," says Garcia, and Lola feels a wave of disappointment that she can only think the word her man is allowed to speak aloud. "Who?"

"We don't know. Whoever he is, he's evaded our tails so far."

"You been following Darrel?"

"We follow all our people."

The implication that Los Liones has been following the Crenshaw Six sends a ripple of excitement through Lola. They are important enough to distrust.

"That's how we know Darrel has set a time and place for the first drop with this new supplier. It's scheduled for tomorrow night at midnight. There will be two million in product, a corresponding two million in cash."

"Where?"

"Venice." El Coleccionista holds out a hand, and Lola realizes he is ordering her to get him a pen.

She finds herself scurrying to the junk drawer and makes a deliberate point to slow herself. Middle management, she repeats in her head, middle management. If El Coleccionista's boss, rumored to be a fat man eternally clothed in a linen suit, were propping himself against her Maytag, the hurry would be justified.

Lola digs in the junk drawer to the left of the washer and hands a ballpoint and scrap of paper from a local appliance store—RINCON BROTHERS—WE DON'T OVERCHARGE—to El Coleccionista. He scribbles an address and hands it to Garcia.

"Three-way intersection, part residential, part commercial."

"You're giving me a lot of information about this drop," Garcia says, a question in his tone.

Lola finds herself in an awkward position, poised by the junk drawer, squeezed between El Coleccionista and the door. She wonders why the fuck Garcia's boss doesn't tell her to get the fuck out. He has a pen and paper, some cookies, and coffee. What else can she do for him? The answer stings—to this man, Lola is not important enough to send away.

"We want your . . . organization to make sure Darrel King never gets his product . . . and that his new supplier never gets his money."

Funny, Lola thinks, the assumption on the cartel's part that Darrel's new supplier is a man.

"That it?" Garcia asks, and Lola is sure El Coleccionista can see her man is trying to play it cool.

"We would like you to use whatever means at your disposal to uncover the identity of Mr. King's new supplier."

"Like?"

"Couriers." El Coleccionista holds out a hand again, and Lola is unsure what he wants until he points a hairy finger at the plate of cookies. When Lola holds it out, he takes three more cookies and puts them all in his mouth at once, grabbing another even as he chews.

"You want us to . . . get information from the couriers."

"Using whatever means necessary."

Torture. Maim. Kill. Lola thinks of human bodies sliced and bleeding, of meat torn from bone, of screams and the smell of flesh turning from fresh to rancid. Even under Carlos, the Crenshaw Six, or Four, depending on the month, didn't have the need to take many lives. At most, they doled out a few good beatings, taking teeth, driving up dental bills for bangers with no insurance. Still, she knows this is their break, and she knows what Garcia's answer will be.

"Sure," he says, too casual, and she wants to tell him El Coleccionista would thrive on seeing the weight this assignment has placed on Garcia's shoulders.

"Do you have any questions?"

Ask him why, she thinks, *ask him why the cartel won't do it themselves.* They've certainly got the men and the firepower. She thinks again of the town in Mexico El Coleccionista helped destroy. But that was Mexico.

"Why the Crenshaw Six?"

Okay, Lola thinks, *not exactly, but still good.*

"We can't disrupt this drop ourselves. To do so would risk exposure. The Los Angeles Police are putting pressure on Darrel King in order to get to me . . . to my boss," El Coleccionista corrects, and Lola catches the middle management man's eyes darting around her laundry room, as if the cartel leader whose identity no one seems to know is watching.

"We will help," Garcia says. The man's evasion of Garcia's question puts Lola on edge. Why did the cartel approach the Crenshaw Six? They have gangs operating in every incorporated city of Los Angeles, the Westside and Venice included.

Of course Lola knows why. The Crenshaw Six are disposable to the cartel. They control a minimal number of cartel corners. This assignment, disrupting a drop between a midlevel but heavily armed and guarded trafficker like Darrel King and a supplier with access to two million in what Lola guesses is heroin, is a potential shit show. But if the Crenshaw Six can pull it off, they will have proven themselves to the cartel.

"You will be wondering about compensation." El Coleccionista sighs, as if he himself floats above the material needs of man. "If you succeed, you will receive ten percent of the product and cash recovered, as well as control of Darrel King's territory."

Lola's heart catches in her chest like it did the first time she saw Carlos, leaning against a locker at Huntington Park High School, when she was fourteen years old. Holy fuck.

"Of course, you could fail," El Coleccionista says. "And if you do . . ." The man finally shoots a quick look at Lola before taking a sip of coffee. A slurp, and he continues, "We will take her, we will open up her stomach, and we will pull out her guts until she dies."

Garcia gulps the threat like air, his face reddening with visible fear, but all Lola can think is 10 percent of four million and all of Darrel King's territory. She recognizes this rare feeling—it is not fear, but ecstasy.

Los Liones has given the Crenshaw Six the break it needs. Garcia's fledgling empire will continue to spread into other neighborhoods, and one day no one will remember Darrel King's name.

If the people of Huntington Park had their way, no one would remember Los Liones, either. But for now, the cartel is a necessary evil, the medicine the people here must swallow to keep their drug fiefdoms up and running. Here, if you want to graduate to middle class, the only career choice to make is which side you're going to sell for, and the drug trade looks a lot like any other service industry—hooking customers, building up a client base, and turning a profit, paying your debts, making a life for your family that's better than the bullshit God served you.

Lola can see the citizens of her neighborhood between the streaks of her laundry room window. El Coleccionista's request for a meeting has frozen the barbecue into an anxious tableau. Smoke rises from a charcoal lump of burnt meat the men have neglected. The bulky women from the kitchen stand hip to hip near the back door, arms crossed over ample bellies. Nearby, the younger women cluster in a circle, their heads touching. Lola wonders if Kim is imparting what she thinks are the meeting's minutes before any of the participants have emerged. Kim could do this—tell everyone with a frightening degree of certainty what was occurring in Lola's laundry room, despite not being invited to the meeting. Then Lola remembers she wasn't invited to this meeting either.

But I am here, Lola thinks. *I wasn't invited, but I am here. And if we fuck this up, I am the price. We have to do this. For us. For them.*

Lola feels an outpouring of love for these people, her neighbors, but she is not them. She and Garcia have a good two hundred grand in cash they can't clean, but even if they could, they wouldn't advertise their good fortune. Lola would keep her cracked linoleum and her ancient appliances. In the drug business, the only way to stay safe is for no one to know you're someone.

Still, the cartel has offered a break to Garcia, and he must take it. To the neighborhood, it will look like Lola's getting more by virtue of who she's fucking.

For women, isn't that always the way?

THREE

STAKE

Lola cracks open a bag of generic cheese curls, resting her Pumas on the Honda's dashboard. It is near noon on Sunday, the day after the barbecue, and the sun over West Adams glows bright and hot on her skin.

Outside, black children race across vast front lawns. Unlike Huntington Park, in this neighborhood there is no need for kids to play in a fire hydrant's spray. Sprinklers pump back and forth, cooling skin, and mothers call their babies in for hot lunches. The houses are three stories with long, wide porches and rounded towers that remind Lola of storybook castles.

"What they call them things?" Garcia asks Lola, pointing to the second story of the house across the street. He sits behind the wheel, his seat cranked back. His fingers fiddle with the cap of an unopened soda, as if he's not sure he should drink it. Like Lola, he doesn't know how to behave on a stakeout, because this is their first.

"The castle things?"

"Yeah."

"Expensive," Lola says, and Garcia laughs.

Darrel King's house is a sprawling gingerbread complex with a wraparound porch. Pink and green foliage threads the latticework that runs up what Lola decides to call the castle towers, one on each side.

"Don't think the new supplier's gonna show up here." Garcia sighs.

"Course not," Lola says. "But you gotta know your enemy."

"Hard to know him when he hasn't shown yet."

Garcia's shoulders sink in the passenger's seat. They've been here for over an hour, not realizing that Darrel would be gone so early on a Sunday morning. There are no cars in the driveway, and the detached garage, its roll-up door wide open, is empty.

"We know he's got lookouts," Lola says, jutting her chin toward the corner, where a lanky teenage boy in tan boots kicks at the curb.

"One kid," Garcia says.

"You didn't look behind us," Lola says, indicating the rearview, where three more teenage boys have dragged a rickety basketball hoop into the street.

"They're watching us."

"Doubt it. No one's come to scare us off. Don't know why Darrel King bothers having lookouts if they're not looking. You hungry?" She holds out the bag of cheese curls.

"Nah," Garcia says. "Just . . ."

"What?"

"You called Darrel the enemy."

"Yeah?"

"Fucking strange. Just yesterday, I was runnin' a few corners. Now . . ."

"Crenshaw Six is in the same league as Darrel."

"Not yet. Not till tonight," Garcia says. He is still feeling fear instead of honor at the cartel's assignment. She resents him for this luxury. The cartel has recognized him as a diligent soldier. They couldn't even be bothered to throw Lola out of the meeting.

Lola had tried to make Garcia forget his concerns last night. She'd been out of her clothes and on top of him as soon as El Coleccionista's coffee cup was upside down on the drying rack. She'd pushed her man onto the linoleum, sticky with cleaning suds and smelling of lemon and pine, and straddled his thighs with her own as she took him in her hands and guided him inside her. He had closed his eyes, but she kept hers open so she could see the pleasure she gave him. The feeling of her pushing down on him satisfied her, but more than anything, she found herself craving the power of grinding on top of him until he cried out, a fierce, deep growl at once masculine and vulnerable.

It was only after, lying next to him on the hard floor in a sweaty clean lemon haze, that she was thankful she knew how to pretend affection when she felt resentment. She hadn't had this skill the first time her mother sent a man to her little girl's bedroom. The ability to pretend came a couple of years later, after Maria Vasquez had pimped Lola out to so many men she was numb, and then, somewhere after the apathy, Lola realized she'd gotten good at what she considered her job—sex. Through it all, Lola had tried to convince herself a man could force pain on her without causing permanent damage. Then, fourteen-year-old Lola met eighteen-year-old Carlos, and he took her out of her mother's house and made sex a pleasure.

"Chocolate cake was good," Garcia had murmured then, breaking Lola's late-night reverie. Lola could see he was half asleep but felt the need to pay Lola a compliment that wasn't "thanks for the sex."

"Kim made it," Lola had said without anger, thinking Kim could stay in her kitchen with her recipes and her cake and her jealousy.

Garcia had tasted what Kim could offer. He had even knocked her up. Three years before, around the time of Carlos's murder, Kim was elbow-deep in hand-me-down onesies and burp cloths, used gifts from well-meaning neighbors, when Garcia was driving her to the doctor and crashed into a semi. He blew a red light, killing the unborn baby they'd made together. They hadn't been able to survive that.

Now, in the shadow of Darrel King's gingerbread house, there is no time to wonder if she and Garcia would survive the same tragedy. A black Escalade purrs up the street. In the rearview, Lola sees the bouncing basketball abandoned. By the time the Escalade pulls into Darrel's driveway, the three players are boys on three separate corners, keeping watch. Even Garcia sits up straighter, now that Darrel King is home. Lola keeps her kicks on the dashboard, her fingers wrapping around a handful of cheese curls and crushing them to powder.

Her first glimpse of Darrel is muscles bulging beneath a white collared shirt. His suit is gray, tailored, his tie a regal purple that pops against the starched white of the shirt. He walks around the back of the Escalade with a smile on his face, and when he opens the passenger door, an older black woman in a hat and floral print dress that reminds Lola of her own duvet cover takes his hand to descend.

Darrel King missed the first part of their stakeout because he took his mother to church.

Lola feels a pang of guilt. Their business has intruded on family time, and, although Lola has only set foot inside churches for weddings and funerals, she can appreciate the souls who are innocent enough to believe in a higher power.

Darrel's mother gestures to the corner boys, all four standing at attention, and when Darrel shoots them a look, they act as casual as they were before his arrival—slumped shoulders, the offhand toss of an orange ball into a dingy street hoop net.

Of course, Lola thinks, Darrel can't have more foreboding and efficient lookouts because his mother doesn't know her son is a drug lord.

Before Darrel can get his mother inside, the screen door opens and a tall, statuesque white woman in a white T-shirt and faded jeans emerges. A ropy black braid falls to her waist, and, from her creamy-looking skin, Lola puts her age at no more than twenty-five. She holds two glasses of iced tea, but when Darrel reaches for one, she withdraws it. She says something Lola can't hear, and Darrel laughs. He gives her a church polite kiss and disappears into the house before Lola remembers her camera phone. She scrambles for it, realizing too late that her fingers are coated in the orange yellow powder of pulverized cheese curls.

If Garcia notices her failure to get a single photo of their new enemy, he doesn't say anything.

Darrel's girlfriend holds out a glass of iced tea to the black woman, and the two settle into wicker rocking chairs that begin to move in harmony as they chat. Lola wants to hear what they're saying, but even with the Honda's windows down and the engine off, the breeze, the sprinklers, and the joyous shouts of children drown out any hope of surveillance.

Still, Lola snaps a photo, and she takes her eyes off the live scene to focus on the image she's captured of two women, one old, one young, one black, one white, one a mother, one a daughter, spending a slow Sunday afternoon on the porch like the world's standing still.

Garcia clears his throat, and when Lola looks up, she sees his head cocked toward the Escalade, the plates, the only valuable intel this stakeout has offered. She snaps a quick photo of the numbers and letters by which the California DMV knows Darrel King.

"Who's the girl?" Garcia asks.

"Must be Darrel's girlfriend." Lola shrugs, her eyes going back to the picture instead of to the porch, preferring the frozen image to the two living breathing women across the street. "And she gets along with his mother. Shit must be serious."

"That what makes something serious?" Garcia asks.

Lola shrugs again, because she likes that Garcia often picks fights with her mother and avoids her company—not that this makes any impact on Maria Vasquez, who has never seemed to realize that no one in her family likes her. It is this fact that drives Lola crazier than anything her mother has done in the long trail of fuckups she calls a life.

"I'm hungry," she says, which is true. She also feels a burning to get the fuck out of this nice, historic place with its castle houses and well-fed children.

Garcia starts the car and pulls away from the curb, but Lola's sharp breath causes him to slam on the brakes.

"What?" he asks, but Lola can't answer.

Garcia doesn't know the girl on the corner, ignoring Darrel's lookout as she waits to cross. Lola has only seen her once, but still, she recognizes the glasses, the long hair scraped back in a sharp ponytail, and the slender frame underneath a loose cotton skirt. Even on a Sunday, this girl, Amani, carries books in her tiny arms, her skin a shade darker than Hector's or Lola's. Amani belongs here.

"What?" Garcia presses, his adrenaline up because Lola doesn't scare easy.

"Nothing," Lola says, then, quick, "No one."

She hopes the revision is true.

FOUR

BROTHER

The abandoned house reeks of mildew and wet dog. Lola, skinny arms crossed over her flat chest, stands in the corner of the second-floor bedroom that faces the intersection of California and Electric. Lola hadn't known there was a real Electric Avenue until she read El Coleccionista's scrawl identifying the intersection below her now.

She found the house earlier this afternoon, after their visit to Darrel King's neighborhood. She had pulled up a map of the Oakwood section of Venice online, clicking until she could see the designated location for the drop, a parking lot backing up to a residential neighborhood. It had taken her only a few clicks through the Venice real estate pages to land on this foreclosed home, an abandoned gem with vantage points of the two streets—California and Electric—that run perpendicular to each other, converging in a "T" in the northeast corner of the parking lot El Coleccionista had identified as the drop's location. From this house, Lola promised Garcia, they would be able to see anyone entering or exiting the parking lot.

Now, Lola peers through the lookout house's window to the actual parking lot across the street. It borders the back of a storybook brick building that houses several stores. She can't see the entrances to the stores from here, because they face Abbott Kinney, one street west. Instead, Lola faces the concrete and Dumpsters and back entrances that border the rear parking lot. She can tell from the sign that rises above the building that it houses a spray tan salon, a pet store, and a doughnut shop. The latter must have pissed off the strip mall landlord, because the last three letters of its flickering neon sign have burned to dark. From here, it looks like the shop offers only dough.

Lola glances down at her feet, her black-and-white Pumas now atop a wood floor cresting and falling, a wave frozen with water damage. A bare bulb sizzles above her, casting the soldiers of the Crenshaw Six in meager light and ample shadow. Lola watches the men load their automatics and talk shit.

Garcia is quiet, meticulous with his weapon—checking the clip, the safety, but Lola's eyes land on his muscles, stretched to bursting under his brown skin. He stands tall, shouldering his automatic in front of a splintered glass background. By the time the Crenshaw Six arrived here, neighborhood thugs, possibly bangers, had long since pilfered the house, shattering windows with small stones and gutting walls for copper wiring. Everyone has to watch their feet to keep from stepping on glass shards.

Lola wonders if the previous visitors belonged to the Venice 13, whose soldiers, she learned today, have worked this neighborhood at the behest of the Mexican Mafia for decades, or the Venice Shoreline Crips, the black gang whose existence sparked a war between the Mexican and black gangs throughout Los Angeles. She has done her research, she thinks now, feeling proud of herself for posing these questions. She wonders if she will even catch a glimpse of any of these foreign bangers tonight, although she doubts they roam the streets of Venice, an upper-middle-class bohemian refuge near the sea. If you have money and are willing to have your house or car broken into every couple of years, Venice seems to be the place to live. Here, moneyed families plan trips to the mega Whole Foods in their multimillion-dollar digs while gangs peddle powder on the next block. Venice is the high and the low, coexisting in relative peace.

"I told her, look, yo, I dig you, but I'm a young man. Field calls."

Jorge's voice interrupts Lola's thoughts, but she knows he's all talk. His girlfriend, a curvaceous Mexican Lola would call fat if she were being honest, has given Jorge a shiner for fucking around before, a prune of a bruise that framed his left eye. Jorge told the guys he took a beating from a neighboring gang, but Lola knew the truth. Yolanda, his fiery fat Mexican, wasn't willing to put up with his shit. Lola didn't blame her. Unlike most neighborhood men, Jorge, who, like Garcia and Marcos, is twenty-eight, doesn't have an excuse—abusive parent, skeevy uncle, drugs, no money, no food—for fucking up or fucking around. He comes from a blue-collar family, his father a mechanic, his mother a secretary at a dentist's office. Jorge earned straight As at Huntington Park High School his freshman year. Then, like Lola, he met Carlos at the confused age of fourteen. Like Lola, he started off worshipping Carlos. Unlike Lola, Jorge never grew into questioning Carlos's leadership choices. He never became a threat to Carlos. Lola was a different story. Jorge knew, and still does, how to diffuse tension with humor. He is, and always has been, the Crenshaw Six jester. Lola can't imagine the Crenshaw Six without him. It is his home now, even if that isn't the way the world is supposed to work.

"Field don't gotta cuddle after I tap that shit," Jorge says now, and the gang erupts in laughter. Even Marcos, with his prison-hardened black beady eyes, cracks a smile as he jams a magazine into the chamber of his weapon. Marcos had a stepfather who left him bruised and battered and bleeding when he was a child. Marcos has every excuse to be here, prepping a weapon he's not afraid to use on the second floor of a foreclosed house.

"I feel you." The voice that strains to be heard over the ruckus causes Lola's heart to leap, because it belongs to Hector. What does her eighteen-year-old brother know about the field? But of course Lola knows he knows plenty.

Lola is the only person who knows her baby brother lost his virginity at sixteen. She caught him, in between sheets roughened with months-old boy sweat and body hair, with Amani, the girl Lola saw earlier today in Darrel King's neighborhood. Lola had warned Hector only once—Amani lives in the wrong neighborhood and has the wrong skin color. Amani's older brother runs with Darrel King's guys. Their relationship couldn't be. Lola made Hector break it off before anyone else in the Crenshaw Six found out. It's like Romeo and Juliet, except for Hector and Amani, suicide is the best-case scenario. Not everyone is lucky enough to pick the where, when, and how of their death.

Lola hasn't told Hector she saw who she hopes is his former girl today. Only bad things could come of reminding him the girl is still living and breathing and reading. It would be better if Hector fell hard for a bad news brown girl, someone with a kid to support and a back-of-a-truck couture habit that would make Hector feel both necessary and tortured. The ghetto train wreck in Lola's imagination would get Amani off his mind. Then she remembers Hector's show at the barbecue yesterday, his flirting with the prowling skank for Lola's benefit, and his subsequent disappearance while Lola listened and Garcia talked with El Coleccionista. He had given some excuse to Veronica—Maria needed something plunged or wired or patched. Now, Lola wonders if Hector left the barbecue early to see Amani.

Either reason for his departure makes Lola unhappy. She doesn't like Hector spending time with Maria, because she still remembers an afternoon eleven years ago, when she was fifteen, Hector seven. She had pushed open the thin wood of their front door and smelled cooking, but she couldn't detect the residual fried meat scent of the empanadas her mother made when she was fresh out of one of her many rehab stints and vowing to make sure her little ones didn't starve. Instead, the house smelled of burning and chemicals, and when Lola stepped into the shoebox living room with its stained shag carpet and rickety television stand, she had seen Hector sitting with their mother on the floor. He was mimicking the way Maria Vasquez sat, her calves curled under her, bare toes touching hip bones.

Maria had stretched a square of generic tinfoil on the coffee table, and Lola understood that her mother was trying to teach her seven-year-old son to cook. Lola understood how a spoon could serve as a tiny pot and how a lighter could be a stove. What she didn't understand was how a white powder finer than sand and packed in a freezer bag no bigger than a special edition postage stamp could satisfy any kind of hunger.

But the part that made the least sense to Lola was that her mother was offering to share her heroin.

Lola had grabbed Hector by the arm and shouldered him, whimpering, into the kitchen to run times tables while she chopped peppers and fried meat for dinner. Maria had appeared in the doorway only once, and a single look from Lola sent their mother scattering for her coat and all the loose change the sofa cushions could yield. Maria had disappeared for three weeks after that, and Hector had gotten his first *A* in math.

When Maria showed her face again, Lola packed up her baby brother and marched to Carlos's house, the same house she shares with Garcia now, and made a deal with her boyfriend: *Keep us, I'll keep you and your house, but Hector is off-limits for your gang.* The arrangement worked for years, until it didn't.

Now, Hector catches Lola watching him, and she feels like she has intruded on what should have been a private bonding moment with him and the guys. Is this what it feels like to be a mother, when your last child is no longer a child?

She has to stop her thoughts. It is almost midnight, the hour designated for the drop between Darrel and his new supplier.

It is time for her to go to work.

FIVE

GOD LAUGHS

Lola takes the creaking wooden steps of the foreclosed house two at a time, ignoring the danger of a leg plunging through rotted wood. She weighs ninety-eight pounds with jeans, sneakers, and wet hair. Most of the world doesn't notice her, and she likes that no one can see her coming.

Lola feels her muscles cry out as she heaves open the front door, a monstrous splinter that was once painted the same orange red as paprika, just widely enough to squeeze through. She's guessing artists owned the house, artists who had money . . . until they didn't.

Out in the street, the ocean breeze hits her. When water sits in the streets of South Central after a pounding rain, Lola smells human filth, wasted cooking, and the metallic tinge of blood. Here, on the Westside, the salt water carries hints of escape and hope. She could plunge in with her clothes still on and wash away her roots, let the sea carry her where it wants. Here, for a few seconds, Los Angeles is quiet. Lola closes her eyes, the air still around her. She wonders if she's imagining it, or if she hears salt water foaming on the beach four blocks away. Her fingers and toes tingle, remembering the packed damp of wet sand squishing between them. Maria took her children to the beach only once, making them peanut butter and jelly on tortillas for lunch, not knowing neither of her children could stomach grape jelly. The experience proved what a twelve-year-old Lola already knew—she was not equipped for any world but her own. Even Venice, twenty miles west of Huntington Park, disorients her.

Lola takes in the neighborhood houses—white-trimmed bunga-lows, sprawling modern monstrosities, butter-cream cottages with fluorescent peace murals splashed across the sides. She knows from the real estate website she looked at this afternoon that each of these places is worth a good two million. She knows the identities of each of the residents, from the television producer and his fund-raising housewife who live in the modern monstrosity, to the female entertainment lawyer who works while her unemployed husband takes care of their three kids. Lola hadn't known until this afternoon how Google could eat up hours, creating an appetite for learning hard facts about people and places. She learned that the Oakwood section of Venice earned the nickname "Ghost Town" for reasons no one seemed to understand. She learned about the decades-old gang war between the Venice 13 and the Shoreline Crips. She had told herself she was casing the neighborhood, but in the process she was wondering what it meant to inhabit a two-million-dollar house by the sea, to work while your man stayed home, to shoulder the burden of an upper-middle-class lifestyle you had to strive to keep.

Now, she looks at the entertainment lawyer's family's white-trimmed bungalow. It is directly across California from the fore-closed house. Lola sees the swing set and the doghouse in the front yard. A dog could be a problem. Lola would never shoot a dog, and Garcia knows better than to let any of the men try it.

Lola finds a spot to keep watch behind a scraggly bush in front of the foreclosed house. It is summer, and the sky doesn't turn true black until what her mother used to call the witching hour. She can see clear down all three streets that lead to the burned-out dough sign—Electric, which runs north to south on the western side of the foreclosed house, Sixth, which runs north to south on the east-ern side of the foreclosed house, and California, which runs east to west in front of the foreclosed house. The brick building's rear parking lot and its glaring dough sign are on the southwest corner of California and Electric.

Lola's eyes sweep the block for buffed Escalades or tricked-out Benzes, drug vehicles of choice. Nothing. The Crenshaw Six would never use a flashy vehicle for a drop. Any unwanted attention, down to a casual compliment from a passerby, is not worth the potential loss of cash, powder, and freedom. It is better to have a dependable car no one will remember. Perhaps Darrel King and his unknown supplier follow that rule, too. Lola does a second sweep for nondescript cars with a living, breathing human inside. Nothing. The dealers' vehicles are probably a couple blocks away from Ground Zero. The Crenshaw Six's own transport, a used minivan Jorge borrowed from his mechanic father's shop, is a block and a half over. Lola had particularly appreciated the "Baby on Board" sticker stuck to the rear window. That shit always makes people, cops included, think twice before getting too close.

Lola looks across the street to the doughnut shop's rear entrance. At this hour, it must be closed. There are no cars in the parking lot, where a lone streetlight casts a cylinder of fluorescence onto the blacktop. Lola watches for the couriers to appear with their token dog crates or gym bags from Electric or California. She has seen hundreds of drug deals, mostly small fish palming bindles and cash on South Central corners, but she's never crashed a drop worth this much before tonight.

Lola makes sure to stay quiet and small out here. No sudden noises or movements. She is wallpaper, sticky and flat and clinging to any surface that will have her. She is the lookout, not the hero. The plan is for two bodies to drop by the end of the night, and Lola wants to make sure she isn't one of them.

The Crenshaw Six's plan to intercept the cash and its corresponding value in heroin makes only two assumptions. The first, that there will be two couriers, one representing Darrel King with the cash, the other representing his new and as-of-yet unknown supplier, whom the Crenshaw Six has deemed "Mr. X," with the heroin. Jorge will accost Darrel King's courier when he or she is approaching the drop site and take him or her hostage first. Jorge will then hand this courier's cash off to Hector, who is young and believable as a lowly courier. Hector will walk the cash to the appointed site of the drop, the parking lot, where he will pretend to be Darrel's courier. He will meet Darrel's unknown supplier's courier, get the heroin, and take him or her hostage.

Lola suspects her theory that the dealers are several blocks away in their Benzes and Escalades is true. The same can be said of any backup. She's certain even an aggressive supplier like Mr. X would think twice before sending his soldiers in to shoot up an area where four million in cash and powder are at stake. No one wants the police swooping in and scattering minority bodies, pocketing powder and marveling at the bulk of two million in cash.

But the Crenshaw Six has a contingency plan, in case Darrel's new supplier is a cowboy. Lola found them the only empty house on the block. Marcos will stay on the second floor, weapon at the ready to shoot any unexpected gang guests. From that vantage point, one Darrel and his new supplier won't have, he can pick off any backup bangers on the ground before the sound of the shot rings in their ears.

Lola's place is in the bushes, watching for these uninvited thugs, aggressive police, or any random pedestrians out walking dogs. The Crenshaw Six is against collateral damage, because white Westside lives bring attention from authorities that would have otherwise ignored the stray bullets and spilled blood. If nothing goes wrong and they live through the drop itself, Garcia, whom the enemy can't be allowed to see because they will identify him as the Crenshaw Six's leader, will be waiting behind the wheel of the minivan. He will whisk them and their two courier hostages back to South Central, where the "questioning" as to Mr. X's identity will begin.

The second, and larger, assumption the Crenshaw Six has made is that nothing will go wrong.

Now, Lola hears the clicking, one-two, one-two, one-two. She recognizes the sound—spaghetti skinny stilettos on concrete—but the first click is quieter, the second louder, echoing off the beach bungalows and modern monstrosities that line the narrow night street. Whoever's walking in those shoes has never worn them before. Lola knows the girl who appears heading north on Electric will be limping, and when the girl does, ten clicks later, she is.

Lola takes her in, a tiny shadow skittering through the ghastly light of a lone streetlamp. The girl slows in the darkness, maybe because she doesn't feel the need to hide. Or maybe she needs more time to pick her way through the cracks and crevices that might snare her and her too-high heels. She wears her dirty blond hair scraped back in a messy ponytail. Her skirt, leather, doesn't cover her knobby knees, and the black wife-beater on top hangs loose on her frame. Her arms are stringy, her tiny lumps of biceps fighting tight, young skin. Lola sees she's carrying a black gym bag.

The courier staggers under her burden. Whatever's in there, white powder or green paper, knocks her off balance with each step.

Which side does she represent? Darrel or Mr. X? Lola remembers Darrel's lookouts from today's stakeout—all black. This girl is white, so Lola is going to guess she belongs to Mr. X.

Jorge and Hector must have made the same judgment call, because they allow the girl to get closer to Lola's hiding place and the strip mall parking lot. Lucky for Lola, Mr. X's courier's eyes are on the dough sign. Lola sinks back into the bushes, catching a glimpse of the girl's face as she passes. Tiny red pocks, closed up and healed now, dot her high cheekbones. For an instant, Lola thinks she sees bruises under the girl's wide, green eyes. But she's wrong. They're dark circles. This girl is tired, but it's the pockmarks that give her away. Meth got her.

Lola spares no pity for addicts, but she wants to know what made this white suburban dropout pick up the pipe in the first place. Most days, she can tell what drove someone to addiction—abuse, force, wounds, stolen youth—and she doesn't waste time asking when she already knows the answer. The question that keeps her up most nights is why she and Hector aren't languishing in alleys with needles in their arms.

Lola sinks back farther, and for a second, the meth girl stops. She turns and blinks into the darkness, alone in the middle of a narrow street, a staggering amount of some kind of currency on her shoulder.

Lola holds her breath for a long second, and the girl forges her path forward, clicking an uneven beat across the street toward the empty parking lot. She lands under the glaring sign, staring up at the letters, then looking left and right, although she's already crossed the street. Satisfied she sees no one, she stands still.

Lola glances behind her at the foreclosed house's second floor, where she knows Marcos has his weapon aimed at the point between the girl's eyes.

Lola hears the creaking of the bungalow's screen door, followed by a big dog's rough, warning bark. The wolf sound sends a tingle crackling up Lola's spine. A German shepherd lopes across the even spikes of green grass that make up the entertainment lawyer's yard. The dog goes batshit, running the length of the property's white picket fence. From somewhere inside the house, a sleepy male voice calls, "Enough, Watson." *The unemployed husband,* Lola thinks, as the wind picks up, stirring the palm fronds above her. She squeezes her eyes shut and wills Watson to shut up. It works. Watson claps his jaw shut and retreats into his doghouse.

That's when Lola sees another woman heading west on California, about a hundred feet from the parking lot. Tall, sporting thigh-high spike-heeled boots like a second pair of feet, this woman's heels cruise across the pavement in even clicks. She balances a gym bag on her shoulder like it weighs nothing. With her peachy cheeks, perky breasts, spin class calves, and designer leather, she is the antithesis of the girl who's already landed in the parking lot.

It takes another twenty feet for Lola to recognize this woman as the one she saw in West Adams earlier today, sitting on Darrel King's porch and sipping iced tea with his mother. Then, she was wearing jeans and a cotton tank, her face naked except for startling blue eyes, her black hair roped into a long braid that hung all the way down her back. Now it is blown out, slicked down, and so shiny Lola can see its gleam even in this cobalt blue night.

Darrel King's girlfriend has dressed for this drop. She has the cash, so Lola's assumption was correct—the meth head has the heroin. But what the fuck is Darrel's girl doing out here on the street, making a drop?

Shit does not add up.

But Darrel's reasoning for putting his girl on the ground is above the Crenshaw Six's pay grade. Lola feels a surprise tinge of jealousy that Darrel's girl gets to be out there in the street, flaunting her salon hair and her couture calves like she belongs in the spotlight.

Darrel's girl keeps heading west, crossing under a streetlight a few feet from Lola. California is perpendicular to Electric, so the meth head courier can't see Darrel's girl yet. Another twenty feet, though, and the game is up. *Where is Jorge?* Lola thinks, just as the jester's two meaty hands reach out and grab Darrel's girl, dragging her and her bag full of cash out of the light.

Across the street, the shepherd shoots out of his doghouse. Watson picks up speed, paws on the picket fence. He whimpers in a high pitch, competing with the whistling wind. Lola has been looking out for cops and thugs, but she's unsure what to do about Watson as the screen door to the entertainment lawyer's house opens. A fit white man in silk pajamas emerges, rubbing sleep from his eyes. Shit. They can't have rich white witnesses, because they can't kill rich white witnesses.

"Back inside," Mr. Entertainment Lawyer mutters, and Watson bounds up the patio steps and into the house.

As soon as Mr. Entertainment Lawyer disappears behind the dog, Hector appears on California, the gym bag Darrel's girl was carrying now on his shoulder. Lola feels a surge of warmth as she watches her baby brother's even steps. In this moment, Hector is a true soldier, sure of his assignment, and Lola knows Amani hasn't crossed his mind. Amani is pleasure. This is work.

Another twenty feet and Lola sees Hector round the slight three-way corner to enter the parking lot. She sees her brother see Mr. X's meth head disaster of a courier—small, blond, pockmarked. She sees Hector's step falter, slightly, as if he's felt a rock in his boot.

Then Lola's baby brother keeps moving, his pace quicker, striding toward the baby blonde, who stands up straighter, the beginnings of alarm tingling somewhere deep inside her fucked-up nervous system. *Why is Darrel King's courier coming at me like this?* she must be thinking.

Slow down, Hector, Lola thinks. *Keep cool.*

Hector has known both couriers would end up dead at the end of this night, and that that outcome is the best-case scenario. If the Crenshaw Six can keep the body count at two drug- and cash-toting criminals, they will have won. Hector has known, Lola thinks; this is not a surprise to him.

But of course the blond girl is a surprise. She is not a tatted-up, muscled thug with a growl for a greeting. She is slight and vulnerable and fucking dangerous.

Hector is close to Blondie now, and she stands her ground, or tries to, looking back down Electric, the way she came. Looking for someone, Lola thinks, because someone dropped Blondie off somewhere back there in the Venice dark before she emerged from the shadows and started fucking up Lola's world.

Lola sees her baby brother's hand go to his waistband. *Grab your gun,* Lola thinks, trying to will Hector to raise his gun on Mr. X's courier, to take her and her product so they can get the hell out of this foreign territory.

"Hi," Lola hears Blondie say to Hector, and the second Lola hears the girl's voice—high and sweet and broken—she knows it is over.

At least take the drugs, take the drugs. Lola squeezes her eyes shut and tries to exert her will over Hector, just as she did with Watson. This time, it doesn't work.

Hector's hand goes from his weapon to his side, and Lola hears the single word he utters to Blondie. "Go."

Blondie stares up at him, because he's got a good foot on her, even in her dress-up heels.

Lola is on her feet and sprinting across California as Blondie takes off south on Electric, which borders the other side of the parking lot. Even the meth head girl has the good sense to kick off her heels. She is faster than Lola would have figured for a frail addict. She must know she is running for her life.

Lola feels the woosh of a bullet flying past her ear before the shot rings out, an explosive wake-up call to the balmy night.

Marcos. The thought of the beady-eyed felon pumping bullets into the salty air soothes Lola. Marcos is watching over her.

There is a scream, Watson's mother the entertainment lawyer, maybe, and Lola knows their time to contain Mr. X's meth head and retrieve the heroin is limited. There will be a hysterical call to the police inside Watson's house, and a quick response time because this is a neighborhood that needs to seem safe.

Blondie moves toward the darkness south on Electric, as fast as she can, the heavy gym bag acting as some bizarre shoulder shackle. Lola wonders if Blondie will have the good sense to die with that bag on her shoulder rather than drop it. The meth head loses her boss's two million in product, she'll be lucky if all Mr. X does is pump a bullet into her Swiss-cheese brain.

Marcos's second bullet sings toward the meth head, but, to Lola's surprise, the girl stops and looks back at the foreclosed house. She must see the buzzing light in the second-story window, she must realize someone up there wants her dead. Yet she doesn't move. A thousand fucking dark corners of this street, and she just stares up at the window, trying to put it together.

Marcos fires again, and this time, the bullet wakes up Blondie. She sees Lola running toward her, she feels the bullet rocket past her and sink somewhere in the concrete behind her, and she freaks the fuck out.

Blondie the meth head drops the fucking gym bag carrying two million in product, right in the middle of Electric Avenue, and takes off at a sprint. This is one of the many reasons Lola would never hire an addict, she thinks as she strains her eyes, trying to see south on the darkened street, but the blond girl has disappeared. All she sees is the gym bag, resting at the far edge of the dough sign's sick pallor of light.

Lola is halfway across the parking lot, running diagonally over the asphalt, going for the gym bag, when she remembers Hector. Her baby brother stands in the exact spot where he warned Mr. X's meth head.

"Come on," Lola says to him now, and Hector has the good sense to follow her at a sprint.

Lola hears an engine gaining momentum and volume, speeding toward her from California. When she turns, she sees the Crenshaw Six's minivan, a turquoise-and-tan can of dented and dinged metal, swinging a sharp left onto Electric. Garcia is behind the wheel.

She and Hector are still a hundred feet from the bag Blondie dropped, and now Lola sees headlights flash on two hundred feet south on Electric. Blondie's getaway car. They need to get to that bag, fast.

"Stop," she says, stepping into the street. The Crenshaw Six van's tires squeal on cracked concrete, and Lola sees smoke rising as the old piece of shit struggles to keep from running her over. The fender lands three inches from Lola's knees.

She slips into the passenger's seat next to Garcia. She is putting on her seat belt when she sees Hector still in the street, waiting for orders.

The whole van is quiet except for even breathing, and when Lola turns to face the Crenshaw Six soldiers, she sees Darrel's girl, passed out in the back, the gym bag full of cash zipped up next to her. She sees Jorge sitting with his head in his hands. She sees Marcos's jaw tight and grinding. They all know Hector fucked up. They all saw it.

Lola speaks to Garcia now. "She dropped the bag."

"Who?"

"Skinny bitch."

"Where?"

Lola lifts a finger toward the edge of the neon sign's light, a hundred yards down the street. The bag looks gray in the sick glow.

Lola feels the entire van quiver with new hope, and she takes the opportunity to throw a "Get in" to Hector. He does, still standing when Garcia's foot slams the gas to the floor mat.

Lola feels her heart leap up as Garcia nears the bag, and Hector shifts in his place beside the door, a shaking hand on the handle. "I can get it," he says.

Garcia looks to Lola, his eyes asking if he should trust her brother with this task. Hector wants to prove himself. Lola raises her chin, her version of a yes, and Garcia nods to Hector.

Hector leans forward then back, letting his weight roll the door open so he can lean out, asphalt flashing under him like television static, to grab the bag. Lola watches her baby brother's fingernails—which she trimmed for the first decade of his life—almost reach the bag's dusty gray handle. But then she hears it. Another engine, this one lower, more like a purr than the van's smoker's rattle. On instinct, Garcia's foot presses down on the gas. The van jolts. Hector's fingers fly past the bag's handle.

"The fuck?" Jorge asks as they all see Blondie's getaway car, hauling ass north on Electric toward the van, toward the bag, toward them.

Lola doesn't recognize the man behind the wheel of what she now sees is a Chrysler—he's a blur of white and blond, a cleaned-up WASP version of the meth head courier. He doesn't belong with the car. He belongs in a luxury SUV, a Mercedes or a Benz or an Audi, and not the tricked-out, tinted window, lowrider kind. This dude belongs in the for-real, two-and-a-half-kids-toting SUVs parked in two-car garages attached to two-story houses and fake turf lawns.

Blondie the courier has parked her skinny ass in the passenger's seat, her face awash with blank terror. She's pointing her own finger toward the bag, but the WASP ignores her. He sees it. And he sees Garcia.

Both vehicles shoot toward each other, and somewhere too far in the distance Lola swears she can hear the exotic dull roar of waves crashing on sand before the familiar humdrum wail of sirens.

"Cops," she warns Garcia.

Garcia presses harder on the gas. The Chrysler comes at them, high beams scorching Lola's eyes. Lola reaches for Garcia's hand. They could be a couple out for a relaxing Sunday drive. Her hair escapes its ponytail in wisps, and her fingers lock with Garcia's.

Lola hears the crash before she feels it, metal crumpling on metal, and she tucks her head, bracing herself. The impact makes her mind go dark. It's a few seconds before she can look up to see who won.

When she does, it's not the Chrysler, spinning and smoking against the minivan's crumpled hood, that she notices. It's not the rising wail of an LAPD cruiser's sirens, or even Watson, the dog whimpering and clawing at his screen door. It's the edge of the neon sign's light, still blinking dough, even though the bag of heroin is gone.

"Lola. Are you okay?" Garcia says. Lola sees him through blurry eyes first, then he comes into focus—muscles and bone and cotton. Lola sees the WASP in the Chrysler doing the same thing. How much time has passed? Who could have come and gone when they were all coming to?

The sirens are a piercing, rhythmic shriek now. Lola knows that a black-and-white will take the corner in front of her at a pace not meant for a surface street. When they get here, the cops will undoubtedly pursue the brown people in the shitty minivan first.

The Chrysler's engine coughs. The WASP is trying to start it, but, to Lola's surprise, he isn't swearing. He has one hand on the wheel, one on the key.

Garcia tries the same thing, but the minivan doesn't bother to sputter. It is dead.

"The fuck we do now?" Jorge says.

Lola hears the Chrysler's engine turn over, and the WASP slams the car in reverse, shaking it free of the minivan's collapsed hood. As the Chrysler switches gears, pummeling toward California, Lola sees its passenger door open. Blondie rolls out, tucked in a ball, her knees pulled to her chest, like this is a fucking fire drill. Lola can't tell from where she sits in the van if the WASP pushed her, or if she was smart and tried to get out herself. The Chrysler has disappeared around the corner by the time Blondie lands on pavement; Lola can see she is shaking and crying. But she is alive.

The black-and-white makes a blistering entrance now, tires squealing and kicking up asphalt pebbles as it appears in front of them on Electric.

The Crenshaw Six is holding a white woman hostage. They have a gym bag with two million in cash and a minivan whose engine won't start, Baby on Board sticker be damned. They are fucked.

Lola doesn't have to look at Marcos to be able to read his mind. He's not going back to prison.

"Give me the bag," she says, and one of the men hefts Darrel's girl's bag up to Lola. If they can scatter some cash, the cops might go after it first.

"We can't leave that," Garcia says.

"Gotta distract 'em. You got any better ideas?" Lola says, pissed at herself now for not fucking the fear out of her man. She feels everyone behind her tense. Lola catches Hector looking at his hands. Lola hopes his face is burning with shame. She also hopes these cops have a soft spot for women.

Her hand goes to the passenger's-side door. She's ready to emerge and scatter some cash, when Hector reaches through the center console and grabs the gym bag from her. She knows she should stop Hector from fleeing the minivan, but she doesn't. When he is out, she sees his gun abandoned on an empty square of seat.

Two LAPD officers, one fat, one skinny, emerge from their black-and-white with guns drawn. They yell at Hector to freeze.

Lola draws a sharp breath in the long second between the cops issuing the command and Hector dropping the gym bag in the middle of the street. She doesn't fault the cops, who see fucked-up shit every day so the rest of the country can live in ignorance. Lola is certain these two officers are responding to a call of shots fired. Now they've got a muscled Mexican standing in the street with a gym bag. Hector could be armed. He could have a bomb in there. Instead, he has something much more powerful—cash.

Hector raises his hands above his head in surrender. For a second, it is a standoff, and she is sure her brother is going to prison. You can't be brown with two million in cash and not be arrested on suspicion of trafficking. She sees the skinny cop holds his gun with a shaking hand. She thinks these guys are rookies, which could be good or bad.

Blondie whines at the side of the street, where she's collapsed, unnoticed, just outside the scope of a lone streetlight.

"Shit," Lola hears the fat cop say.

"Check the bag," the skinny one says to the fat one. "I'll see who's over there."

Lola can see the fat one doesn't like the skinny one pretending he's the boss. But the fat cop lets his resentment go and heads for Lola's brother. He keeps his gun raised on Hector, whose hands remain in the air like a seasoned criminal. Her brother would be good at his job if it weren't for damaged girls he thought he could save.

"What happened to your car?" the fat cop asks.

"It's not mine," Hector says.

"What happened to it?"

"Some white dude hit it and ran."

Lola is proud of her brother for the partial truth. The fat cop takes it as a smart-ass answer and moves on.

"You wanna tell me what's in that bag?"

"It ain't dangerous," Hector says.

As he speaks, Lola catches Hector looking not at the fat cop with a gun trained on him, but at the skinny one approaching Blondie. Jesus Christ. Her brother still wants to protect Blondie. Lola wants him to keep his eyes on what really matters here—again, the cash.

Hector doesn't move as the fat cop steps forward and frisks him. He's still watching his addict white girl.

"He's not armed," the fat cop announces to his partner, who has found the frail girl and could give a fuck.

"Are you okay?" the skinny cop asks, and Blondie looks up at him with wide eyes.

Lola looks back at Hector, who's biting his lip in frustration. It seems everyone here wants to save Blondie.

Lola can almost feel the burn of Hector's cheeks on her own as he watches this scrawny cop lay a blanket across Blondie's shivering shoulders.

No one is paying attention to the fat cop, who's on his knees now, unzipping the gym bag with clumsy fat fingers.

"Holy shit," a man's voice says as the bag opens. But it's not the fat cop. It's Hector, his eyes wide with panic. He's looking back at Lola, asking her what to do.

"Hector?" she says, not too loud. She wants him to know he can ask her what to do. But she doesn't want to give the cops his name before they've even asked.

"The fuck? This some kind of joke?" The fat cop stands. He's holding a rectangular stack in his hand, but it's not green. It's white. Darrel's girl wasn't carrying cash. She was carrying paper.

"Aw, fuck," Jorge says somewhere behind Lola. Out of the corner of her eye, she can see Garcia's fingers gripping the steering wheel.

The Crenshaw Six has just lost four million in cartel assets.

"She's hurt!" the skinny cop calls to the fat one. "We need to get her help."

The fat cop looks over to Blondie, who's shivering in the balmy night. He looks to Hector, an unarmed idiot carrying around a heavy bag of worthless paper. And he hesitates. Fuck.

"Did you hear me? She needs a medic. Call it in."

"There were shots fired."

"And he's not armed."

"I need to check the car."

"Get her help first."

Lola wants to kiss the skinny cop full on the lips.

"Run," Lola says, as the fat cop makes his way toward the black-and-white to call in the actual emergency here, a white girl with skinned knees and teary eyes. "Passenger side."

The entirety of the Crenshaw Six, minus Hector, emerges stealthily from the minivan on the passenger's side. Just because the cops can't prove they took a shot or arrest them for carrying around a gym bag of paper, they are packing heat. And they don't want to end up on any LAPD radar. At least not before they've had the opportunity to recoup their millions in losses. Like an army, they move through the overgrown weeds of what Lola imagines is some hippie surfer's yard. Marcos has Darrel's girl gathered in his arms like she weighs no more than a newborn. He can move silently even with a heavy load, and the way he's carrying Darrel's girl looks almost romantic.

"Abbott Kinney's one block over. Lots of bars. We can break up. Disappear," Lola says to Garcia.

Garcia nods agreement, and like that, they break up and disperse. Lola hears the skinny officer telling the fat one to bring him the first aid kit.

Hector is still standing in the street, and Lola backtracks to the van and steps around it to look at him. Her baby brother sees her, and Lola mouths, *Go.*

He obeys, running toward her, knowing he should not choose now to beg forgiveness.

"Abbott Kinney," she says to him, thankful she took time this afternoon to case the neighborhood. She and Hector duck into an alley that smells of piss and trash, just like any other alley, and Lola finds solace in the fact that rich and poor shit stinks the same.

Then, as they emerge onto Abbott Kinney, they almost collide with a white woman tossing a cashmere wrap over her shoulder and tucking her arm under that of her male companion. Lola and Hector both mutter their apologies, but the couple continues at their relaxed pace, early for a dinner reservation Lola hears them say, so they'll sit at the bar and have a drink first. Why not?

Because, Lola thinks, the Crenshaw Six just lost four million dollars in cartel cash and heroin. The best they can hope for tonight is not to go to prison.

"Lola?" she hears Hector say.

"Yeah," she says.

"I'm sorry," he says, and she realizes they, too, have fallen into the relaxed pace of the Venice nightlife.

She hates it. She wants out.

"Let's go," she says, and they duck around a corner, where Hector hotwires a Prius and drives the speed limit back to Huntington Park. Lola hates that he is letting her ride in silence out of respect that comes too late. She hates what she knows is coming for him. And for her.

SIX

DARREL'S GIRL

The sun peeks over the eastern edge of Los Angeles, illuminating the alley outside the storage facility. Lola has been waiting here for an hour, watching dark turn to dawn. The swirls of liquid beneath her Pumas could be anything from car wash runoff to blood. She thinks again of the similar stink of the Venice alley. She wishes she had a cigarette, not that she has ever smoked, so that she could look like she has a reason to be here, waiting. But timing, in this instance, is crucial. She can't go inside until she gets the okay.

So she waits. This section of Huntington Park is industrial. Warehouses stretch up to the next block, which is home to a car wash and a greasy spoon diner. Leaning against the storage facility's brick wall, Lola can hear the beginning of the barrio's Monday morning rumbles—televisions blaring with bad news, a child's bark of laughter, a bicycle skidding over a pothole that will never be fixed. The sun burns pale pink and yellow toward the east, a bastion of safety on the rise that will be gone again in twelve hours. Gone, too, will be the innocent sounds of the inner city waking up to some sort of sick hope for a new day. Darkness will replace that hope with loud pops that might be vehicles backfiring, or gunshots. There are always screams, usually female, that go ignored. People turn up their televisions so the sounds of game shows and canned laughter emanate from their flimsy windows, shit glass behind rusted bars, muting everything else.

When she was young, Lola took refuge in alleys. Lola's mother didn't call her home for dinner or homework. Maria called her home only if she had a man waiting to hand over some more bad white powder she needed Lola to "work for." But here, in shadows like these, Lola would hide from the dark things that happened in her mother's own bright kitchen. She talked to strangers—none of them ever did the harm television told her they would. That harm came from within her own home, where, night after night, she didn't want to go, and where she feared falling asleep—her mother considering it some kind of mercy to bring a man into her daughter's bedroom for pleasure after Lola's eyes shut. As if a man on top of her wouldn't wake Lola. But in her mother's mind, it was the most kindness she could do for her daughter. Maria needed her drugs. Maria didn't have cash—she had Lola.

"They're ready," Jorge says. He is fast, appearing on the doorstep where before there was nothing. But, as the sun appears, Lola wants just one more minute out here.

"Okay," she says, then, "How's Yolanda?"

Jorge didn't expect the question. Sweat drenches his forehead, blood dots his wife-beater like so many imperfect polka dots. His mind is not on his home life, because they met here first thing after everyone made their own way back from the fucked-up drop.

"She's good," Jorge says.

"Thought you told her you had to play the field," Lola says.

Jorge laughs. "Lola, you know that was bullshit."

Lola smiles, feeling the warmth of Jorge confiding in her when he'd lied to the men in the gang.

"Even if I wanted to cheat, Yolanda don't trust me to leave the house without knowing where I'm going and when I'll be back. I say I'm going to the store, she asks for a receipt. With one of those time stamp things. Movie, same thing. She don't trust nobody. Some of those talk shows say that can kill a relationship."

In this case, Lola thinks, *the television is right.*

"So you're not? With some other girl?"

"Fuck no, Lola," Jorge says. "Yolanda'd cut off my dick and feed it to my dog."

"She say that?"

"In those very fucking words. And she keeps her word," he continues, and the way he says that last part, Lola can tell Yolanda's dependability has endeared her to Jorge.

Lola would say the same for herself. Three years ago, the cops picked up Jorge as a person of interest in a stickup the Crenshaw Six (the Crenshaw Four at the time) had pulled the night before. A jilted banger from the victim's crew had described Jorge, given a partial plate even, that led back to Jorge's father's shop. Carlos hadn't asked Lola where she was going that day. He probably thought she was headed for the library. Instead, she made the trek to the police station in Bell, the next neighborhood over from Huntington Park. She had told the desk sergeant at the tidy office that she was there to speak to the detectives who had picked up Jorge Ramos. She had waited with her bag on her knees, her two hands resting atop it, her fingers fiddling with nothing to do. She had behaved like an innocent because she was nervous. Back then, Carlos barely let her play lookout. But when the detectives sat her down at their metal desks and offered her coffee, she told them with tears in her eyes that Jorge was her man, and that he had been with her all night. He had no record, how could they do this? And whether or not the cops believed her, the fact that Jorge wasn't in the system, coupled with the victim of this particular crime—a drug-dealing parasite they had better things to do than protect—meant Jorge was out in time for lunch with Lola. She hadn't saved his ass, but she had prodded the cops to remember they shouldn't waste their time on gangs sticking up gangs, especially when no bodies dropped.

After tacos at a Bell bodega they both agreed weren't as good as any in Huntington Park, Lola and Jorge had returned to their own neighborhood, she to Carlos, him to Yolanda. Carlos had heard Jorge was out, but neither Lola nor Jorge ever mentioned how this came to pass.

Now, in this stinking home alley, Lola can't remember if she already had it in her head what was going to happen later. Thinking of Jorge, of how he will always be loyal to her, she has forgotten why she is here. But the forgetting has made her ready.

Jorge holds open the streaked glass door for her, then remembers she hates that and mutters, "Sorry." She holds up a hand to let him know it's nothing. Then she is inside.

A long, dark hallway leads Lola to Darrel's girl. Jorge's uncle owns this place, and he's agreed to let the Crenshaw Six use it on occasion only because the economic meltdown of 2008 fucked him. The Crenshaw Six had planned to bring both Darrel's girl and Mr. X's courier here, but that didn't work out. Lola thinks now that Garcia should throw him a few extra bucks to put a lightbulb or two up in this hallway.

Then she thinks of the paper that was supposed to be two million in cash and how they could have lit the entirety of Huntington Park. Now, El Coleccionista will have her guts and her pain and her screams. Unless she can do what she came here to do.

After a few turns, winding through neat grids of metal roll-up doors, Lola finds the number she's looking for—"2348." She knocks twice, a simple code so no one will forget it. Three seconds and the door rolls up like a flimsy window blind, revealing Garcia.

Lola sees Darrel's girl, awake now, her wrists bound with zip ties, sitting in a straight metal folding chair. It is not the only chair in the room. Others are folded and stowed in the corners, along with a matching table, as if the Crenshaw Six uses this facility for weekly poker games. In truth, the chair came in a set Garcia bought at Target. Like hot dog buns or potato chips, you can't buy just one metal folding chair.

Garcia's cell rings, and he answers with a barked, "Yeah." Instantly, his tone changes. "Yes, yes I understand."

When he hangs up, he looks to Lola, who knows that was El Coleccionista, calling with a grace period. The cartel wants to punish the Crenshaw Six by taking Lola's life, but they also want their money back. If the Crenshaw Six can come up with the four million they lost at the fucked-up drop, maybe Lola will escape this whole debacle with her life.

"Cartel leader wants to meet with the leader of the gang that fucked up this drop. Before they take you."

"Guess that fucking sucks."

"Guess so."

"How much time?" she asks Garcia.

"Till Thursday. Seventy-two hours. Meet the leader, give over the stuff, or . . ."

Seventy-two hours to live. Lola has never thought of a bucket list before. The term seemed too innocent, too white, too much for big dreamers. She thinks she might like to go on a roller coaster again. But is that it? Then she thinks of Maria Vasquez, of making sure her mother has food on the table, that she'll rid her refrigerator of expired food instead of eating it, and now Lola's pissed that she can't even think about her own death without her mother creeping in like a slithering disease.

Lola takes a single step toward Darrel's girl, whose name, the soldiers have found out, is Mila. When Lola looks back, Garcia has disappeared, and the rolling door slaps shut.

She is alone with Darrel's girl.

The dried blood on the woman's lip has browned. Garcia and Jorge have been in here with her a good two hours, and they have done their jobs—roughing Mila up without hurting her. They have played bad cop. As opposed to Marcos, who returned from prison a sociopath and would have actually been bad cop.

"Hi," Lola says to Darrel's girl, her voice tiny, shy.

Mila looks at her, chapped lips curled in a snarl. Her mascara has smudged, but Lola doesn't know the source—sweat or tears. Her hair, clearer in the bare bulb's light, is not cobalt, but a wild tangle of dark reddish brown, flying loose from her head. Her clothes, the black miniskirt and red camisole, rest on her lithe body, askew. But Lola knows it would take only a little hot water and a cloth to make Mila look like a million bucks again. She is that kind of woman—put-together pretty even in her darkest hour. Still, Lola feels the disappointment in her chest—she liked the Mila she saw, drinking sweet tea with Darrel's mother in the light, then cat-walking in the dark.

"I brought you some water," Lola says, retrieving a bottle from her cargo pants pocket.

The bound woman can't take it, of course, so Lola twists the cap and waits for Mila to open her mouth. She will. She is human. She needs water. She needs Lola.

It takes five minutes, by Lola's watch, for Mila's pride to crumble and her mouth to open wide. In that time, Lola doesn't move from her position over the metal folding chair, water bottle poised like a gun, uncapped, and Lola ready to pull the trigger.

But it's not a gun, because Lola's job is to play good cop.

Lola watches the clear liquid trickle into Mila's open mouth. When a few drops spill out the side, Mila cries out, sad, but Lola shushes her.

"It's okay," she says, still soft and shy, looking at her feet. "I have another bottle."

"Okay," Mila says, and Lola feels the relief in her voice even before she leans her tangle of auburn hair against Lola's exposed midriff. Lola feels the stick of day-old hairspray against her skin, and Mila stays there, glued by what Lola is certain is a higher-end version of Aqua Net.

When Mila has had enough water, Lola pulls up another metal chair. She sits, putting herself on Mila's level.

"Darrel loves you," Lola offers after clearing her throat. She tries to steady her voice. If Mila knows her as anything, it is the lookout, a low position in any gang.

Darrel's girl is silent for a few beats, but then she speaks, her voice a low whisper, as if she wants to talk to Lola but is afraid whoever roughed her up might be listening. She doesn't fear Lola, because in Mila's mind, they are equals. Women in a man's world. The realization gives Lola hope. If Mila discounts her, Lola might be able to get Mila out of this room alive, despite the Crenshaw Six's original plan of torture and death. The original plan is done. Now, the plan is for Lola to live.

"Yes," Mila says.

"Fuckin' dangerous. A man like that loving you." Lola's voice gains momentum.

"It was a lot more dangerous being out on the streets. I was an addict," Mila says, and Lola guesses from the way she talks she's just another girl from the suburbs gone wrong. Otherwise, she'd have been "hooked" or "fucked."

"Don't know about that. Lot safer, being nobody," Lola says.

"Is that who you are?" Mila asks, and Lola knows it's not a challenge. Mila has lowered her voice, trying to take Lola into her confidence.

"Tell me about the paper," Lola continues.

"What paper?"

Lola shakes her head in disappointment. "They fuckin' told me you were gonna do this."

"Do what?"

"Deny you knew someone put paper up in that gym bag. Was supposed to be cash."

"I don't know . . ." Mila says.

Lola lowers her head into her hands. "I told them you would talk to me. You would tell me the truth."

"I am."

"Fuck," Lola stands and heads for the door. She puts her hands to her temples, a gesture of despair that can be read across cultural and economic divides.

"Wait!" Mila calls out. "I don't know anything about any paper. I saw Darrel put the cash in the bag."

"And it just turned to paper like fucking that?"

"He put the money in the bag at the house. After that, I don't know what happened."

"How much money?" Lola says, returning to her place like a preschooler finally engaged in storytime. She needs to test Mila.

"I don't know. A hundred thousand, maybe."

Lola levels her eyes at Mila. She doesn't have to say anything for Mila to admit her lie. Maybe Darrel's girl was testing her, too.

"Okay . . . I knew it was two million." Mila pauses, then offers in the shy, hesitant tone Lola used at the beginning of their conversation, "Look, I've never done this before."

"What? Dropped cash for Darrel?" Lola asks, knowing the answer. Mila has never dropped cash for Darrel. Mila shouldn't be here. She is an innocent. The thought makes Lola taste the salt and bile that comes before sick in her throat.

"No. He wouldn't let me. He thought it was too dangerous."

"Maybe you should have listened."

"Maybe," Mila says. "It's just . . . I got tired of depending on him for every need. Of asking for permission every time I saw a pair of shoes I liked. I never wanted to be a trophy wife. That's what my dad used to call it, a woman who lived off her husband."

"You and Darrel married?"

"No. Sort of. Not yet. We had talked about it."

"Talk means shit."

"I know."

"Okay. You didn't want your man keeping you. So what did you want?"

"Three years ago, I was an econ major at UCLA. A semester away from graduating. But I went to too many parties, did too much coke, my dad stopped paying my tuition."

Lola's heard the story before, straight out of an after-school special meant to scare. "But you're clean now."

"Because of Darrel. He saved my life. I'm not leaving him."

"You should go back to school."

"Darrel says so, too." Mila sighs. For the first time, Lola sees the girl beneath the thick makeup lines, the grown-up hair. Mila's older than the meth head waif who couriered for the other supplier, but not by much.

"He's a smart man, Darrel. You should listen to him."

"Maybe," Mila says. "If . . ."

"If what?"

"If you let me out of here."

"Tell me where that two million is, I'll have 'em give you a hot meal and cab fare home."

"But I've seen faces. That man, Garcia—"

"No secret he's a banger."

"Still . . . isn't that how it works? He thinks I'll tell Darrel who took me, even if I won't, even if I swear—"

"You ever think maybe Garcia wants to get caught?"

Mila stops, and Lola feels her own stomach shrink up and her heart catch, and all the nausea that she has heard comes with talking to someone you know is already dead rises to her throat. Mila doesn't know where that two million in cash is. Now that Mila has told them that the money does, in fact, exist, and that Darrel wasn't just planning to rip off his new supplier, Mila is no use to them. Still, Lola has to try. It is her job.

"Why would he want to get caught?"

"Credit."

"For what?"

"For killing Darrel's girl."

Mila works at the dried blood with her tongue, using the scab forming there as a pacifier.

"I shouldn't have asked Darrel to let me do the drop," Mila says.

"You asked him?"

"He said he'd let me do it, to get me off his back."

Lola shifts her weight back in her chair. She needs a few seconds to think. Darrel King, who runs South Central, lets his lovable babe of an ex-econ major girlfriend do a two-million-dollar drop with nothing but plain white paper for backup.

Again, Lola thinks, *shit does not add up.*

"Who was Darrel's new supplier?" Lola asks.

"I never met him."

Lola sighs again.

"I mean, I saw him—"

Now Lola sits up.

"White, blond hair, blue eyes, some sort of old English name I'd never heard before."

Lola longs for a little notepad to write these facts down. Leads, the cops call them. Even without a notepad, Lola knows Mila's describing the WASP behind the wheel of the Chrysler. Mr. X.

"Where'd he get that much stuff, if it wasn't coming from the cartel?"

Mila looks at Lola with disbelief. "You mean you don't know?"

Lola doesn't answer, because she never answers a question when she does not, in fact, know.

"Afghanistan," Mila says. "It's where the high-end heroin comes from now. The kind they have at raves and hedge-fund parties. None of this blue-collar stuff the cartel peddles."

Lola feels a surge in her stomach, more anger than pity now, for this white-collar bitch who just insulted her kind. She is happy for the change. It gives her the cold she needs to do what she has to do.

"Least the cartel's not funding terrorists," Lola says. She has learned a great deal from CNN, which she uses as background noise when she's doing other things—cooking, folding, thinking, fucking.

"Look, I've told you everything I know. I don't know where the cash is."

"I believe you," Lola says, and she's telling the truth, just as Mila is.

"Can you talk to the leader? Garcia? Can you tell him I've told you everything?"

"Garcia's not the one you have to convince."

"But . . . he's the . . . banger. He wants credit. You said."

"I didn't say he was the leader."

"Then who—"

Mila doesn't get to finish her question, because Lola shoots her between the eyes.

SEVEN
FRY

Lola watches the last of the chicken empanadas sizzle and pop in the orange Teflon skillet Garcia bought her last Christmas. The skillet and its companions—smaller skillet, Dutch oven, grill pan, all orange—came from a set endorsed by a celebrity chef on the Food Network. The woman on the skillet's packaging wore a flowing orange floral top that matched her cookware, her smile stretched into a grin on the glossy cardboard. White teeth, fake tan, loose-fitting top to hide the rolls that spilled over her too-tight jeans—white people would classify her as "cute." Lola wondered how much time the woman had spent trying to outrun cute and reach pretty before she embraced who she was and made a fucking killing.

Lola has never seen the lady's show, but as she fries dough in oil now, she narrates in her head the way she imagines this woman does. "The key is to make sure you let your oil get hot enough before adding the empanadas. Otherwise you end up with a greasy mess. Bad for your tummy in more ways than one."

It's seven a.m., and the day of Mila's death has dawned. It's early for empanadas, but Lola likes to cook after she kills. She made the same empanadas almost three years ago to the day, in this same kitchen, after her first body dropped.

From the living room, she hears men shifting their weights in stiff chairs, the creak of a floorboard, a lone cough and an immediate, "Sorry." Tension. The men of the Crenshaw Six aren't speaking. Garcia is with them. Lola knows he's sitting in the hunting armchair, its deep red cloth dotted with horses and hounds. Someone dropped it on a curb in Bel-Air a couple years ago. Garcia brought it home for Lola, even though they could have just as easily dropped some cash at a Crate and Barrel for something more classic.

The pattern on the chair was a foxhunt, Garcia had explained to Lola. During a hunt, he said, fat white men rode their horses into the ground to trap a small fox. The fox, meanwhile, ran from the hounds set after it by these very same fat white men. When Garcia had finished speaking, Lola had taken a black marker to the men in the pattern. She had scratched out their eyes and their red jackets and their sausage-casing thighs scrunched into tight white pants. The horses and hounds she left unmarked. It wasn't their fault some entitled motherfucker got bored and decided to turn them against the fox.

All people everywhere, rich or poor, skinny or fat, are animals. Looking for a fight. Looking to turn everyone against the weakest.

Mila was weak, but thought she was strong. Lola killed her because she had gotten everything she could out of her—she bled Mila dry before she shot her between the eyes. And yet, Lola hadn't lost any sleep over Mila. She may only have seventy-two hours left on Earth, but she needs her rest if they're going to have any hope of getting the cartel's four million and Lola's life back. She also needs her rest to deal with Hector.

This morning, before the kill, she had sent Hector home, thanking him for his willingness to sacrifice himself for the rest of them to escape the scene. Still, she heard the nagging voice in her head—he wouldn't have had to sacrifice himself if he hadn't fucked up and warned Blondie. He had gone back to his apartment with a clear conscience, because Lola, whom he still sees as his sister, not his leader, hadn't punished him then. Hector thought this meant she, his sister, had forgiven him. In truth, or at least the truth she tells herself, she merely had other things to do, like shoot Darrel King's girl.

The reality is Lola was too tired to punish him. She had known she would have to deal with her baby brother with a clear head. Of course, the clear head would only make what she knew she had to do more difficult. Spent and hungry, she could ravage anyone. Rested, fed, and caffeinated, balance restored, she was more forgiving.

Together, after the kill, she and Garcia had brushed their teeth side by side in their cramped bathroom, and Garcia had left the toilet seat up after he peed. They didn't mention Hector or the drop again as they fell into bed, backs down, watching the ceiling fan whir through the thick air above them. Garcia had started snoring within two minutes, but Lola hadn't been able to stop thinking— not about Mila or Hector, but about the blond meth head and her stick legs and her shoulders sagging under the weight of so much heroin.

Now, two hours later, Lola hears Garcia's voice, deep and sure, from the living room. It rattles the skillet. The empanadas shake. "We did what we set out to do. We kept that shithead Darrel from getting his supply."

Lola hears murmurs in response. *Damn straight. Fuck yeah, we did.* Same old shit. Tension dissolving into stale ghetto air saturated with fry grease and engine exhaust. Garcia can do that. Let the tension out of a room with a few words. But her part, the punishment, is still coming.

Standing over this sink, its cracked white enamel showing thin black veins, Lola thinks back to three years ago. She was making the same dish, empanadas, but on this day, that was her only duty. Sure, Carlos let her serve as lookout, which she'd done on their last heist a couple days before, the one that landed Jorge at the Bell Police Department with no alibi till Lola showed. In the other room, she'd heard Carlos giving a pep talk, similar to the one Garcia is giving now, albeit with lower stakes—glad our homeboy Jorge's home. *Home, home, home,* Lola remembers thinking. She was moving in a trance that day, too, and again because of her brother. Because of Hector.

Now, there is a whine at Lola's feet. Valentine looks up at her, eyes green like olives, chestnut brown coat. When Lola hoisted the pit over the fence to freedom, Valentine's ribs were showing. Ribs on a pit bull should never show. If they do, you know someone's training them to fight, starving them, making them mean with the promise of food on the other side. Food or death. Those are the choices. Her mother taught her that, at least. The knowledge has kept her alive.

Lola turns to the Dutch oven, where two chicken breasts, boneless, skinless, bland, boil in rolling water. Lola lifts them from the pot and shreds them with two forks. She is always amazed that flesh comes apart so easily, crumbling under tines. She mixes the chicken with white rice and adds a pinch of salt. She wants Valentine's stomach to accept the food, so she keeps it bland and easy. She spoons the concoction into Valentine's pink bowl and sets it in front of the dog. She has done this for her dog every morning since she stole her from that fighting ring a year ago.

"Stay," Lola says. The pit keeps her eyes on Lola's. Lola wants the pit to know she doesn't have to fight anyone for her food. She doesn't have to knock Lola over to get to it. Lola will let her have it, if she just pauses to accept her circumstances. "Okay."

The pit sticks her snout in the pink bowl and gobbles. Lola gets down on her knees and scratches the dog's ears. Lola wants her to get used to having people bother her while she eats. She doesn't want Valentine turning on anyone because she needs food. Lola vows in the pit's ear now that she, Lola's girl, will never want for food ever again. Is she promising to keep herself alive, then? Will Garcia remember how much Valentine eats and when and which brand? If you change a dog's food, it can fuck with their stomachs.

Valentine gobbles her food, oblivious to the promise, but Lola leans against the counter, at peace.

"We kept Darrel from his drugs. We sent his new supplier's courier running scared." Garcia now. Calm. Sure. But he has nothing else to say, because everything after the running scared, they fucked up. Her baby brother fucked up.

That was not the case three years ago, when Lola knew Carlos was holding up a shot glass with one hand and pouring tequila for the soldiers with the other. *Today, we have something to celebrate,* she remembers hearing him say. *Today, we are not the Crenshaw Four, but the Crenshaw Five, because today, we welcome Hector into our ranks.*

When Lola had peeked around the corner, she had seen the men surrounding her baby brother with their pungent shots and piercing barks of congratulations. Lola had seen Marcos dole out a gut punch to Hector as her brother took a shot. She had seen her brother choke on it, and she had seen Carlos laugh. She had seen Jorge catch her looking and lower his glass. He knew that, for her, her fifteen-year-old brother's indoctrination into a gang wasn't something to celebrate. Garcia had seen her, too, and done the same.

The condition for her moving in with Carlos years before had been that he wouldn't touch Hector. He had agreed. She had believed him. For years, he had kept his word, through Lola's college classes, through her suggesting ideas for his gang to do more— *There are six corners,* she had told him, *that no one in Huntington Park wants to touch. You can do more than stick up other gangs. I do more,* Carlos had said. *Then let me,* Lola had responded. And he had let her serve as lookout on the job in Bell a few nights before he came after Hector. He wouldn't change the gang name from four to five for her—she was a woman, she cooked his food and washed his shorts, which up until she found econ and business and chemistry had been fine. But he would let her keep watch from the bushes outside the rival gang's living room window. He would let her peek through the bars to watch the stickup go down.

But once Jorge, Garcia, and Marcos had taken the money and run, Carlos had stuck behind. Lola had watched her man, the man with whom she'd shared a bed for years, kick another man, this one bound and defenseless, until he told Carlos something. Carlos had disappeared into the hallway, but Lola followed him on the outside, from the living room to the front bedroom, where Carlos took a knife to the rival gang leader's mattress. Lola remembers being able to spot the wet pools of drool or some other bodily fluid on the sheets all the way from the window. She remembers wondering what the hell Carlos was doing. And she remembers the mountain of cash that jolted upward from the force of Carlos's knife.

Great, Lola had thought, *more for everyone.* Except later that night, when the men sat drinking and dividing their profits, Carlos never told the other men about the cash. Lola didn't mention it then, but when she was sitting at the same vanity she uses today, brushing her hair before bed, she had met his eyes in the mirror and asked him if he was going to tell the others about the cash. Carlos had laughed and smoothed her hair and asked didn't she want to live in a castle. He had kissed her and soothed her, and she knew from his kindness not to mention it again. So she didn't.

Still, the next night, she had caught Carlos in the living room, showing Hector how to load an automatic. She had half expected Maria Vasquez there too, offering Hector the spoon and the flame and the powder. *Is this what motherhood is,* Lola had wondered, *trying to stop the devil?* She had dropped her backpack on the floor and gone to start dinner while, in the other room, Carlos was doing what he promised Lola he never would—bringing her baby brother into the gang. Carlos was trying to punish Lola for knowing his secret.

Now, on the day she is to punish her brother, Lola hears silence in the living room. The empanadas are ready. She doesn't want them to burn, so she scoops them up with a flat spatula, rusty from wear and wash, blots them on store-brand paper towels that don't like to soak up grease or coffee or blood. She has no platters or chipped china that's been passed down through generations.

"What we didn't anticipate was losing the merchandise," Garcia says, continuing to the bad-fucking-news portion of his speech.

Valentine tilts her head, spying the plate of empanadas Lola hoists in her taut arms. It is time. The pit trails Lola into the living room. Green shag carpet, rickety white wood tables, and dim lamps. Their shabby home. Their home. Nothing else matters.

"And Darrel's girl," Garcia says.

"Mila," Lola says, soft. Hector looks at her—he heard. But he turns back when he sees she didn't want anyone to hear.

Lola stays quiet as she moves through the room, offering empanadas to each member in turn—starting with the least powerful. She cooks to delay the inevitable.

Hector takes only one with a murmured, "Thank you." As she moves up the chain of command, the men take two, even three. She understands Hector's appetite well enough to know he was too scared to take more, so she circles back to him before she gets to Garcia. The men will leave three on the platter for her. Hector takes a second empanada with a grateful smile.

"We didn't get the shit," Garcia continues. He doesn't mention Hector's fuckup. He doesn't have to. "And Los Liones doesn't give a shit how we get it back. But we in for some serious heat, 'less we make this shit right."

"What kind of heat?" Jorge says, mouth full. Marcos grunts his approval of Jorge's question. The ex-con eats bent over, shoulders protecting his food as he shovels it in with no time for air.

Garcia looks to Lola, then, his eyes on her, says, "We have till Thursday to deliver the cash and the drugs." He is not telling the whole truth.

"Or . . . what?" The whole room shifts to Hector, who looks surprised he spoke.

Garcia looks to Lola again. She gives a slight nod. She wants this part to hurt.

"Or they take Lola."

Somehow, the sentence makes Lola want to laugh. The cartel still thinks she is the girlfriend, but if they take her, they're sure as shit never getting their currency back.

"Take her," Hector repeats, and the confusion in his voice angers Lola. She doesn't know what she wanted—tears in a room full of bangers wouldn't do anything to further Hector's position here. Still, she wanted her baby brother to be smart enough to realize "take her" encompassed any number of action verbs—cut her, maim her, rape her, kill her. She wants Hector to understand that, because he couldn't pull a gun on Blondie, he has saved one lousy tweaker's life only to jeopardize his own sister's.

"Valentine." Lola gets the pit's attention. Lola lowers the last empanada to the ground, leaving it under the pit's nose. "Stay." The dog does. Then, "Okay." Valentine gobbles up the empanada. It's gone in two neat bites. Everyone's stopped eating to watch Lola and Valentine's act. The entire room holds its breath, sticky thigh skin pressed to edges of rickety chairs.

They are all awaiting their leader.

Lola turns her back on Hector and pads into the kitchen. She peels the paper towels damp with grease from the now-empty empanada platter. Valentine nuzzles and sighs at Lola's feet, where she drops into a circle of brown fur, exhausted.

No one in the living room has spoken or moved. They are waiting for her.

It wasn't like that three years ago, when Lola could hear the celebrations and the fucking around and the male preening. Carlos wanted her to hear Hector's happiness. Carlos wanted to punish her for knowing he was stealing from his own men.

Lola knew where Carlos kept the guns. She had gotten one from the safe that morning, waking up knowing Carlos had trapped her brother. Guns and money are like drugs. One taste and you're hooked. There was no going back for Hector, just as there would have been no going back for him had Maria succeeded in giving him his first dose of heroin. But Lola couldn't—and still can't—punish her mother.

That day three years ago, Lola had turned the empanadas just as she had today, not wanting them to get anything past golden. She had figured she had about two minutes, three tops, if she wanted to get back to the kitchen in time to move them from skillet to plate.

She had marched into the living room while Carlos was speaking.

"Gonna go far, my man," Carlos was saying to Hector, his arm around the boy's shoulders even as Lola put a bullet between his eyes.

Was it premeditated? Lola didn't know. She still doesn't. She had gotten the gun from the safe hours before, yes, but had she known what she was going to do before she was relegated to kitchen duty while Carlos tried to take her whole world away?

"The fuck?" Marcos had said as the bullet wound between

Carlos's eyes seeped blood. Lola hadn't known they would need a tarp. Maybe she hadn't known what she was going to do.

"Why?" Jorge.

Garcia had placed a hand on Hector's shoulder and pulled him back from the carnage.

"He was stealing from us," Lola said, and when she returned to dump the extra cash, a hundred grand, on the coffee table, Garcia, a quiet soldier Lola had known since her high school days but barely noticed, was the first to bow his head to her. Jorge followed Garcia's lead. It was only Marcos whose loyalty was still in question. Hector was Lola's brother. Hector was a given, and with her as leader, she thought, she could protect him.

By the time Garcia and Jorge had rolled Carlos's body in a plastic tarp, burned off his fingerprints, and deposited him deep in the Angeles National Forest, the city's most popular body dump, Lola had added herself to the gang's roster. Carlos never let her join in any official capacity. Still, despite his death, she had decided to keep him in the count. Not to do so would make the neighborhood suspicious. Besides, Crenshaw Six sounded better than Crenshaw Five.

She had picked up the phone and called Kim first. Had she seen Carlos? He didn't come home last night. Okay, okay, she would let the cops know. Two Huntington Park PD detectives had come to ask rudimentary questions. They wore suits and ties and complimented Lola on her coffee, then exchanged knowing glances when she mentioned Carlos may have ripped off a few people he shouldn't have. Right now, he was just a missing person, but Lola knew something worse had happened. At least she was sticking mainly to the truth, she had thought. The detectives did not disagree with her theory that Carlos might have been killed, but there was no body. Lola had asked if it was true what she'd seen on those cop shows, that it was almost impossible to solve a murder without a body. The detectives had said yes, that was true. Then they had closed their notebooks and promised to be in touch. She had given them coffee in Styrofoam cups to go. For a couple of months, they had called to update her about their lack of updates on Carlos's case. What they never said to her was that it was no fucking wonder Carlos went missing after sticking up gangs for their loot, that they'd bet their pensions his killer was the last dude Carlos stole from, and that maybe he should have considered the consequences to his actions. Lola appreciated this omission on the detectives' part. She also appreciated that they'd solved the case in their own minds, and with the police department budget and resources what Lola knew they must be, that had to be enough. Lucky for her, since she was the real killer. The only wild card now, three years later, is Kim. If Carlos's sister ever finds out Lola is the true leader of the Crenshaw Six, she'll be gabbing to the cops before Lola can shoot her between the eyes.

Now, Lola scoots a trapped foot from under her snoozing dog. Valentine shouldn't have to see what Lola has to do. She grips the chipped countertop, just for a second, then turns her attention to the knife block. She has to take the butcher knife, even though she knows it might be labeled irrational, ripe for a woman's hysterics. She can't lose her shit. Violence must always have a purpose, one greater than standing by, doing nothing. Saving a baby, stopping a thief, making sure a soldier obeys orders.

In the other room, Garcia speaks, low, to Hector, "You break your sister's heart. You know that?"

"What?" Hector asks, and his ignorance sticks in Lola like a barb that can't be dug out.

She grips the butcher knife, so large it looks comical in her tiny hand, and strides into the living room. Everyone freezes in a twisted diorama, the kind Lola made in grade school—pilgrims and Indians feasting together at Thanksgiving, slaves tossing off shackles, George Washington on a rearing horse. Heroes who had jack shit to do with little Lola, granddaughter of shitting-in-a-hole poor Mexican immigrants living in South Central under her junkie mother's watch.

In this diorama, everyone has turned to Lola. Everyone is looking to her to see what they're supposed to do.

But Lola is the leader. Lola must do this particular dirty work.

When Hector sees her coming for him, he doesn't know to move. She is his sister. She has never so much as laid a hand on him. But he has seen what she did to Carlos in this very room, Lola thinks, just as he has the good sense to let his feet struggle to get under him, to help him get up and run away, but his heels give out, and his ass lands right back in his chair. No one's touched him. Still, he's a prisoner.

Marcos and Jorge have dragged out the tarp. Garcia tilts up Hector's chair so they can spread it under him. It pleases Lola, to see her men working as one.

"Lola. What the fuck?" Hector asks his sister. But she is not his sister. She is his leader, and she can't allow him to be a boy. "I said I was sorry."

Lola resists the nagging urge to tell him he should have thought of that before, that he's only saying these things out of fear. He's not sorry he helped Blondie survive. But she doesn't want to sound like his mother. She's not his mother. No one was his mother, and no one was her mother, and she's fine, and he fucked up.

"What are you doing?"

Hector's saying all the things an angry, entitled child would say. He told her he was sorry, he must be thinking, and isn't that enough for his sister?

Still, his petulance cuts her more than a pleading apology, because it reminds her that he is hers. In that moment, she knows she can't kill him.

She touches Hector's cheek and feels his whole body relax under her palm. It takes both her small hands to hold one of her baby brother's. The right one. She raises it to her heart so he can feel her life beating there.

"Thank you . . ." he whispers. "Thank you."

"You're welcome."

In one quick movement, Lola draws the knife and tries to slice clean through Hector's trigger finger. She wants it to happen fast, to punctuate her "you're welcome," but it turns out slicing through bone and sinew is rough work. She has to jump on Hector's lap, to take his hand in hers, to anchor herself as she saws and he cries out. The whole thing takes a good fifteen seconds.

As blood spurts and Hector screams beneath her, Lola feels her own heart beating steady.

EIGHT

COMMUNION

The scent of recycled fry grease assaults Lola as she enters Mamacita's Bodega and Taco Stand. It's nine a.m. now, four hours after she shot Darrel King's girl between the eyes. Already Juan and Juanita Amaro have fired up the grill behind the small lunch counter so that it's too hot to cook eggs.

Juan, sleeves pushed up, mans the smoking apparatus, playing the different meats—beef, pork, chicken—like his own personal symphony. Juanita presides over the cash register, a manual apparatus that requires her to press hard at the keys with crooked, bony fingers. Mamacita's customers must be prepared to wait while Juanita rings them up, then wait some more while she scrawls a handwritten receipt.

Lola wonders if Lucy is here, somewhere in the small back break room, the Amaros maybe using the ancient television with its grainy picture as babysitter.

Lola picks up a plastic basket with one handle missing. She swings it onto her left forearm and strolls the aisles, not sure why she's here, other than the fact that she woke up and needed to leave the house. Since Marcos took Hector to County for stitching she hasn't been able to set foot in her living room. It's not because she thinks the hospital will ask too many questions. Hector is a brown banger with a missing trigger finger. No cops are gonna show up at Lola's door wanting to know what happened. They know all they need to know—this banger can't shoot. Lola has done them a favor.

Mila, Darrel's girl, is another matter. Mila was white, and Mila was sleeping with a drug lord. Mila will be a person of interest.

Lola's fingers lift cushions of bagged white bread and sweating jugs of milk into her flimsy basket.

"Lola?"

Veronica. The only women out shopping at this hour are over fifty. The girlfriends are asleep in twisted sheets, sticky from a night of trying to keep their men at home.

Veronica kisses Lola on the mouth and asks, "What are you doing here so early?"

"Shopping."

Veronica makes a face at the white bread in Lola's basket. "What you gonna make with that?"

Veronica makes migas for breakfast, and her lunch meats keep company with tortillas. Lola knows this, because Veronica made lunch for a schoolgirl Lola at least three times a week. In Veronica's mind, white bread should have no place in Lola's home.

"French toast," Lola mumbles, and Veronica frowns. It irks Lola that the older woman's judgment stings.

"Maybe you can fatten up your brother," Veronica says, shrugging.

"What?" Lola's voice comes out too loud. Juanita looks up from her place at the register, and Juan turns down the vent. Are they trying to eavesdrop?

"Hector's too thin." Veronica tsks, a small cluck with her tongue to the back of her lips.

You fix him then, Lola wants to say, but she doesn't want Veronica accepting the challenge. Hector is her child to screw up, then fix again.

"Lola," Veronica says, pulling her into the freezer aisle, where iced, meat-filled doughs and frozen pizzas surround them. Now Juanita peers over her register and Juan his grill, information as

much a commodity to them as the tacos and cheap groceries they
peddle. "The man at the barbecue—"

"A friend," Lola says, knowing Veronica is referring to El Coleccionista.

"Bullshit," Veronica says. "We didn't raise you blind."

"'We' didn't raise anyone."

"You're too hard on your mother," Veronica says, but the words
are rehearsed, recited, meaning nothing. Veronica believes her best
friend, Maria, ruined her children's lives, and for that, she will never
forgive her. Still, obligation forces her to utter this same sentence
every time one of Maria's offspring dares to imply she wasn't a good
mother. Because they are her children, and she is their mother, and
that is the way of it.

"Okay. He's cartel. So what?"

"So the ladies of the community are concerned. About his . . .
leadership."

"Garcia knows what he's doing," Lola says.

"He gets in bed with the cartel, chica, he's not the only one
who'll suffer." Veronica pulls Lola closer, as if she's divulging a
secret, which of course she's not. "Did you know Los Liones comes
after families, too?"

"Garcia knows what he's doing," Lola repeats. She wishes she
could tell Veronica the truth—that she, Lola, is the leader of the
Crenshaw Six, and that she knows what the fuck she's doing and
would Veronica just lay off for once? She is so close, then she
thinks of Kim, and of the bullet she, Lola, put between Garcia's
ex-girlfriend's brother's eyes. She thinks of Kim's monthly phone
calls to those poor overworked detectives who complimented Lola's
coffee. She thinks of how, if Kim knew Lola was really running
things, Kim would know, somehow, who had murdered her brother.
Kim would scour the seven hundred thousand acres of the Angeles
National Forest herself. And Kim would turn Lola in. Lola is safer
in the shadows, because her own neighborhood doesn't know to put
a target on her back.

Los Liones, of course, is a different story, because they do come
after families, and she has sixty-eight hours to live.

"You put a lot of faith in one man," Veronica is saying.

Lola doesn't respond. She reaches behind Veronica's puffy black hair, streaked with frazzles of gray, and grabs a package of ice cream sandwiches. The box seems to wilt as soon as she takes it out of the freezer case. Even with the window unit blowing cold air, it is still summer inside Mamacita's.

When she reaches the register, Juanita Amaro pretends to add some figures on a calculator. Juan turns back to his grill.

Lola places her basket on the counter, her shoulder sinking as the weight is lifted. She hadn't noticed the weight until it was gone.

"This all?" Juanita asks, painting on a smile. She has a missing front tooth she can't afford to get fixed.

"Eight tacos, pork and beef," Lola says, reaching for her wallet. Then, to her own surprise, "How's Lucy?"

"Huh?" Juanita asks, the smile gone.

"Lucy. How is she?"

A look passes between the old couple, and it takes a moment for Lola to realize she's not breathing.

"She's fine," Juanita recovers.

"Back with her mother," Juan says, looking down at his wrinkled hands and greasy apron. So Lucy is with Rosie, the Amaros' junkie daughter. Lola recognizes the look between the couple as shared shame. But Rosie is Lucy's mother. What else could they do?

Still, the fact that they let her go angers Lola.

"Forget the tacos," Lola says. Because what else can she do to punish them besides give them less of her dirty money?

NINE

SMALL VICTORIES

Lola is surrounded by sick—a white electric stove with two burn-
ers, a dish rack, a refrigerator that rattles and hums its way through
the thick summer heat, and the smell of dead fish coated in bright,
strong lemon.

Lola hates this place. She scrubs at a stain that won't come off
the linoleum. The knees of her cargo pants are black from grime,
her forehead coated in a slick sweat that will keep coming, she
knows, hours after she leaves this shithole.

She has come here today, as she does every week, to commune
with past sins, although the past sins are not her own. She atones
because no one else will.

The bucket of soapy water has long since turned from clear
and clean to dark and muddy. Lola tosses the scrub brush into the
bucket, letting the dirty water slosh out the sides. She likes this feeling of leaving something a little unclean—it is the least she can do
to spread a tiny torment of her own.

Lola grew up too fast in this kitchen, this house, and no matter how much industrial-grade, lemon-scented cleaner she uses, she
can't wash off the stink and the ruin that coat it—and her.

"I made tea." The voice behind her is soft, feminine, faded. Her
mother holds out a mug of lukewarm water and tepid brown swirls.

"Thank you," Lola says, and she gets off her knees, because her mother doesn't get to see her like that. She arches her back, letting her spine pop, and thinks twenty-six is too young for a body to make these noises. She has no doubt this is the place that aged her.

Lola takes a sip of the tea and wants to spit it out—it is some herbal crap that her mother has taken up, now that she's clean and wants to imbibe anything that claims it will keep her that way. Yet what would it matter now if she were using? She has no children to raise, no job to go to. Maria Vasquez will die of some long illness that costs a lot of money and pain. Why couldn't she have taken up heroin in her golden years, when it might even have done her some good, relieved her of some loneliness?

Lola says only, "It's good."

"Green tea with fenugreek," Lola's mother says, and then, because her mind hasn't held on to the specific alleged attributes, adds only, "It's good for you."

"Tastes like it," Lola says, hoping her mother understands the implied insult, but Maria Vasquez just looks through Lola to the dirty window behind her. She is clean, but her brain is Swiss cheese, with holes where there should be room for smiles and laughter and the memories of all the fucked-up shit she did when she was high.

"Place looks better," Maria says. She is telling Lola she's a good housekeeper, a good woman, doing what she is supposed to do— caring for her aging mother. Garcia's mother is also aging, but she had sons—three of them, with three different fathers who disappeared the requisite year after their respective children were born. Granted, Garcia's mother moved to Santa Fe years ago, but she cleans her own house and cooks her own meals. If she'd had daughters, Lola knows, she would do none of this—she would fade faster into their maternal care. She would stop moving. Then again, Garcia's mother wasn't a junkie, just a young girl who wasn't careful with what little birth control she could get her hands on.

A timer dings, and Lola retrieves kitchen towels to remove a Pyrex dish from the oven. The enchiladas she's made will feed her mother for the week. Maria can't be trusted to keep useful kitchen items like oven mitts or ladles around the house. Lola buys them for her, and they disappear. Lola's first thought is always *Did she pawn them for drug money?*, but what useless things to pawn. The heroin you could get for a couple of oven mitts would kill you, and the television, a fifty-inch flat screen courtesy of Garcia, is still mounted on the living room wall, watching over the tattered furniture that sags underneath even Lola's insignificant weight.

"What happened to the oven mitts I bought you?" Lola asks her mother.

"I use paper towels." Maria shrugs and sips her tea.

"Paper towels don't keep your hands from burning."

"Huh," Maria says, as if she's never realized this. If Lola gave a shit, she would go to her and turn her palms over to see if they were streaked red.

"Are you selling them?" Lola asks.

"Why would I do that?"

"I don't know. I buy them for you, but they're not here. So where are they?"

"I don't . . . I can't remember," Maria says as it finally dawns on her this conversation has jack shit to do with oven mitts.

"Forget it," Lola says, because she always stops the conversation, whether it's about oven mitts or getting out of the house or cleaning her own toilet, when her mother realizes Lola is telling her she's a shitty person and she wishes she would just die.

Lola does not ever want to say that to her mother.

"What did you make?" Maria asks, falling back on etiquette, and Lola is thankful. She doesn't want to think about the things she did on this dirty kitchen floor to earn Maria some smack money.

"Enchiladas."

"I can't have beef. My cholesterol."

"They're chicken," Lola says. Growing up, she and Hector ate Spam and hot dogs and sugary fruit punch three times a day. They watched their mother shoot up. Lola did things with and to men, so Maria could shoot up. And now Maria's concerned about her cholesterol.

Maria looks to her tea, maybe reading the brown swirls there. Then she says, "I'm sorry." Lola doesn't know what this particular sorry encompasses—her mother does apologize constantly now. She's sorry about the dirty dishes in the sink, or the linoleum that won't get clean, or that Lola has to come over here every week and make sure her conditions are livable, just because Lola is her daughter and these things are expected. "I should have known you'd remember about the beef."

Lola prefers the apologies like this, doled out like a thousand tiny pinpricks to Maria's heart. For an instant, Lola wants to take her mother in her arms and squeeze until blood and guts and life fluid inch through her pores like garlic from a press. It is a mixture of love and hate, this thought, and it frightens Lola. She is used to only hate where her mother is concerned.

"Make sure you eat these enchiladas within the next three days. I don't want you keeping spoiled food in your fridge." Lola grabs her bag, a Prada knockoff that velcros shut.

"That's it? You're going, just like that?" Always wanting more, junkies.

Lola opens the back door to go, then, just to ruin her mother's day, tosses it over her shoulder, "Hector's in the hospital."

TEN

TWO BIRDS, ONE STONE

Mamacita's mingled smell of grease and salt, maybe from the ocean, maybe from food or urine, hits Lola's nose again at seven a.m. the following morning. Forty-six hours to live. Or does she have forty-eight? She can't remember. Being with her mother does that to her, makes her mind weak. She will err on the side of caution and go with forty-six.

She is standing outside the Amaros' bodega with Kim and Veronica, mugs of cooling coffee in hand. Together with other Huntington Park residents, they form the audience for the clusterfuck of a death dance that's happening behind the yellow crime-scene tape in front of them. Even though Huntington Park has its own police department, a dead white girl must warrant some kind of joint task force pissing contest. Huntington Park PD is here. LAPD is here. So are the sheriffs. Everyone must want to be a white girl's hero.

"I hear she's that King boy's girl," Veronica says through clenched teeth. Lola knows the reason for the clenched teeth—Veronica also doesn't want the cops or the neighborhood thinking she's gossiping—it's a thing here. No talking within a hundred feet of the police.

"Uh-huh," Lola says, to say something.

"What she doin' here?" Kim asks. "This ain't her hood."

"Running with the wrong people." Veronica tsks, and Lola finds herself thankful to find her surrogate mother's signature move directed at someone else, even if that someone is the first woman Lola killed. "White girl." Veronica tsks again. "No wonder cops are here so early."

Lola takes stock of the token fat white man across the tape, his belly spilling over an off-the-rack suit, sweat already spotting the tight fabric bunched under his arms. The lead detective. From what she's overheard, his name is Tyson. He carries one of those tiny spiral notepads she wanted when she was questioning Mila.

"Where's McMillan?" Tyson thunders, not bothering to keep anything secret from the wide-eyed brown people eavesdropping on the other side of the tape.

"On his way, sir," a clean-shaven uniform with a crew cut pipes up.

"Did you explain that his presence at the drop scene makes his appearance here im-fucking-perative?"

"Not in so many . . ." The rookie trails off, and Lola has enough time to remember the other rookie, the one with the shaking hand, and his fat partner, who both clambered to help Blondie while Hector was trying to turn himself in. Is McMillan one of them? If they had any sense at all, the two uniforms would have taken one look at meth head Blondie and known they needed to call Narcotics. But how had they connected Mila to the drug drop, unless the meth head was a rat?

That's when Lola spots him, parked in a tow-away zone fifty feet from the taco stand off Alameda. He steps from his dirty-as-fuck car, some sort of American-made sedan that looks exactly the same as any other American-made sedan. His eyes are sunken ghost white blots in crinkled skin—he's hungover. Gel smooths back his long brown hair. He sports a uniform of leather jacket, torn jeans, and Styrofoam gas station coffee cup.

He wasn't one of the uniforms at the drop. Maybe those two called him in later, if Blondie told them what she was doing shivering and pockmarked on a residential block of Venice.

This McMillan dude is a narc. Lola doesn't know him, she's never seen him. Still, she could have made him a thousand yards away.

The narc sniffs the air, unaccustomed to the smell of fried meat and masa drifting toward him from the banged-up bodega in front of him. He spots Juan and Juanita Amaro, two sets of arms crossed over two aprons streaked with unidentifiable red and brown. Juanita's hair escapes the bun at the nape of her neck, flying free from her face in wisps courtesy of the brisk early morning air. Juan looks at the pavement, Juanita at the uniformed officer trying to take their statement.

The narc starts to cross under the tape, but another uniform, a doughy kid with bright blue eyes, stops him. The narc flashes his badge, but the kid shakes his head. "Homicide only."

"Good," Lola hears the narc say. "I can go back to bed."

He turns his back on the kid and starts toward his car, keys out, ready to make his escape. Lola has to fight to keep from running after him. She wants to find out what he knows about the drop. She wants to know if the cops found the gym bag full of heroin. More important, she wants to find out if he knows the identity of Mr. X . . . or the tiny meth head who had no business being on the corner that night.

"He's with me." Tyson. The fat homicide detective. "Get your ass back here, McMillan."

McMillan the narc gets another couple of steps in before the voice booms louder. "Bubba." McMillan's first name. Bubba stops. Lola recognizes a power struggle in the standoff—and finds herself rooting for Bubba, the underdog. Lola knows Tyson outranks him. Homicide trumps Narcotics, every time, even though the prison sentences are often shorter.

Still, Bubba makes a show of fumbling with his keys, pretending to search for the one that fits his driver's-side lock.

"Going somewhere?" Tyson calls, his voice loud enough to wake the residents who live in the tumbledown pile of bricks and shit-showered "courtyard" across the street.

"Home," Bubba responds. "Boot there says it's Homicide only."

"Fuck him," Tyson says. The doughy kid is standing right beside him, but the rookie absorbs the insult, feet squared under his shoulders, arms at his sides. "He's an ex rent-a-cop on a power trip, isn't that right?" Tyson directs the question at the kid, and Lola thinks she can see his Adam's apple bob, a gulp mixed with fear and resentment. The gesture, even if it's only a reflex, makes Lola like the kid—he wants to talk back to Tyson. "Get over here, Bubba," Tyson rumbles, his back turned to the kid and to Bubba.

Lola watches Bubba cross the street, duck under the crime tape, and try for a sympathetic smile for the kid. The doughy uniform rejects it, his eyes on the street, looking for anyone who might challenge his authority. Unfortunately for him, the weary, wary neighborhood residents know to steer clear of the cops, even when they're bleary-eyed from working three jobs or coming down off last night's high.

"I gotta go," Kim says. "Gotta do my shopping."

Veronica gives Kim a hungry look—Lola knows the older woman wants to stay. "Shopping can't wait?"

"Nope."

"But this—" Veronica gestures to the cops and the yellow tape and the bodies lined up to see the body.

"What you mean, 'this'? Bodies always be droppin'," Kim points out.

"Not white ones," Veronica says, her voice so loud the crowd turns. Lola shoots them an apologetic smile. They're all trying to hear what the cops are saying, and here these two women have to go arguing about shopping and race.

"Yeah. 'Xactly. They don't give a shit about Carlos 'cause he's brown. Why should I stay here pretending like I care about some dead white girl?"

No, Lola thinks, *he was brown. He's dead. I killed him.*

"I'll stay," Lola tells Veronica, both because she has no intention of leaving and because she knows Veronica doesn't want to be at a murder scene alone. Like buying vodka solo on a Friday night, it wouldn't look right, even in this neighborhood.

"Thank you," Veronica huffs, and Kim disappears into the

crowd. Lola wonders why Kim doesn't rush the police now, in the flesh, demanding answers about her brother's case. People are so much more difficult to deny in the flesh, when they're not crackling, filtered voices over a telephone line. But she knows what Kim knows—in Carlos's case, no one is listening. And that is good for Lola.

Lola doesn't have to strain to hear Tyson give Bubba the rundown. "Proprietors came in early to get ready for the breakfast rush. Found the body at four thirteen a.m."

"Body? Here I thought you got me out of bed to bust some twenty-dollar junkie pro who ripped you off."

"You don't want to help, I call someone else."

"You had anyone else, you wouldn't have called me," Bubba says.

"Evidence of torture, epis under the nails," Tyson continues. Lola notes his refusal to acknowledge Bubba's comment and takes it as a confirmation of its truth. "She fought."

"Good for her," Bubba says, and he sounds like he means it. "This isn't my department. I arrest corner boys and watch them make bail three hours later, remember?"

"Maybe I can change that," Tyson says, voice lowered, some conspiratorial hint in his tone.

"Bullshit," Bubba says. "Why did you call me, Tyson?"

"Because you responded to what those boots thought was a drug deal gone bad two nights ago. How'd you happen to be there thirty seconds after the unis called it in?"

"I was in the neighborhood."

Tyson moves closer to Bubba, and now Lola has to drift two casual steps closer to hear. "Your colleagues, how they treatin' you, now that you're out?"

Bubba's eyes lower to his shoes, some shame driving them down.

Tyson continues. "Don't answer. I can guess. They wouldn't piss on you if you were on fire."

Bubba doesn't object.

"Fucking narc who has to go to rehab. Goddamn shameful."

Lola looks to Veronica, to see if she's getting all this, but Veronica has found another ear to bend, now that Kim has left. This one's a skinny teenager, his eyes hardened with too much life, but that doesn't stop Veronica.

"You should be getting ready for school or work, not out here watching some dead girl—"

With Veronica distracted, Lola wanders closer to the two sidelined cops. She ponders Bubba McMillan—a narc who had to go to rehab. A narc, or former narc, who was conveniently thirty seconds away from a drug drop gone wrong. A narc who might have found two million in heroin.

"Heard you picked up a new CI at the scene. Some girl. What was her name?" Tyson again.

"She didn't give it."

Lola realizes they're talking about the blond tweaker, the one who caused Hector to lose his trigger finger.

"And you didn't ask. Always protecting the scared little addict girls."

"Yeah, especially them," Bubba says, and his acknowledgment shuts Tyson up. But only for a few seconds.

"Heard there was no cash at the scene. No product. Your girl must have told you it was a drop. She the courier?"

"There any coffee here?" Bubba asks.

Lola decides to take Bubba's nonanswer as a yes. Blondie told him the scene was a drop, and she was the courier. She hopes the little injured victim gave up her boss's name, too.

"She tell you who she worked for?"

"She did that, she'd be dead."

So? Lola thinks. Of course Blondie couldn't have given up any information Lola didn't already know.

"So where is she?"

"Confidential."

"She gave up Darrel King. Now his girl turns up dead." Of course the cops know Darrel, one of the largest players on the L.A. drug scene. They don't know the Crenshaw Six, or Garcia, or her. The thought pleases and saddens Lola all at once. "I want to talk to your CI."

"I didn't arrest her. Didn't find any drugs on her."

"And you don't know where she is now?"

"Didn't say that. I will say I'm not taking you to her."

"You think I want to go wading through junkies at some crack house?"

"Crack's not her thing."

"Fuck you."

"Fuck you back."

"Can you at least bring her in for a friendly conversation?"

"Maybe."

"When?"

The two walk farther away, their voices fading, and Lola has to think fast. She ducks under the tape and smacks into the squishiness of the rookie uniform.

"I'm sorry, ma'am—"

"Emergency. I need to talk to the Amaros. It's about their daughter." The rookie doesn't know what to do, so Lola grabs onto his arm, as if she's going to faint. "Please. Just one minute, and I'll leave."

The doughball relents with a murmured, "Just this once," as if he will see Lola at another murder scene, where she will once again ask to speak to the witnesses who found the body.

Lola hurries over to the Amaros, and Juan nods a greeting to her. "Lola—"

"You okay?" she asks, but she doesn't listen to their responses. She needs to hear what Bubba and Tyson are saying.

"Tomorrow afternoon, Pacific Division," Bubba says, and that's it. He leaves Tyson standing next to the weathered picnic table, a few to-go wrappers skittering across it because some of Mamacita's patrons couldn't be troubled to walk the five paces to the rusted metal trash bin and deposit their dinner remains last night.

For the first time, Lola sees her, sprawled on top of the table, arms and legs akimbo. Left arm flopped over one side, right arm above her head, as if she is sleeping. Her legs are spread, hanging one to a side. Her too-short skirt is hiked up above her thighs, and her camisole is unbuttoned to expose her breasts. The bullet hole is a gaping red, perfectly centered between her wide-open eyes. Mila. Dead.

Lola likes what Jorge and Marcos did, putting her on display like this. Mila would have liked it, too. She is the center of attention, as any suburban girl who turns to cocaine likes to be.

But Lola doesn't have time to admire her boys' handiwork. She has only forty-six hours to return the cartel's cash and heroin. She needs to find a way into the meeting between Tyson and Bubba's meth head CI at Pacific Division tomorrow.

Beside her, Juan Amaro speaks in an uncharacteristic ramble. "Found her this morning when I was opening up. Who would leave her here?"

Me, you irresponsible old fuck, thinks Lola, who's been pissed at the Amaros since she found out they gave Lucy back to her junkie mother. She wanted to figure out a way to get them back for that, to hurt their business, and now there's Mila, sprawled on a picnic table—the first dead bird—and the Amaros—out of business for the day—the second dead bird. And there is Lola, the stone.

ELEVEN

FAVORITE

Half an hour later, Lola lounges in her living room recliner, feet up, head back, mouth open as she dozes. Home from Mamacita's, she dreams of El Coleccionista's boss, the person who has ordered Lola's death. In her dream, the boss is a woman not unlike herself—though she's well dressed in a white Prada suit that seems to repel the Mexican desert dust. The boss sips her coffee in the shade of a Mexican hacienda, the white stucco walls matching her suit. In her dream, Lola looks down at her own white shirt—a cotton wife-beater—and the baggy cargo pants that make up her standard uniform. She does not belong in a Mexican hacienda. She can't be here.

Her eyes fly open, taking in the recliner's pattern of fat white fox-hunters, the sound of children screaming outside her barred living room window. She belongs here, and she knows El Coleccionista's boss is not a woman, but a man who has evaded both identification and law enforcement for the past decade.

Valentine whines at the foot of the foxhunting chair—needs to pee—and Lola digs herself out of the cushions with the slow, resentful movement of a person much older than her twenty-six years.

"Let me get your leash," Lola says, padding to the front door. She retrieves the old roped leather from a row of hooks, lined up like fallen question marks under a smiling pit bull. Garcia didn't

see the need for coat hooks. Carlos had had the same attitude—
Who needs coat hooks in L.A.? *Well, you don't have to use them for
coats,* Lola thinks now as she clips the leash onto Valentine's collar.

Lola opens the door without checking the peephole. Minus her
soldiers, no one in the neighborhood thinks she has enough power
to want her dead. But now, in the fishbowl between sleep and wake,
she thinks of Kim and of Carlos and has a flash of Kim walking
toward her front door with a sawed-off shotgun in one hand, a chocolate cake in the other. Still, Garcia can be out of bed and down the
stairs with his .45 in three seconds. Lola has timed him, though of
course she would never tell him that.

But the men she sees sitting in a black SUV at her corner are not
from her neighborhood. They are brown, like her, and clean-cut,
but they wear suits and hair product and sunglasses. Government?
No, Lola thinks, as she and Valentine hustle out the front door and
closer to the SUV. *Those suits are tailored. Those men are not government. They are cartel, and from the looks of their wardrobe,
they are several steps above El Coleccionista's pay grade.*

Lola feels a surge of fear and then pride that she has finally
graduated from middle management.

Then she sees Lucy, wandering across the street between Lola
and the cartel's SUV, a filthy Donald Duck backpack on her shoulders, a teddy bear propped like a baby on her hip.

"Lucy!" Lola calls, a note of panic in her voice before she
remembers these men are watching her. "Your mother know you're
out here?"

Lucy freezes in the middle of the street and stares at Lola, recognizing her. Lola wants to tell the girl she's sorry for the sharp
tone, but she has to make it look like she doesn't give a fuck, or
Lucy's life could be in danger.

Lola moves toward Lucy, the dog fighting to pee on the other
end of the leash, so that it's quite a picture they make—Valentine,
the lifeline, squatting on the single patch of ashy grass at the curb,
Lola holding the dog's leash as she inches into the street, Lucy frozen there with her Donald Duck backpack, trademarked merchandise Lola knows must have fallen off a truck for a ghetto kid to be

carrying it around. Crumbs, toast or bread from days ago, dot Lucy's dark hair, and she smells of dried sweat and grease. Has she been at Mamacita's? Lola's heart plunges—did Lucy see Mila's body?

"Lola," says Lucy. She doesn't talk much, and she seems to be trying out Lola's name for size. Valentine approaches, and Lucy launches onto Lola's leg, clinging to it, eyes squeezed shut. "Don't."

"She's friendly," Lola promises.

"She fights," Lucy says. To her, that is the role of a pit bull, and Lola doesn't want to ask why she knows that.

"No. She's not like other dogs," Lola says, and Lucy's eyes watch hers without meeting them. The little girl sees she is clinging to Lola's leg and removes herself, clearing her throat in some sort of embarrassment at affection that should be beyond her years.

Tentative, Lucy reaches out a hand, and Valentine licks the dried sweat from the girl's palm. Lucy tilts her head, tickled, but unable to giggle. *Someone should teach this child joy,* Lola thinks.

"Did you run away from home?" Lola asks.

Lucy nods.

"What about your grandparents?"

Lucy shakes her head.

"You don't want to live with them?"

Lucy shakes her head again. Lola wants to ask why, but they are standing in the middle of a ghetto street, in the crosshairs of a couple of bespoke-suited cartel henchmen.

"Are you hungry?"

A nod from Lucy.

She tosses a glance to the cartel soldiers in the SUV and says, too loud, "Let's go inside and call your mother."

Five minutes later, Lola places a chipped blue plate of scrambled eggs and pico de gallo in front of the girl. She has heated tortillas, which she places next to the eggs, but Lucy stares at the food, gulping and gaping. She is hungry and overwhelmed. Lola feels her longing, her desire to set upon the food like a starving wolf, to devour it with sharp bites, feeling the metallic tinge of other blood on her gums.

"Eat," Lola says. Then, realizing she gives the same okay to

Valentine before she allows the dog to approach her bowl, she continues, "It's for you. All of it."

Lucy bows her head, quick, little fingers folded into little fists clasped together. Lola realizes she is praying, and, on instinct, she, too, bows her head, clasps her fists, brown hands rippling with veins, blood, life. Lola is strong. But by the time Lola has figured out what to say to God, Lucy has finished her own prayer and is tucking into the food, her hand gripping her fork, determined to shovel as many eggs as possible into her mouth at once.

Lola finds Lucy's dedication to getting fed admirable. She does not know what to make of her own determination to feed the girl. She has never wanted children because to her, they would be extensions of herself she must let roam around a dangerous world where someone, anyone, could extinguish them to get at her. She does not need any more Achilles' heels. And she does not want to have to teach a child what it takes to survive in this particular world.

Hector, she thinks now, *Hector in the hospital.* Not her child, but she raised him, and look what happened.

"I'm still hungry," Lucy says when she's scraped the blue plate clean and folded the last tortilla into her tiny o-shaped mouth. A second later, Lucy seems to realize she's spoken words she might not have dared utter in front of her own mother, words that might seem like a complaint and therefore earn her a backhand or three hours in a tight closet with no light or water. Lola does not have to be inside this girl's head to read her mind.

"I'll make you more," Lola says, and she rises to return to her skillet, cracks more eggs into a bowl, whisks them with whole milk, salt and pepper. She scrambles them in heated butter, not letting them get brown and scabbed. The food Hector's getting in the hospital must be horrible. "You want bacon?"

Lucy nods, eyes wide with hope and hunger.

Over the second helping, Lola nods to the Donald Duck backpack, abandoned on the floor, the zipper opened wide enough for her to see several changes of underwear, a toothbrush, and some pajamas. "You trying to get to your grandparents?" She knows the answer from the street but wants another stab at the truth.

Lucy shakes her head. "I'm not supposed to bother them."

Lola doesn't ask where that edict came from—Rosie or the Amaros themselves. She commends herself on her decision to display Mila's body at Mamacita's. Fuck them for not taking care of what's theirs. She does it for her own fucking mother, because she understands the rules of the world. Still, she's relieved Lucy hasn't been near her grandparents today. If she had, the little girl would have seen one more dead body than she needed to.

"Bet they're worried about you."

"They don't know."

"Know what?"

Lucy takes a pause, chewing her bacon. Lola fried it crisp so Lucy could take quick, easy bites. She knows Lucy is buying time.

"Is it your mother?" Lola asks. "You don't have to say. Just nod your head."

Lucy nods her head.

"She gone?"

"No," Lucy says, and Lola thinks the saddest thing she's ever seen is a five-year-old girl sighing. Of course, it's not the saddest thing Lola has ever seen. Maybe she is just wishing it were.

"She home?"

Lucy nods. "With her new boyfriend. He likes me." With those words, Lola knows everything. How is it such a common story that anyone, ghetto or not, could fill in the blanks and determine Lucy's reasons for running away?

"I'll call your grandparents." Lola will make them see their obligations to this girl.

"Don't." Lucy stops Lola, who's scrolling through her cell, searching for Mamacita's number in her contacts.

"They'll take care of you, Lucy," Lola says, hoping it's true. They know their daughter is an addict disaster and an abusive mother. They'll have to make sure Lucy has a roof over her head, clean clothes, food. They'll even hug her a couple times a week, especially if Lola sends Garcia down there threatening to burn down their lifeblood.

"They know him," Lucy says.

Shit. Lola doesn't want to tell Lucy her grandparents will believe her. She's not that stupid, to take people's inherent goodness as a given just because they run a successful business and feed her soldiers some damn good bulk tacos on occasion. Lucy has her reasons for thinking they won't listen, and if Lola just sits very still, Lucy will tell her what they are.

"He's their landlord's son," Lucy says. From the way she sounds out the word *landlord,* Lola can't be sure she understands its meaning, but Lucy does seem to have grasped that her grandparents need this man, her mother's new boyfriend's father, to keep their business up and running.

Lola hates when children have to be so smart.

"I see," Lola says. Her mind spins—the Amaros' landlord's son is a pedophile. Could her two birds, one stone theory work here? She could burn down his property, ruin their business, clean up her community, one pervert at a time. Lola might have only forty-five hours to live. Destroying a pedophile seems like a worthy item to add to her bucket list.

"Can I stay here?" Lucy asks, stealth, trying to dart in under Lola's logical to-do list so she'll get an answer from the heart, that unguarded vessel somewhere at Lola's center.

Would keeping Lucy here, in a stucco shambles of a house that serves as a gang's headquarters, be worse than letting her return to her mother and her new man? No, Lola decides. Guns and drugs are not the worst things in the world for a child to see. They should be, but they are not.

In response, Lola rises and removes the toothbrush, pajamas, and underwear from Lucy's Donald Duck backpack. She puts the dirty clothes into a small pile for the washer, but she leaves behind one pair of underwear—pale pink, except for blood where there never should be for a girl this young. Lucy will never have to see them again.

TWELVE

ANYTHING

A wrought-iron fence, six feet high to Lola's eye, borders L.A. County Hospital. The building itself is imposing—tiered and stacked at varying heights. She enters expecting courtrooms and jail cells.

Instead, she finds a bustling emergency room—one waiting patron bent over a trash can, a janitor poised with a mop nearby; another—alone, female, wedding ring, sunglasses—holding her broken arm. *Domestic,* Lola thinks with some satisfaction. At the reception desk, she finds a bright nurse, no more than Lola's age, her red hair scraped back into a ponytail, her green eyes shining with an energy Lola suspects must come from knowing you're doing good in the world, asking her if there's a problem with the child and saying, if so, they can see her right away.

Lola has forgotten about Lucy, that the little girl hadn't said outright she wouldn't stay in the house alone with Garcia, but Lola had known better than to put that decision on a child. Now, she finds she is gripping Lucy's hand so tight it must hurt. Still, she can't bring herself to ease the pressure, and Lucy doesn't seem bothered. The little girl is staring up at the nurse in what Lola decides is awe, and she knows the pang she experiences from the realization is jealousy.

"Hector Vasquez," Lola says, her tone brusque, like she's got more important shit to do. She is behaving the way she expected the nurse to. She had braced herself for a *Calm down, ma'am, you'll have to wait,* or a *You'll need to fill out the forms correctly, in block letters, black or blue ink, before the doctor can see you.*

"Oh," the nurse says, and Lola forgets the jealousy, forgets her expectations, and thinks only that in sparing her brother, maybe she's killed him anyway.

"Can we see him? I'm his sister."

"You're Lola?" the nurse asks. Hearing her name come from this white bright happy woman's mouth throws Lola.

"Yes."

"He's been asking for you." The nurse doesn't even have to look at her computer. "Mr. Vasquez has been moved to the third floor."

"What's on the third floor?"

"A room to keep him comfortable."

"Comfortable?" The word here, where misery and bustle combine, seems out of place.

"He's septic."

"What?" Lola's hand grips Lucy's even tighter now.

"The wound he sustained from the meat slicer was infected."

So that's the story Hector invented. A meat slicer. She guesses you could call a butcher knife a meat slicer. She likes Hector for telling some skewed version of the truth.

"You can go on up. Elevator's just down the hall on your left."

Lola moves at a repressed run toward the dinging elevator. She wants whoever's there to hold the door, now that she knows her brother wants her. He's not expecting her; she wasn't even thinking she would come here until she was in her car with Lucy in the backseat, the safest place, Lola figured, despite her lack of car seat. She drove with the speed of traffic, knowing that was safer than driving slow, her eye remembering to glance in the rearview to see if the cartel SUV was following her. It wasn't. She had to console herself then, remind her ego that the cartel thought Garcia was in charge. They are watching him, not her. Then she was pulling into the hospital parking lot, seeking the lone empty spot and thinking that she put her baby brother here.

Now, running for the elevator, she remembers she meant to bring muffins or migas or something for Hector, and she's forgotten. Shit.

"Hold the door," she says, too loud, and she catches a glimpse of a stocky man in a shitty suit spotted with sweat pressing what must be the Door Close button, because the doors do just that, leaving Lola and Lucy stranded.

"Motherfucker," she says, then sees Lucy pursing her lips not in judgment, but fear. She can't have a temper around this little girl.

"I'm sorry," Lola says. "I didn't mean that."

"He should have held the door for us," Lucy says.

"Yeah," Lola agrees, glad the girl seems to have some sense of right and wrong despite her junkie mother and her worthless grandparents.

The third floor is quieter, the people in the waiting room in less pain. The television there plays a game show on mute. On the floor in front of a middle-aged man, a child plays with toy cars, making them crash into each other head-on before losing interest and starting to rip pages from gossip magazines that have felt the touch of a thousand thumbs.

Lola spots Marcos outside a door toward the end of a low, white corridor. He drove Hector here yesterday morning with orders to stay until Lola's baby brother was released. Now, Marcos has his hands in his pockets and is rising up and down on his tiptoes. Lola wonders if this is an exercise he learned in prison, something to help pass the time without freezing the muscles, but when she gets to the end of the corridor, she sees another man around the corner, this one in his fifties, wearing hard-soled loafers and a cotton sweater that only partially disguises his burgeoning gut. Like Marcos, this man has his hands in his pockets, and he's rising up and down on his tiptoes, waiting outside a door that holds someone sick.

Marcos is copying this man, pretending to be a person.

The thought breaks Lola's heart a little, her soldier faking humanity in a hospital. Then she remembers there are no rules of etiquette to follow in the face of death and sickness, and Marcos didn't fucking call her to tell her her brother was septic.

"The fuck?" she starts in, then remembers Lucy and mutters "Sorry" to the little girl.

"Just words," Lucy says in a singsong Lola hasn't heard her use before.

"I was gonna call you . . ." Marcos says. He's trailed off without Lola holding up a hand for him to stop. "But I didn't know if you'd want that. After you sliced him like that."

Now Lucy looks up at Lola in alarm, and Lola hisses at Marcos. "I have a kid with me."

Marcos notices Lucy for the first time. "Why you got a kid with you?"

Lucy and Marcos are both looking at Lola for an answer now, but Lola doesn't have one.

"It was an accident," Lola says to Lucy now. "The slicing thing."

The little girl nods and looks away, and Lola sees, in the girl's motion, Lucy's deciding to accept the truth Lola has conjured for her.

It pisses Lola off, having to lie to Lucy like this. She takes two steps toward Marcos and speaks in a hushed tone so the little girl can't hear. "They said he was asking for me. You sure you didn't just want to let Hector die without saying good-bye to his sister?"

"Shit, Lola, he ain't dyin'," Marcos says.

"He fucked up."

"No shit."

"Were you punishing him?"

"Nah, man, that's your job."

Lola could take this as insubordination, that Lola hasn't done her job, but she can see in the way Marcos is looking up and down the corridor, making sure no one is listening, that no one is watching her, that he doesn't mean it that way. Marcos doesn't speak in subtext. He doesn't know how. The lines of logic and decency that divide humans from the animals don't exist for him. This close, he smells of raw flesh, as if his mother didn't cook him long enough in her belly and now he's poison to anyone who tastes him.

Three years ago, Marcos didn't bow down to her over Carlos's warm dead body. She had alibied Jorge, and she knew Garcia wanted to fuck her despite Kim and her endless folding of washed onesies for their unborn child. Marcos was different. Marcos was created by the stepfather who beat him. Lola knew Marcos had been looking for the man since he got out of prison a few months back. It seemed the evil stepfather had jumped ship, leaving Marcos's mother as soon as he knew Marcos was getting out. The man knew to run scared. He had disappeared, poof, and Lola knew Marcos must have been asking why he couldn't have done everyone a favor and vanished fifteen years prior.

Lola also knew Marcos didn't understand how to find someone. He only understood how to kill them once they were found.

The day she drove him out to the desert, past bakery restaurants meant for retirees and dollar stores advertising discounted junk on their marquees, Marcos had sat up straight in his seat. He hadn't wanted to come with her, but Jorge had told him to. Marcos was like that, scary to one person, obedient to his true friends. Lola already loved him for it.

She had pulled up in front of a small, Spanish-style house with a clean pickup parked outside. She said, "Open the glove box."

The gun Marcos took out was unregistered, the serial numbers filed off.

Marcos looked at her, unsure what to do. He didn't know that he was waiting for her orders, but Lola did. She knew she had won him before she even gave him his prize.

"Your stepfather lives here."

She didn't have to tell him not to let anyone see him. She let him out without another word and said she would be at the dollar store two blocks away when he was ready.

Fifteen minutes later, he found her in the aisle that held cleaning supplies, stocking up on generic toxic shit for her mother's apartment.

"I'm ready," he had said. And he was.

Now, outside Hector's hospital room, Lola nods toward Lucy. "Take her to get something to eat," she says to Marcos.

Lucy looks to Lola as the rancid, raw man approaches her.

"He's going to take you to get some food," Lola says. "He's all right. He won't take you anywhere there aren't other people."

Marcos knows to walk beside Lucy, his hands in his pockets, playing at casual to frighten her less. Lola wonders if he learned these things, how to show surrender, from being a child in a house where he must have wanted to disappear. Has he learned what not to do from his early abuse? Has she?

Hector's closed hospital door beckons, and while she wants to stay out here contemplating the cycles of abuse and whether or not they can be broken, she must go in. She was anxious to do it only five minutes before. Now, she has to force herself to turn the door handle and push, too hard, as if she's expecting resistance on the other side.

There is none. There is only Hector, propped up in a hospital bed, watching the same game show the waiting room patrons are ignoring. His hand is bandaged, and Lola can see a digit there, wrapped in gauze. They must have been able to reattach the finger. He's sipping what looks like lemonade from a straw and calling out, "Sixteen fifty! Sixteen fifty!"

He looks content.

Lola doesn't want to interrupt, wants to give him this serenity, but he sees her where he was expecting someone else, a nurse, maybe, and he turns down the television volume and puts down his drink. It saddens her, Hector's need to sit up straighter when she enters a room. Was he like this before? Or was he just her brother then?

"Hey," she says.

He bows his head in response, and Lola thinks of Marcos with his acknowledgment in words.

"I meant to bring you food."

"It's actually not so bad here," Hector says. "They got cheese-cake."

"Oh. That's good."

"Would you like to sit?" Hector casts his eyes around for a chair.

"Sure," Lola says, and she takes a seat on the very edge of the bed.

Hector shifts so she can have more room.

"How are you feeling?"

"Fine. Think they're just being overly cautious. Must have been a slow night." He tries a smile, and Lola responds in kind.

The television hums a catchy tune that hurts Lola's ears, then there is a commercial with a wrinkled celebrity sitting at a modest kitchen table, trying to sell reverse mortgages, whatever those are, to senior citizens. The word *reverse* strikes Lola as wrong—why would you want the reverse of what you worked so hard to get?

"Must have," she says after too much time has passed for it to qualify as a response to Hector's observation.

"Lola," Hector says, knowing she is somewhere else.

She covers his bandaged hand with hers and bows her head over it, kissing his hand, the gauze, his blood.

"Lola," Hector says, and his tone is sharper now, correcting her.

"I'm sorry," she mutters.

"I'm the one who should be saying that," Hector says, his cheeks flushing, not with humiliation, but with anger. "I'm the one who should be kissing your hand."

Lola sits back, crossing her arms. How is the reverse mortgage commercial still playing? She guesses senior citizens have nowhere to go in the middle of the day. Even if they wanted to get up for a snack, it might take them more than thirty seconds to cross their dated living rooms, to walk from armchair to refrigerator. They would have to hear the commercial. They would have to hear about the benefits, the importance, the need to call right now.

Her heart pounds and thumps then, and she wants to bolt. Hector was content without her here. He was at peace. She interrupted and upset the balance. Now, he is angry because she came here and reminded him he owed her something. That was not her intention. She came here as his sister.

"I'll do anything," Hector says. "What can I do?"

"Nothing."

"When's the deadline?"

"Forty-two hours."

"Lola," Hector says.

"Don't worry. It's not gonna happen."

"It's my fault," Hector says.

"No," Lola says, and he gives her a look that tells her not to lie to him. But that is her job, to protect him. Not to punish him.

"I'm gonna fix this, when I get out of here."

"What are you going to do?"

"I don't know."

"Then why'd you say it?"

Hector shakes his head and shrugs. "Sounded good."

Lola smiles at him. "Can't do that shit. Talk out of your ass like that."

"Learned it from you," Hector says, and Lola laughs loudly, competing with the game show jingle.

"I'm gonna make it up to you. I'm gonna fix this," Hector lies to her.

"I know you are," Lola lies back, a parent just wanting her baby to go back to sleep so she can get on with her day.

THIRTEEN

THE PACIFIC

"Three pearl necklaces, my best diamond earrings, and a set of Ginsu knives—not the kind for sale on television." The woman in front of Lola dictates her stolen possessions to a desk sergeant at the LAPD's Pacific Division. All Lola can see is the woman's back—she's blond, with the bob haircut, khaki Capri pants, and pastel cardigan of a smiling mother in a Swiffer commercial. She wears a diamond the size of a bullet on her left ring finger. Seeing the woman's weighted finger makes Lola think of Hector, and she has to look away.

From what Lola has gathered, Pacific Division operates at a slower pace than most precincts surrounding South Central. Maybe it is a particularly slow day here, but so far she hasn't seen so much as a cuffed prostitute grace the double doors since she arrived half an hour ago. The single perpetrator the cops have thrown in holding is a streaker—although the guy could just be a drunk who had the bad luck to take a piss where he didn't know people were watching. This issue—streaker or drunk—necessitated debate between ten detectives, all in off-the-rack suits and clip-on ties, slurping stale coffee into their mustaches as they deliberated.

"Could you describe each knife separately for me, ma'am?" The desk sergeant doesn't look up, his pen scratching paper as he fills out a robbery report. Lola prepares to wait another half hour. In her neighborhood, the only knife that would concern police would be one stuck in a throat.

In her neighborhood, no one wears matching cardigans. There, a single detective might bring in a different suspect on five different murders in one night. There, the interrogations were like therapy, with the detective giving the suspect coffee, the suspect pushing it back toward the detective. Eyelids got heavy. Cop and perp held each other up, needing each other, going through the dance they knew they had to, until the station or prison spit the perp back out to wash, rinse, repeat, and come back to the cop, faded and comfortable as an old T-shirt.

When did it stop? Never. Symbiosis was natural, Lola had learned in eighth-grade science class.

She imagines a world with no crime. No cops. No lawyers. No judges. She imagines the people who would be out of work and starving because crime had fed their families.

Who was anyone to judge her? She was keeping these assholes in their clip-on ties and American sedans. Everyone was always yammering about change, revive the neighborhood, her neighborhood, but no one was prepared for what came after better schools, cleaner sidewalks, full bellies, and arms full of healthy, bulging veins. Then what? Then there must be new ways to judge people. People will find new ways to make outcasts, because as always, some must suffer. Some people have to be less, so others can have more.

"Ma'am?" The desk sergeant speaks to Lola. The Brentwood woman has vanished, most likely to a German SUV parked far enough away that no one will scratch it. Lola wonders if Garcia has seen the woman walking to her car, crying into her cell phone as she describes her harrowing ordeal to another sympathetic sheltered ear.

Lola made Garcia wait in the car because he has visible gang markings. She does not, having never felt the desire to show off her loyalty. Besides, she is a woman. She can be here in peace.

Lola clears her throat as she contemplates the desk sergeant—tall, broad, older, probably in his fifties, with an eighties-style mustache that's still more pepper than salt. He wears a thin gold wedding band. She's guessing he's got kids, maybe a grandbaby. She bets he wants to retire alive, and that's why he's here, behind a counter, taking down tedious descriptions of steak knives.

"Ma'am? How can I help you?" the desk sergeant says. His smudged name badge reads "Tom," and his voice is not unkind. She must be his daughter's age, and he must see the sadness in her that she tries to keep hidden. He is a cop after all. Lola has found that, try as she might to despise them, many police can read a person in five seconds flat—hopes, fears, hungers. Then again, many can't.

"I need to report a missing person," Lola blurts out the lie. She's no good at stammering or faltering. She barrels ahead like a runaway train, leaving chaos in her wake.

"How long has the person been missing?"

"Almost forty-eight hours," Lola says. The timing is crucial.

"Almost?"

"Almost."

She has heard from other people in her neighborhood—cousins and friends and enemies—that the police won't do shit for a missing person if it hasn't been forty-eight hours. Even if said missing person is white.

"How long until it's been forty-eight hours?" Tom asks with a sigh. She had hoped for an impatient desk sergeant, but Tom's sigh bleeds empathy. She's in trouble.

"Forty-three minutes," Lola says.

Tom pauses, lifting his pen from paper so that the whole station suddenly seems quiet. Lola knows this can't be—there are detectives hunting and pecking at computers, and the streaker or alcoholic conspiracy theorist in holding hasn't shut up about 9/11 being an inside job. Lola understands the man's wish that there were something more, but she knows what happened happened, and people died the way they died, and there was nothing beyond that.

Tom sighs again, and Lola thinks, good, he'll refuse her request, and she will stomp her foot with feigned hysteria and say she will wait right over there on that bench where she can see the entrance and the exit and the entire fucking bullpen. She will wait out that forty-three minutes until she can march up there to Sergeant Tom and proclaim a fake missing relative she sure as shit doesn't want the police to find. And maybe in the meantime Sergeant Bubba will trot in here escorting her skinny meth head mark, and she can follow someone out the door and over the rainbow to her missing cash and heroin.

Instead, Tom says, "Give me a name."

Caught, Lola stammers her brother's name. "Hector Vasquez."

"He live in the area?"

Lola shakes her head.

"Address?"

Lola gives it, picturing Hector where she last saw him—at the hospital, watching a game show and asking for another piece of cheesecake.

Sergeant Tom peers over the spectacles Lola hadn't realized he was wearing until now. Another sigh. "This is Pacific Division, ma'am. If you'd like to report your brother missing, you'll need to go to your local police station in Huntington Park—"

Red tape. Lola had counted on it. She hadn't wanted to give a name, but she had needed to stall for time. It's brazen, for sure— giving a false report. Maybe she wants the police to punish her. But the cartel will do that before the cops ever have a chance. She doesn't know whose gauntlet she'd rather run—the cartel will make her death painful and long, Lola's guessing up to three days, but rotting a life away in prison with bland food and steel bars? Not for Lola. She wants to go out screaming, not sighing like poor content Sergeant Tom here.

"Okay. Okay, I—" Lola thinks fast. "I just gotta wait for my ride. Can I sit over there a few minutes?" Lola does her best to look tired. It's not difficult.

Sergeant Tom beckons for Lola to lean closer. "When you go to file your report, ask for Detective Mattingly," he says. "Richard Mattingly." He scratches out a quick note on the back of a business card. "Tell him Tom Wiederman sent you."

Lola takes the card. Sergeant Tom has excellent penmanship. Lola admires his dedication to his job, to helping her find her missing brother who isn't missing, even though she is brown and in the wrong neighborhood. Lola finds comfort in a person, cop or criminal, who can remain kind despite all the hate they've seen humans hurl at other humans. She can't figure out if it's mercy or naïveté, but she respects it.

It's too bad Sergeant Tom's help will go unused.

"You want something to drink while you wait? Bottle of water? Coffee?"

"So you'll have my DNA?" Lola says, too quick, because she shouldn't crack a joke now, when she's supposed to be worried about a missing relative.

"Well . . . yeah," Tom says, a smile playing at one corner of his lips, and Lola smiles back.

"Water," Lola says, and in seconds she's sitting on the bench with the view of the double doors and the bullpen, sipping cheap bulk bottled water. She could sleep here, with the bustle around her, although she could take some added action—a heated interrogation, a few token pimps—to help her relax. She'll have to settle for the streaker, who has shouted his way to sleep in holding, and the two detectives discussing last night's game—hockey, football, what does it matter. After today, she has one more day to live. She imagines more noise, more chaos, and her eyes flutter and close like some modern damsel in distress.

The woman who bursts through the double doors holding the tallest Starbucks cup they sell is a tiny storm, heels clicking, breath hurried as she pats several flying wisps of chestnut hair into place. She's wearing a tailored skirt and silk blouse. She can't be much more than five feet and a hundred pounds. Lola likes this game—it's like sports stats. Height, weight, reach. How else can you measure a person at first sight?

"Hey, Tom," the woman says, and she chucks her empty Starbucks cup into the wide can next to Lola as she's already pouring another from the communal pot near Tom's desk. She rips open a packet of powdered creamer with her teeth, a little animal.

"Andrea," Tom gives her a respectful bow of his salt-and-pepper head.

"That her?" The woman named Andrea jerks her chin toward Lola, and Lola sits up, because she didn't know the woman had even noticed her.

"Who?"

"Bubba's girl," Andrea says, and Lola realizes this fury of a woman has mistaken her for Sergeant Bubba's meth head CI. Andrea is looking for the same person she is—the small blonde from the drop.

"Nah, he's not here yet," Tom says. "You want me to take you to his desk? He bought his own chair. Real comfy."

"Smart. Your chairs are shit."

"I don't mind them," Tom says, and Lola sees a flash of hurt flicker across his face.

"Yeah, well," Andrea says, not finishing the sentence as she whips out an iPhone and starts to tap out an e-mail.

"You buy your own chair?" Tom asks, as if the concept of bringing one's own furniture, the kind you pick out yourself, is foreign to him. Of course, Lola has never heard of it either. If someone were to give her an office, with a desk and a chair, she wouldn't think to replace the furniture. It would be rude, wouldn't it?

"D.A.'s office gives you a decorating stipend. A very small stipend. Then you pick your own chair," Andrea says.

So she is a prosecutor. And she's here for Bubba's meth head. But surely not to prosecute, not if Blondie is a CI. They must have some sort of case against someone—Blondie's boss, Mr. X, the WASP from the Chrysler? Lola chugs some water. If she can get that clean-cut white man's name, it might be worth more to the cartel than the heroin and the cash combined. He is their sole competition.

"Where's the lineup?"

"Room Two," Tom says.

"Ugh. Bad lighting."

"Bad lighting in all the rooms," Tom says. "How's Jack?"

"Fine. Working."

Lola notes the wedding band glinting with tiny diamonds on Andrea's left ring finger. It's not gold, but not silver, either. What's the really expensive metal? Platinum. Andrea's wedding band must be platinum.

"Sure, a shrink's always on call," Tom says.

"Don't let him hear you call him that."

"I wouldn't," Tom says, and he and Andrea laugh. "Don't you want to sit down? Bubba's probably stuck in traffic. Who knows how long he'll be?"

"Yeah, I'll sit," Andrea says in a resigned tone, as if it's a punishment. She turns to Lola. "You mind?"

"Fine by me," Lola says, and the tiny woman sits, toe tapping on the hard tile floor. She hunches over her cell, tapping toes and fingers, incapable of sitting still.

Lola has cultivated the skill of calm over years of exhaustion. She is used to the world spinning around her. She is used to staying still in a storm so that no one notices her. It is the only way she has stayed alive. In Andrea's world of platinum wedding bands and workaholic shrink husbands, it doesn't matter if someone notices her. Andrea is at the top of the food chain, and there is no predator who can take her down. To Lola, she is an exotic species, a professional woman who walks into a room wanting others to know she is there. Andrea does not have to stay in the shadows.

Lola feels the urge to lay her head on the woman's shoulder, to wrap her body around her. *Stay still,* she wants to whisper. *Stay still.*

The double doors inch open, and Lola spots a broad back in a familiar leather jacket. Sergeant Bubba. When he turns to face the station, Lola sees the tiny blond meth head with him. She has traded her miniskirt and high heels for sweatpants and sneakers, and she looks twenty years younger—if it's possible for a twentysomething tweaker to look six. With her thread-thin hair, scraped into a messy ponytail, and scrawny skinny legs, lost somewhere deep in cotton fabric, she reminds Lola of a neglected child.

Blondie is not high, Lola can see that, but she has the wandering, confused eyes of someone taking their very first step on the road to recovery. Someone discovering the world anew, and maybe not liking what they see. Lola used to see the same look on her mother's face, every few years, every few state-run rehab centers—baffled at how the world off drugs grated and edged and stung. Of course, her mother was on heroin, and Blondie here's only struggling with meth. Her brain might be Swiss-cheesed, but she won't suffer the same physical withdrawal that kept Maria Vasquez shivering and sweating for days.

"Bubba." Andrea stands, her eyes on her phone's screen.

"Andrea," Bubba says, steering Blondie toward the bullpen.

"Tyson joining us?"

"He's sitting this one out."

Andrea nods to Blondie but speaks as if she's not there. "Let me guess. She won't talk with him present."

"Something like that."

Lola wonders if Bubba is telling the truth or claiming Blondie doesn't want Tyson there because Bubba can't stand the fat fuck.

"Any idea what intel she's got?" Andrea continues to ignore Blondie, whose eyes dart from doors to vending machine to Sergeant Tom, who tries out a kind smile she doesn't seem to understand is meant for her.

"She'll tell you inside."

"Room Two," Sergeant Tom says, and Lola thinks she hears a buzzer as Sergeant Tom presses a button somewhere under his counter. Then they're disappearing, Andrea leading the way, with Bubba behind her, his hand on Blondie's elbow.

But Blondie looks back one more time—is it the Doritos in the vending machine that have caught her eye, or maybe the stale cheese Danish?

Lola had planned for this moment, because of course Blondie might remember her—to her, Lola is the woman from the drop who ran after her when that nice Latino boy couldn't pull a gun on her.

"You." Lola hears the soft cracking voice of a girl who's forgotten she can speak.

"Huh?" Bubba turns to Blondie, who's staring at Lola, the flicker of recognition gaining light until it is a surefire flame.

To Lola, the seconds pass like long drops of blood drawn from her veins. Does she want Blondie to turn her in? Does she want to get closer to this case than she had planned?

"Nothing," Blondie says.

The word drains Lola. She is nothing. She ran after Blondie, sure, but she didn't catch her.

Blondie's about to disappear into the interview room when Lola hears it, soft. It's Bubba's voice, like gravel, as he says one beckoning word. "Sadie." Blondie's name.

FOURTEEN

WESTSIDE

Lola yanks open the passenger door and slips into Garcia's Honda Civic. "I have a name," she tells him in a whisper, because Lucy might still be sleeping in the back, as she was when Lola was able to slip out of the car and leave her alone with Garcia.

"The girl?"

"Sadie." Lola tries it out and finds saying the name sends her salivating and licking her lips.

"Just a first name?" Garcia asks, trying to mask the disappointment in his voice. Does he not want to hurt Lola's feelings, or does he not want to piss her off? It only strikes her now that Garcia saw her slice off her baby brother's trigger finger—the only part of his body that would make him money in gangland. Garcia must be questioning her loyalties. If she can turn on blood, she can turn on him, he must think. Is Garcia protecting her feelings now because he loves her or because he fears her?

Lola stops these destructive questions. It's like an older man asking if his plastic wife loves him for his money, or a trophy wife wondering if her rich husband loves her for her fake boobs. Yes and yes, but so what? Whatever the reason, you're together, digging, building, and fighting.

"Don't need a last name," Lola says. "She's in rehab."

"Which one?"

"Easy to find out." Lola pulls out her cell, ready to call Hector. The hospital discharged him several hours after her visit, when a bus crash flooded the emergency room with bleeding bodies. They needed his bed, but they gave him pain pills in exchange.

Lola knows Hector will welcome the tedious task of calling every rehab center in L.A. County until he finds a meth head named Sadie. It's a task that no one else wants, and he can start to prove himself again.

As Lola is about to dial, she remembers Lucy, the sleeping girl in the backseat; or she's assumed Lucy is sleeping, because everything back there is still. And the dog—Valentine—should be snoring, but there is only silence where the pit's gentle whir should be.

Lola turns to the backseat she suddenly knows will be empty.

"What the fuck?" This is Lola, losing her shit, and she's standing outside her body, watching her sinewy limbs scramble from front seat to backseat, as if she can tear up the upholstery and find Lucy there.

"I'm sorry." She hears Garcia trying to reach her. "I must have drifted off."

Garcia can sleep anywhere—the bed, the sofa, a kitchen chair, where Lola's seen him face-plant into steaming enchiladas and keep snoring. This quirk of his was funny only an hour ago. She wonders if that's what having kids does—takes qualities that were funny in your partner and molds them into liabilities.

"Cartel assholes," Lola says.

"They didn't follow us. Weren't even outside when we left."   -

"You don't know for sure." Lola thinks how it's scarier not having the Mexican men in their tailored suits outside her door. When she sees them watching, she knows where they are.

Now they might have taken Lucy. The thought blurs her vision, springs sweat from her pores, mixes up her brain like eggs before they go in a skillet. She sees red.

She has to save Lucy.

The blur of upholstery and bodies, hers and Garcia's, comes into focus as Lola's thoughts fall into one coherent piece. "She's too young to be out alone," she says, and Garcia looks more afraid now that her voice is steady than when she couldn't speak.

"She's not alone. She has a pit bull," Garcia points out, but Lola doesn't want his calm. She wants him to feel the weight of fault on his strong shoulders. He should be out of the fucking car now, panicked. Where is his guilt? She must make him feel it.

"Valentine could've run into traffic. Dragged Lucy with her," Lola tries.

Lola knows this scenario would never happen, because Valentine adjusts her behavior to match her particular master. With Garcia, she pulls at the leash and chases squirrels. She knows he can handle it. With Lola, she plods along, dutiful, the leash lax, and if she perks up at a random South Central rodent, she lets it go with a heavy heart and a pitiful look back at Lola. With Lucy, Lola knows, Valentine will be vigilant, head up, eyes open and meeting anyone who dares to cross a five-foot radius.

"Valentine wouldn't pull that shit," Garcia says, and Lola sees blood when she looks at him. She can't pierce his pragmatic armor—is it because he's a man? Then she remembers—Lucy is not his child. Lucy is not her child. If she can remember that, she has a better chance of getting Lucy back.

"We'll split up," Lola says, and Garcia nods, his movements quick and efficient, but not urgent. They break apart to search their respective halves of the police station's parking lot.

As Lola weaves through the cars, she calms herself by trying to tell cop vehicles from criminal ones: unmarked Crown Vic, cop; tricked-out Impala with custom window tint, criminal. After about ten cars, she gives up. The game is too easy, and the realization unsettles her, the old saying about judging a book by its cover ringing in her ears. *Yes,* she thinks, *judge.* That is called instinct, and whatever nagging feeling about a person grabs you and won't let you go is probably right. How shitty.

"Lola!" She hears the little girl's voice then sees her five spaces away, standing on the curb facing the busy main street, Valentine by her side.

Lola feels a drowning rush of relief. Then she sees they're not alone. A tall man, middle-aged with a slight paunch, bends over to pet Valentine. He wears a Hawaiian shirt and khaki pants, casual loafers with no strings.

Lola thinks of Maria and her childhood and the white men like this who would only venture into the ghetto to fuck a poor brown child. She breaks into a run, unable to cover the short distance as fast as she'd like.

"Hey!" she shouts. Valentine looks up, caught, because that is what Lola says when she wants Valentine to stop doing something—chewing furniture, eating tree bark, eyeing a Chihuahua like so much lunch.

"Hey," the man responds with a casual wave that matches his casual clothes, clothes Lola's instinct tells her he spent hours picking out this morning to appear nonthreatening.

She fingers the switchblade she shouldn't have been able to sneak into an LAPD precinct but could and did. Her pocket is large, and it swallows her hand like a favorite blanket. The knife's aluminum handle cools her fiery palm.

"Nice day, huh?" the man continues. "Sunshine, just the right amount of breeze."

Lola shouts something to Lucy in Spanish, she doesn't know what. Something about stepping away from the man, getting down. It is not meant to make sense. It is meant to scare the white man, because he has a minority bearing down on him, and can't he see her hand in her pocket? Doesn't he, shouldn't he, expect her to pull a weapon? Shouldn't he back the fuck down? Isn't that what running, shouting, hand-in-pocket brown-skinned woman means?

No, Lola thinks, and it's the woman part that sticks, that deflates her status from terror red to something like light lavender.

"I found your daughter," the man says as Lola reaches them. She makes it a point not to breathe hard, despite her screaming lungs and red cheeks. She keeps her mouth sealed in a single straight line of plump lips.

"She's not—" Lucy starts, then catches Lola's eye. Lucy must see some sadness there that Lola didn't know she had, because Lucy doesn't say that Lola isn't her mother. Instead, she says, "Thank you." Then she, too, seals her mouth in the single straight line, and Lola finds the imitation charming. And smart. An unreadable face will help Lucy once she's out in the world. Although maybe Lola's face is not as unreadable as she thought, if a five-year-old can decipher a fleeting dash of pain there.

"What's your name?" Lola turns to the middle-aged man.

"Harry."

"Your real name."

The man chuckles. "Why would I lie?"

"It's what criminals do," she says.

In a single swift motion, Lola whips the knife from her pocket, flipping the blade out. The metal is two inches wide, glinting in the bright sunshine they're having from the nice weather the casual man pointed out. The blade looks as thin as a single sheet of paper. It is surgical, precise, clean. Its tip comes to a sharp point, which Lola holds toward the man's paunch. He steps back, hands up.

"We're outside a police station," he reminds her.

"And you're lucky I don't turn you in."

"Your word against mine," he says, and Lola realizes she was wrong—he did see how it was before, when she was running at him. He knew to judge her by skin color, but he wasn't judging the physical harm she could do to him. He was judging what a cop would believe from her versus him, and he won every scenario. "I'm betting you or whoever you're picking up here wasn't on the right side of the bars."

"The fuck you know about it . . ." Lola mutters.

"Hunch," he says as he holds up a badge. "Harry Rauch. Vice."

Lola feels the knife handle in her sweaty palm, where she's still holding it, frozen in pouncing position even though she knows she's misjudged this man. "You gonna arrest me?"

"Nah. You're one of the few actually takes care of your daughter."

His surprise mercy forces Lola's knife hand to her side. She takes Valentine's leash and Lucy's hand. As they walk past Crown Vics and lowriders, Lola remembers her game—cop or criminal. Maybe it's not that easy.

They find Garcia back at the car, his cell phone out, dialing. "I called ten times. Everything okay?" he asks, even though he must be able to tell from Lola's sagging shoulders that it is not.

"Yeah," she lies.

Valentine leaps into the backseat with Lucy, collapsing against the little girl's tiny thighs with a contented sigh. Lola would like to think Valentine would have come to Lucy's aid if some dangerous man were to make a move, but maybe Valentine has forgotten that people can do her harm. Unfortunately, it's all Lola can remember, a fact that could have gotten her in big fucking trouble ten minutes ago. Assault with a deadly weapon. On a police officer. Sentence would have to be life. Or death. Fuck. When did she start seeing every stranger as a fatal struggle?

"Want to go to the beach?" Garcia asks, his voice too high, his suggestion absurd. They have never been to the beach together. They have no towels or flip-flops or bathing suits. Garcia is grasping, trying to find something to restore balance. But Lola doesn't think she can look at a wave crashing against sand without feeling a fierce isolation from the other beachgoers, dressed appropriately in bikinis and sarongs. She will not look right in her cargo pants and wife-beater. Garcia will take off his shirt, revealing tattoos snaking across sweating brown skin. The white people will look twice at them, then they will scoot away, foot by foot, until they have crossed some invisible line where they feel safe. Lola, Lucy, and Garcia do not belong here.

"Lola," Garcia says, and she hears a panicked edge in his voice. Her heart floods with love for him, worried about her, and she sinks into the Honda's upholstery, where she belongs, with him, her sleeping pile of would-be daughters next to her.

"Let's go home," she says.

FIFTEEN

BROTHERHOOD

Three hours later, Lola wakes to sunlight fading on the other side of her bedroom curtains. An insistent ring drowns out the dull drone of Garcia's snores. The landline. Only three people have the number.

"Yeah?" she says. They don't have caller ID for the cheap plastic phone with big buttons and an answering machine that runs on tape. Lola expects her mother's fading chirp on the other end, telling Lola not to worry, but her pipes have burst or her hot water's not working, and does Lola know the best plumber to call? Maria Vasquez assumes her daughter worries about her. She never calls on her son for any of her "emergencies," because it is Lola's job, not Hector's, to take care of her. The work of nurture falls on female shoulders. It is the same across classes, races, and religions. *Fucking bullshit,* Lola thinks.

"Lola?" It is Hector, his voice an octave higher than normal, the octave reserved for uncertainty and questioning, as if he's thinking someone besides Lola might answer the phone. But there is only Garcia, a sliver of restful drool wetting the pillow beneath him, and Lucy, asleep in the next room, cuddled up with Valentine and a Spanish-English dictionary, the sole book Lola could find in the house. But Lucy is bilingual, and Lola sighs now, thinking how use-less she must seem to the girl.

"Yeah," Lola says, not a question this time.

"It's Hector." His voice jangles with nerves.

"I know, honey," Lola says in the voice of a mother. She needs him to tell her what's got him scared. That won't happen if he's scared of her, too.

"It's . . . something's happened. Can you come over here?"

"Where?" Lola asks, wondering if the cartel has decided to skip her and go for Hector instead. She's got one more sleep by her count, though, and she had planned to call Hector to get started on the search for Sadie as soon as she woke. The drugs and cash are either with that wisp of an addict or her cop protector, and Lola doesn't consider either of them a match for her.

"Mom's," Hector says, and Lola knows this particular drug prob-lem has jack shit to do with the Los Liones cartel.

Twenty minutes later, she's standing in her mother's bare living room, taking stock of the stripped space. Television, stereo, furni-ture, all gone.

Lola moves at a stroll into the bedroom, where the faded flo-ral duvet cover, differing from Lola and Garcia's only in color, is folded neatly under the two feather pillows. But when Lola opens the dresser, her mother's jewelry box is empty.

"I called earlier, to see if Mom needed anything," Hector says. He clasps his hands together, and Lola notes with some satisfaction that he is able to intertwine his fingers, including the bandaged one, in a pose fit for a nervous prayer. "I was at the store. Needed coffee. Thought you were probably busy."

Lola hears judgment where Hector meant none—*You were probably too busy to take care of your own mother.* She knows he meant to help her, to start taking over some of Maria's care. After all, Lola will probably die tomorrow because of his fuckup.

"Uh-huh," she manages. She wants him to see her stroll, her slender finger reaching out, slow, to take in the emptiness. She wants him to see that their mother's disappearance does not alarm her. Of course, if it were just their mother missing, Lola might not know what the hell happened. Lucky for them, Maria Vasquez took all the shit fit to pawn with her, so Lola knows the score of the game she has watched play out countless times before.

Their mother is back on smack, and she needed cash to get her next fix, and maybe her next, and maybe even her next after that.

Lola imagines Maria pacing in an alley identical to the one where Lola stood waiting to talk to Mila. Maria will be waiting for the protection of darkness, when the dealers emerge from the shadows like so many rats.

Drugs are Lola's business, too, though. Does that mean she can't judge these alley sloths, preying on street addicts? Who does she think she's getting drugs for? White-collar hedge-fund managers or movie producers? Who is she to say her mother doesn't deserve a fix?

"Lola?" It's Hector again, in that questioning voice that rakes at her heart. "What do you think . . . where do you think . . ." He trails off, because he already knows the answers to his unfinished questions.

Lola throws an arm around his neck, pulling him down to her level so she can kiss the top of his head. His hair smells like freshness, and it's still damp from the shower. She wonders what he had planned tonight, before their mother went and fucked up their lives a little bit more.

"Shouldn't be surprised," Hector says, Lola's lips still lingering on his hair.

"She was doing better," Lola lies, because she doesn't believe any addict is ever doing better. They're just at the top or bottom of their respective lifelong roller-coaster ride, waiting to drop, or waiting to climb up from rock bottom.

"Yeah," Hector says, and Lola can tell he doesn't believe it either. Does the realization mean he's growing up?

"You had dinner?" Lola asks, because she wants out of here. She'll keep paying the rent, maybe drop by every couple of weeks to check mail and wipe down the dust until her mother decides this time she's getting clean for real. Then the cycle will begin again, with Lola making enchiladas and mopping floors every week, both of them pretending Lola's helping and Maria's recovering.

"No," Hector says, and they're almost to the front door, Lola about to tell him to lock it behind him, when he asks, "Why do you think . . . this time? Some bad news shit or something?"

Lola remembers her last conversation with Maria. Her parting words. Hector's in the hospital. The realization smacks her, shaking her body from the top of her head to the ends of her toes, pinched in her cargo boots. She had taken such care to make her parting words to her mother sting. *Your son. In the hospital.*

And now, instead of buying some fucking flowers and candy and going to hold her son's hand like a decent mother, Maria Vasquez has pawned all her shit for heroin.

Lola has fucked up. In her hurry to deliver alarming news to her mother, Lola forgot about Hector, her younger brother, who somewhere deep down in his young bones thought this recovery would be their mother's last, that Maria would kick her habit and start worrying after her children—were they getting enough to eat, would Hector ever think about settling down, why hasn't Lola had a baby yet?

But all these questions have always been too much for Maria. Their mother lives in the moment in a way Lola never could. She has a focus and determination to achieve a single goal—scoring her next fix.

Lola's to-do list runs much longer—shoot Darrel King's girl, retrieve cash and heroin, learn to withstand cartel torture. She has lost control of all the webs she's been spinning, and she's entangled Hector in a way she didn't see coming.

She must learn to think twenty moves ahead. Until she does, she's no leader.

"I told her you were in the hospital," Lola says.

Hector looks at her, but Lola holds her chin high. She wants him to tell her it's her fault that Maria relapsed, but he doesn't say anything.

"So?" Lola asks, unsure what to think of Hector's silence.

"You got your reasons." Hector shrugs. She wishes he would rail at her, maybe take a swing. She wouldn't punish him. They're alone. She could tell her other Crenshaw Six boys she'd taken a tumble down the stairs her house doesn't have.

"Hector," she says, and he looks down to his shoes. She takes his broken hand in hers, and he lets her. "If the others hadn't seen, hadn't heard . . ." Lola trails off, knowing it's true. If there had been no witnesses to Hector's fuckup besides her, she would not have punished him. He is her weakness and her strength, her only blood.

"Fuck that," Hector says, and when his eyes meet hers, they are blazing. "You went easy." He jabs a blaming finger close to Lola's eye, and she thinks of the consequences of Hector's single word: *Go.* Two million in cash. Two million in heroin. Her life. Her slow death at cartel hands. Hector is right. Any other soldier she would have slashed at the neck and watched him bleed out on her living room floor.

"I need your help," she says, because she has to say something to get them both out of these scary shit thoughts. "Need you to call around, find a rehab center."

"Rehab? You think Mom—"

"Mom's not in rehab," Lola says. Hector is quiet again, and Lola imagines he is both absorbing the blow of their mother's relapse and marveling at his sister referring to Maria as her mother.

"I know," Hector says. "Stupid fucking thing to say."

"Not really," Lola says. "She were smart, she would be. But addicts—"

"Fucking stupid," Hector says.

Lola doesn't know if Hector is referring to Maria for relapsing, or himself for believing she wouldn't.

"So who'm I looking for?" Hector asks with a deflating sigh, and Lola knows the anger has seeped from him. Hector is ready to work for her again. It shouldn't be this quick, their grief, but it has to be, because they've got shit to do.

"Girl named Sadie."

"No last name?"

"No last name. But you find it out."

"Wanna tell me who she is?"

"Tweaker from the drop."

Hector's eyes meet Lola now, his tongue flicks across his lips, as he recognizes the description of the girl he warned because he couldn't pull a gun on her. His eyes flick to his sewn-on useless finger. Lola looks too, and when he catches her looking, he hurries to speak.

"I'll find her. You thinkin' she's a lead?"

"She's our only one," Lola says.

SIXTEEN

THE TWEAKER

The thin scraggly blonde behind the counter smiles at Lola when she enters. Unlike Sadie, this blonde is tall, sporting baggy jeans and a plaid flannel shirt that camouflages any hint of breasts, hips, or ass. Her skin has the translucent skim milk hue of someone who's had the fat of life sucked from them. Lola doesn't have to hear her story to know this woman's a recovering addict.

It is Thursday, the morning after her mother disappeared, the day Lola is set to meet with the cartel. She has until nightfall to trade their loot for her life.

Hector did his part, calling every rehab facility in the county. He started with the state-run places, figuring their tweaker Sadie couldn't afford one of the private facilities that dot the coast of Malibu. Both he and Lola had Sadie pegged for a suburban runaway whose family wanted nothing to do with her. The pockmarks mapping Sadie's face told Lola she'd been fighting her meth addiction long enough to alienate parents and cut off any supply of cash they had ever been foolish enough to give her.

But they had been wrong, because here Lola is, on a sunny morning, dressed in a pair of designer jeans, feet encased in ballet flats too delicate for South Central streets, where they might pick up a shard of beer bottle glass. Garcia had starched and ironed her shirt, a white button-down she'd worn when she waited tables at a local Mexican restaurant in high school. Here in Malibu, she could pass for middle class, perhaps a foster sister of the blond tweaker she'd come to find.

"Who you here for?" the tall blonde asks, but Lola sees someone catch the woman's eye on the other side of the counter. It's a fat white twentysomething man in jeans and a baseball cap. "Brian, why aren't you in group?"

"I wasn't feeling well," Brian says, and Lola can tell by his proper speech and total belief in the bullshit lie he's telling that Brian is used to getting his way. Mommy and Daddy are definitely footing his bill, and she wonders what he's in for. Probably coke. Rich white men always do coke, because they can't see the harm in taking a hit to be more productive, make more money, get more women. They don't see the harm, because when you have money, there is no harm.

Fuck you, Brian, Lola wants to say.

"Get your ass to group," the tall blonde says, and just like that, Lola likes her.

Brian turns and plods away, hands in his pockets, a fuck-you gesture of humility. Lola hopes he relapses under an overpass where some criminal element will gut him for five bucks.

The tall blonde turns back to Lola. "I'm sorry, doll. Who'd you say you were here for?"

"Sadie Perkins," Lola says, trying the tweaker's full name out for the first time. She likes the whitebread Pilgrim feel of it, and for a second, she imagines it is her own name. What would she have done if she'd grown up in a two-story ranch house far from South Central? What would she have done if she'd had a mother who defrosted vegetables every night for dinner, and a father who taught her that a man should come home every night to his wife and children? What if she were true middle class, instead of just dressed like it?

She sure as shit wouldn't have said yes to meth. But then again, maybe if she shared Sadie's story, she would have. Like any good detective, Lola has done her homework on the meth head. She thinks she understands the girl's brokenness, and once she knows that about someone, she can ply them and trick them and play with them.

"Sadie. . . ." the blonde says as she scans a clipboard. "Right. Sadie's on kitchen duty. She's real good at baking. I just need you to sign in here." The woman passes her a different clipboard, and Lola wonders how many clipboards, charts, and planners it takes to keep a hundred recovering addicts in line.

Lola signs her full name. She's not on any of the LAPD's gang rosters. The name Lola Vasquez means nothing to anyone.

"Lola. Pretty name. I'm stuck with Ruthie." The blonde smiles. "You a friend of Sadie's?"

"I'm her sister," Lola says.

The lie doesn't register as any sort of red flag with Ruthie, even though Lola is brown and Sadie is white. Ruthie picks up the telephone, an old beige contraption with a red bulb flashing at the top. When she speaks, Lola hears her calm twang reverberate across the facility's tile floors.

"Sadie Perkins, your sister's here to see you."

Lola doesn't sweat the public announcement. Her research uncovered a sister in Sadie's past, five years older. The sister, Meredith, is married now, with two small boys. Her husband is a chemist, and she stays at home. Lola imagines Meredith has severed contact with her drug addict sister, not wanting Sadie's pockmarked skin and stringy hair to grace her clean carpet and granite countertops. Lola imagines the announcement will intrigue Sadie enough to pry her away from her domestic domain.

Lola is right. Less than ten seconds after Ruthie summoned her, Sadie rounds a sharp corner, feet slipping across clean tile because she is hustling. Flour smudges one cheek, and Lola catches the little blond girl trying to wipe it off with a finger wet with spit. In that moment, Lola's heart breaks a little for Sadie, trying to look and be okay for her sister.

Then she remembers she's going to die tonight if this bitch gets away with stealing the cartel's shit.

Sadie approaches Ruthie, eyes scanning the waiting room where Lola stands, clutching a respectable shoulder bag.

"Where's my sister? She's here?" Sadie asks.

"She's right there," Ruthie says, her voice soft, and Lola doesn't have to worry that Ruthie suspects her of foul play. She is gentle with Sadie, because of course Sadie is in a delicate state, too delicate to see what or who is right in front of her.

The real test lies in Sadie's reaction to Lola. She kept quiet at Pacific Division, maybe out of some split-second loyalty to the woman who couldn't catch her. Or maybe Sadie was questioning her ability to distinguish between brown ladies.

"Oh," is all Sadie says, and Lola hears a beep as Ruthie buzzes her in.

Lola walks to Sadie. The girl keeps her arms at her sides, until she remembers Lola is supposed to be her sister. Then, she raises them, stiff and unbending as two raw asparagus stalks, and Lola leans in for a quick air kiss. She doesn't want to touch this girl's cheek with her lips. To Lola, addiction is as contagious as the common cold.

"Hi."

"Hi."

The two pause, until Sadie must feel Ruthie watching them. "This way," Sadie says, and Lola notes the girl's small hands, clasped together, kneading skin and knuckles like flat bread dough.

The room Sadie turns into is wide and tall, with floor-to-ceiling glass windows that overlook the Pacific. This morning, the ocean spits frothy waves onto sand already darkened with dawn's wetness. Leather sofas dot the room, and Lola feels the cool of the sleek modern cushions through her khakis as she sits.

Two sofas away, a skinny man in jeans and a black T-shirt plays checkers with a plumper version of himself. Father and son, Lola guesses from the lines that crease the plumper man's ruddy skin. She's also guessing it's alcohol, not manual labor in the hot sun, that has reddened the older man's cheeks. She wonders if the son has the same problem, or if his addiction involves a less "respectable" substance, like heroin. Lola pities alcoholics—she knows it might be the hardest addiction to kick, because it's legal and it's everywhere and everyone asks why you can't have just one. Nobody pulls that shit with heroin. If they've got it, they keep it for themselves.

"Sit," Lola says to Sadie, because the girl is still standing above her, hands clasped, kneading.

Sadie obeys, but she doesn't sit in the leather armchair across from Lola. Instead, she sits right beside her on the sofa. Sadie curls her skinny legs under her nothing body and kicks off her shoes.

It has been a long time since Lola's attended a meeting and the other person felt comfortable enough around her to remove their shoes. She considers it a slight now, and she wants to make Sadie pay.

"Put your shoes back on," Lola says.

"You can take yours off. It's more comfortable," Sadie says, a pleading note of kindness in her voice. Sadie wants her approval. The realization eases the tension Lola didn't know was in her spine.

"Okay," Lola says, and her red ballet flats splat on the floor like two long drops of fresh blood. She catches Sadie looking at her toes, painted with clear polish. Lola doesn't bother with color on her nails, because color fades and chips and smudges. With clear, you can't see the flaws.

"Do you want something to drink? We have soda," Sadie says, as if it's a delicacy. But of course Lola knows caffeine and nicotine are the two main food groups of rehab.

"I'm okay," Lola says, finding her own hands resting on her clutch purse like the nervous middle-class estranged sister she's portraying.

"Okay."

They sit like this for an instant, Sadie with her legs curled under her, Lola with nervous hands on her purse. The father and son continue to play checkers in silence. In the absence of anything to say, Lola listens for the ocean waves crashing on sand, but the window glass is thick and impenetrable.

"I like the ocean, too," Sadie says.

"It scares me," Lola says before she has time to think she

shouldn't be showing fear. Although here, sitting on cold leather cushions overlooking the Pacific in reflective silence, it's hard to see the girl who's too close to her as any sort of worthy adversary.

Whatever happens to Lola, whether she finds the cartel's stash or dies trying, Sadie's fate is sealed. She works for Mr. X, someone who entrusted her with two million dollars' worth of heroin, and those drugs are gone. Either way Lola's fate swings, Sadie's dead. Lola wonders if Sadie realizes this fact, but if she does, why writhe and fight her way out of this world in rehab?

"I knew you wouldn't be my sister," Sadie says. "Meredith . . . she doesn't want me around."

"She has kids." Lola finds herself defending Meredith.

"I don't blame her. If I were around them, and I needed . . ." Sadie trails off, leaving unspoken the part about her possibly getting high and driving with her sister's kids, or leaving them unattended, or forgetting them in a hot backseat. Sadie can't say the words Lola can imagine. "I'm glad you're not her."

Lola realizes Sadie is terrified of her sister allowing her back into her and her children's lives. She's terrified she'll fuck it up, because statistics and experience tell her she will.

"Who do you work for?" Lola asks, because as much as she enjoys the calm of the room folding over her like a light blanket as she dissects the addict across from her, she can't forget her purpose here.

"Him," Sadie says; her eyes are on the checkers game, as if she's willing the son to make the correct move.

"Who's him?"

"I'm trying to forget about him," Sadie says, her eyelids fluttering closed. Lola wonders if that works, closing your eyes in hopes that the world you've built around yourself will disappear. She prefers to look, because if she's painted herself into a corner, she wants the best chance of finding the exit.

"Did you take my drugs?"

"Your drugs?" Sadie asks, her eyes open now. Like most people, Sadie never saw the harm in Lola, who's stalked her from police station to rehab, changing Pumas for ballet flats. Sadie would never think to cross the street if she saw Lola walking on the same sidewalk. No one would, and the thought both comforts Lola and pisses her off. She wants respect, and she wants invisibility.

"My drugs."

"I don't know," Sadie says in a way that lets Lola know she's telling the truth.

"Why were you there that night?"

"Paying off a debt," Sadie says.

"Dropping heroin to pay for meth."

"Something like that. Actually, exactly like that," Sadie says, and the corner of her mouth turns up in a sad smile she won't let spread.

"But you lost the drugs."

Sadie's head hangs in a nod of acknowledgment.

"Your boss know you're here?"

Sadie shakes her head.

"He will. It was easy to find you," Lola says in a chiding tone, as if she's the one who's trained Sadie to fly below the radar, and Sadie has let her down.

"I can't hide from him," Sadie says. "Why try?"

"Why try to get sober if you know he's just gonna kill you?"

A triumphant whoop punctuates the question, and Lola wants to ask the father-son fuckups if they could please keep their emotions in check while the women talk business?

"I was trying before. I had been clean for seven hours and twenty-nine minutes," Sadie says. "Then he came to my apartment. He told me I had to do one last job."

"You've done drops before?"

"Smaller ones. Five thousand. Maybe ten. It was the"—Sadie pauses, searching for the right word—"easiest way of paying for my habit."

Lola knows without Sadie having to say it that Sadie didn't want to blow dealers for meth. Lola wants to tell Sadie she understands, that once you've done sex work you didn't want to do, you're utterly fucked. Instead, she just says, "Yeah."

"You're not a user," Sadie says.

"No."

"You don't care for users."

"No."

"Then why are you talking to me?" Sadie asks.

Lola pauses. "I knew you didn't belong out there," she says. "You were in over your head."

"You lost two million dollars' worth of heroin. It sounds like you might be, too," Sadie says. She picks a piece of lint from her pants and rolls it between her fingers with a tired sigh. She moves like she knows she has a to-do list miles long, but the sofa is so comfortable, why bother? She does not move like someone whose drug trafficker boss is going to come after her and make sure her death is long, painful, and memorable.

Why isn't Sadie worried? The only explanation that makes sense to Lola is that she must have someone more dangerous and more powerful than her boss on her side.

"You were still at the scene when we left," Lola says, her thoughts racing as she tries to piece together this little tweaker's puzzle.

"I think so. It's blurry. You were in a van."

"Nice memory," Lola says.

"I read somewhere they're good for drive-bys. That gangs prefer them because of the sliding doors?" Sadie poses the question to Lola. Lola hasn't said she's part of a gang, but, like Lola, Sadie has started putting together the pieces of the puzzle that is Lola. Brown, drug drop, guns, minivan. All the parts add up to gang. Yet the way Sadie poses her question lets Lola know she, Sadie, doesn't consider herself part of a gang. She is white. She works for a clean-cut white man who supplies large amounts of heroin to what he must consider small fish like Darrel King. Even in the drug business, Lola realizes, there is classism. She wants equal footing with Sadie's boss.

"Yeah. Then we drop them, burn them, get another one," Lola says, answering Sadie's question.

"Huh," Sadie says, and Lola likes her tone, like she's realizing Lola has thought of something her privileged white-ass boss never would.

"You were at the scene," Lola prods, deciding to cash in on this tidbit of respect.

"Yeah. You guys were going after the bag . . . there was the crash . . . and . . ." Sadie pauses, bumping up against her boss's name and reversing. "He left, too. Left me out there."

"And the cops found you. At a scene where they knew shots were fired. You told them you were a courier. Why didn't they arrest you?"

There it is, the question that had evaded Lola until now, because of course Sadie should be in a rickety holding cell with cheap hookers and addicts, awaiting arraignment. Instead, she is here, on a cushy leather sofa by the ocean, her legs curled under her and her wisp of a body leaning too close to Lola.

"Haven't you heard? I'm a confidential informant."

"You were a CI, you'd have to give up your boss."

"Who says I didn't?"

"You're alive."

"So far," Sadie says with a sigh. "They never even asked about him."

Lola stares at Sadie, unable to tell if she's lying or if she just believes what she's saying so much she's forgotten it's a lie.

"The sergeant just drove me out here. He told me he knew I could use some help."

"What sergeant?" Lola asks, but she already knows his name.

"Bubba."

"He paying for this place?"

The question hits Sadie like a ringing slap, and Lola sees the flash of confusion on her face. Sadie, freshly sober, has not stopped to consider who's footing the bill here.

"Somebody's paying. I don't think it's your papa," Lola says.

Sadie's eyes rise to meet hers, and Lola sees the first hint of anger there. Sadie uncurls her legs, shrinking from Lola like a wounded dog.

"You don't know anything about my father."

"Roger Perkins. Fifty-two years old. Birthday, January fourteenth. Lives at four three two Avenue Mariposa, Woodland Hills."

Sadie scrunches into the sofa, her white face growing whiter as she tries to disappear into the couch cushions.

"They can't ask him," Sadie says into the cushions. "He can't afford it."

"Shit no he can't. Hasn't done much of anything but grieve since that psycho killed your mama five years ago."

Lola knows every addict has a hole in them, somewhere deep only drugs can touch. She knew she needed to find Sadie's to get the truth from her. She had to find the place to stick the knife, and, in Sadie's case, it was simple. Unlike molested or abused children, living their darkness in secret, Sadie's was plastered all over Woodland Hills newspaper articles that turned up in a simple Internet search. Her mother, Carol Perkins, a hairdresser, had been shot by a young man, a customer who'd been obsessed with her for months. The man's name was Dusty, and, in court, he told the jury he'd killed Carol because she had closed her shop five minutes early and refused to give him a quick trim. He had thought he was special. What a dumbass.

"Please. Do you think . . . will they go after my father, to pay for this place?"

"Doubt it," Lola says. "You got a cop who doesn't book you, brings you to Malibu after a failed drug drop where four million combined in cash and heroin goes missing. You really think that cop stashed you here out of the goodness of his heart? Or do you think he wanted to get you out of the way so he could make off with the stash your boss thinks you lost?"

Sadie's eyes flit left and right, searching Lola's face for signs of bullshit. Lola knows she will find nothing.

"How is this getting me out of the way?"

"Your boss sees you weren't arrested. He finds you here, private rehab, costs upward of twenty grand a month. He sees who checked you in—Sergeant Bubba. He assumes you turned over his drugs to the cops and are gonna testify against him."

"But I don't know what happened to the drugs. And I'm not giving him up—"

"Didn't say you were. Said that's the way Sergeant Bubba's making it look. Which is a pretty damn good way to make sure he gets to keep two million in heroin and make it seem like you fucked over your boss. Not him. Boss kills you, stops looking for the drugs. Bubba retires. End of story."

"You said two million. In heroin."

"That's how much there was."

"You didn't say anything about the two million in cash I was supposed to get."

Lola remembers the gym bag full of paper Mila was carrying. Sadie's right—this part of the mystery she hasn't solved.

"Yeah. I didn't," Lola says.

"How do I make this right?" Sadie says, and Lola can see from her pleading holes of green glass eyes that she doesn't know she's already dead.

Lola almost feels bad as she lies. "Help me get that heroin back to your boss."

"How?"

"Start by telling me his name."

Sadie pauses, a shorter pause than Lola would have thought. Then she tells Lola what she wants to know.

SEVENTEEN

NAMING NAMES

Eldridge Waterston. The name reeks of class, of Ivy League and polo and champagne on the golf course. When Sadie first told Lola her boss's name, Lola had made her repeat it, and Sadie had said she understood, it was an odd name, but it wasn't an alias. Lola didn't think anyone would think to use Eldridge, which Lola hadn't even known was a name, as an alias.

Garcia has her repeat it now, in their bedroom, as Lola braids her hair at the vanity mirror. She notices a crack in the glass but doesn't mention it. Garcia will not let her out of the house with such a bad luck omen staring them both in the face.

"The hell kind of name is that?"

"Fucking fancy one," Lola says.

It is dark outside. Lucy is asleep in the next room. Lola's seventy-two hours are up. She is sitting at her vanity mirror preparing to answer to her own boss, the legendary fat man who heads the Los Liones cartel.

She has braided her hair because it comforts her. Soon, she will slip into a gray cotton hoodie for the same reason. For her, this meeting could mark the beginning of the end of home.

Lola can't retrieve drugs from a dirty cop who's pocketed them. She can't get to Darrel King to get the cash he traded for paper in the duffel bag he handed to Mila. But Lola can give the cartel boss Eldridge Waterston. She can hope the name of the cartel's sole competition is worth four million dollars, even though she knows it will buy her a quicker death at most.

She finishes her braid, winding a black elastic band around her thick noose of hair. When she looks up, she catches Garcia watching her in the mirror. Lola sees his Adam's apple bobbing where he's gulping back a little extra saliva. He is nervous. He must have seen the crack in the mirror.

"You got your piece?"

Lola gives him a kind smile. "You know I can't show up armed."

"Then let me drive you. For backup. We'll swing by, pick up Hector on the way. He wouldn't choke at the other end of a bullet if it's your life on the line."

True, Lola thinks, *but irrelevant.* One of the conditions the Collector's boss has insisted upon is, of course, no weapons or backup. The cartel boss must be expecting the unknown Crenshaw Six boss to plead for Lola's life, and maybe he's willing to strike a deal for Eldridge's name, maybe not. Either way, Lola hopes she has the element of surprise on her side. She can guarantee he does not expect Garcia's girlfriend to sit across from him and talk terms.

"No," Lola says, placing her brush on the vanity next to the tools of her daily face—moisturizer, eye cream, mascara. She straightens her supplies into a neat row. She realizes she wants Garcia to argue with her, to force the issue, but he won't. In this moment, she is not his girlfriend. She is his boss. "Gotta go. Can't be late."

"You're right," Garcia says, his head down. Lola wonders if he doesn't want to look at her face in the broken mirror anymore.

She takes her fake Prada bag from its hook next to her plaid fleece robe. She hopes she will make it home tonight to slip her arms into the robe's warm crevices and stick her cold feet against Garcia's until he wakes up and begs for mercy.

"You need anything? Water? Might get thirsty."

"I'm fine," Lola says, and since he won't look at her, she cups his stubbly sharp cheek in her hand and makes him. "I'll be back."

"Damn straight," he says. He pulls her close in a grip that cracks her back as he presses his lips, so tight, to hers. The kiss isn't passionate or sad—just desperate.

"You'll take care of Lucy?"

"Yep. Got the breakfast casserole you made. Twenty minutes at three fifty."

"And peel her an orange or something."

"We got juice."

"It's not the same," Lola says. She wonders, if she's not back by breakfast tomorrow, if Garcia will pour orange juice for Lucy with one eye on the phone, too worried about Lola to remember her instructions. Or will he overcompensate, thinking if he just subs in real oranges for juice, Lola will come back.

She doesn't kiss Garcia again before she walks out of their bedroom, because no kiss will be right for a last one. The fact that they both know it could be the last has charged the moment too much to make it mean anything.

At the front door, Lola pulls her soft gray cotton hoodie over her black hair and wades into the night. The air around her sticks like a glaze. It is a phenomenon foreign to Los Angeles but common to South Central and its adjacent outposts. Here, the heat rises from cracked pavement and crumbling blacktop. It is present in every escalating conversation, from the poor mother trying to convince the cashier to let her take that extra loaf of bread on credit, to the gangbanger explaining to the trial member what he must do to earn initiation.

For most gangs, that task involves doing something to a woman. That won't be the case for the Crenshaw Six, should Lola ever decide to initiate a new member. She fantasizes about sending her would-be soldiers to terrorize white professional men, single guys with no families who earn six figures and play the field. The kind of guys Maria brought home to take a turn with her daughter. Guys who think they are invincible. Lola dreams of having her men show them they are not. It is important for her fantasy soldiers to see the type of man who has looked down on them all their lives looking up at them, begging for mercy from the blade of a knife.

But of course this fantasy will never come to pass. Even if Lola survives tonight, the Crenshaw Six can't terrorize white men without taking major heat and fire from LAPD.

"Hey, boss," Jorge says, holding open the back door of a red Dodge Neon.

Lola stares at him.

"Don't like the car? Best I could do on short notice. My dad's pissy this week. But I got some fake plates. Cartel can't trace it."

It touches her that Jorge thinks the cartel can't trace a shitty Neon back to the ghetto. The cartel SUV has disappeared from the street, probably because it was never following her or Garcia at all. Those henchmen were there to be seen, Lola has realized.

"I don't ride in back," she says to Jorge.

"Yeah, you sit up front with the assholes like me. It's why I like you."

Lola smiles, and Jorge knows it's okay for him to smile, too. She can feel his sigh of relief—his gallows humor is working. It's why she's letting him take her, because all her other men—Garcia, Hector, Marcos—would be too somber, driving her to what might well be her death. Garcia might be pissed at her later, if he notices her car still in the driveway, but what can he do? She is his boss. Jorge was her choice.

"Buckle up," Jorge says, stretching his frayed belt over his muscled chest.

"You go to the gym, Jorge?" Lola asks as he puts on his left turn signal and pulls into the street. There is no traffic, but Jorge is careful.

"Three times a week. Rest of the time, I run from Yolanda. She got this one spatula thing, it's got holes, and it pinches when she hits me."

"Why's she hitting you?"

"How much time you got?"

The question hangs between them in the electric night air. Lola turns up the radio—hip-hop—and the beat fills the silence.

Lola feels out of her league, as she has every time she's left her own neighborhood past eleven p.m. The clubs that line the Sunset Strip belong to the twentysomethings, the ones who came here to be actors and ended up getting fucked up on cheap beer and X every night. The five-star restaurants of Beverly Hills are filled with late-night diners, the bars of Silver Lake packed with hipsters in skinny jeans and glasses they don't need. Lola has never been in any of these places—she has seen their patrons only from a car window, observing without them ever knowing she was watching.

The address El Coleccionista's boss gave is on National. As Jorge signals for the exit off the 10, Lola scans the neighborhood. She has only glimpsed this part of town from the freeway on her way to somewhere else. She sees a Von's, its parking lot empty at this hour, and several stucco apartment buildings, brown and light brown, with names like Cheviot Vista or Cheviot Manor. Just like every neighborhood from Santa Monica to Compton, there is a Starbucks, sandwiched in a strip mall between a dry cleaners and a cheap Mexican takeout place with "salsa" in the name.

"There." Lola gestures to the Von's lot, because they're closing up, and because there's a cluster of cars—Acuras, Lexuses, BMWs—near the address where she's supposed to go. She is meeting El Coleccionista's boss in a strip mall, the same strip mall with the Starbucks and what she assumes is a shitty Mexican joint.

"Big fucking spender," Jorge says what she's thinking. "Boss, you sure about this?"

No. "Yes."

"I'll be waiting."

"I have to go alone."

"I leave you, Garcia's gonna whip my ass."

"Where'd you tell Yolanda you were going tonight?" Lola looks over at Jorge. He's gripping the steering wheel, leaning forward to case the parking lot, looking for guns until he realizes Lola wants him to look at her.

"Out."

"Out?"

"Yeah, drinking and shit."

"She buy that?"

"Fuck no."

"Why do you stay with her?"

Jorge looks at Lola like the question never occurred to him.

"Yolanda's a good woman. I just like to bitch."

Lola wonders about Garcia, if he fought hard enough to drive her here. Did she test Garcia by asking Jorge to do it? Did he fail?

"Thanks for the ride," Lola says.

"I'll pull around the corner and wait."

"You're one man. They have hundreds."

"So that's it?"

"Go home. Take Yolanda some flowers so she doesn't beat your ass."

Lola shuts the Neon's door, and that's that. She doesn't wait to see if Jorge is going to pull away immediately or wait until she's inside. She doesn't want to be late.

The address El Coleccionista has given leads her to a small, darkened restaurant across the parking lot. A bell rings when Lola enters, and a thin Japanese woman in white shirt and black pants scurries to her, fast and silent. *In another life,* Lola thinks, *this hostess could have been an assassin.*

"Good evening," the woman says in choppy singsong English. Lola thinks of her mother, of Maria's inconsistent English that always sounded more native when she was fucked up. That state of being relaxed her, kept her from second-guessing vocabulary and pronunciation. Maria could have gotten a job with that version of her English, if it weren't for her red, dilated pupils and lolling neck, her regression to newborn status. Lola used to try to hold up her mother's head, until she realized the burden was both too heavy to bear and useless. Unlike a newborn, her mother would never learn. Wherever Maria is, she's on the hunt for her fix.

"I'm meeting someone," Lola says, her hands removing her hoodie, because it's caused several patrons to take a second look at her. Most of the diners look the same—men in casual collared shirts and designer denim, women in flowing silk and tighter designer denim. All white. All plucking a single piece of raw fish over rice from a plate the size of a saucer. No one using soy sauce. Lola recalls the luxury sedans in the parking lot, and it strikes her that everyone in this tiny strip mall sushi restaurant is wealthy.

"Yes," the Japanese woman says, bowing. She turns her back to Lola and shuffles through the ten or so two-top tables. Lola realizes she is supposed to follow, but the tables are close together, and she has to squeeze through several of them on her side. She earns admiring looks from the men, disgusted ones from the women. It's the same in her neighborhood, and the thought comforts her.

The Japanese woman turns a corner to a single table. "Yes," the Japanese woman says again, lifting an arm to the patron sitting at the table.

There, Lola finds a fat Mexican man in the same casual collared shirt and designer denim as the white men in the restaurant. His mouth is full, his eyes closed as he enjoys the piece of raw fish that pokes out from the corner of his cheek. He looks the way Garcia does when he's on top of her, about to finish, wanting it but not wanting it to end.

Lola waits until he swallows to clear her throat. She won't sit down until he asks her. There is a code of business conduct, even among those who traffic in violence and weakness, although when she looks at white-collar industries—real estate, hedge funds, stocks—she can't say they traffic in any product much different from her own. They are all of them looking to exploit, to squeeze pennies and dollars and power from people who need what they peddle.

The boss stares at her, and she sees the surprised recognition in his eyes. Whatever assets this man has—luxury cars, whitewashed haciendas, high-class hookers—he does not have a poker face.

"Lola," he says. She wonders if that's how the whole cartel views her, as a girl not worthy of a last name, because sooner or later Garcia will give her his.

"Yes," she says, because her last name doesn't matter. He knows her true identity now. She is the Crenshaw Six boss. She is out of the shadows, a marked woman if he decides that's what he wants her to be.

"Please, sit," he says, standing and putting his napkin aside to pull out her chair.

The Japanese woman, who has disappeared without Lola

realizing it, returns with a saucer and chopsticks for Lola. These chopsticks are not wrapped in white paper or made of cheap, splintering wood. These chopsticks are smooth black, and Lola guesses that they are bamboo. The only sushi Lola has ever tried came from another strip mall joint. There, the salmon tinged her tongue with something that tasted like formaldehyde smelled, and the rice was cold and crumbling, expanding in her gut with the liquid sodium soy sauce.

"Are you hungry?" the man asks.

"Yes," she says. She ate an early dinner with Garcia, barbacoa chicken and vegetables—enough calories to fuel her, not enough to weigh her down if she needed to run.

The Japanese woman returns again, this time with a teapot and a small, round cup. She takes away Lola's clean saucer and replaces it with another. On it, there is a small rectangle of white rice covered with a thin slice of pinkish fish. Lola sees specks of silver skin still on the pink.

"Mackerel," the Japanese woman says. "No soy sauce, please." She bows and disappears.

The cartel boss remains silent as Lola fumbles to take up the entire roll. He looks away, out the window, until she manages to get the rice between her bamboo sticks. She appreciates his pretend ignorance of her lack of social graces.

When she puts the roll in her mouth, it stings her tongue, her throat, the insides of her cheeks. It lights them up, setting them on edge—it's everything—lemon, butter, fish, the sharp silver snap of the skin.

Holy fuck, Lola wants to say. She feels her eyes close and roll back in her head, and she wonders if the man across from her knows this is how she looks during sex.

When she opens her eyes, though, she sees he is still not watching her. He must have known the face she would make, must have thought it too private. She feels guilty for watching him earlier.

"I hope you like sushi," is the only thing he says now, his eyes returning to her.

"Yes," she says, and she wonders if he must think this word is the only one she knows. Maybe he will ask if they should speak Spanish. The thought of having to speak her mother's native language embarrasses her, although she prefers the sound to English.

"I'm happy to meet you," the man says, pouring her more tea. "And you must have liked that look of surprise on my face."

So he knows his weaknesses. Good rule for a cartel boss . . . or the leader of an up-and-coming gang. She knows her weakness— she owes this man and his organization four million dollars. She'd trade her poker face for that amount any day. And she wonders if this dinner will be added to her tab. The thought sends a chill flickering up her spine, and she imagines this is how a middle-class person racking up debt to afford a house and two cars somewhere where bullets don't ring feels.

"I didn't mind it," Lola says to the cartel boss, who gives a hearty chuckle. He is playing the jolly fat man. A Santa Claus with a hit on her head.

"And here I thought it would be Garcia sitting across from me. That he was running your whole little operation and pretending not to be."

"He could."

"You're selling yourself short," the boss says. "Women do that."

That stings, because he is right. Lola sinks her teeth into her dry lips to keep from apologizing, another feminine weakness. She's not fucking sorry. She's just trying to live in the world and duck under, not break, those glass ceilings she keeps hearing about.

She occupies herself with the next course, which the waitress bows onto their table with another, "No soy sauce, please."

"I suppose you want me to call off the hit on your head."

"I wouldn't mind it," Lola says. The boss chuckles again. "But my time is up, and I don't have your money or your drugs."

The fat man sits back with a sigh, placing his napkin on the table.

"I do know where your drugs are."

"Then why don't you get them back?"

"I can't," she says.

"You seem like a determined woman," the boss continues.

"A cop has them." Lola does not mention that, if her hunch is

correct, said cop failed to check said drugs into evidence. She pictures some creaky floorboards in Sergeant Bubba's house, a patch
of wood that doesn't match the cheap fake hardwood he bought so
as not to attract attention. Dirty cops piss her off. There are cops,
and there are criminals, and you pick a side and stick with it. Any
deviation strikes Lola as weak.

"And the money?"

"Switched out for a bag full of paper before the drop."

"A fact you must have gathered from Mr. King's . . . girlfriend.
Before you shot her, of course."

"She wasn't much good to me after," Lola says.

"In that case, it seems you have something in common with her."

This barb stings. But Lola nods. She can take a punch.

"I'm giving you a chance to plead your case," the fat man says.
"Don't squander it."

Lola says, "I have a name."

"A name worth four million dollars?"

"That depends on how you use it," Lola says, recovering. She
is hungry, so she pops the next no soy sauce piece of fish in her
mouth like a pizza roll. She has given up the chopsticks. The fat
man does not reprimand her. The rich white people who surround
them glance at her, then look away, fast, because, Lola is sure, they
don't want to appear racist.

"Whose name?"

"Darrel King's new supplier."

The fat man sits back and motions for more green tea. Lola gestures for the waitress to get her a cup, too, and she sips the bland,
hot liquid as she waits for the boss's, her boss's, response.

Before this assignment from El Coleccionista, Lola flew under
the radar, with random low-key, low-cash drops. She had always
assumed that, somewhere far up the food chain, the cartel supplied her middleman, Benny, although Benny himself had never
met anyone belonging to the organization. With no true power or
infamy, Lola could command her own soldiers. She led her own
pack with no orders from anyone. She grappled and scrapped and

made something of her gang until the Los Liones cartel noticed and wanted more.

Now, sitting across from the fat man, she realizes she fucking hates not being her own boss. Even if she pays off her debt, Los Liones runs her neighborhood. Either she stays small and quiet like everyone else in her community who fears these invaders, or she succeeds and eats someone else's shit.

"Okay," the boss says. "You give me the name. If it checks out, you live."

Lola takes another sip of tea to excuse the flushing she feels rising to her cheeks from the tips of her toes.

"With one condition." There. She knew the ass-fucking was coming, and she feels safer now that it's here.

"You infiltrate his organization."

"How?" Lola asks, then wishes she hadn't. She doesn't want to do things the fat man's way. She wants freedom to be creative.

"That's your problem."

Lola wants to reach across the table and smack her lips against his cheek. She doesn't have a chance, though, because he's still talking.

"You have one week."

Impossible. Lola knows the fat man can read the thought on her lips, which are dancing upward on one side into some sick twisted smile. Why does she get off on the thought of an impossible task?

"If anyone can do it, et cetera, et cetera," the fat man says, responding with his own hungry smile. Then the smile disappears, and he says, "I'm sorry."

"For what?"

"I still have to punish you."

Lola came here ready to sit down across from this man and face her own death. She was not prepared for punishment. Yet she knows the fat man will not do his own dirty work. She wonders if there will be thugs in the parking lot, Mexicans with large belt buckles and sharp blades. She wonders if her torture will be the same as it is for a man—pliers and fingernails, digital removal—the standard stuff, the kind of thing she doled out to her baby brother. Maybe they will leave her alive with no face on which to trade. They like to take away their victims' most valuable commodity.

The Japanese woman returns with two more mismatched saucers, his with flowers, hers with blue houses.

"Tuna toro. No soy sauce." She pads away, command issued.

Even knowing she will be punished, Lola finds her hands gripping the chopsticks, preparing to take up the fish and feel it against the inside of her cheek. She craves the sting. The fat man takes the fish between his own chopsticks, and Lola follows his lead. She is used to letting the man across from her think he is in charge.

Lola takes her bite at the same time as her boss. She lets it light up her mouth, enjoying the comfortable silence between herself and the man she expects to cause her pain tonight. She is glad she is not here on one of the upper-middle-class white people dates that surrounds them. Lola hears a man's too loud laughter, a woman chattering about a movie she and her date saw that night—the central characters were poor people, and the woman didn't think the dialogue was authentic.

Lola has never spoken with Garcia like this. They have been two people on a path, scrounging, digging, building an empire for themselves. They sit across from each other at their kitchen table, each not wanting to get up and leave the other. It is a cage, their relationship, but one that gives them the illusion of safety.

Lola doesn't know why she is thinking of Garcia now, turning her mind inward to look at her own relationship. Is it because she doesn't think she will survive the night? No, she has decided, tonight this man must send her a message. She will be given a chance to receive it. She will live through the night, but she might need several days to recover. She wonders if Garcia is preparing their bed—clean sheets, clear liquids, bland foods. But if Lola herself had only expected life or death, how could Garcia anticipate she would return home alive but damaged?

It is strange for her to be sitting across from another man at a date restaurant, a man who will do things, physical things, to her later. That must be it. She does not fear death; she feels she is betraying Garcia with this man.

Is it rape he's planning? The thought has occurred to her only now. She leads like a man, she expects to be punished like one. The thought of rape causes her to feel something akin to disappointment, like she'd thought she had finally broken through some sort of drug lord glass ceiling. But it could be she is merely a woman to this man.

"Don't rape me," she says, quiet but clear. She will not say please.

The fat man pauses over his tea. He looks confused, as if he hadn't thought of that. But she is a woman, he is a man, and there is a punishment to be exacted.

"You make it sound like an order," he says finally.

Lola has always been better at giving orders than making requests. If her orders aren't followed voluntarily, she finds a way to finagle the result she wants from the recipient. Hector fucked up the drop. She took his trigger finger. Now he wants to do as he's told. But this man is not her brother.

"I didn't mean to sound like that," Lola says.

"You didn't want to beg."

"I don't beg," Lola says, and again, she has spoken too quickly, letting emotion cloud logic. She should have stated this as a fact, not a defense.

"Good. I don't like beggars," the fat man says. "And I don't like rape."

Lola wants to laugh at this. He is the head of a cartel, a shadow leader like herself, a man whose name the authorities don't know and most likely never will. The idea that he does not enjoy taking women by force seems silly to her.

"I don't like rape in business," he clarifies, and she finds some satisfaction in his confession. He considers her a colleague, not a woman. "Lola," he says, leaning forward, and Lola knows the reprimand part of her punishment has begun. "You failed to bring us the merchandise and the money we requested."

"I sent a message to Darrel King."

"You took his woman's life. And you have nothing to show for it."

"Darrel will know not to seek out another supplier on our watch again."

"All you've done is anger him."

"No. We have broken him."

The fat man considers Lola's theory. "No," he says. "You haven't heard the last from Mr. King."

"Could be," Lola says, not wanting to concede that the fat man is right. They have not heard the last of Darrel King, but right now, she needs to focus on escaping the cartel and tonight with her life.

"You have one week to infiltrate the organization of Mr. King's new supplier. You will find his supply so that we may take the four million from him. Who is he?"

The question is fast, and Lola responds in kind. "Eldridge Waterston."

Like every other fucking person, the fat man makes her repeat the name.

The fat man remains silent as he lays three hundred-dollar bills on the table. When his eyes return to Lola, he says, "You understand I have to take you outside now."

"I understand."

Their chairs scrape against the concrete floor as they both rise. She lets him touch her elbow, guiding her through the small space. People must think they are on a date. Maybe they think the fat man is paying Lola for her time, either as a prostitute or a gold digger. She wants to put up her hood, to frighten off the lustful looks of the men, to cover her silk black hair and heart-shaped face. She wants them to know she doesn't belong here, letting a man pay for her expensive dinner. She's not like that.

Then they are out the door, into the warm Los Angeles night. The parking lot seems empty, even though most of the patrons are still inside the restaurant. Maybe Lola is just now noticing all the places bad things will happen to her. There are many, even in an open parking lot. Which of the weak men and chattering women inside would call the police if they heard Lola screaming? Lola guesses most would dive into their own cars and save their own skin, dialing 911 only when they had gotten far enough away to ensure their safety.

But a person can feel a world of pain in thirty seconds.

The fat man turns to her as a black car pulls up. The driver scurries from his seat and crosses behind the car to open the back door.

"It's been nice meeting you," the fat man says. "I'll be in touch."

"Yes," Lola says. "Thank you."

Then he disappears into the back of the car, which Lola now recognizes as a Bentley. Garcia would have known it in an instant, but Lola often confuses the luxury sedan with something less, a Lincoln or a Cadillac. She feels again that she has let Garcia down.

The driver returns to his own seat, and Lola watches the Bentley turn right onto National, no traffic there to delay its departure.

She gets a few seconds of breath, in and out, here in the parking lot. When she looks up, she can see stars. All around her, Los Angeles is silent.

She feels the first blow to her right ear like a fist of fire. The pain blinds her, and she finds her arms reaching forward, grasping for something, anything in front of her. Is she trying to orient herself, or is she looking for something to stop the pain? But no protection is coming, not in this parking lot in the dark with the stars above her and the self-involved white people behind her.

Garcia will take away her pain, but first she must get to the other side of it. That she must do here, alone.

The second blow catches her gut, and she sees a man in front of her, in dark jeans and a black T-shirt. She catches a glimpse of his face, recognizing him as one of the two men from the SUV outside her house. Up close, he is handsome, more handsome than Garcia. His fist plunges into her belly, pressing through flesh to meet bone. Something inside Lola cracks, and she knows she won't remember anything else.

She will fall now, she thinks, and she does.

EIGHTEEN

MAMACITA

Lola wakes to bright hot sunshine and a pounding in her brain. She feels the pour of yellow-tinged light through the bedroom's faded floral curtains. She should sleep, she knows, but the pain makes it impossible. Then she remembers she is not hungover, and that sleep will not help this pain.

Lola feels heat at her stomach and looks down through what she knows must be a puffy eye to find Lucy, curled up, catlike, stringy hair on Lola's tummy. It feels natural to have the girl here, safe, in Lola's bed.

Lola reaches a hand over Lucy and pats the comforter for any sign of Garcia. She feels rumpled sheets, the cotton cooled. He's gone. Lola hopes for breakfast—eggs and toast with crispy burnt strips of bacon. Garcia's cooking skills apply only to the morning meal. He takes pride in telling Lola it's the half-and-half that makes the eggs, and that setting the toaster on defrost results in a bread that's equal parts crunch and softness.

The pain wallops Lola in the face like an unexpected uppercut, and her appetite disappears.

She did not have a chance to discuss her conversation with the fat man when Garcia picked her up off the parking lot pavement in that Cheviot Hills strip mall. The aftermath floods back to her in flashes now—coming to, hearing footsteps hurry past her, a woman's whine asking if they had to call 911, and a man's voice responding they would, in the car. *The men who did this might still be in the neighborhood.*

Lola remembers pawing for her cell phone on wet concrete, then finding Garcia's number ten times on her missed-call log. He was easy to get on the other end of the line, and Lola had a brief flash of their dating life—him not wanting to call her too much, her not wanting to be too quick to respond. In her blanket of pain, she had been glad that all the games were over, and that he would be there soon to scrape her bloodied body off the pavement.

She must have passed out after the call, because she doesn't remember anything until she was sitting in Garcia's passenger seat, a cold compress on one side of her face, a heating pad on her shoulder, Gatorade in her hand. Lola remembers thinking Garcia must have thought she caught a cold instead of a beating. He should have known better how to care for a person in the aftermath of violence—surface stab wounds, minor gunshots—outside of a hospital, because for people in their business, secret medical treatment is a necessity. Then Lola heard Garcia saying her name, over and over, a question, asking her to respond, to let him know she was alive, and she realized then he must have been too scared to gather proper supplies. She forgave him in her pain, but she made a note that she should have all her boys sign up for EMT courses. She remembers being glad he did not ask why her car was still in the driveway of their home, but she knew his lack of suspicion must mean she was fucked up bad.

The next thing she remembers is waking up here, with Lucy by her stomach, and Garcia's place in bed cold.

She hears murmurs from the kitchen instead of the popping of bacon fat in a pan. Lola recognizes the singsong lilt of her mother's best friend even though she can't make out Veronica's words. Every few seconds, she hears Garcia's response—a low growl that means he's listening. Lola taught him that, to acknowledge her when she spoke. She's glad her mind seems sound.

Lola throws back the covers and crawls out from under Lucy's sighing sleeping head. She can hear Veronica's words now, a string of statements disguised as questions.

"Why would she be out alone at that time of night?" Translation: Lola brought this on herself. "Doesn't that seem strange to you?" Lola's not acting like herself. "And you're sure she doesn't need to go to the hospital?" We need to get her to a hospital.

Lola hasn't looked at herself in the mirror, but she figures she can make a grand, energized entrance, demanding bacon and coffee. Her appetite for pork fat and caffeine should tip Veronica off that everything's fucking fine.

A knock at the front door interrupts her plan. It can't be much past seven in the morning. This news, whatever it is, can't be good. Lola's mind flashes to Maria, and she finds herself hoping for a cop on her doorstep, delivering the news that her mother is dead. She imagines the LAPD would send a rookie to get his feet wet with a poverty-stricken addict's family before they let him loose on some Westsider's pretty blond dead daughter.

Lola practices her face on the way to the door. She must give the expected reaction to an addict's death—tired and sad, but not surprised. Then she remembers her puffy eye, her pounding temples, the blood she fingered on pavement last night that must have been hers. She can't answer the door to a cop.

"Whoa, whoa, whoa," Garcia says, and Lola feels his strong hand on the small of her back. "You should be in bed."

"I'm fine," Lola says.

"You need to go to the hospital," Veronica says, appearing behind Garcia with a mug of coffee. Lola can tell Veronica wants to be more hysterical, but her mother's friend will have to finish her second cup of caffeine before she can muster the waterworks and wringing hands she figures will get Lola to an emergency room.

"I'm fine," Lola repeats. "Someone's at the door." Garcia checks the peephole as Lola, impatient with the pounding and Veronica's muted worry, asks, "Is it the cops?"

"Cops?" Veronica pipes up, having just thrown back half her mug with the expert toss of an alcoholic over a shot of scotch. "Do you know who did this to you, honey?"

"Yes. No," Lola says, her brain foggy. She takes a moment before she faces Veronica. "Mom's gone." Veronica will give her less shit for not telling her about Maria's disappearance if Lola acknowledges Maria as her mother.

"What?" Veronica's eyes widen over the rim of her coffee mug, and Lola can't tell, could never tell, over decades of maternal disappearances, if Veronica's shock was genuine or feigned for the sake of Maria's children. Either way, it makes Lola hate Maria even more, because either way, her mother would always have a friend in Veronica—to cover for her, to be on her side even when she didn't deserve that second, third, or thirtieth chance. Addicts are lucky like that.

"She's using again," Lola says.

"That can't be," Veronica says.

"It is," Lola says over Veronica's feigned shock or her naïveté. Whichever it is, Lola can't give a shit right now.

"It's not the cops," Garcia says. "It's Rosie Amaro." Lucy's mother.

"How's she look?" Lola asks. She wants to know what she's dealing with. If it's sober sad Rosie, Lola will brew a fresh pot of coffee. If it's Rosie on PCP, Lola will grab the baseball bat she keeps in their coffin of a front hall closet. She bought it on sale specifically for unexpected visitors she doesn't have an excuse to shoot.

"Pissed," Garcia answers.

"Go hide Lucy."

"Lucy Amaro is here?" Veronica asks, her voice pitched up to shrill.

"Veronica. Go pour yourself another cup of coffee."

"You're awfully bossy this morning, missy," Veronica says, but she disappears into the kitchen as Garcia heads out to stash Lucy in the spot only Lola and Garcia know.

Lola takes her first moment alone to look through the peephole at Rosie Amaro. The woman is sick thin, with ripped tights and a second-skin short skirt. Black curls spring from her scalp in tense tight coils so that now, with her back to Lola, Rosie gives the impression of a ghetto Medusa.

Lola remembers Rosie from high school. She was quiet, head

always bent over a book, a target for girl bullies with their labels: skank, fat skank, skinny skank, stinky skank. Lola wonders if these poor excuses for insults gnawed at the hole in Rosie, letting in enough sadness so that heroin became the answer. *No,* Lola thinks, *calling someone a skank every day for a few years should not make an addict.* But maybe Rosie isn't as strong as Lola.

Lola herself had gotten the skank label a couple of times in high school, from a girl bully jealous of her and her book smarts and her curving pear hips. Lola hadn't gotten sad. Instead, she had channeled all her anger into fucking the bully's boyfriend so good he would never go back to the abusive bitch. But she was younger then, fourteen, and the boyfriend she fucked was Carlos, and she has to wonder now if that skank label set her on a path she could never reverse.

Lola sucks in some air before she swings open the front door. Rosie stops pacing and spins on her heel, toes tapping, arms crossed over her flat chest.

"Where's Lucy?" Rosie asks.

"What?" Lola squints in the sunshine. Her right eye is swollen shut, but she can tell it's another banner day in Los Angeles— seventy-five, sunny, not a single cloud in the sky. Even here in Huntington Park, where drive-bys leave little bodies bleeding out on cracked sidewalks, the sky smiles down like it doesn't have a fucking care in the world.

"Lucy. My daughter. Where the fuck is she?" Rosie darts toward Lola, who straightens up. She's sick of playing tired dumb even two seconds in.

"You don't want to do that," Lola warns.

"Oh, yeah?" But Rosie stops, because she's taken notice of Lola's appearance. "The fuck happened to you?"

"Rough night," Lola says. With Rosie this close, Lola can tell she's not high, but she is coming down off something. Rosie can't even hold one-eyed Lola's stare for a single second. It is in this state between highs, when the need for another fix grows like a malignant tumor, that Lola has found addicts to be at their most dangerous.

"I want to talk to Lucy," Rosie says.

"She's not here," Lola says, even though she hasn't discussed Lucy's wishes with her. Is there some deep want in the little girl to go back to her mother, to give Rosie her hundredth or even thousandth one more chance to give a shit? Lola wonders what it would take for Rosie to win Lucy back—some cinnamon toast and a tuck into bed with a teddy bear instead of Rosie's boyfriend?

"My parents tellin' me you have her."

"No, they're not," Lola says, because she hasn't called the Amaros to let them know Lucy's here. They're pretending not to know Rosie's letting their landlord's son grope their granddaughter, so in Lola's book, they can go fuck themselves.

"Well." Rosie deflates, bluff called. "They said Lucy likes you."

The outside acknowledgment of Lucy's feelings for her makes Lola's chest swell until she's almost beaming at this skinny skeleton of a mother. She has to cover, fast.

"She'd like you, too, if you'd stop pimping her out to your boyfriend." Direct, but it throws Rosie off whatever game she thinks she's playing with Lola. Lola wants to assure Rosie they are not in the same league.

"The fuck?" Rosie says, with a too-loud laugh that confirms what Lola knew was true from the moment she found that wadded-up pair of panties in Lucy's backpack.

"You heard me. Skank," Lola throws in, just because it's sunny out, and she got the shit beat out of her last night. She's feeling a little high school.

"You . . . you," Rosie sputters, and Lola finds herself wanting to help Rosie craft a return insult. *Ho, whore, bitch, cunt. Come on, Rosie. You're a terrible person. You can fucking hurl a couple insults my way.* But Rosie doesn't. Instead, she forces herself to breathe, to stand still, to be calm. Must be a trick she's learned in some rehab somewhere over the past decade. "You have until tonight to give her back."

Lola sighs. A cartel boss can give her deadlines, but not this sad sack addict wanting to play at motherhood for a night, probably because her boyfriend's coming over. Lola no longer has time for Rosie and her sick shenanigans.

She opens the door a little wider, palming the bat where Rosie can see as she says, "Get the fuck off my porch."

Rosie stares at the bat, eyes widening. "Lola . . . my God . . ."

Lola raises the bat, hoping for all the world that Rosie will make a scene. Lola wants Rosie to give her an excuse to crack this bat across her cheek.

But Rosie runs. Lola squints through her puffy eye and sees high heels sinking into dewy morning grass, atrophied calf muscles in torn tights trying to put distance between their owner and Lola.

Oh, well. Lola didn't need another complication. She's got shit to do.

She finds Garcia in the bedroom, sitting in a metal folding chair that wasn't there when Lola woke.

"She gone?" he asks.

Lola nods, and Garcia stands, placing the folding chair to one side as together they pry up the floorboards to a wide-eyed Lucy, squatting on a makeshift chair made of cash. Lucy is sitting on the dirty drug money Lola and Garcia have made but can't use. They can clean about ten percent of what they make through cash purchases—gas, groceries, liquor, manicures that include fancy tips and glitter. They hand over big bills for clean change. The rest makes Lucy's seat now.

The little girl's tiny fingers reach up to rub the sleep from her eyes. When Lucy sees Lola's beaten face above her, she asks, "Was that my mom?"

Lola nods.

"Did she want me back?" The hope in Lucy's voice breaks Lola's heart.

Lola nods again. "But I sent her away."

Lucy sinks back down onto the cash and says, "Oh." Her expression of disappointment hurts more than the beating Lola took last night.

NINETEEN

OPENING STATEMENTS

"Could you tell us in your own words what happened that night, Sarah?"

It is the afternoon of the day Rosie Amaro came calling for her daughter. The courtroom where Lola sits reeks of industrial lemon cleaning supplies and the salty meat smell of postcafeteria cold-cut body odor. There aren't many bodies here—jurors of all colors, shapes, and sizes; a thin male judge with white hair who reclines in his large black chair, comfortable being the one in charge; a defendant, white male, thirty, who's looking right at the witness; Sarah, thirty, white, beat-to-shit bruises fading on her face. Lola doesn't have to look at the jury to know the defendant is fucked.

"He promised me it wouldn't happen again. That he would never hit me, that it was just that once. But he lied."

"And just to be clear, you're referring to the defendant?"

"Yes."

"And what is your relation to him?"

"He's my husband."

"Your husband did this to you." The prosecutor times her words so she stops in front of the jury, letting the horror of domestic violence hit them.

"Aw, shit," Hector murmurs, enthralled with Andrea, the prosecutor Lola saw at Pacific Division. Today, the diminutive woman wears a tailored green suit and silk blouse, jacket off, with heels Lola recognizes as a designer brand from the fresh bloodred soles.

Lola bets no one on the jury—from a smattering of doughy white men to a no-bullshit middle-aged African American woman to a sobbing white coed who didn't realize until today that, for most people, the world sucks—will hold Andrea's designer garb against her. Maybe Lola has read it wrong—maybe the judge isn't the one in charge here. Maybe that's why he's reclining, like a security guard on a coffee break. Maybe he has turned his courtroom over to this fiery little storm in green, who closes her eyes now, as if praying for both this woman's safety and the defendant's dark soul. Lola sees Andrea steel herself as she opens her eyes and holds up a hand, a gesture that says she just can't go on. She has to clear her throat before she says, small, "No further questions, Your Honor."

Andrea walks, too slow, back to her chair at the prosecutor's table, which throws off the defense attorney. A clean-cut white man in pinstripes he can't quite pull off, he leaps from his chair, working his squeaky loafers and large, inappropriate smile to bring the jury out of their postlunch pity comas. But Lola can see the twelve are not ready for this shift in energy.

Andrea must sense it, too, because she busies herself with her case binder, a large black object that Andrea's small hands can't quite contain. She takes a sheet of plain white copy paper from her briefcase, so slow, moving with the easy grace of someone who knows eyes are on her. Even seated and silent, she has the jury's attention.

"Mrs. Rollins," the defense attorney begins, and half the jury jumps in their seats, because he is too loud. He is losing his case already.

"Sarah," the woman says, but her voice is too quiet for the defense attorney to hear as he charges on with all the energy of a cavalry horse at war. Too bad Andrea has just created a somber air that belongs more to a battle's aftermath, when people want stillness to grieve.

"Did you cheat on your husband?"

"Yes."

Lola glances at the jury to see if they recognize this asshole's victim-blaming, but not a single member of the twelve-person jury is looking at the defense attorney. Instead, their eyes linger on Andrea, taping that single piece of white copy paper to her case binder as if she doesn't have a damn thing better to do. What's so important about that piece of paper, Lola wonders, that now is the time to tape it to the front of her binder?

Lola cranes her neck, and she can make out the words *State of California v. Rollins*. The case name. A simple administrative task Andrea's secretary should have taken care of weeks ago, but here Andrea sits, in court, tearing another piece of tape from her roll and centering it over the white sheet before sealing it to the binder.

"Objection, Your Honor. Relevance." Andrea doesn't look up as she tears off another piece of tape.

"Sustained."

Lola doesn't have to listen to any more of the defense attorney's questions to know he has lost his case. Of course, she didn't come here this afternoon to watch a jury convict a wife beater, although she considers that a bonus. She came here to find Andrea, the woman who had taken such an interest in speaking to Sadie the other day. A simple Internet search turned up the prosecutor's full name—Andrea Dennison Whitely. With three names like that, Lola figures Andrea's either rich or a serial killer.

Maybe both, Lola thinks. The woman seems like a multitasker, prosecuting a piece of shit domestic violator while building a case against the Westside's most notorious new drug trafficker—Eldridge Waterston. It's the only reason Lola could think of for Andrea to make the drive to Pacific Division for one lousy meth head. She must want the head of the snake, and, in this instance, her wants coincide with Lola's.

Lola has one week to infiltrate Eldridge Waterston's organization, but she has to find him first. Sadie has no idea where her boss lives, and the only other person who might know is sitting in front of Lola in this courtroom, taping paper to a binder and winning her fucking case.

The judge calls for a break as soon as the defense attorney realizes his cross strategy—which so far consists of insinuating that a battered woman is a slut—has failed.

Lola and Hector trail out of the courtroom with the other spectators.

"What do we do now?" Hector asks.

They're in Van Nuys, walking down a long corridor walled in windows. Potential jurors line the hall, jackets and bags clutched to them, ready to make their exit as soon as some voice of authority booms the words, "You're excused."

Lola answered a jury summons once. The defendant was a quivering white college dude caught on a possession charge. When the judge had asked if anyone had a reason they couldn't serve on this particular kind of case that they needed to tell him in private, Lola had raised her hand. She had summed up her entire childhood for the judge in his private quarters with no tears. "My mom pimped me out to older men for drug money." The judge had listened with kind eyes, then said, in a firm, genuine tone, "I'm sorry. You're excused." Talking to that judge for ten seconds, Lola had known for the first time what it must be like to have a father. She had found herself wanting to take back the words, to spend a week or two with this man who ruled with kindness and quiet strength. When she went home that night, she had searched for him on the Internet and found a quick bio: UCLA undergrad, Harvard Law, admitted to the bar, charities, married, two daughters. The judge's biography reminded Lola that she did not belong in any part of his world, except maybe the charities, and she never wanted to be helped. She wanted to be the helper, or maybe that was the wrong word for it. She wanted to be the one in charge of telling other people what was best for them and making them do it. It was then Lola had realized she didn't need a father figure; she was the father figure.

Now, following Andrea the prosecutor toward the cafeteria, Lola doesn't know how to answer Hector's question. She doesn't know what to do next. She watches Andrea, her heels clicking, her head bowed over her phone, not seeing the heads she turns. But Lola knows, even if Andrea's not looking back, that the woman senses everyone's turning to her, their true north.

"Let's see where she goes," Lola says to Hector, because she doesn't want to give her little brother the impression she hasn't designed a foolproof plan that will land them on Eldridge Waterston's doorstep before dinner.

She hadn't expected company on her courthouse stakeout, if that's the proper term, but Hector had called this morning, on the landline, so Lola knew it was a personal call, nothing related to the Crenshaw Six. If it was a business call, Hector would have used one of the many burner phones Marcos is in charge of obtaining and discarding, over and over again, like paper plates good for a single backyard barbecue.

"Any word?" Hector had started their morning conversation without a hello.

"Would have called if there were," Lola had responded. Most likely, there will be no word from their mother until she's cuffed as a criminal or bagged as a corpse.

"Okay," Hector had said, and Lola could hear restless in his voice. In their family, a restless day, a day where one might seek a substance to soothe, is not a good one. Hector has never been a user, but he, like Lola, is one snort away from being consumed by their genetic quicksand.

"You busy today?" she had asked. "I gotta track someone down."

"Sure," Hector had replied, and they had both hung up as their personal conversation drifted into business waters.

Now, sister and brother watch as Andrea purchases five soggy egg salad sandwiches from the courthouse cafeteria. She has smiles ready for the workers, knows their names—Harry, Lana, Renaldo— and tips well.

"No way she eats that shit," Lola mutters.

"Egg salad? It ain't bad," Hector says, because he doesn't mind any "salad" drenched in mayo and pressed between two pieces of spongy white bread.

Outside, in the courthouse square, Andrea strides past vendor tents and carts peddling everything from scarves to hot dogs. She heads for underground parking, but Lola sees a homeless man and woman in her way. On instinct, Lola pats her pocket for a weapon—a simple blade would do.

"Hey!" the homeless man calls to Andrea.

"Hey!" the woman by his side repeats. They have the dirty, waifish look of regular humans gone to drugs. Even in the ninety-degree heat of Van Nuys, the couple, for Lola assumes they are together, wear bulky down coats that swallow their skeletal frames.

"Hey," Andrea responds, stopping, because the homeless man and woman have blocked her path to the underground parking garage. She looks up from her phone but keeps tapping on its touch screen.

"We saw you yesterday," the homeless man says. "You drive a real nice car."

Hector looks to Lola now, splinted hand feeling for his own weapon, but they are both unarmed. No heat would have made it through the courthouse metal detectors. Should they step in, he's asking, but Lola's gut tells her Andrea can handle herself.

"I do," Andrea responds to the homeless man. "Audi. Red. Too flashy, if you ask me, but my husband wanted to surprise me."

"What's your husband do?" the woman asks, and as Lola takes two steps toward the scene, she catches the scent of homeless human—onions, sweat, cheese, fear.

"He's a psychiatrist," Andrea says.

"Must be nice," the homeless woman says, and Lola notices the woman's wistful look as her eyes dart from her own tall, drug addict, mental case of a life partner to the blue sky above her. What if.

Andrea holds the bag of soggy courthouse sandwiches out to the couple. "Lunch. Egg salad."

They both reach for the bag, but the wife, smaller and quicker, wins.

When Andrea starts for the parking garage again, she is moving slower, the clicks uncertain taps on the pavement. Why let people see her like this, a little downtrodden, a little tired? But Lola and

Hector are the only two people with Andrea in this far corner of the courthouse square. The vendors are bright lines in the distance, weaving among one another, bobbing for business.

"We can't follow her to her car," Hector says, low, to Lola. It makes him nervous, being alone with his sister and this other woman. It hasn't occurred to Lola until just this minute that Hector doesn't know what they're doing tracking Andrea. He knows Eldridge's name, knows this prosecutor might have started a file on him, but he doesn't know how Lola plans to solicit information from Andrea. He must think Lola's going to beat the shit out of this woman, and he doesn't want that to happen. Hector excels at tedium—calling rehab centers, observing in a courtroom—but the one time she allowed him to explore his potential to kill or maim, he failed her. Despite taking his trigger finger, Lola has given Hector a second chance. Everyone in the Crenshaw Six must be willing to pull a trigger if Lola deems it necessary. He seems to know he is on probation, that Lola could raise the call to violence at any time, and it's making him jumpy.

Lucky for him, Lola does not want him to go after Andrea now. She is not the enemy. She is a source of information. Lola needs her trust. Or her sympathy. She thinks back to the woman testifying in the courtroom. *Who did this to you? He did. Your husband.*

"Hit me," Lola says to Hector now.

"What?"

"You heard me."

"Lola, you already got a black eye, your fucking cheek's all puffed up—"

"I said. Hit me." Lola speaks through gritted teeth, because Andrea has paused at the parking garage elevator, her profile toward them. She can see them, if she chooses. If they wait any longer, they lose her to a slow-moving metal box and her red Audi and her psychiatrist husband.

"I don't—" Hector hesitates.

Lola turns to face him. "Don't fuck this up, too."

Lola sees the flash of hurt feelings across her little brother's face turn to anger. Good. A second later, she feels his fist connect with her puffy cheek, an explosion of knuckle popping swollen cells.

Lola's not acting when she screams.

"Hey!" She hears Andrea's voice, deeper now, downright fucking scary.

Above her, Lola sees Hector through watery eyes, his hands folded, feet hip-width apart, a soldier waiting for orders.

"Hector," Lola whispers to him. He bends closer. "You did good." Hector bows his head in silent thanks. Lola hears a thud of bulk on concrete, then the quick clicking of Andrea's heels as she flies toward them. Lola can see the prosecutor has dropped her briefcase near the elevator. She can see files spilling from its discarded belly.

"What do I do now?"

"The briefcase," Lola says. "Eldridge's file." Hector nods and starts for his mission, but Lola stops him. "One more time. The stomach. Use your foot."

Hector plugs the steel toe of his boot into Lola's tummy and runs.

"Hey," Andrea shouts again, and Hector looks up at her, because Andrea's voice commands attention, and Hector, the little brother, the constant soldier, craves orders and structure. Andrea is all these things, and she is smart, getting this assailant to look her in the eye so she can study his face. Lola wouldn't be surprised if her brother bowed down and begged Andrea's forgiveness. But he is Lola's soldier, not Andrea's, so he takes off running.

Andrea watches him for no more than a second, and Lola can see the prosecutor memorizing stats: height, weight, race, distinguishing marks. Maybe Lola shouldn't have added the stomach kick, but Hector had wanted more orders, and she had needed a reason for him to be standing over her. *No more second-guessing,* she thinks.

"You okay?" Andrea asks, bending down, balancing her body on her stilettos like it's nothing.

"Yeah," Lola says. She feels Andrea's hand on the small of her back, tiny and strong, lifting her into a sitting position.

Now that the two women are on the same level, Andrea studies Lola's face. Lola wants to look for Hector, to see if he's sifting through the briefcase files looking for Eldridge's, but she can't look away from Andrea.

"Jesus," Andrea whispers, her hand reaching out to touch Lola's face: the black eye, the puffy cheek. Lola winces in half pain, half pleasure, as Andrea's fingertips brush her busted lip. "Was this . . . did he do all this?"

"No." Lola shakes her head, pleased that she can tell this woman the truth.

"If you've got more than one man in your life who'll do this, you're hanging with the wrong crowd," Andrea says.

No shit, Lola thinks, although she doesn't consider her boys— Garcia, Hector, Marcos, Jorge—the wrong crowd. Where she lives, they are the only crowd. And though she's had many men in her life hurt her, Lola's troubles originated with one woman, Maria Vasquez. Even now, missing on the streets, Maria has not allowed her children to move on with their lives. She should've done the polite thing years ago and died quiet with a needle in her arm.

"He's okay," Lola says. Another truth. She likes being honest with Andrea. She peers over the prosecutor's shoulder and sees Hector grabbing a manila file, then darting off, silent, hopping a concrete wall to somewhere. *Shit,* Lola thinks. *He took the whole file. Andrea's gonna fucking notice that.* Lola's got no one to blame but herself. Her orders weren't specific enough.

"You think it's okay for someone to beat the shit out of you in a courthouse parking garage? I'd hate to see what you think is okay behind closed doors," Andrea remarks.

Lola wants to interject, to tell her that, come to think of it, she does have bad luck with parking structures and lots. Both recent altercations have occurred in these public places, and Lola can't remember the last time someone fucked with her behind closed doors.

"Do you need an ambulance?" Andrea asks.

Lola shakes her head. The truth.

"Will you press charges?" Andrea asks, her voice indicating she knows Lola won't. Lola feels a pang slice through the pain in her stomach. She is sad to let Andrea down.

"I'll think about it," Lola says, a flat-out lie, but one she hopes will keep this particular connection open, in case she needs Andrea again.

Andrea presses her business card into Lola's hand. Her palm is sweating, and the card sticks to skin. She hates that—her body betraying her poker face. This whole on-the-fly confrontation has unnerved her. She feels guilty, deceiving this woman. But why?

"Call me," Andrea says. No if you want to press charges, no if you need to talk. It is an order.

Walking back to Hector's car, slow, one foot in front of the other, Lola sees the homeless couple passed out in the courthouse square, the detritus of egg salad and plastic wrap surrounding them in a makeshift border. Lola notes the single leftover sandwich and guesses they couldn't figure out how to divide it.

Lola's about to pass their sleeping, smelly bodies when she sees another square business card among their trash. Lola walks up and swipes the card, expecting to find it identical to the one Andrea gave her.

Instead, the card Lola turns over reads NEW HORIZONS REHABILI-TATION FACILITY, with an address in Malibu. It's the same place Sergeant Bubba stashed Sadie Perkins.

TWENTY

FLAMES

Lola carries Eldridge Waterston's file with her as she walks from Hector's lowrider to her front door. The file isn't as thick as she would have imagined for an up-and-coming Los Angeles drug lord. She wonders now how long it will take Andrea to realize her folder on Eldridge Waterston has gone missing. Will she connect the codependent, cliché domestic abuse couple from the parking structure to the file? Or will Andrea, like most upper-class citizens, dismiss the fighting man and woman as irrelevant? It would be easier for the Crenshaw Six if Andrea forgets Lola's existence; yet part of her wants Andrea to piece it together and seek her out.

Lola hasn't opened the file yet, because she needs to look at the case Andrea is building against Eldridge Waterston without distractions. Hector drove her home in silence, but Lola could feel his adrenaline pumping in the driver's seat. She could feel that, even if he would never admit it, part of him, that male, testosterone-driven part, had gotten off on hitting her. He would go see Amani now, if he is still seeing her, Lola had thought as she got out of the car, weary with the hatred she must carry for her brother's secret girl. It's too bad. In another world, Lola might have liked to sit across from Amani at a kitchen table and bitch about their respective men.

Lola stops on the welcome mat, feeling a lump under its worn edges. The mat Garcia purchased doesn't read welcome or bless this home. Instead, it has a picture of a cat, curled up asleep on a hearth. There are no words, and Garcia hates cats. He bought it four weeks after Kim's miscarriage, four weeks after they lost their family, and six weeks after Lola murdered Carlos. He had watched Lola shoot Kim's brother between the eyes, and he had bowed down to her. After that, there was no question of a life with Kim. The car accident was an accident, yes, but it drove him to where he belonged—Lola's. Three years ago, when Lola had asked Garcia why he had brought her that mat, Garcia had explained it was the only one at the store, and they needed to make sure they never tracked blood into the house. He had unrolled it in an even square and pressed the edges down with his weight. Then, he and Lola had walked inside, and he had never left.

The envelope poking out beneath the cat mat now is the standard brown of offices everywhere, not that Lola has ever worked in one. It appears to be a hand delivery, with no to or from address, only "Garcia" scrawled in Sharpie on the front. Like Eldridge's file, it will have to wait until she has time to focus on it.

Lola pushes through the door and finds the first waft of home both welcoming and overwhelming, that same feeling women across the globe get, crossing their thresholds at the end of a long day knowing domestic chores and chaos await them. She checks off her own list of chores—start dinner, get clean sheets for Lucy, figure out how the fuck to infiltrate Eldridge Waterston's organization using the information in Andrea's file. Somewhere at the end of that list, Lola tacks on "find junkie mother," but if her list were on paper, this last item would be in smaller print, an optional obligation.

Lola hears female laughter in the kitchen, guttural, the kind of laughter that involves a tossing of hair. She finds Kim at her kitchen table, in her chair, across from Garcia. Lucy sits between them, her hand in Kim's, and Lola feels the urge to leap onto Kim, to tear her black hair from its roots. Something is frying on the stove, and Lola takes stock of the skillet, her skillet's, handle, calculating how many seconds it will take to get from the kitchen doorway to the skillet, then to get the skillet from the stove to Kim's face.

"Lola," Garcia says, standing fast, as if Lola has caught him dick-deep in Kim instead of sitting across from her, his hands to himself.

Lola doesn't answer.

"Kim," Garcia says. "I need to talk to Lola."

"Just a sec," Kim says. "Hold still, Lucy."

Lola sees that Kim is painting Lucy's nails, bright red, and she speaks for the first time, keeping her voice even despite the angry froth she feels building in her throat. "No."

"What? Oh, Lola, turn down that skillet. Butter's gonna scorch," Kim says, as if she is the one to give the orders in Lola's kitchen.

"Kim," Garcia says, because he can see where this is going, and Kim can't.

"I'm almost done," Kim protests, and Lola hears a hint of whine in her voice. Lola can see Garcia hears it, too, and it turns him off. Lola never whines. She can protest in silence.

"You have to leave," Garcia says, and Kim looks up at him, finally getting it.

"Lola," Kim says, standing now, too. "Nothing happened."

"I'll make sure it doesn't burn," Lola says, flicking her wrist at the food on her stove, her tone so polite it makes Kim back out of the kitchen on tiptoe.

When Lola hears the front door shut behind Kim, she springs into action. She turns off the flame under Kim's skillet, then dumps the entire concoction—beef and onions and butter, some sort of filling—into the trash can.

"Can you take this outside, please?" she asks Garcia in the same polite tone she used on Kim, more electric than a Taser, and Garcia cinches the trash bag and heads outside without a word. Lola watches him from the kitchen window, sees him moving with the slow trudge and hanging head of a wounded animal.

"Lola?" It's Lucy, her voice louder and clearer than Lola has ever heard it.

"What is it, honey?" Lola says, her own voice shifting from polite to genuine as she kneels in front of the girl.

"I don't like this nail polish," Lucy says, and it's more words than Lola has ever heard the girl say at once. Lola relishes the girl's adamant tone, and she wants to tell Lucy to always speak like that, to know what she wants and go after it.

Instead, Lola takes the nail polish remover and one of the cotton balls Kim had spread on the kitchen table. *Bitch can't even paint nails without fucking up,* Lola thinks as she wipes the bright red from the little clear squares that are Lucy's fingernails.

By the time Garcia returns from the trash bins, Lola has cleaned off all the polish.

"Kim just dropped by. She didn't tell me she was coming," Garcia tries.

Lola knows Garcia is telling her the truth. She understands women like Kim, the ones who drop by and cook up a stick-to-your-ribs dinner and watch your kid and take their place at the kitchen table like they've earned it. The way to a man's bedroom, Lola thinks, can be through the kitchen. She understands now why it jarred her to find Kim in her place, cooking on her stove, painting Lucy's nails across from Garcia. It made Lola wonder if this was what Garcia's life would have looked like if he hadn't been driving Kim and their unborn child into a T-bone. Would Garcia be sitting at Lola's kitchen table, or at Kim's? And if he ever were to sit at Kim's kitchen table again, would he feel obligated to rat out Lola, to tell Kim Lola's the one who did her brother?

"I understand," Lola says, and it's the truth.

"She's a piece of work," Garcia says.

"I understand," Lola repeats, to let him know she doesn't want to hear any impression Kim has left on him, good or bad. Either way, Lola knows Kim has marked Garcia, her man.

"Never did like her empanadas," Garcia mutters.

"Got a file on the guy," Lola says. She doesn't feel comfortable naming names in front of Lucy. She doesn't want anyone thinking the girl has any information they might later try to extract with larger, scarier versions of the tools Kim used for Lucy's manicure.

"How?" Garcia asks, then, noticing her face for the first time, "Did someone hit you again?"

Lola shoots him a look, but she's too late. Lucy looks up at her, seeing her squirrel-puffy cheek and her two black eyes. Lola wonders why Lucy didn't notice this morning, then remembers with a nice salty sting that Lucy's mother showed up, giving her daughter false hope that mothers can change for the better. Lola had wanted to give Lucy some sort of speech to temper her excitement, something about how you can't trade a raspy old Chevy for an Escalade. But Lola doesn't know cars, and she had wanted Lucy to have a single good morning before she started dosing out the real fucking world like so much sick sweet cough syrup.

"Lola," Lucy mumbles, reaching out two fingers to press on Lola's puffy cheek. Lola holds in the pain so Lucy can explore the marks violence left on her face. "Who did this to you?" Lucy asks in a tone more suited to a badass boyfriend bent on revenge.

Lola does not want to launch into a dose of her own reality—*see, Lucy, sometimes you fuck up big-time, and sometimes you have to swallow your pride and take your beatings.* She doesn't want Lucy thinking Lola's reality is standard procedure. Yet part of Lola does want to tell the girl all her accomplishments, to make Lucy see Lola is someone she can be proud to know.

One day, Lola thinks, *but not today.* Today is for deceit, the calming salve one spreads over wounds not to make them go away, but to forget they are there.

"Took a bad fall," Lola says. "High heels and stairs. Together, no bueno." Lola tries out a smile on Lucy, and the girl gives her one back, but only with one side of her little round mouth. Lucy doesn't buy it, but the little girl's not going to contradict Lola.

"You tired?" Lola asks. She and Garcia need to figure this Eldridge shit out, alone.

They have only six more days to infiltrate Eldridge's organization. Lola feels a patter of excitement in her chest now, thinking of this, strangely, as an opportunity. She will meet Eldridge Waterston. Somewhere in her heart of hearts, she appreciates this clean-cut white dude giving the bloodthirsty cartel thugs a run for their money. If Eldridge Waterston could drive the cartel out of her neighborhood, Lola could control not only the drug trade but drug violence and drug deaths. She could rule her little kingdom, the only one that matters, with a fair hand and an open heart. But there is no autonomy in the ghetto. You're either working for the cartel, working against them, or working to stay off their radar.

Lucy gives Lola a quick kiss on her puffy cheek and says, "That will make it better. I hope."

Lola pulls Lucy a little closer and whispers into her hair, still stringy despite the daily washing and vitamin regimen Lola has implemented, "Sleep tight. Don't let the bedbugs bite." She learned that last bit from Veronica as a child, because Maria never whispered any good-night nonsense over her children. The first time she heard it, a young Lola had sat up in bed and demanded Veronica bring her some Windex so she could kill all the bedbugs. But Lucy says, solemn, "I won't," and she pads away on silent feet.

When Lola looks up, Garcia has already spread the contents of Eldridge Waterston's file over the kitchen table. He has disappeared the nail polish and manicure tools, erasing Kim's visit and reminding Lola this table is her domain, for business, domesticity, and the occasional pleasure when she and Garcia are too impatient to walk the fifty feet to their bedroom.

"Wife's name's Amanda, a.k.a. Mandy," Garcia says, then squints at what Lola imagines is Andrea's handwriting. "Thirty-seven."

"Eldridge?"

"The wife."

"How old's Eldridge?" Lola asks. She likes to measure her own progress at twenty-six with others both inside and outside her profession. Life expectancy shrinks when you enter South Central, so it's best to make your mark young, before someone shoots you in the fucking head, either on purpose or by accident. Lola hopes for the death she deserves. She doesn't want to be collateral damage—an unfortunate bystander in someone else's story.

"Thirty," says Garcia, and Lola can't help liking this drug lord she's never met for loving an older woman.

"He cheat on his wife?"

"File doesn't say."

Lola digs through the papers until she finds a few pages filled with Andrea's atrocious scrawls. She finds the part about Eldridge's domestic life and picks out every other phrase. "Attentive husband."

"Doesn't stray." "Home for dinner every night. Six o'clock or Mandy gets pissed." Lola chuckles, imagining this older woman, the only person who can poke at Eldridge Waterston with a spatula or a steak knife, demanding to know where he's been. "Loves dogs," Andrea's scrawl continues, another tick in the positive column Lola has drawn in her mind. "One son, Henry, ten months." Thank God or whoever the fuck's watching from the sky that Eldridge didn't feel the need to continue what Lola now knows is a family name—on his legal documents, he's Eldridge Waterston III.

"How we gonna do this?" Garcia asks her. "This dude gonna know we workin' for the only other game in town."

"Why? Because we're brown?"

"Yeah," Garcia says. He's right, but Lola doesn't have an answer for him yet. She's considered putting on a Spanish accent and going in as a housekeeper, but then she would have to clean toilets and change sheets, and Lola has never been a fan of strangers' bodily fluids. Besides, housekeeper would put her in Mandy's orbit, not Eldridge's, and Lola wants to sit at the boys' table for this game.

The leader of Los Liones wants her to find Eldridge's stash. Not the recreational dime bag of weed in the freezer marked "oregano," but the bricks of heroin stacked high as a house in some secret place. The fat man has not tasked her with stealing the stash—she doesn't have the manpower for that mission. Finding it requires brainpower; stealing it will be the simple part—whoever has the most guns wins.

Garcia can see Lola's thinking, so he switches gears, removing the manila folder with his name in neat Sharpie written across it. Lola had meant to open it herself, before Kim's attempted theft of her kitchen, her man, and the little girl who's not Lola's to steal.

"What's this?" Garcia asks.

"Found it under the mat," Lola says.

Garcia opens it, removing a single sheet of plain white copy paper. On it, someone has cut and pasted different letters in different fonts and colors, all of them from the slick paper of magazines.

She reads aloud the words the letters spell: **"We know it was you. Now we have her."**

"The fuck?" Garcia says. "Know it was me what?"

Lola's mind races back to the storage facility where she sat across from Mila, Darrel's girl, befriending her so she never saw the shot coming. She recalls the picnic table display of Mila's body, and she wonders what Garcia would do if someone gave her that public death.

He'd go batshit, as Darrel King has done now. Lola doesn't know how he found the Crenshaw Six, but she does take strange comfort in his inability to discern their true leader.

Lola turns over the note, because the magazine letters are big, taking up too much space. On the back, she silently reads the rest of the note. *Two million dollars by next Friday. Or she dies.* Darrel King has given her the same deadline as the cartel.

"It's a ransom note," Lola says aloud. "From Darrel King."

Garcia lets this sink in before he asks, "Who's her?"

Lola doesn't have to think before she says, "My mother."

TWENTY-ONE

INSIDE MAN

Garcia had wanted to debate the ransom note. How had Darrel King found him? Lola had remained silent during the one-sided conversation at their kitchen table. She was thinking about dinner, about her stove, the one Kim had marked by frying up some god-awful beef and onions. She had still been able to smell the grease.

When Lola had risen and started pulling healthier ingredients from the refrigerator—lean ground turkey, bell peppers, tomatoes—Garcia had stopped asking questions. Lola had known what he wanted to ask her but the words, smartly, stopped on his tongue—*Don't you want to get your mother back?* Easy question for Garcia to ask. His mother had decamped from Huntington Park a decade ago. Now she spent her years in Santa Fe playing bingo and asking when Garcia was going to make an honest woman of Lola. As far as everyone in the ghetto is concerned, Santa Fe might as well be Switzerland. Darrel must have taken the closest asset of Garcia's he could find, besides Lola, who was untouchable because she had Garcia's constant protection.

Darrel had pegged the wrong man as leader of the Crenshaw Six. He hadn't been able to find the group responsible for Mila's death for several days. And he had kidnapped the one person in Lola's life she wouldn't take a bullet for. No wonder Darrel was stuck in middle management, Lola had thought. She knew that, if she really wanted, she could get her mother back without handing over a single dollar. She would not feel the same confidence if Eldridge Waterston had nabbed her mother. But Eldridge Waterston would know not to act from emotion, kidnapping the first person you could get your hands on instead of waiting to slice your enemy's true Achilles' heel.

Lola didn't want a fight over her mother. She liked to save war for something that mattered, and last night, standing over her stove, sipping a cold beer and frying ground turkey, Lola had felt peace waft over her, the peace of knowing that, right now, her mother was Darrel King's problem.

Now, sitting shotgun in Hector's car, Lola feels battle itching at her skin. Hector has parked a hundred feet from Eldridge Waterston's front door. Garcia and Marcos have parked one street over, so they can follow Eldridge if Hector and Lola lose him. Lola had left Lucy in Valentine's care. Lola has more confidence in the pit bull's ability to protect Lucy than she does in Garcia's, or even her own. So why is she so nervous sitting here, on what's proven to be a tedious stakeout so far?

Lola wonders if the restless feeling crawling through her skin stems from her mother's kidnapping, which she has neglected to mention to Hector, or from sitting here, on the Westside, an outsider among multimillion-dollar houses and pristine landscaping executed by hardworking civilians and ex-cons from Lola's own neighborhood. What is it about the Westside, Lola thinks, that demands manual labor and shitty hourly wages to make someone from the ghetto feel they belong?

It is not the Westside that's bothering her today. It is what she wouldn't allow herself to consider last night when she reclaimed her stove. Maria was kidnapped, yet all the valuables in her mother's shitty life were missing from her apartment.

Maybe Maria hadn't relapsed by the time Darrel King got to her, but Lola knows her mother must have been on her way to score.

"You hungry?" Hector asks now.

"No," Lola says, and Hector looks away from Eldridge's frosted glass front door to Lola. Lola realizes her mistake—she is always hungry. "Yeah. Just don't want to miss him."

"It's okay. I'll go."

"Okay," Lola says, too quick, because the thought of Hector's absence has dissipated the tension pulsing through her body. Fuck. Should she tell him about their mother? If she does, she'll lose his focus on their current mission. Fuck Darrel King and his middle management kidnapping bullshit. Even if Lola decided to hand over two million in cash she doesn't have, she knows most kidnappers don't release their victims alive. She tries to convince herself that she is protecting her mother's life by sitting on her ass doing nothing to save her.

"You okay?" Hector asks.

"Yeah," Lola says, and she exhales deep when he shuts the driver's-side door. She has never understood why Hector still insists that Maria is his mother. Biologically, yes. But practically, Lola fucking raised him. Lola wiped up vomit, Lola tucked him in, Lola read bedtime stories and packed healthy school lunches on a goddamn budget. She taught him a lesson with a knife and a stitched finger. Is she refusing to help her mother because she is jealous of Maria?

Fucking second-guessing. Woman shit.

Eldridge's frosted glass door opens, and a woman emerges. From this distance, Lola can tell she's in her late thirties, with curly chestnut hair and a nose that's a tiny bit too large for her narrow face. She is skinny with curves—hips and boobs—but a flat, barely sagging ass formed from a combination of age and not eating enough. The woman wears her flaws like she knows they're there and could give a shit. Lola feels instant respect for this woman, who she knows must be Mandy, Eldridge's wife. No fucking wonder he married her.

A few seconds later, Eldridge emerges from the same door, locking it behind him. The door and the house don't look so massive on him as they do Mandy. He is larger, broad shouldered and fit, with trimmed blond hair and no facial scruff. He carries a car seat, and Lola sees a fat, smiling towhead of a baby strapped beneath a blanket there.

"You have your keys?" Lola hears Mandy's question to her husband.

"Yep," Eldridge says, and Lola hears a smile in the drug lord's voice, like he's fucking thrilled his wife is questioning his ability to remember his keys. Does Mandy know that her husband is running designer heroin from Afghanistan in direct opposition to the cartel? If she did, would she doubt his ability to remember both their baby and his keys at once?

"Wallet?"

"Check," says Eldridge, leaning over the car seat to make a funny face for the baby.

"And tonight . . ." Mandy starts, climbing into the passenger's seat.

"Lars and Amelia at seven." Eldridge shuts the door on Mandy's side before clicking the car seat into the bulky Mercedes SUV.

They are leaving. Lola doesn't have time to wonder where Hector is with the food. She scoots over to the driver's seat and turns the key. As she's pulling out of the parking space, she hears a thud on the car's roof and brakes. Hector jumps in, carrying white paper bags stained with grease.

"Burgers," he says, and Lola floors it.

Lola knows Eldridge isn't driving his wife and baby to whatever storage facility he uses to stow millions in heroin. She is curious— where does a drug lord take his family on a Saturday afternoon? The beach? Brunch, a meal Lola has never experienced?

Neither, it turns out. Twenty minutes later, Lola signals to turn right off Venice Boulevard and onto a cobbled street with pay parking. Pedestrians cross the cobbles, making their way from H.D. Buttercup to Room & Board. The bar across from the pay parking, Father's Office, is bustling with an afternoon crowd—men in jeans and button-downs; women in tight jeans, flowing tops, and high heels. Lola wonders how they cross the cobbles in heels. She has no problem in her Pumas.

"The fuck is this place?" Hector asks.

Faced with throngs of upper-middle-class families wrangling

little ones back to their respective luxury SUVs and strapping young
flying limbs into car seats, Lola has no fucking idea how to speak in
statements. She can only ask questions. "Looks like . . . a shitload of
furniture stores?"

When they get out of their car and start to follow Eldridge,
Mandy, and the baby at a safe distance, Hector points to a nearby
sign. "Says it's 'Helms Bakery District.' I don't see no bakery."

Lola sniffs the air for buttered and sugared dough. Instead, she
gets fried meat and sweet onions from Father's Office. She hears a
waiter tell a patron no, they can't make their signature burger with
no onion. No substitutions. *Must be nice,* Lola thinks, *being able to
be an asshole to a customer.* She wonders if part of the bar's appeal
to this casual white crowd is they get treated like shit. For them,
bad treatment must be a novelty.

Eldridge holds the door of Room & Board open for Mandy and
the baby.

"What do we do now?" Hector asks. "Wait out here?"

Hector has just suggested the first and most important guideline
of a stakeout—wait. Don't leave to go to the bathroom. Piss in your
Big Gulp. But Lola wants to know what the fuck Eldridge Waterston needs from a furniture store.

"We go in," Lola says, opening her door.

Inside the long, high-ceilinged building, Lola sees furniture for
miles, shaped and sculpted into would-be rooms. It's a giant dollhouse, beckoning Lola to come play pretend. Mandy pushes the
stroller through a Polo-and-khaki-clad family of five, Eldridge two
steps behind his wife as she cuts a weaving line through bodies, not
stopping to think twice or apologize if she runs over a stray toe here
or there. Even Lola would say sorry for that, but she guesses apologizing to strangers has nothing to do with whether or not you're
a good person. Decent, maybe, but there's a difference between
decent and good.

"Look at this shit," Hector says, pointing to a child's bedroom
built right into the store—bunk beds, red-and-yellow-striped com-
forters, matching desks and dressers. Room & Board has designed

this haven that belongs to no one for siblings. Gender neutral, it's the kind of room she and Hector could have shared and both felt at home. Instead, they had shared an oversized L-shaped sofa, with Lola on the long side until Hector outgrew her. Then they switched. When Maria pawned the sofa, they moved to the floor. Then Lola found Carlos.

"Nice," Lola says now, as if the room has glided over her, harmless, instead of sticking in her ribs like a blade she didn't see coming.

"You heard from her?" Hector asks. He must have been thinking of that same sofa and of Maria.

Lola shakes her head. If she wants to be technical, she's telling the truth. She heard from Darrel King, not from Maria, but she knows she can't hide behind technicalities. Just because something's legal doesn't make it right.

Legal. Lola has spotted something. A little green blur, appearing and disappearing, moving faster than the rest of the light Saturday crowd.

It's Andrea, the prosecutor, dressed down in jeans that fit too well to be cheap and an evergreen cotton sweater. Hair pulled back in a careful ponytail with no strays. She's got a man beside her. He's much too tall for her, with dark hair, glasses, and a button-down plaid shirt. The psychiatrist husband. What are they doing here at the same time as Eldridge Waterston? Lola remembers the New Horizons card she found in the junkie homeless couple's lunchtime trash. Sadie's rehab. Sadie, Eldridge Waterston's courier. What is the connection?

"What now?" Hector asks. He scratches at his splinted finger but stops when he sees Lola staring, unable to look away from what she has done. Hector hasn't seen Andrea, because he has followed stakeout rules and kept his eyes on Eldridge. The drug lord is admiring a stainless-steel dining table Mandy is showing him.

I don't know, Lola wants to tell Hector. Follow Andrea. Keep following Eldridge. Find Maria and pay the ransom, or at least tell Hector the good news that their mother might not have gotten around to relapsing—she's just been kidnapped. Lola has to take a breath before she calls up the fat man's orders. Infiltrate Eldridge

Waterston's organization within the week. She has to get Eldridge to trust the Crenshaw Six enough to let them know where he keeps the drugs.

Lola watches Eldridge smile and nod at his wife's potential purchase, happy to be spending a Saturday with her. She remembers his respectful tone when answering Mandy about his car keys and his wallet. From where Lola's standing, Mandy seems to be a housewife with too much time on her hands, reveling in dinner with the neighbors or full-price dining tables, but Eldridge treats her as an equal.

Lola had thought she would have to send Jorge or Hector to speak to him. But now she knows she can go herself.

TWENTY-TWO

THE OFFERING

That night, Lola paws through the dirty cash she and Garcia keep under their bedroom floorboards. Funny how dirty money can look clean and crisp as a starched hotel bed—an anomaly Lola has heard about from some of the honest women in her neighborhood who spend their days and nights making them up. Lola keeps meaning to look into buying a cash business—a nail salon or a car wash— but the neighborhood will talk if Lola Vasquez decides to try her hand at making other people's hands or cars sparkle. Everyone here thinks Garcia is a two-bit dealer, one who earns enough cash to wash his car and manicure his girl every seven to ten days, but not enough to purchase those businesses outright. Garcia does that, everyone in the neighborhood's gonna be filtering in here to kiss the ring, looking for work and favors and for Garcia to make all their fucking problems go away.

Lola doesn't mind the idea of helping her neighbors. The cartel might control the neighborhood, but Lola knows the individuals who make up the populace—their favorite foods, their financial situations, which of their relatives are in prison, which ones are out but fucking up enough that they'll land their asses in a cell eventually. No, Lola thinks as she counts cash, she doesn't mind helping her neighbors, but she wants hers to be the ring they kiss.

Maybe she is tired of leading from the darkness. Still, if she emerges from the shadows, Kim will know Lola murdered her brother Carlos. Lola can't say for sure how she knows this, but she does. Kim will know Lola wanted more, that Carlos wouldn't give her anything beyond designer clothes and a spatula. Kim will know Carlos had to be the alpha, but so, apparently, did Lola. Lola will go to prison.

Then she remembers her alternative, her potential few days left on Earth, and she knows prison isn't the worst thing. Maybe she is just tired of answering to men. But here in Huntington Park and South Central, the cartel is king, and Lola knows there is no room for autonomy. Yet.

"Lola?" Lucy's small voice interrupts her count. Lucy sees the cash, sees Lola's face screwed up in concentration. "I made you lose count."

"Nope," Lola lies.

"I can help."

"You count?"

"Yeah," Lucy says, reaching for a stack of cash. Lola wants to reach out and grab the money before Lucy can, but she doesn't want to disappoint the girl, who's biting her lip in concentration as she begins to count. "One, two, three . . ."

Lucy makes it to ten before she starts over at one.

"You know what comes after ten?" Lola asks.

"One."

Lola can't say no to Lucy, her hopeful eyes looking to Lola to tell her she's got the correct answer.

"Ever hear the number eleven?"

"Yeah," Lucy says. "At the store."

Mamacita's. Lola can't help thinking how Rosie Amaro found time between needles and dicks to seek out her daughter, yet the Amaros, Lucy's on-and-off guardians, have not. Lola turned their store into a violent crime scene where no one will want to touch the tacos for a couple weeks. Shouldn't their lack of business free up their time to give a shit about their granddaughter?

"Eleven, twelve, thirteen . . ." Lola finds a piece of scratch paper but no pen. She grabs red lipstick from her vanity and starts to write. In bright red, the numbers look like a countdown, or up, to some bloody murder. Together Lucy and Lola recite them, all the way up to twenty, giggling when they flub and clapping when they finish.

"Lola," Garcia interrupts. Lola detects a hint of reprimand in his voice. Lucy must hear it too, because she shuts her mouth and tucks her head under Lola's arm.

"Yeah?" Lola says, inserting a hint of leave-us-the-fuck-alone in her voice. She doesn't like his tone, the father trying to work on the Anderson account, doing the important work, while mother and daughter frolic too loudly in the other room. Not that Lola knows a goddamn thing about the father who knows best and the mother who dotes. She knows only that she has worked hard to get Lucy to the point where she can stand to be alone in a room with Garcia, and he is fucking it up.

Garcia hears her impatience and tempers his voice. "Think you should be . . . doing that?"

"Teaching Lucy to count?"

"With . . . money," Garcia says, and Lola hears the word he wants to say but doesn't. With *drug* money.

"Better than nothing," Lola says. She feels the blood rush to her cheeks—what kind of mother teaches her child to count this way? What kind of mother doesn't have the strength to tell her daughter no when she reaches for the stack of drug money in the first place?

Valentine chooses this moment to trot up to Lucy and lick the little girl's face from mouth to forehead. Lola keeps her voice even as she says, "Lucy, you mind feeding Valentine? She looks hungry."

Lucy hops up and runs out, Valentine on her heels, tail wagging, mouth open and stretched to the corners in a sweet pit bull smile. Lola is happy Valentine has found someone in this house worthy of her unconditional protection. Lola and Garcia have guns, Lucy has Valentine, and Lola is glad everyone has his or her own set of armor.

"I'm sorry," Lola says to Garcia, her head hanging.

"It's okay."

"I didn't want to tell her no," Lola admits, but when she tries to look at Garcia, she can see he doesn't know what to say. She wonders if he has the same problem with her—his lover, his boss. He can only question her choices. He can't tell her no.

Unsure, Garcia places his rough palm on her shoulder and changes the subject. "How much you thinking?"

"A hundred thousand."

"Jesus," he whispers.

"Price of doing business," Lola shrugs. "We go in there with some five grand bullshit he's not gonna think we're serious."

Lola has considered every possible way to infiltrate Eldridge's organization, but she is tired of playing a role. With Eldridge, she wants to be herself—Lola Vasquez, up-and-coming queenpin who can help him move his product in South Central and its surrounding colorful shitholes. She'll help level the playing field between Eldridge, the underdog, and the cartel, the surefire favorite. But Eldridge won't listen to any of Lola's speechifying unless she makes him an offering.

"Who you gonna send?" Garcia asks.

Lola can't take the money herself. In their business, couriers carry the dirt, the cash, the drugs. She can't lower herself on bended knee to Eldridge Waterston and present him with a hundred thousand dollars in cash. Leaders don't concern themselves with these menial tasks—unless, of course, a courier's transport goes missing, as Sadie's did. Couriers who fuck up can start wars between leaders.

Lola is banking on Eldridge wanting some kind of war with the cartel; otherwise, she, the woman who would be his rival if she were on the same level, would have no leverage. What she's offering Eldridge, besides a hundred grand, is intelligence. The cartel fucked up his drop. How does Lola know about this fuckup? 'Cause she's the one they hired to make sure it happened. And now she doesn't like how they're doing business. If the cartel asks, which they won't, she will make like this last part's a lie. But of course she wants her neighborhood to belong to her.

"Hector," Lola says, because she doesn't want to send Marcos in anywhere there's a baby. Jorge is still scarred from driving her to her meeting with the fat man. He saw the bruises and had to excuse himself.

"Hector's pretty hung up. On your mom being gone," Garcia observes, a cautious tone creeping into his voice. Lola doesn't like that Garcia feels he has to use that tone any time he says something she might not appreciate. Then Lola imagines Garcia telling her flat out not to send Hector, that she is wrong, and her mind is two rooms away in the kitchen, to the knife block and the stove, where she imagines skin sizzling. Then Lola has to take a deep breath because she just scared the shit out of herself.

"It'll be good for him. Take his mind off her."

Lola thinks of Maria, and of Darrel King, thinking he'd lucked the fuck out, snatching Lola's mother. He could have snatched anyone else in her life—Hector, Lucy (and the thought pings her heart), even Marcos—and she would have answered his demands before the deadline. Maybe not in the way Darrel planned, but she would have given him a response. But he took Maria, the woman he thinks is Garcia's would-be mother-in-law. Would-be if Garcia ever takes Lola down to the courthouse, signs a couple documents, and smashes cake in her face. Will they do that, Lola wonders, are they that kind of people, the kind to make promises and pledges when they don't know what blood life's going to throw at them?

Lola asks, fast, to see if she can get Garcia's honest opinion, "You think Maria's worth two million?"

It doesn't work. Garcia pauses, considering his next words, and, even though she is two rooms away from her kitchen, Lola's mind again flashes to the stove and the knives and blood and heat.

"She's your mother. You don't do something . . ." He trails off, not wanting to talk regrets and mistakes.

"We don't have two million dollars," Lola says, as if she would spend it on her junkie mother and not, say, Lucy's college fund. Funny how it's only been a few days and Lola's already planning Lucy's future, a brighter one, here under this roof with her.

"Darrel thinks we do."

"The fuck would he think that?"

"'Cause he sent Mila away with a duffel bag of cash. We grabbed Mila. We grabbed the bag."

"Bag was full of paper."

"Maybe Darrel didn't know that," Garcia says.

Lola thinks back to Mila, the recovering addict who was an econ major at UCLA before the drugs took her. She thinks of Mila's pleas, her swearing she had seen Darrel put the cash in the bag, that she didn't understand why Darrel would send her into a drop with paper instead of cash. He loved her, he did, Mila swore.

Damn right he did, Lola thinks now. Darrel King loved that slick damsel-in-distress Mila enough to let her swipe two million in cash from under his nose. He loved her enough to get desperate after her death and grab his rival's mother-in-law instead of taking the time to capture Garcia's true love. He still loves her enough not to believe a goddamn word Garcia says if he goes into some ransom meeting proclaiming Darrel's love Mila stole his cash, ripped him off, betrayed him.

Lola is glad she hasn't wasted any more grief on a girl who would steal from her man to set herself up. She wonders what the hell Mila's plan was at the drop, when Sadie the meth head would have checked the duffel. Had Mila even had a plan, or had seeing two million in cash blinded her to logic? And once she had the cash, what then? Was she planning to set up a grown-up lemonade stand, peddle H and coke and X to a bunch of suburban yuppies, out of Darrel's reach? No, Lola thinks, girl like that, recovering addict, college dropout, she'd use the dirty money to go straight. Stocks or hedge funds. Lola pictures Mila in cardigan and khakis, her worst vice sipping white wine at lunch with her girlfriends. Would she remember the day Darrel picked her drug-addled body from the street and got her clean? Or would she deny him to her rich white girlfriends as a mistake, telling them a story only filthy enough to elicit their envy at her harmless wild streak?

Doesn't matter. Mila's dead. The only time Lola should waste on her now is finding where the fuck she stashed two million dollars between the time Darrel gave her the duffel and the time she showed up in Venice armed with a short skirt and a bag full of worthless paper.

Lola's mind harkens back to the crime scene, Mila's body sprawled on Mamacita's outdoor picnic table, the gentle morning breeze electrifying the neighborhood lookie-loos, Lola among them. She remembers Detective Tyson, calling in a favor to the washed-up narc . . . Sergeant Bubba. The cop she thinks took Sadie's two million in heroin and forgot to check it into evidence. If he were helping Tyson investigate Mila's death, could Bubba have found where the dead woman stashed the cash and forgotten once again to log it into evidence?

Lola feels a pang of acid and bile in her stomach. She hates corrupt cops. They work for the people who can't protect themselves. They are paid to be good, and when they don't play their part, the results can wreck lives. She plays her part—the ambitious ghetto girl out to make a name for herself in the only world she can. She is a criminal. She is bad. But she's good at it. Why can't Sergeant Bubba be good and be good at it?

"What's up?" Garcia asks. His hand brushes her cheek, and Lola longs for him to question her decisions here, now. She wouldn't think of her knives. She would listen and consider. But he doesn't, and she doesn't, and Lola thinks it's no good wishing for the people she loves to change.

"Thinking," she says. He wants a precise answer, precise orders, and she doesn't have either. Her mind leaps and stalls like a car dying on a busy interstate, trying to land anywhere safe.

You should tell Hector about Maria, Lola hears, in Garcia's deep, strong voice.

"I can't," she says.

"I didn't say anything," Garcia says.

Lola lifts her tired body from the floorboards, cash counted.

"Lola. You okay?"

Lola doesn't answer. Instead, she hands the neat bound stacks to Garcia. "Get these to Hector. Tell him to put the word out, he's looking for a sit-down with Eldridge. He's got an offering for him, from the leader of the Crenshaw Six."

Garcia nods, letting her nonanswer go. Again, part of her wishes he would press her, but she's talking business again, and his hand is no longer on her cheek. There is no room for questions once she starts making statements.

TWENTY-THREE

MOTHERS

Lola grips the steering wheel even though she put the car in park five minutes ago. The parking space is good, she thinks, too good if she wants to stay hidden. But she is too tired to consider putting it back in gear, sussing out another spot, and making sure she has a clear view of Darrel King's sprawling West Adams house.

Alone this Sunday, she takes a longer look at the man's home, thinking it looks like an enlarged gingerbread house, brick with white vanilla icing draping the roof and trimming the various arches and cupolas. She guesses at the square footage—low three thousands, similar in size to Eldridge's modern structure, but Eldridge's real estate is in Venice, close to the beach, and easily worth a million or so more than Darrel's just because of the placement of the earth beneath it.

Lola isn't sure what she's doing here, other than she didn't want to sit at home while Garcia helped Hector put the word out that he was looking for Eldridge Waterston. It'll take a little time before Lola gets the go-ahead to meet Eldridge herself, to propose providing him intel on his rival, the cartel. Lola has five days until Friday. She'll have to play both sides, Eldridge and Los Liones, even though the only side she gives a shit about—her own—is one that doesn't exist to either of them.

Darrel's huge wooden block of a front door opens. Lola wonders if Maria will emerge, but of course a hostage isn't free to open a front door. Lola does recognize the woman who comes out. She is midfifties like Maria, but black, all curves and long, red painted fingernails. This Sunday afternoon, Darrel's mother has exchanged her church dress for designer jeans and a flowing floral top. Her feet toddle along in wedge sandals. Today, looking closer, Lola can tell by the woman's sure movements, her command of the porch and the way she gazes on the rest of the neighborhood with sharp eyes, that she leads Darrel's household.

Darrel's mother takes a seat on one of the large wicker chairs. She sips from her coffee mug and surveys the neighborhood. Lola would love to emerge from her car and join the woman on the porch, to find out how she sees her corner of the world, but this is not Lola's neighborhood. In this neighborhood, her skin is wearing the wrong color.

Mrs. King, as Lola now deems her, because she can't imagine calling this woman by a first name only, sees three restless boys at the corner. The lookouts. Lola can see now that they can't be more than sixteen. They have the fidgety faces and hands of those with no satisfying outlet for their time and energy. The sight of them brings Mrs. King to her feet. Darrel's mother is so pissed Lola can see the woman's furrowed brow from her parked car.

"Sherman Moore. You got a good reason you're not home helping your mama?" Mrs. King has the booming, sure voice of a principal.

"Yes, ma'am," the tallest of the three pipes up. The other two hide snickers in their overstuffed jackets, storage facilities for bindles and blades, Lola guesses. If the cops were to drive by, these three would be fooling no one.

"What would that reason be?" Mrs. King continues.

"Workin'," Sherman replies.

"I don't see any work happenin' on that corner."

Sherman is silent. Lola checks to see if the boy has the tormented look of a child wanting to rat out an adult to another adult. She's guessing Sherman isn't home helping his mother today because he is both looking out and dealing for Mrs. King's son. But Lola sees

Mrs. King's chiding has started a change in Sherman. He stands up straighter, his chest puffs out, and Lola can make out the beginning of muscles rippling under the sweatshirt he has outgrown. None of this bravado is frightening to Lola. The only thing that surprises her is when Sherman's eyes go dead. He does not like Mrs. King's scolding. Even from here, Lola can tell he would have no problem taking a life.

"Yes, ma'am," Sherman says in a flat tone.

"Don't you 'ma'am' me when you don't mean it."

Now Sherman looks right at Mrs. King, and the dead behind his eyes would make bumps pop on even Lola's arm if she weren't carrying a blade.

There is quiet between Sherman and Mrs. King now. The kid is standing up straight not out of respect, but defiance. *Darrel King better be careful,* Lola thinks, *or this lieutenant of his is going to make a play to become king.* From Mrs. King's silence, Lola gathers the older woman can see what her son can't—that Sherman Moore is dangerous.

"You get on home now," Mrs. King says finally, but the big block front door behind her opens and Darrel emerges.

"Momma," he interrupts. Lola again takes note of his muscles, rippling this time beneath a cotton T-shirt and jeans with just the right amount of bag. She pictures him sweaty for a little too long, skin gleaming in sunshine, then she remembers this man is her rival. Yet his eyes are kind as he reaches out a gentle hand to touch his mother's arm. He will let her think she's the boss. "I'm starving. You make me some eggs?"

"Don't see the point, you just eating the whites. Barely any nutrition there," Mrs. King mumbles, but she disappears inside with a smile. Lola feels a pang at her lost opportunity at daughterhood—why couldn't she have a pain-in-the-ass, up-in-her-shit, love-smothering mother like that? There is no point asking this question. She has what she has, and she makes what she makes of it.

Darrel King turns to Sherman. "She giving you trouble?"

"No, sir," Sherman says. *This kid is stupid smart,* Lola thinks, respecting his elders, never giving more answer than the question requires.

"Didn't think so," Darrel says, and his voice contains a smile that Sherman, cautious, mirrors.

"Want us to stay here?" Sherman asks. Then, too late, "Sir?"

If Darrel has noticed the initial omission of feigned respect, he doesn't show it.

"Better move on down the block," Darrel says. "She catches you out here again, she's liable to call your mother." With that, Darrel turns his back on Sherman and company. The other two boys take this movement to mean the end of their conversation.

"Hold up. We gettin' a piece of the next package or not?" Sherman. Stone-cold killer, even if he doesn't know it himself yet.

Darrel turns toward Sherman. *Mistake*, Lola thinks. She would have kept walking as she answered. Let the little shit see his question wasn't important enough to stop her. But she can see Sherman doesn't care about the answer. He just wants to be the one to end the conversation.

"Yeah. There a problem, Sherman?" Darrel asks. Again, Lola thinks, *Mistake*. Darrel is opening a bunch of tiny doors that add up to a coup.

"No. Sir," says Sherman, then, to the other two, "Time to get the fuck on outta here."

Sherman leads the way down the block, the other two following with the plodding, tired movements of young people who have seen too much for their years. She feels for Darrel, living his own lie, hiring teenage guards to protect his domain and keep his mother in the dark. Even Sherman didn't give her, a twentysomething woman, a second glance, despite her skin color. It could be that Sherman considers the job of lookout beneath him. Still, Lola can't say a more dedicated guard wouldn't have done the same. She is underestimated in every neighborhood, including her own.

As she watches the three boys turn a corner, she spots an oddity rounding the opposite one. The timing is too perfect—to appear just as the three corner boys disappear—and the couple, or one of them, doesn't belong. The girl is black, of this place, but she moves with the quick, darting moves of a sitting duck. It's because of her companion—brown skin. Lola doesn't have to see any more of him to know he shouldn't be here, with this girl, walking in broad daylight like he belongs. Idiot.

Then he gets closer, and Lola sees him just as Darrel does. She picks out the familiar gait, the eyes, the slight shrug of one shoulder. Hector. Her brother. Out for a tense Sunday afternoon stroll in rival territory with his girl, Amani. A flash of anger explodes in Lola's heart, but it turns to sadness quick as a douse of cold water extinguishes a flame. Why is Hector putting himself in danger? Has Maria's disappearance so affected him that he doesn't give a shit if he lives or dies? Lola's not going to let her baby brother ruin his life grieving for their washed-up drug-ridden asshole of a mother. But Darrel King has already seen Hector, and, whether or not he recognizes him, he knows Hector doesn't belong.

Lola doesn't think further than getting out of the car, letting Darrel's eyes land on her. Target her. Hate her.

"The fuck . . ." she hears her rival utter. Good. She has the elements of both surprise and confusion. Darrel doesn't have any more of a plan than she does, so utterly ridiculous are the circumstances in which Hector's appearance has put them. To Darrel, it must look like Garcia can't control his girl and her baby brother.

"Hey!" Lola calls. Hector sees his sister, and Lola's heart softens as she sees his face go from could-give-a-fuck to oh, shit.

"Lola?"

"Get your ass over here," Lola says, but she keeps moving toward Hector. She has to get him in her car. She has to get him out of here. She's not going to wait for him to come to her.

"Is that . . ." Amani speaks with quiet questioning.

"Amani!" Darrel shouts to her. "What you doing out here? You need to get on home. Now."

For a second, Lola and Darrel lock eyes—two parents calling their star-crossed children inside where they can protect them.

"Hector, goddammit, I said get over here," Lola says. She's losing her shit on the inside, pissed as all get-out, but she has to play up that Darrel terrifies her. The more scared of getting shot she looks, the more Darrel won't feel the need to shoot them.

"Lola. This is Amani," Hector tries, standing up straight, defiant, but Lola has no time for his naive sense of justice. If he wants this girl to fuck and love and feed him, he has to get fucked and loved and fed in private.

"Nice to meet you," Lola says to Amani, because as far as Lola can tell, Amani is smart and kind and takes good care of her baby brother. Lola doesn't mind—as long as it's behind closed doors.

"Amani," Darrel calls again, and this time Lola hears the implied countdown in his voice. She has to get Hector out of here.

"Hector," Lola says, out of breath as she reaches the couple. "We have to go."

"Why?"

Lola fights the urge to say because she said so, something their own mother never said because even Maria had the good sense to know her judgment was a few steps below questionable.

"Because he's gonna shoot you," Lola says.

"What if I don't care?"

"After he shoots you, I gotta shoot her," Lola nods to Amani, who accepts Lola's statement without surprise. The way of the world.

Hector's eyes blaze at Lola. She wants to slap the gullible rebel out of him, to get him to see she knows what's best. She wants to tell Amani she seems like a lovely girl, that it's just business.

When Lola turns to get Darrel back in her eyeline, she sees the gun in his lowered hand. A warning, subtle but clear. He's keeping the weapon where Lola has to strain to see it, by his side. He's giving her a chance to get Hector out of here.

"Come on," Lola says. Hector sees Darrel with his gun. He looks at Amani.

"Go with her," Amani says.

"You sure?"

"Yeah," Amani says. "You have to."

At least this girl understands you have to obey the rules, even if they're not fair. Amani is an adult. Hector is behaving like a child, and Lola blames herself.

She would have killed any other soldier who fucked up her drop.

When Hector moves in to kiss Amani good-bye, right here in the middle of Darrel King's concrete and potholes, Lola feels hot flushing up her cheeks.

"Fucking idiot," she says, disgust soaking her voice so that Hector, surprised, has the nerve to look wounded. *Fucking puppy love,* Lola thinks, although she can tell Amani feels her same disdain for Hector right now. The girl pulls away from Hector's lips and crosses her arms over her chest.

"I gotta go," Amani says.

"I'll call you," Hector says, and Amani nods in response, crossing her arms tighter and turning her back on them both. She wants to get home, a place she belongs, in this neighborhood, away from Hector.

Lola doesn't tell Hector to come on now. Instead, she turns and walks toward the car, and he follows like a kicked puppy, lovesick eyes on Amani's retreating form. Lola sees Darrel clenching the gun at his side, waiting for them to get the fuck off his streets.

Inside the car, Lola starts the engine as she says, "You were supposed to be hooking up a sit-down."

"Wanted to see Amani first," Hector says.

"You think she respects that? Man who can't get his shit done without letting his woman say jump first?" Lola says.

"You tell me," Hector tries. Lola swallows the pinprick pain, keeping her face stone.

She has to remind herself Hector is only eighteen. He must be smarting from her calling him a fucking idiot. Or she must be making excuses for him.

"I'm gonna drive you home. Then you're gonna get in your car, drive out to Venice, and get this shit done," Lola says.

As she speaks, she hears the sound of Darrel's front door opening. Mrs. King walks out onto the porch. Darrel whips around, tucking pistol into pants with the ease of a man accustomed to living a double life.

"Looks like Darrel's scared of his momma," Hector says with a laugh, and Lola doesn't like the low, bullying rumble she hears in his delight.

"So?" Lola challenges him, and Hector's laughter stops. For a second, Lola thinks she's gotten through to her brother, but the thought evaporates as the front door rumbles open and shut again, and a second woman with a second coffee mug emerges from the house in a ring of shared laughter.

Maria. Manicured and coiffed to match Mrs. King. She takes a seat in the wicker chair opposite Darrel's mother, the two women gabbing in fits and starts, sipping, rocking, bonding.

"Jesus," Hector says. Lola knows she should feel some sort of thankful that Maria is okay, but seeing her mother safe and happy, all she feels is nothing.

Lola puts the car in gear as Darrel looks at her, caught keeping his two-million-dollar hostage healthy and polished. He must know from the look on Lola's face that he's never going to get his two million dollars for this version of Maria—clean, smiling, gossiping.

"That's Mom. She's here," Hector shouts, despite the fact that Lola's sitting right next to him. "Where you going?"

"Home," Lola says.

"What the fuck?"

"We got shit to do."

"Darrel has Mom."

"Never seen her happier," Lola says.

Hector stares at her. "You knew. That she was here."

"Yeah," Lola says, casual. She puts foot to gas and guns. If Hector were to stop, drop, and roll into the street, to run back for Maria, Lola would respect him. Instead, he sits, mute, in the passenger's seat, letting her drive him away without protest.

Hector is still a boy. Lola has to change that.

TWENTY-FOUR

GROUNDED

The barista hands Lola a repurposed, recycled, brown paper coffee cup peppered with proclamations of Earth friendliness. His name-tag reads, "Gordon," and he's too handsome to be frothing lattes behind a thick wooden counter forever. *Actor,* Lola thinks. Lola's not in the entertainment industry, but even in her own head, the term *actor* carries equal parts awe and disdain—awe for the hotness, disdain for the idiocy of anyone willing to stand in front of others and be judged, day after day.

"You have a nice day now, Lola," Gordon says with a smile. What is it with this kid? She notes that sweet, dear Gordon spelled her name correctly, the block letters written in Sharpie identical to Darrel's ransom note.

Lola finds a table near the window where she can see the coffee shop's comings and goings. This place is not Starbucks. The line stretches out the door—hipsters in skinny jeans and Converse, middle-aged hippie ladies with wiry orange and straw-colored hair, yuppie couples with dogs instead of babies, and a few daring tourists trying to comprehend the concept of coffee as religion. While Lola often buys her daily dose of caffeine at a neighborhood bodega where they leave the dregs percolating for hours, she can appreciate a cup of coffee that undergoes an actual brewing process.

She scans the line of people out the door again, but there's no sign of Eldridge.

Earlier, Lola had sent Hector out the door with the briefcase of money and a warning that he shouldn't come back until he had unloaded the offering on Eldridge. The ride home from Darrel's had been silent, but Hector had obeyed her orders once they were back in their own neighborhood. He had delivered the cash to Eldridge, who wanted to meet the leader of the Crenshaw Six this afternoon, Monday, at this very coffee shop.

"Excuse me, excuse me." Lola hears a voice that shouldn't be familiar but is. When she looks to the entrance, Lola sees Mandy, Eldridge's wife, ramming the baby stroller through the coffee shop's door, rolling over toes and disgruntling patrons.

"There's a line," growls a hipster man who's too old to still be a hipster. Lola might be a banger, but even in the hood, people can unite in their shared hatred of these pretentious, trust-funded, pale faces. This particular man's skinny jeans encase his chubby thighs—fabric fighting fat—and his gut spills over the top, an exposed sack of flab between T-shirt and denim.

"I know, I know." Mandy sighs, as if she can't believe the injustice of it either. "But the baby's crying and I've got to get home before my decorator arrives."

The baby is not crying, but cooing up at his mother, happy as a goddamn bug in a rug. The old hipster has no idea how to respond to Mandy's entitlement, and Lola catches herself smiling.

As Mandy weaves her way to the front of the line, other patrons step back, letting her pass. They have overheard the conversation with the aging hipster and must not feel like fighting a losing battle. When Mandy arrives at the counter, she booms, "Good afternoon, Gordon," as if she's known him her whole life, but Lola can tell even friendly Gordon doesn't have a fucking clue what to do with this particular woman except stare at her. "How are you today?"

"I'm fine. Good." Gordon gulps, as if Mandy's wielding a gun instead of a stroller. She doesn't hear Gordon's response, because she's turned to coo at her baby. The whole line inhales, about to express impatience at this woman who not only cut the line but now can't be bothered to place her order. Then they remember the aging hipster and everyone holds their breath.

Lola can't take her eyes off Mandy, even to tell the person grabbing the chair across from her that this seat's about to be taken.

"Gonna use that," Lola says.

"I know," a man's voice responds, and then Eldridge Waterston is sitting across from her. "My wife's something else, isn't she?"

"That your wife?" Lola asks as if she didn't know. Eldridge turns to her with a short yell of a laugh, sharp as a sniper's rifle ring. The coffee shop patrons turn as one to face Eldridge.

"Honey? Do you want anything?" It's Mandy, voice singing across the sea of puzzled patrons and landing like a kiss on her husband.

It amazes Lola how, if you act like you own the place, you can.

"No, thank you, sweetheart," Eldridge responds in drippy sweet dulcet. Lola wonders if this gushy husband and wife duet is an act or some sick version of a too-healthy relationship. She and Garcia would never soak a public place in their aching affection. But maybe every happy relationship is happy in its own fucked-up pleasures.

"You sure you're at the right table?" Lola asks. "Only two chairs."

"My wife doesn't like to sit still," Eldridge says.

"Doesn't seem like it," Lola says, taking a sip of coffee and letting the caffeine arm her like so much steel.

"If you'd prefer to pretend you haven't done a little intelligence work on my family, I'm fine with that."

Lola tries out a blank stare on Eldridge, then scraps it, because her resting face tends toward anger.

"I have to give you credit. You stayed at a respectful distance. You expressed no aggression. Most importantly, you did not approach us when we were with my child."

"I would never hurt a child," Lola blurts, her head shaking the universal signal for no, no, no. She wants Eldridge to know her intentions as a paid stalker are honorable.

"Thank you." Eldridge bows his head. He keeps it down so long Lola wonders if he might be praying, and, if so, should she join him.

"I appreciate that," he says suddenly, head snapping back up, blue eyes locking in on Lola's brown.

Lola decides to ask the question that's been burning in her gut since Eldridge sat across from her, certain he had the right person. "Aren't you going to ask where my boyfriend is?"

"I don't ask unnecessary questions," Eldridge says.

"Why is that question unnecessary?" Lola asks. Eldridge makes her want to speak in complete sentences.

"I know where he is," Eldridge says. "Home, in Huntington Park, looking after the little girl you're harboring from her heroin addict mother."

Lola fights the instinct to sit back, pushed by the power of Eldridge's words. He knows about Lucy. This information frightens her more than the fact that he must have had his own spies running down the Crenshaw Six all day. Lola doesn't flatter herself thinking he might have been watching them longer than that. Until Hector dropped a hundred grand in Eldridge's lap, Lola is certain the drug kingpin had never heard of what he must consider a ragtag bunch of bangers. Lola fights through the pulsing of fear and heart inside her to retrieve another logical thought. Unlike Darrel King and the cartel, Eldridge does his homework. Even though the fat man had his men watching her house, they were looking at the man—Garcia— and failing to notice her. Eldridge was expecting her.

The question strikes her, swift and strong as her closet baseball bat—Whose side should she be on? Right now, she's playing Eldridge at the fat man's behest. But has she chosen the losing team?

No, Lola thinks, *it's too soon. Be here. Now.* She once felt silly telling herself to be present, but she knows sitting across from this man is not a simple conversation over coffee. Together, she and Eldridge are brewing a war. The only thing Lola regrets is she can't be Eldridge's actual opponent. In the world of Eldridge and the fat man, Lola is the person brought in to stir up shit, fuck up drops, and incite violence and mayhem and bloodshed so someone else can come out on top.

"We're similar souls," Eldridge remarks, bringing Lola back to the coffee shop, where, nearby, Mandy paces in front of the glass case of baked goods. She scatters patrons with the stroller, which, in her capable hands, becomes a lawn mower spitting out anyone in its way like severed blades of grass.

"How so?" Lola asks.

"I also don't harm children," Eldridge says.

"That's good," Lola says, and relief floods her body as she thinks of Lucy.

"And I don't believe you meant me harm, conducting a bit of espionage."

"I wanted to make sure you could be trusted," Lola says.

"You can do better than that," Eldridge says.

He's right. She tried a lie on him, and it didn't fall right.

"I wanted to see what kind of person you were," she says, effortless, because it's the truth.

"Much better," Eldridge approves. "Why did you want to see what kind of person I am?"

"I'd heard about you."

"Of course. You visited Sadie." Not a question.

"Yes."

"Do you think she absconded with my wares?" Eldridge asks, eyes raised and expectant over the rim of his mug.

"No," Lola says. She hesitates, because she wonders if ratting out a dirty cop this early into their first shared cup of coffee is overkill.

"Do you have any theories? On who did?"

"Don't know enough about your enemies."

"And my friends?"

"Just Sadie."

"Sadie is a harmless addict who will spend the rest of her life feeling guilty that she serviced a few men to feed her habit."

Lola gives a short laugh, surprised at his honesty. She feels her own pang of guilt at the harsh sound. Even though she holds a requisite amount of disdain for a sheltered suburban girl like Sadie, she can't imagine knowing childhood as a safe home, hot food, and two loving parents, then having one of those secure pillars extinguished

in a puff of violence. Sadie's childhood prepared her for content-
ment and security. Lola's childhood prepared her for injustice and
hurt.

"You paying for her rehab?" Lola asks.

"I don't believe in rehabilitating addicts," Eldridge says.

"Because it's bad for business?"

"Because it doesn't work," Eldridge says.

Mandy approaches their table. Lola can see the baby peering
up at his mother with wide, adoring eyes, mouth open, smooth lips
longing in a little circle.

"I'm going back to the house. Sandra's coming at four. I wanted
her to start at noon so she'd be out at a decent hour, but it's fine,"
Mandy says. Lola can tell by the slight grit of her teeth on the word
fine that it is anything but. "We can ask her to sit with us at dinner."

"Okay," Eldridge says.

"It's not," Mandy says. "Sandra won't want to eat with us. She'll
want to finish cleaning she can get back to her own kids, her own
family, but she'll feel obligated, so she'll sit with us and no one will
talk and then she'll ask to be excused. It's sad, really." Mandy sighs.

"You don't have to invite her to sit with us."

Mandy gives Eldridge a look one might bestow on a challenged
child—pitying and affectionate. She gives his styled hair a little
shaking up, moving it despite the large amount of product there.

"That's not how it works, sweetie," Mandy says, dropping lower
to kiss her husband on the lips. Lola wants to feel insulted by Mandy's housekeeper diatribe, but she can't muster anything besides
agreement. Mandy is right. Every domestic worker cleaning someone else's house and rearing someone else's child wants to get back
to their own families, their own lives. Their bosses want to treat
them like family, invite them to eat at their tables to assuage their
own guilt—yet they also want their employees to refuse the invitation. But who can say no to a request from the people responsible
for one's livelihood?

"Hello," Mandy turns to Lola. Does she know who Lola is? Does
she know about her husband's booming business, scattering heroin
and warm bodies like her baby stroller cutting through a crowd?

"Hello," Lola says. "Hi" doesn't feel right, not for Mandy. Lola appreciates the woman's formality.

"My husband tells me you've done some impressive work in the field of pharmaceutical distribution."

Lola can't tell from Mandy's term—pharmaceutical distribution— if she knows about her husband's illegal empire, or if he's concocted an alternate, legitimate business that satisfies Mandy's curiosity without Eldridge having to lie to her too much. *Besides,* Lola thinks, *who's to say what's more dangerous? Illegal heroin or legal Oxy?*

She stays away from pills. People in her hood are suspicious of doctors and prescriptions and professional help. And unlike West-siders, they are immune to the cheap thrill of buying illegal shit.

"Could say that," Lola says, then despises her glib response. Mandy blinks, unsure she heard her right, and Lola suspects Mandy's face will transition from confusion to pity in a few seconds.

Instead, Mandy dismisses Lola with, "I'm running late. It was nice to meet you."

Lola watches her go, feeling a pang of sadness that she would be more nervous sitting across from Mandy at coffee than she does now, in her element with Eldridge. But Lola has always known she is faking it on the woman's side of the world. She can style her hair and apply eyeliner, even if it takes her a few tries, but she can't commiserate about failed brownie recipes or foods forbidden during pregnancy or husbands who can't keep their dicks in their drawers.

"You mentioned your offering came with a piece of information."

"Yes," Lola says. "You were going to sell your . . . stuff to Darrel King. He was supposed to bring you two million in cash."

Eldridge doesn't confirm or deny the figure.

"He had a courier. With a bag." Lola's heart beats faster now. This is the part of her speech that makes her feel like a rat. "But the bag was full of paper. There was never any cash for you." This last part isn't entirely true. Lola believes there was cash, that Darrel kept his word, but that Mila kept the money.

Eldridge pauses, chin tilted. He doesn't look Lola in the eye the same way most people might when trying to figure out if she's lying. "An interesting theory," he says. "It makes perfect sense."

Lola sits back, knowing it can't be this easy to infiltrate Eldridge's organization. Something is coming, the proverbial other shoe, and in this case it's steel-toed.

"The cartel doesn't want me supplying one of their largest customers. They're upset Darrel found me. So they send you in here to provide me false information about a decent customer. As if this information will keep me from supplying him."

Shit. Eldridge has called Lola out as a cartel spy. *It's true,* she wants to say, *all true, except not, because,* she wants to scream, *I don't want to be under the fat man's thumb. The fat man couldn't be bothered to research me. All I want is four million dollars, in heroin or cash, I'm not picky, and I'll pay off the fat man and work with you.*

But Lola can't turn her back on the cartel. It is a dream fueled by caffeine and Eldridge's ballsy sweet wife and this coffee shop filled with people with real careers and real futures. None of it is for Lola.

"That's not true," Lola says, but it comes out flat. "Darrel's courier didn't have cash to give you. I'm trying to help."

"Well, of course you'll have to prove that, if you want to do business with me."

I do, I do, Lola feels her caffeinated insides cry out as she sits in silence, waiting for her orders. She expects Eldridge to tell her to run point on a drop, to see if she can get through an exchange without stealing the goods herself. She can do that. She can slink up a side street in a leather skirt and thigh-high boots, she can stand under a burned-out doughnut sign, and, unlike Sadie, she knows to hold on to the stash when the shots start.

"You say Darrel King betrayed me. If that's the case, he's no friend to my business. I wouldn't want Mr. King claiming he got away with what's mine."

Lola hopes he's not sending her to steal from Darrel. She doesn't want to have to explain to Maria Vasquez why she's leaving her mother hostage and making off with cash instead of the other way around.

"And I imagine you have some sort of beef with the man, what with him kidnapping your mother," Eldridge continues. Here, he does look Lola in the eye, and when he doesn't see the requisite sadness there, he smiles. "Not that you're in any hurry to retrieve her. Still, I imagine you'll appreciate my task all the same."

"What's the task?"

"Kill Darrel."

TWENTY-FIVE

MISSED CONNECTIONS

Lola covers the ground from coffee shop to car in five minutes. Record time, considering Venice businesses play hard to get by forcing their customers to pay for parking ten blocks away. She wants to call Garcia, to tell him she can't do it. Darrel might have tried to go behind the cartel's back, but he is still one of their largest and most consistent customers. She kills Darrel, the fat man kills her, open and shut. She doesn't kill Darrel, she doesn't earn Eldridge's trust, the fat man kills her, open and shut.

In either scenario, Lola sees her own throat slit, her body disappeared and left on the lawn in a vat of lye for Garcia to discover. Not that Garcia would ever know for sure that the bits of bone and skin in the vat were Lola's. Lye is a cartel favorite because it makes it impossible to test DNA. Because loved ones can never identify their dead, they can never have closure.

Lola clicks on her right turn signal, taking some comfort in the idea that she is a safe driver, especially for a dead woman. She stops short of the pedestrian crosswalk, more than she can say for the honking douchebag behind her. Lola glances in the rearview and sees the man she expected—white, sunglasses, BMW, too much product in his hair. She regrets that she doesn't also keep a baseball bat in her backseat for emergencies like putting an entitled motherfucker in his place. The gun in her glove compartment would be overkill.

She has to settle for a middle finger stuck out her driver's-side window. She sees the man behind her put his hands to his sticky hair, then slam them back to the steering wheel. Lola delights in his rage, building until the BMW can no longer contain it. The man opens his door and spills from the car in a fit of red, puffy cheeks. He's headed for Lola.

Bring it, she thinks, and when she turns her face up toward the man, she has no fear to give him. It surprises him, her lack of feeling. To his credit, he rallies, ripping the sunglasses from his eyes to reveal piercing blue pupils.

"Did you just give me the finger?"

"Yeah," Lola says, looking away to change the radio station. Something with bass. Something ethnic. Something that will give this motherfucker pause.

The combination of her bored eyes and the nonwhite people music works. The man sputters his way back into his sunglasses as he says, "You should be careful about that. The next guy might not be so understanding." Before she can answer, he turns and walk-runs back to his car, fast, like he's gotta take a piss.

Lola puts her own car in gear and starts forward, almost banging up against short legs in denim and heels. Her eyes travel from the spiked red-soled shoes all the way up to the green cashmere shirt and matching eyes.

Andrea. The prosecutor.

Lola thinks back to Room & Board, of seeing Andrea there with her white-collar, dressed-down psychiatrist husband. Maybe a prosecutor building a case against a drug lord might happen upon said drug lord on a weekend furniture shopping trip, but what's the likelihood Andrea's here by chance, seeking coffee from the same pretentious shop Eldridge frequents?

None. No chance.

Lola tries to make the pieces fit—two million in heroin missing, dirty cop Bubba, cash for paper, Darrel, Eldridge, Andrea, Sadie's

New Horizons rehab. Lola can't work them into their respective places.

She wants to fling open her car door and run back to the coffee shop to observe the two. They won't be at the same table. It's too public. Lola just wants to see one look, one nod between them, but what will that answer? That Eldridge knows Andrea's watching him? Or is it more nefarious, an acknowledgment that they'll meet up later to discuss their true business, whatever blurred gray havoc that might be?

Lola realizes she's been sitting in the crosswalk for too long. A glance in her rearview tells her the BMW douchebag wants to lay on the horn but is too scared shitless. She waves a sorry to him, and his mouth opens and closes in impotent surprise.

Lola white-knuckles the steering wheel all the way to Huntington Park. She pulls into her driveway fast and hard, parking askew, because there's a cocktail of nerves and adrenaline building in her tummy and chest. She knows she's dead whether she chooses the fat man's path or Eldridge's, but she doesn't want the same fate for Garcia and for Lucy. She can't leave Lucy out, because Eldridge knows about the little girl.

As Lola pumps arms and legs, heart skipping, begging for air, she thinks how much of her life is sitting across a table from a man, waiting for orders. In that way, she is like so many other women.

"Hey," Garcia says as Lola slams through the door.

"Hey," Lola spits out, breathless, tired. Lucy and Garcia are sitting on the floor, playing a shabby version of Candy Land Lola has never seen before.

"We got it at a yard sale," Garcia explains. Lola notes the subject and verb, the complete sentences he, like Lola, is using because he knows a child is listening. The effort melts Lola, and she sinks to the floor with them.

She feels Garcia's questioning eyes on her as Lucy moves her piece toward the pink puffy princess at the board's end. He wants to know how the meeting went, but Lucy forces them to practice patience.

"Lola wants to play, too," Lucy says, and that settles it. Lola joins the game, and for the next half hour, she works her own way through the Candy Land board, her only concern making sure Lucy wins this game of chance.

When Lola has shut the white bedroom's door on a sleeping Lucy that night, she returns to the living room and curls into the foxhunting chair, laying her head on the armrest and sighing. She has assumed the position she wants—no longer putting on the costume of strong—but her vulnerability masks an ulterior motive. She needs Garcia's advice, not his agreement, and she wants him to feel safe giving it.

"White man wants me to get rid of Darrel," Lola mutters into one of the foxhunter's fat pasty thighs. The fabric smells of dog breath, sweat, and the remnants of many nights of fried meat eaten in front of the television. Home.

Garcia waits for her to finish her thought, but she has nothing.

"What do I do?" Lola asks, putting on a distraught tone. She is so used to reinforcing her voice with the boom and strength of a leader that she doesn't know how to sound vulnerable.

"You do it, cartel comes after you."

"I don't, Eldridge knows I'm a fucking rat and comes after me. Maybe you. Maybe Lucy."

"I can take care of myself," Garcia says, unable to pass up an opportunity for masculine bravado. It's such a typical banger reflex, but Lola likes the shortness in his tone, the talking back to her she needs right now.

"Can you take care of Lucy?" Lola doesn't mean can Garcia protect Lucy. She means can he raise her, after the blood has drained from Lola's body, and there is nothing but hours of Candy Land and feedings and naps and adding and subtracting on worksheets after school. Lola sees a flash of Kim in the kitchen frying up dinner while Lucy scratches pencil on paper at the kitchen table.

No, Lola thinks. *I can't die.*

"No," Garcia says. "Not without you. And I won't have to."

"You can't know that."

"Not gonna let nothing happen to you," Garcia says, proper

grammar dropped as Lola watches him swallow what she thinks must be tears. Still, she can't help but think Garcia's use of a double negative implies he will, in fact, let something happen to her.

"Something doesn't fit," Lola says, remembering Andrea.

"Lot of shit like that in this world." Garcia sits on the foxhunting chair's footstool. He isn't sure what to do with his hands, so he starts stroking Lola's ankle bone. He should have known to go for her shoulders, her neck, her feet even, but the awkward gesture soothes Lola.

"No, I mean with that prosecutor . . ."—Lola was about to call Andrea a bitch but finds she can't—". . . lady."

"Huh?"

"Andrea with the three names. Saw her outside the coffee shop today."

"Rich people," Garcia says, shaking his head at the coffee habits of the privileged.

"She was at that funky-ass furniture store, too," Lola says.

"What you thinkin'? They workin' together?" Garcia asks.

"Could be." Lola plays at the fabric of a foxhunter's fat ass with her fingernails. "Can't figure why, though."

"Thought you said she was buildin' a case against him?"

"She is." Lola thinks back to the file Hector swiped from Andrea's briefcase. It's been two years since Eldridge got on the DA's radar. Two years, and all Andrea, the tenacious pit bull prosecutor, has to show for her investigation into Eldridge Waterston is a few sheets of personal details like address, phone number, hair and eye color, and his wife's favorite stores. Lola knows Eldridge must guard the actual details of his business—offshore account numbers, storage facilities, trusted lieutenants—with care, but still, a woman as determined as Andrea could surely have thrown the names of a few known associates into the case she's building.

"Where you going?" Garcia asks, because she's pulled her ankle from his calloused hands to tear across the room.

The old desktop whirs and shakes as Lola fires it up. The spinning colored wheel going round and round reminds Lola of her own mind, frozen as it tries to figure out her next move. When the Internet browser finally opens, Lola searches for "New Horizons Rehabilitation Center." The full name. She wants the official website. The rehab facility is the only thing she can think of that connects all the "good" pieces—Andrea, the fierce prosecutor who dropped the center's card on the homeless couple; Sadie, Eldridge's withering addict courier who's flourishing there, not knowing who's paying her bill; Sergeant Bubba, the dirty cop who dropped Sadie there before he disappeared two million in Eldridge's heroin.

The website appears in bright, peaceful pixels. Lola feels Garcia standing behind her, afraid to touch her now that she's back in work mode. She tries to click on the "Staff" link, but the computer fucks up and sends her on a virtual tour. Lola clicks through the photos of this Malibu wonderland—white sheets, ocean views, massage therapy, organic, gluten-free bullshit menu. The computer doesn't let her go back until she's seen the entirety of this facility open only to people who have fucked up their lives.

"Must be nice," Garcia mutters, looking at the same pictures.

"No shit."

The spinning wheel relents, and Lola navigates her way to the staff page. The first name there stops her heart like a miniblast of heroin.

Dr. Jack Whitely, Founder.

The photo next to the name shows the clean-cut, handsome man who accompanied Andrea to Room & Board. Here, he wears a white coat and professional smile. The picture is a head-and-shoulders shot, so Lola can't see the wedding ring she knows is there.

Lola remembers Andrea telling the homeless couple her husband was a psychiatrist. And Eldridge's courier Sadie is staying at his rehab facility on someone else's tab. And Andrea is everywhere Eldridge is.

They are working together, Lola knows it now, but she can't decipher the benefits of what she presumes is their symbiotic relationship. Eldridge, drug lord going up against the cartel. Andrea, no-nonsense prosecutor assigned to investigate Eldridge. Bubba, Andrea's friend on the force.

Andrea stalls out the case against Eldridge. Why? What's in

it for her? Lola looks back to the Malibu castle Andrea's husband runs. Money. It must be. Is Eldridge paying Andrea tribute to let him keep doing business in what he considers his city, and she considers hers?

They are both wrong, Lola thinks. *This city is mine.*

TWENTY-SIX

BLINDSIDED

The next morning, Lola serves hot coffee in Styrofoam cups to Marcos and Jorge. They are standing on her porch. Lola can't see much farther than her driveway because of the fog. It is too early.

"Nothin' yet, boss," Jorge says.

Marcos grunts at Jorge, a reminder that they don't know who's watching. The legit population of Huntington Park rises early for six a.m. shifts and long commutes that would become insufferable if they waited until rush hour. To anyone watching, it should look like the gang boss's girlfriend is serving coffee to her man's soldiers.

"Sorry," Jorge says.

Lola holds up a hand to let him know it's nothing. "You checked his apartment?"

"His apartment, your mom's place, all of it. Hector's not there."

Amani, Lola thinks. *If Hector's not at his place or Maria's, he must be with Amani.* But she can't tell her men that.

"You want us to get your ma back?" It's Marcos, licking his lips. To him, Hector, the wayward brother, is already dead.

"I'll deal with her later," Lola says. She knows Marcos just wants an excuse to shoot some people, but she reads a subtext he didn't intend—*Why don't you give a shit about your mother?*

She sends them into the fog with coffee refills and blueberry muffins removed from individual plastic wrap. It's the best she can do this early.

Lola tries Hector's cell phone at nine o'clock sharp. Bangers don't keep bankers' hours, but she can't bring herself to start making business calls before what the real world considers a civilized time. If she's being honest with herself, her call to Hector isn't business, it's personal; but she's not, so it's not.

"Hey, got a job for you. Hit me back," Lola says. She knows she has more of a chance of Hector returning her call if there's a task assigned to it. You have to return your boss's call. You can tell your sister to fuck off.

"Still nothin'?" Garcia asks.

Lola shakes her head. She scatters organic fresh berries over Lucy's pancakes before setting the plate in front of the wide-eyed little girl. Their trip to Whole Foods yesterday, a first for all three of them, cost almost a grand in dirty drug money. They loaded two carts full of fruit, vegetables, gummy vitamins, bottled water, and all natural soaps for body and hair. Still, no matter how many times Lola washes and combs Lucy's hair, it dries in clumpy strings that make her look dirty. Lola has heard that it takes seven years for all the cells in a human body to be replaced. If she cares for Lucy for seven years, perhaps she'll have a whole new girl, one who has forgotten her childhood traumas and turns up her nose at nonorganic produce. Maybe Lola can replace Lucy's sullied innocence with naïveté.

"What you up to today?" Garcia asks.

"Gotta get Lucy to school," Lola says, even as she begins wrapping some hummus in a spinach tortilla. She doesn't know what else to put inside, but Lucy's first school lunch is missing color. Lola grabs a red pepper, a cucumber, and some tomatoes from the refrigerator. Should she put cheese on hummus? She doesn't want to send Lucy to kindergarten with peanut butter and jelly. She wants to make an effort, but now she's afraid she's just fucking up, that Lucy will go hungry, or, worse, suffer ridicule from the other children.

It is Tuesday. Lola has until Friday to pick her side—Eldridge or the fat man. She hasn't decided what to do about Andrea, because she doesn't know the extent of the prosecutor's partnership with Eldridge.

Either way she goes, Lola has decided there's a decent chance she won't survive the week. That's why she's picked out a private kindergarten for Lucy. She filled out an application on paper first, before she typed her responses into the computer, but she answered the questions differently in her head. Why do you think your child will thrive at Blooming Gardens? *Because she's survived more abuse and trauma in one day of her childhood than most of your wealthy bullshit angels will their entire lifetime.* Tell us about your child's likes and dislikes. *Likes days when she gets at least one meal. Dislikes being molested by her junkie mother's boyfriend.* How does your child react when faced with a problem? *She gets wide-eyed and doesn't let herself cry, because crying where she's from only earns her a beating.* Does your child have a nut allergy? Lola had typed NO in all caps in response to this last question, because she believes nut allergies are a luxury reserved for people who can afford to be picky.

Lucy needs fruit in her lunchbox, Lola thinks, frantic.

"Apples," she says. "Do you like apples?" she asks Lucy.

"I don't know," Lucy responds. The answer doesn't surprise Lola, who washes an apple twice and dries it with a paper towel before placing it next to the hummus wrap in the lunchbox Lucy picked out. The little girl had ignored the superheroes and princesses in straight gendered lines, going instead for a solid bright red square that reminds Lola of the color of fresh blood.

"You gonna eat something?" Garcia asks, serving himself from the stack of pancakes on a platter in the center of the table. He moves quickly, slapping butter onto the cakes and dousing them in syrup, then shoveling large bites into his mouth without stopping in between. Lola notices Lucy doing the same, and she can't tell if the girl is imitating Garcia or trying to quell a hunger that won't stop burning inside her. Lola's not going to implement any kind of table etiquette for Lucy. The girl needs to eat, however she wants, whenever she wants. Lola doesn't want mealtime charged with any more stress than it already is for Lucy, who shows up at the table when Lola calls unsure if there will be nourishment for her. Lola wonders how many times Rosie offered what little food she could afford to a man over her own child. Lola's heart beats in rage as she daydreams about what she will do to Rosie if they're ever alone. She thinks back to the story of El Coleccionista, drawing and quartering a man with four ropes and four cars, tearing him limb from limb and making sure it took a good half hour. When it comes to creating painful and novel deaths, the cartel wins every time.

Lola contemplates what possible torture the fat man will cook up for her, if she obeys Eldridge and kills Darrel King. Her life has become one awful romantic comedy—which man will she choose to serve? Lola wants her own ending.

"Not hungry," Lola tells Garcia. But when Lucy looks up at her, not understanding, Lola sits at the table and fills her own plate. The cakes turn to dust in her mouth, and she chews too long before another questioning look from Lucy reminds her to swallow.

"When does school start?" Lucy asks. She had sprung from bed this morning, bouncing with anticipation at the thought of going somewhere children outnumber adults.

"Half an hour," Lola replies, and Lucy looks to the clock, seeing if she can figure out where the hand will have to be for them to begin their journey.

Twenty minutes later, Lola straps Lucy into the booster seat they shelled out three hundred drug dollars for yesterday, and the two are on the road. Garcia wrote Lucy's name on both backpack and lunchbox last night. He and Lola had hovered in the living room, not discussing Lola's business predicament, but laying out everything Lucy needed for school: pencils sharpened to a perfect point, more crayons than the supply list required, clean clothes. They hadn't had a drop to drink, but together they got soused on the items before them, the stepping-stones to a decent life.

Now, Lucy drinks in the world as Lola drives them west from South Central, no sign of the cartel in their rearview. Blooming Gardens Elementary School is located in Culver City, a neighborhood that, from Lola's research, seems to be up-and-coming. She hadn't wanted to chance sticking Lucy in with true Westsiders, little Brentwood bitches and burgeoning hedge-fund managers. Together, Lola and Lucy watch the landscape change from window bars, lowriders, and taco trucks to day spas, wine bars, and two-story strip malls.

"Pretty . . ." Lucy breathes in wonder at one of these structures unique to Los Angeles, painted the color of sick skin and containing a Coffee Bean, a vegan restaurant, and a sterile nail salon.

Lucy is a true Angeleno, Lola thinks, *admiring the beauty of a stacked strip mall.*

"It is," Lola agrees, because she loves this town, too.

Blooming Gardens is on the corner of a residential street. Lola notes the dead end nearby, which is good, she thinks, to prevent traffic from mowing down small children. She pulls in to the drop-off line and eyes the SUVs, the luxury foreign wagons, all washed and buffed to a gleam. Mothers in matching workout tops and pants kiss little darlings good-bye. Fathers in starched collars dole out bear hugs and 'atta boys before pulling away, already firing up their Bluetooths to get the day's business going.

Lola doesn't want to drop Lucy with a kiss and a smile. She wants to walk her inside, so she pulls to a stop at the curb and puts on her emergency blinkers. She feels flutters in her stomach—nerves she never felt venturing into school for the first time. To her, school meant eight hours away from home and heroin. She wishes the public schools in Huntington Park had gone through June and started up in early August, as Blooming Gardens does, instead of allowing her hot, stifling summers trying to fill the days with hope that wasn't there.

"It's nice," Lucy observes.

Lola nods, unable to speak for the choke in her throat. She doesn't know whether to take Lucy's hand, or if the affectionate gesture will embarrass the little girl. Lola decides against it, since her parking job has drawn stares. Lola has never been good at getting close to the curb, and now it feels like all the parental eyes are turned on her in collective judgment.

As she and Lucy walk their gawking gauntlet, Lola realizes these parents could give a shit about her parking job. They are looking at the car itself, a Honda peppered with the dents and scratches of a useful life. They are looking at Lola, in her baggy cargo pants and tank top that clings to her trim waist, tight as leather across a bongo drum. Who is she? What does she do for a living? What does she feel her child stands to learn from Blooming Gardens? Is Lucy a scholarship student? Lola feels their application questions searing into her brain as she and Lucy walk.

She feels a light touch at her side and realizes Lucy is reaching for her hand. Lola squeezes the little girl's palm in her own, noticing the sweat there. Lucy is nervous, too.

"It's okay," Lola whispers.

"It is?" Lucy asks, looking at the cruel, higher-class judges that bar the escape routes on either side of them.

"Yes," Lola responds, soaking in the stares of the mothers and fathers in society that matter, the ones who can drop their kids off at private school and pick them up and take them home and feed them organic afternoon snacks and provide encouragement as they bend their precious little heads over homework that both challenges and stimulates. Lola recalls her own childhood, exhaustion at her desk after nights spent cowering in her room, listening to the low growls between her mother and another strange man, the wondering if Maria would send him in to her. She remembers free school lunches, pumped full of sugar, that woke her up for a brief fifteen minutes in the afternoon, then sank her by the time she got home to park herself in front of the television, not watching whatever cheery sitcom she could find. It seemed cruel, to be able to access normal American life on the black box, when Lola's own living room didn't live up to any average standard. Why point out to her, a child, how much of a failure she already was?

"Ma'am," a woman's voice calls. It's half cheerful, half don't fuck with me. When Lola turns, she sees a tall woman with kind, stern eyes. "Can I help you?"

"Yeah," Lola says. "Got a new student. I mean, I have a new student."

Lucy buries her face in Lola's cargo pants.

"School started two weeks ago," the woman says. "Was your daughter on the list?"

Lucy buries her face even deeper, but when the little girl dares to glance out of her nest, Lola sees her cheeks are flushed a rich pink that borders on red. Is the emotion painted on Lucy's face embarrassment or pride?

"What list?" Lola can't keep the edge out of her voice. She is unaccustomed to interrogation.

"The waiting list?"

Lola blinks, and the tall woman shifts her weight. Lola sees something in her relent as she says, "Why don't we go in my office and talk?"

It's only as the woman walks them away that Lola notices the gauntlet of parents she and Lucy were walking has not dissolved, but swollen to what could become a mob if someone were to throw a few choice words and some tear gas.

"Now," the woman says less than a minute later. Her office is a simple square that's a step above small. It's filled with gushing letters from students—"I luv ms lara"—and toys. Ms. Laura forgoes the high-backed rolling desk chair and settles on the sofa with Lola and Lucy, who stares at the dollhouse in the corner. Ms. Laura notices. "Would you like to play with the dollhouse while I talk to your mother?"

Lucy looks up at Lola, who nods, but Lucy stays put. Lola realizes with a bullet-sized pang that Lucy doesn't know what a dollhouse is or how to play with one.

"What's your name?" Ms. Laura asks, leaning forward, her eyes shining at the little girl. Lola recognizes compassion there, not pity, and in that moment, Lola falls head over heels for Ms. Laura.

"Lucy Amaro," Lucy says, too loud, as if she has practiced.

"Well, Lucy Amaro," Ms. Laura says, "you don't have to play with the dollhouse. You can play with whatever you like."

Lucy's eyes light up to match Ms. Laura's, and she squirms off the sofa and goes right to the school director's desk. There, she plucks the woman's empty Starbucks cup from its designated place next to the tape dispenser. Three seconds later, Lucy has settled onto the carpet with the cup and the tape, and Lola wants to cry.

But when she looks back to Ms. Laura, the woman is smiling at her. "She's a very creative child. Most girls her age are already sticking to what society considers a gender norm. Dollhouses, toy kitchens, pink. Even more important, Lucy possesses imagination. She doesn't need frills to be creative."

Lola watches Lucy taping her way around the empty plastic coffee cup and feels her heart outside her body, even though Lola never carried Lucy in her stomach.

"It's an advanced skill, to be able to make something from nothing," Ms. Laura continues, her voice so firm and even that Lola has to believe her. Still, Lucy does not know how to play with a dollhouse. How sad. Lola should have purchased some toys with her drug loot. She has enough to spare on a decked-out dollhouse, one that showcases a cushy upper-middle-class life to whatever-class child frolics at its doorstep.

"I filled out the application," Lola says, her hand shaking as she removes the folded pieces of paper from her pants pocket. "We don't have a stapler," she apologizes, but Ms. Laura waves her sorrow away and glances at the three crumpled pieces of paper Lola printed out last night. The woman grabs a pair of reading glasses from the coffee table, perching them on her nose to read Lola's responses. Lola hears a clock ticking but doesn't dare take her eyes off Ms. Laura to see where in the room time is being counted. The only other sound is Lucy, winding the tape around the coffee cup, fashioning her own version of a spiral staircase.

At last, Ms. Laura looks up. "Wonderful," she says. "Such thoughtful answers."

"Thank you," Lola says, bowing her head to this woman who has welcomed her and Lucy with the same high expectations she might for her wealthy pupils.

"The school year has already begun. We're operating at capacity, and even if we weren't, we do have a waiting list."

"How long is the waiting list? Couple weeks?" Lola asks. She had not anticipated this problem. She thought she could show up and enroll Lucy the same day, any day, especially with the application, typed, no less, as her insurance.

Ms. Laura bites her lip, and Lola can tell she has asked a stupid question. "Longer," Ms. Laura responds, and Lola imagines the years stretching out before Lucy as all her would-be classmates surpass her, living and learning and loving, leaving Lucy behind in her ghetto bedroom with no dollhouse in her future.

And Lola will not be alive to help her.

"Please," Lola says.

Again, Ms. Laura holds up a hand. "I'm willing to make an exception in Lucy's case. We have a select spot for diversity. I can get her in next week."

Lola feels her chest lift, thinking of Lucy here next week, even if she is not.

"I see from her application you're not her mother. We'll just need proof that you are Lucy's legal guardian."

Lola sinks in her chair. Red tape cuts like a fucking knife.

"You're not her legal guardian?"

Lola shakes her head.

"Could you speak to her mother, then? Obtain her permission?"

"I haven't talked to her mother . . ." *Since I threatened her with a baseball bat.*

"I'm sorry, but unless you have a paper authorizing you to care for Lucy, we can't take her at Blooming Gardens." Ms. Laura stands in a way that lets Lola know the meeting is over.

"Isn't there something you could do? We have money. I know it doesn't look that way—"

"That's all right," Ms. Laura says.

"I just have to drive home and back to get it. It's cash. A lot of it."

"No," Ms. Laura tells Lola. It's a firm response, simple and kind. Lola doesn't hear the word often anymore, and she appreciates its finality. Lola knows arguing and bribing are lost causes here.

She stands. "Lucy. Time to go home."

"What?" Lucy asks. "Is school over?"

"Yeah," Lola says. "School's over. Stupid to come here anyway." She has regressed to feeling sorry for herself. Stupid Lola, to think her baby who's not her baby could live and work and play among the semi-elite. Lucy will have to go to some ghetto kindergarten, where she will learn the beginnings of what matters to a ghetto girl—getting the guy, keeping the guy, not being too smart to scare the guy.

Ms. Laura sees right through Lola's self-pity and gives her nothing. Instead, she turns to Lucy. "Keep the cup. And the tape."

Ms. Laura smiles at Lucy, and Lucy smiles back, unaware of the woman's rejection. The little girl thinks she's attended her first day of school, and the realization hits Lola like a goddamn heartbreak tsunami.

In two quick strides, Lola has reached the dollhouse. She widens her arms to lift the two-story structure, and although her biceps bulge under its weight, she feels lighter somehow.

Ms. Laura doesn't protest, doesn't say she can't, or stop that, or she's calling the cops. Instead, she lets Lola take the dollhouse without protest. The lack of confrontation makes Lola feel she hasn't gotten revenge at all.

But by the end of the day, Lucy will know how to play with dolls.

TWENTY-SEVEN

VARIABLE

Lola sits up in bed, legs crossed, elbows resting on knees. She turns Andrea Dennison Whitely's business card over and over between two fingers. One side contains the trappings of a full life—name, title, office information. The other side is blank. Lola wishes her choices were so black and white.

She wonders if Lucy is still staring at the dollhouse, unsure how to play a game where stability and happiness are the prevailing constants. Lola had wanted to show her—*here's how you imagine, here's how you let your mind play.* She had backed off, though, because Lucy had told her on the ride home that dollhouses were her favorite and she loved to play with them. Lola had realized Lucy was attempting to appease Lola, to tell her it was a good thing, Lola stealing a dollhouse from an exclusive private kindergarten.

But Lola's loot doesn't change the fact that Lucy will have to walk the two blocks to barrio kindergarten. Lola will have to keep her fingers crossed some starving child doesn't steal her lunch and trade it for cheap smack money. But Lola is getting confused—what is the age where you turn down the wrong path and can't go back? For her, is it twenty-six?

Lola shakes off the thought and grabs the landline. The phone is cheap plastic, not even portable, its scratchy connection unsuitable for business. Lola considers this a personal call. If Andrea Dennison Whitely chooses to trace it, she will find a landline instead of a burner cell.

"Andrea Dennison Whitely." The woman's voice leaps over the phone, not loud, just right, with a touch of breathless. Lola wonders if she's caught the prosecutor on her treadmill.

"Hi. Um, this is Lola," Lola fumbles. She has to play the part of the abused woman, yes, but Andrea also leaves her tongue-tied and shy.

"Yes?" Andrea says, as if the name means something to her, though of course it can't. Not yet.

"The woman from the parking garage."

"Right," Andrea says, her tone warming, her voice becoming smooth and kind. "How are you, Lola?"

Not great, Lola thinks. *Dead. Can't get my kid into kindergarten. And I forgot to get that life insurance policy no company would ever offer me.*

"Scared," Lola says aloud.

"Have you considered pressing charges?"

"Oh, no. Don't think I could."

"That thought is very common. But I can help you, Lola," Andrea says, and Lola knows the prosecutor must have said these words to countless women on the receiving end of a man's fist. "Come down. Talk to me."

"Someone sees me at your office, I'm dead," Lola replies. The truth.

"Okay. Let's meet somewhere off campus."

"Where?"

"I'm guessing we need to stay out of your neighborhood," Andrea says.

"Would the Westside work for you?"

"Yeah."

Andrea names a diner Lola has never heard of, but she's expecting gluten-free artisan toast and cage-free eggs.

"I'm in court today. Will tomorrow work?"

"Tomorrow will work," Lola says. Tomorrow might be her second-to-last last day on Earth.

Garcia enters with a frying pan, an apron over his jeans. "You want lunch? Be good for us to eat together."

He is right, so Lola lugs her body from bed to table. Lucy carries the conversation, telling Garcia all about what she thinks was her first day of kindergarten. He listens and nods and catches her milk glass before she spills it with an arm waved in careless excitement. Lola feels a sting in her eyes thinking how she will miss these two.

When Lucy goes down for a nap, Garcia follows Lola back into the bedroom. She sprawls on the bed, turned away from him, feeling the urge to pick a fight. Maybe her death will be easier if they go out on a petty sour note. She is seeking separation. She wants to soften the blow for him.

"You should have let her spill," Lola says.

"What?"

"The milk. She's gotta learn."

"Learn what? Coordination? She will. When she's older," Garcia says. Lola sees the flash of anger in his eyes at her own coldness toward Lucy. In that moment, she hates herself and him. *Hold on to this*, she thinks. *It will make you ready to leave them.*

Instead, her hate muscle gives out, and she softens. "I'm sorry," she says.

"It's okay."

"You hear from Hector?"

"Nah."

"Shit," Lola says. She hopes her baby brother's just testing her, seeking her attention in the disguise of punishment.

"Probably holed up with that girl of his." Lola hopes Hector and Amani have the good sense to stay behind closed doors.

"I'll find him," Garcia promises. "You rest."

Lola falls into the musty pillows and mattress she shares with Garcia. She can feel several of the coils below popping into her back. They should buy a new bed. Then she thinks of her ticking clock dilemma and of a fresh mattress and Kim here to share it with Garcia.

"You know where she lives?" Garcia has reappeared, his face swimming above her. He has shifted from house husband in baggy jeans and apron to banger with dangerous shit to do. Lola notes the crease between his eyes. He is getting older.

"Who?" Lola asks, because all she can think is Kim, Kim, Kim. Someone else for Garcia to grow old with.

"Hector's girl."

Lola murmurs, "Somewhere in West Adams."

Garcia gives a quick nod—that'll do—and disappears again. Lola sees her long fingers reaching after him. She forgot to tell him to be careful. While Garcia's girl, Lola, can roam Darrel King's territory with a mere gunshot warning, Garcia can't show his face without becoming a target.

But Lola is tired. She feels herself sinking like a stone in water. She craves a deep sleep that a gun battle couldn't disturb.

Unconsciousness descends faster than she would have expected. She is rooted to the mattress, the same as if someone had chained her. In this dream state, she remembers she has arms and limbs, but she can't seem to move them.

She dreams of Lucy in school, counting to twenty, singing the alphabet at the top of her lungs because she knows she knows it. Lola dreams of allowing a snack with nuts in Lucy's lunch box. Ms. Laura scolds her—Lola has put the other children in jeopardy. Lola promises Ms. Laura it won't happen again. Lola dreams that everyone in the class shows up for Lucy's birthday party. She dreams of candles and a cake, home baked after several sunken failures, and a future for Lucy outside this place. As Lucy's dream life continues, the little girl grows in inches and pounds and words and numbers and hurt and happy. But Lola falls away from her own dream. In her stead, Kim stands over Lucy's thirteenth birthday cake, her famous chocolate concoction that Lola can only copy. When Lucy blows out the candles, she turns to Kim for a fierce squeeze and a smack on the lips.

Fuck that bitch, Lola thinks, and when she wakes to a ringing in her ear, she is saying the words aloud, "Fuck that bitch."

The ringing doesn't stop, and while Lola searches with fingers and closed eyes for its source, she realizes it's not an alarm. Nothing is on fire. It is just her landline, and when she opens her eyes, making the painful journey into consciousness, she realizes the ringing is only a slight chirp.

"Yeah?" she answers.

"He ain't here," Garcia says.

"At the girl's?" Lola asks. She knows Garcia must have debated whether to make this a business or personal call. She would have opted for business.

"Says she hasn't seen him since Sunday. When you dragged him out of here."

"Has he called?"

"She says no."

"Think she's telling the truth?"

"She's got no reason to lie," Garcia says.

Amani might have no reason to lie, but she sure as shit won't tell the truth if Hector has asked her to harbor him and not tell a fucking soul . . . especially not his traitor bitch sister who doesn't give a shit if their mother lives or dies.

"How do you know?" Lola asks.

"I convinced her to be honest," Garcia says, and Lola hears the whimper in the background, low and static crusted through the cheap plastic phone.

"Shouldn't have done that," Lola says.

"Promised I'd find him."

"But you didn't," Lola says, and she hangs up on Garcia. What was he doing, calling her on the landline when one of her soldiers was missing? It helps to think of Hector as a soldier instead of her little brother. But if Hector is a soldier, he is AWOL, and AWOL soldiers return to their commanders only for punishment.

Lola rolls from bed and paws on the floor for her cell phone. On it, she sees three missed calls from Garcia. Shit. She shouldn't have hung up on him. He knew she was sleeping, but he knew she would want him to wake her to hear about Hector.

Lola recalls the dinner table, the spilled milk, her telling Garcia he should have let it fall. Lola despises herself for wanting a child to fail. She despises herself for hanging up on Garcia, who wanted to let her sleep. Even without a psychiatrist, Lola can tell what she's doing—separating herself from those she loves. It will be easier to leave this world resenting her loved ones.

She smooths her cargo pants and checks on the sleeping Lucy. Valentine snores beside the little girl, one ear up for sounds worth waking for—gunshots, screams, doors ajar, the rattle of kibble. Lola can leave them for twenty minutes.

It is late afternoon, and the sun is giving up its light. Lola sees a sky streaked pink and orange, flames forgotten in the wake of a star. Children circle their rusted bikes in the street, toeing the potholed pavement as they spin around in a screech of ancient pebbled blacktop. Sometimes the bike tires uncover other things—empty bindles, discarded vials, cheap beer cans, used condoms—remnants of a fucked-up adult's life.

"Hey," one kid says to her with a respectful raise of his chin.

"Hey," Lola says. She doesn't recognize the kid, but she's guessing she knows his mother. She doesn't bother trying to place a father who must have walked out a good decade ago.

As she keeps walking, pace relaxed, hands in her hoodie pockets as if she's just out for a casual evening stroll, she hears the crunch of rubber on pavement. The kid is following her.

"Hey," he tries again.

Lola stops and looks at him. He's got about twelve years under his belt, maybe fourteen, if his mother forgot to feed him or couldn't afford to. His eyes are large, set deep in his face, and his hair is a sheath of black silk that falls almost to his shoulders. He has to keep flicking his head to one side to get that gorgeous hair out of his eyes.

"Heard you might be looking to hire."

"Don't need anybody to help me cook and clean," Lola says, her inner red flags rising.

"Not talkin' 'bout that," the kid says. "Talkin' 'bout your real business."

Lola likes being recognized.

"I'm good. I'm loyal. I ain't gonna rat on you."

Lola wants to tell him yes, of course, thank you so much. But she can't. She must live the rest of her days, all three of them, out of the spotlight.

"You should be in school," Lola says.

"Five o'clock. School'd be out even if it weren't summer."

Lola takes a long pause, then asks, "How'd you hear about me?"

"Word on the street."

Lola stands, brushing off her cargo pants. She expected to feel more panic than she does at the news that her cover might be blown.

"So what? I come work for you?"

"No," Lola says.

"Why not?"

"Not hiring."

Lola walks away, counting her steps as she nears Hector's apartment.

Then she hears the kid again. "It was your brother. Hector. He was braggin' on you. Told me his big sister was tough but fair. Told me she might could help me with a job."

Lola stops, the shocking part of this kid's words washing over her—not that Hector's big mouth revealed her true identity to a neighborhood kid, but that her rebellious baby brother was bragging on her, acknowledging her talent, her leadership. The words warm her insides as the night air cools off the heated ghetto vibe around her.

"Write down your number. I'll call you if anything comes up," she tells him. He does, and then she's on her way to Hector's again.

There is a single light on in the apartment when Lola unlocks the door. She has a key, but even if she didn't, the lock is cheap and pickable with nothing more than a credit card. The lamp next to Hector's leather sofa gives off a warm glow. In this half shadow, the apartment looks clean. Hector has always been good about putting dirty dishes in the sink, if not the dishwasher. He makes his bed every morning, even though he leaves lumps of sheets and pillow under the comforter. He puts dirty laundry in a pile in his closet. All these habits Lola taught him. Lola, not Maria.

Lola steps through Hector's kitchen on tiptoe. She can't shake the feeling that someone is here with her. She opens the refrigerator and finds the typical trappings of a bachelor banger—a shelf devoted to forties, one devoted to condiments, another to soda. Lola feels a surge of satisfaction upon finding bottled water, orange juice, eggs, and a loaf of whole-grain bread. She has done something right.

In the bedroom, she finds the expected lumpy comforter masking twisted sheets and pillows dented from nights of what Lola hopes involve sound sleep. She finds the dirty clothes pile in Hector's closet, dismayed when she finds no jeans there. Hector and Garcia both are averse to laundering denim, a habit Lola finds disgusting.

The bathroom is a different story. The toilet seat is up, not surprising considering Hector lives alone and his girl can't be caught alive in this neighborhood. A thin layer of grime coats the tub basin and the shower tile. Lola has harangued Hector for his inability to clean a bathroom, but his defense remains constant—if the toilet's dirty, he can put the lid down; if the shower's dirty, he can draw the curtain. Lola has tried explaining to him that when you repress a mess, it's still a mess.

Now she's the one cramming everything under a flimsy lid, telling herself she's too busy to rescue her mother from a drug lord when she just spent five minutes inventorying her baby brother's fridge.

She pads down the hallway to the living room. There, she finds curtains dusted with street grime, blown through the broken window behind them. Lola kneels to find a simple cracked brick garnished with broken glass. Judging by the amount of grime, someone must have thrown it hours before she got here. Tied to the brick with kitchen twine Lola finds another half-assed ransom note: *I have him, too.*

TWENTY-EIGHT

FIERCE

"I'll go alone," Lola had said to Garcia two hours ago. His protests rang obligatory, though, and while Lola considered calling Marcos or Jorge, she decided they didn't need any more ammunition against her brother. Although there are still a couple of days to go before Darrel's deadline comes to pass, he's made what should have been a business matter all personal. Lola wants to finish this quickly, without her men knowing Hector has made another mess by getting himself caught.

Now, crossing Darrel's West Adams street at a light jog, Lola keeps her head down and tries not to attract attention. It is night. It shouldn't be safe for her here. She's about to hang a right onto Darrel's walkway when she catches the corner kid she recognizes as Sherman Moore snoozing in a tinted Sentra right outside Darrel's house. *Some fucking lookout,* Lola thinks, although she guesses Darrel can't help it, if he wants to keep his mother in denial about his business. Then she remembers Sherman's mock civility to Darrel and his mother. Maybe Sherman wouldn't mind if someone were to bypass his snoring ass and shiv his boss.

When she passes the car, though, Sherman's eyes fly open. Lola can't help looking into his deep black holes. He has seen her. And she was right—he is a killer, even if he doesn't know it yet. She waits for him to jump out of the vehicle and pull a piece on her. Maybe Sherman would forgo the weapon and pound her unfeelingly with his fists. She wonders if he even knows he has the power not to feel, the power Darrel can't seem to see but that Lola knew was there from the moment she saw Sherman's face.

But Sherman doesn't move. Instead, he closes his eyes, and, within seconds, his mouth is hanging open in a sleep fit for the dead.

Lola wants to believe her theory that Sherman wants Darrel eliminated. Otherwise, she must accept the more likely cause of Sherman's dismissal. She is a woman. She is small. She is nothing.

She makes her way up the sidewalk to Darrel's fortress of a front door. Sprinklers hiss and churn on either side of her. It's been a dry summer, no rain to cool tension or grow new life.

Lola takes a moment as her finger lingers over the doorbell. It's late. Past midnight. Only tragedy and violence ring at this time of night, but Lola wants to try for something different. Part of the reason she insisted on going alone was that she didn't want to storm the castle. She can play the damsel in distress, she just needs a moment, here at Darrel's front door, to let go of her anger toward Hector. At least for the next hour.

Lola's finger depresses the button, and she hears a chime echo through the creaking house. It takes a minute, then Lola sees a light come on over the broad, wooden staircase. A few seconds later, a woman's painted toenails make their way down the steps, and, over the left foot, Lola sees a nightgown hitched up to expose a fleshy knee.

"We already got religion," Darrel's mother says as she opens the door. But the sight of the brown woman on her doorstep leaves her at a loss for words.

"I'm not here for that," Lola says, letting her voice catch. "I'm here . . . I think my mother is here?" Lola speaks in perfect, unaccented English. She can't let her banger slang upset Darrel's mother, who, truth be told, frightens Lola. It's not that she thinks the woman will pull a gun on her—it's more her maternal spirit, her willingness to answer the door past midnight because she doesn't want anything happening to her son. Lola knows it's natural to fear what one doesn't know, and Lola has never known the fierce maternal love Darrel King's mother embodies.

"Your mama?" It takes a second of squinting at Lola under the porch light, but Darrel's mother makes the connection. "Oh. You have got to be Maria's daughter."

"Right." The word hurts Lola's teeth as it passes.

"You're the spitting image of her."

Now Lola feels heat rising to her cheeks, but she knows she has to keep it together if she wants to gain access to Darrel's house.

"Oh, honey, you look sad."

"No," Lola says, on the defensive.

Darrel's mother seems to have practice with surly children, though, because she ignores Lola and says, "Maria's asleep. But why don't you come in and I'll fix you a plate."

"I don't want to trouble you."

"It's no trouble. Maria's a hoot."

Lola lets the comment pass, but she feels her entire self pulsing against her skin.

A fucking hoot.

"I'm Lorraine. And you're not leaving here without eating something."

Lola wants to pour herself into this woman's flabby strong arms. She wants to tell Lorraine there's a drug lord who wants Lola to kill her son, but that Lola doesn't want to, and not just because the fat man and the cartel appreciate Darrel as a customer. She doesn't want to kill him because Darrel had a chance to kill her yesterday, and he didn't. He let her escape. And yes, Darrel took her only brother hostage, finally hitting the mark of Lola's heart he'd missed when he took her mother, but Hector's predicament is self-made. If Lola sweeps in and cleans up Hector's mess, springing him from Darrel's grip, she will have to punish him. She wants to plead with Darrel's mother, to ask if her son can just do the dirty work for her.

Instead, she leans forward, her hand lighting on Lorraine's forearm. She is going to faint, she thinks, but Lorraine's voice drifts down to her.

"Come on, sweetie. You need some nourishment." A simple solution. A mother's way.

Lola hears her combat boots dragging across Darrel's hardwood floor in short stomps. Now that someone else is the adult, she is too tired to lift her feet.

"I've got some roast chicken, kale with grapes and feta, Pellegrino," Lorraine says, digging around the Sub-Zero refrigerator in the remodeled kitchen. "And you gotta have some fruit, too, but there's nothing wrong with putting it on top of pound cake." Lorraine winks at Lola, their little secret. If Lola were to speak now, she wouldn't have to pretend at the catch in her throat.

Darrel's mother has Lola seated in front of a full plate in under two minutes. Lola looks at the nourishment, made with love and without question for the brown girl who showed up on the doorstep. Suddenly starving, Lola shovels forkfuls into her mouth, letting the chicken and kale and grapes mix there in a painful symbiosis that sets the insides of her cheeks on tingling fire.

"Do I know how to fix you, or do I know?" Lorraine asks with a loud, kind guffaw. She swats Lola's knee with her manicured hand, and Lola wants it to be just her and this mother in all the world, raiding the kitchen and hugging and swatting.

Instead, Lola finds herself shy as she replies, "Thank you." She imagines she must look to Lorraine like Lucy looks to her: too skinny, wide-eyed, haunted. It has never occurred to Lola that she could become someone's lost cause.

"Now. Tell me what you're doing coming to see your mama at this time of night."

"Does the time matter?" Lola asks.

Darrel's mother chuckles, shaking her head as if Lola is a precocious child instead of a rival gang affiliate. To Lorraine's credit, Lola is a woman, and therefore not a threat. Also, Lola would never bring a gun into Darrel King's house. She has settled for a small blade, not enough to kill a man unless she's got soldiers holding him down. It strikes Lola here, over Lorraine's plate of kindness, that she has refused backup and brought a weapon she can't use to inflict a fatal wound. Perhaps she's already picked her side. One thing she knows, sitting across from this mother figure—she does not want to kill this woman's son.

"You're Mila's cousin, then?"

"Huh?" Lola asks, and the flash of disapproval in Lorraine's eyes makes Lola sit up straight in her chair. "Sorry," Lola says. "Who's Mila's cousin?"

"You. Maria's Mila's aunt, so you must be her cousin. Darrel said it was the least we could do, show the grieving woman some hospitality." Lorraine trains her sharp gaze on Lola, waiting to see if she'll contradict her. Lola remembers Sherman Moore, and Lorraine shooing him away yesterday. But she must know her son is a drug lord—where else does he get money for the house, listed on some historical register in the halls of some L.A. government agency, the Escalade, and Lorraine's gourmet groceries and weekly mani/pedis? Still, Lola understands a mother's need to ignore the darker recesses of her child's world. "Course, Maria didn't mention she had any children. But I knew, soon as I saw you. There's no denying you."

Fucking Maria, not mentioning her.

"More pound cake?" Lorraine asks. She can sense the shift in the air, the calm turning to storm, and she treats Lola's anger the same way Lola imagines she treats Darrel's anger: with sugar.

"Please," Lola says. When Lorraine serves her a second slice of dessert, Lola shovels it in, feeling the sweet sugar mixed with the salty, nutty brown butter.

"Course, the boy, he's a different story," Lorraine continues.

"The boy? You mean the one asleep in the Sentra outside?"

"What? Sherman?"

"I don't know his name," Lola says, feeling a twinge of guilt at the lie.

"He's a bad egg, that one," Lorraine says. Lola catches Darrel's mother's furrowed brow, the quick bite of her lip. "My son doesn't see it."

"He's sleeping on the job."

"What job?" Lorraine looks up, sharp, and Lola sees that for all her knowledge about Sherman and power and corruption, she is still in denial about Darrel's profession.

"I don't . . . I'm sorry," Lola says. "You were talking about a boy?"

"Not Sherman. This one looked like you."

Hector.

"He came here last night, said he wanted words with my son. But I could tell he wanted more than words. I called Darrel down. I don't have to listen to any young man's potty mouth," Lorraine says, shaking her head, and Lola finds herself following suit, shaking her head, too, because she taught Hector to respect his elders. Still, she retraces Lorraine's words, something not sitting right.

"You said the boy came here?"

"Yeah, that's right. Rang the bell, same as you, 'cept he was pacing back and forth, pullin' his hair out wanting to talk to my son."

Lola thinks back to the ransom note. Darrel must have had it planted in Hector's apartment after Hector showed up here, half cocked, demanding a meeting with Darrel to which he was not entitled. The fact that Darrel didn't take Hector, just took advantage of her little brother's idiocy, makes Lola want to kill him even less. But Hector—he's a different story. Disobedient. Irrational. Acting love crazed. All for Maria, their sad sack waste of space mother.

"Hey, Momma." Darrel King's smooth baritone fills the whole kitchen like a warm blanket. Lola wants to ask him a question just to hear it again. "You give her all the pound cake, or we got some left over?"

"Well, aren't you being silly? You know I always make two."

Of course she does, Lola thinks. The gentle banter between mother and son surrounds Lola, smothering her in light and comfort right here in rival territory. She and Garcia haven't yet made their house a home, as Lorraine has made Darrel's. *One day,* Lola thinks, then remembers her pending death. *Well, shit.*

When she looks up, Lorraine has disappeared into the depths of the house, and Darrel is sitting across from her with a slice of pound cake the exact same size as Lola's. Lola loves Lorraine for that—giving a woman an equal piece of the pie.

"Guessing you've come to talk business," Darrel says.

Lola can drop the damsel-in-distress act. Darrel must have cracked Hector, gotten him to reveal the inner workings of the Crenshaw Six. But Lola sits over her half-eaten pound cake, wanting to draw out the moment of daughterhood just a little longer.

Then the moment passes, and Lola says, "Yes."

TWENTY-NINE

THE VERDICT

Darrel sets a shot of tequila on the overturned milk crate in front of Lola. He has led her to a detached garage about a hundred feet from the house. Inside, the night air has chilled the structure so much that Lola pulls her hoodie tighter and wishes for a puffy coat. It's late summer in Los Angeles, and the daytime temperature often climbs to the high nineties, but the night is a separate animal— cooler and darker. Lola tries to guess at the temperature tonight. Low sixties. Too cold for Lola to leave the house without a coat. She is a true Angeleno.

Lola slings back the tequila and feels the comfort of alcohol burning as it slides down her throat. Darrel doesn't know from tequila—this brand is something advertised on American television as being suitable for players, athletes, and rap stars. Still, in the cool dark of this particular Los Angeles night, when Lola must decide who's going to kill her, it'll do. No matter her decision, she knows the man sitting across from her is not her killer, and the certainty brings a cozy feeling in her stomach. She can enjoy this conversation with Darrel King.

"Good stuff, huh?" Darrel asks.

"Not really," Lola replies, and Darrel throws his head back in a loud laugh that lets her see the two rows of straight bright white teeth in his mouth.

"Maybe I put something in it," Darrel says. "Maybe that's why it's no good."

"You a rapist now?"

Darrel draws back into his own puffy coat. Her accusation has struck a nerve.

"Didn't say shit about rape." So that's it. She's insulted him by insinuating he's trying to rape her. Fair enough. "I meant poison. Arsenic or some shit."

Lola shrugs and holds out her empty shot glass. A gaudy gold stencil of the Vegas skyline sticks out of the green glass background. It has the wannabe retro feel of something purchased in a cheap souvenir shop on the outskirts of that gambling town, the one Lola will not live to see.

"I gotta frisk you."

Lola stands, and Darrel does, too, and for a moment they are facing each other like two shy teenagers about to slow dance. Then Darrel's hands are on her waist, and her arms are lifted out of the way, letting him at the core of her. She has to remind herself to breathe with his hands on her like this. Then he digs the ineffective blade from her pants pocket, and his touch is gone.

"Nice try."

Lola shrugs. Darrel places the blade on the table in front of them, and his confidence that she won't be able to get to it before he does annoys her.

"Your brother says you don't care for your mama," Darrel says as he pours Lola more burning liquid strength.

"It's complicated," Lola says.

"She seems nice."

"Yeah, well, she's clean. For now." Lola downs her second shot, the alcohol cooling off her nerves enough for her to ask, "She didn't say she had kids?"

"Don't know," Darrel says, looking toward the dart board, the pool table with one broken leg, the buzzing ancient refrigerator that Lola knows is full of beer. The whole place screams man cave. The cool temperature is the only thing that keeps it from reeking of salty dry sweat and faded gas.

"I was straight with you. You be straight with me," Lola says.

"Look, I didn't wanna hurt your mama."

Lola shrugs again—what's it to her?

"I just wanted to get Garcia's attention."

"Really did your research. Thinking Garcia was the one you needed to get to."

"Hey, I got it right in the end. Turns out your brother likes it when someone listens to him."

"Hector likes Maria. It's a weakness," Lola admits. She crosses her legs, taking tipsy pleasure in watching one toned calf bounce off the other in perfect rhythm. Sitting like this, leaning forward to be closer to Darrel, she craves a cigarette.

"And you like your brother."

"I love my brother," Lola corrects Darrel.

"Looks like I did find your weakness."

Lola laughs, and Darrel follows suit. He is mirroring her. She is pulling his strings. He is her ripped gangster puppet. Lola feels a pang of sadness—she wants to be sitting across from a man who is her equal. She feels respect for Darrel, sure, but Lola also pities this banger, huddled in his man cave out back while his mother serves pound cake to strangers like they're family. She can't kill Darrel, Lola thinks. It wouldn't be right. It would be a lioness ripping apart a gazelle. An unfair fight. Then again, isn't that nature's way? Lions don't hunt other lions.

"I want my brother back," Lola says.

"I want Mila back," Darrel counters.

"Why?" Lola asks, and she feels the flare of Darrel's anger like a blast of heat.

"The fuck? Why? She was my girl."

"She fucked you over," Lola says, her voice even. She is going to float above this particular fight on an emotionless tequila cloud.

"Like hell she did."

"So you gave your girl a bunch of paper instead of two million in green?"

"Paper? Fuck you talkin' about?"

"The duffel bag you gave her. We took it."

"And you best be giving it back."

Lola removes her car keys from her pocket. "Check my trunk. Bag's there." A bluff, but she's counting on Darrel not wanting to traipse through the house and disturb his mother.

"With the money?"

"With the paper Mila put there. She took the cash."

Darrel paces now, and Lola pours her own third shot.

"You got a soft spot for traitors," Lola says. The burning of the alcohol is making her generous. She's going to give Darrel a piece of advice that might save his life. "Like Sherman outside. He's asleep."

"He's lazy. That doesn't make him a traitor."

"No. But waking up and letting me pass does."

Darrel stops pacing to think. Then he says, "He's just a kid."

His loyalty to his asshole soldiers is going to be the death of him, even if she's not.

"You're underestimating him. He wants you dead." Before Lola can get the next shot to her lips, Darrel yanks the cheap glass from her hands and downs it himself.

"You don't have to believe me. About Sherman or Mila," Lola says. "But I'm giving you a chance to get your cash back, 'cause I don't have it."

"What chance?" Darrel asks, deflating onto the overturned crate. He's so close to Lola their noses could touch. Or their lips.

"Mila stashed that cash somewhere. You knew her best. Where would she hide it?"

"The fuck should I know? She did this, I don't know shit about her."

Lola hears Darrel's hesitation, his not wanting to believe Lola, but his instincts are sharp enough that he knows something was off in his love for Mila. He knows he loved Mila more than she loved him.

"Where did she go, when she wasn't with you? She have hobbies and shit?"

"She was a recovering addict," Darrel says, and Lola can't tell if he's answering her question, if Mila's hobby was recovery, or if he's hopped his own logic train Lola can only hope will clash with hers. She wouldn't mind walking out of this meeting with a deal to split the two million in cash only Darrel can help her find. "But I would give her cash. Any cash she needed. I paid for everything— dinners, gym membership, beauty salon bullshit she didn't need," Darrel says.

"Mila was recovering, yeah," Lola starts, "but she was also learning econ, business shit, before she started partying."

"Yeah?" Darrel says. It's a question. Get to the point.

"Could be she wanted to start her own thing, get out from under you," Lola says.

Darrel leans closer to Lola, his head dropping to his hands. He hides like that for a few seconds, not wanting Lola to see him absorb this blow. Then his head snaps to like a soldier on lookout, going from sleep to attention in a half-second jerk.

"You full of shit. Get the fuck out my house."

"Give me my brother."

"Kind of woman don't want her mother," Darrel spits at her, but Lola doesn't move. He is having a tantrum in the midst of a business meeting. He is not worth killing.

"What, you don't wanna keep her?" Lola taunts. "She's small. Doesn't eat much. Just gotta watch out for the relapses. That's when she gets expensive."

"Fuck you."

"Where's Hector?"

"Who says he's still alive?" Darrel tries, chest puffed in overt bravado.

Lola stares at Darrel, and the silence fills the cold room until Lola can hear ringing. It's dull at first, but the quiet sharpens it to a point until it's all she can hear. Then there's a knock. One. Two. Three. It's coming from under the floor.

Hector. Alive. Under the floor.

"Let's make a deal," Lola says. "You keep my mother and brother here. Go check out Mila's spots. Gym, nail salon, all that shit."

"Why would I do that?"

"'Cause odds are you're gonna find two million large," Lola says.

Darrel licks his lips, and Lola feels the hunger for cash there. A second later, Darrel is shaking his head, the hunger dashed like glass dropped on hardwood. He wants cash, but he wants to believe Mila, his girl, didn't betray him.

"What's in it for you?"

"Call it fifty percent."

"Call it shit. You killed my girl."

"Your girl straight up fucked you over."

"We'll see."

"So you'll check it out?"

"Ain't gonna find nothing. And when I don't, I'm coming looking for you."

"Don't bother. I know where to find you," Lola says, not adding that she'll be dead by the time he checks out Mila's usual haunts for hiding places. Plus, she knows recovering addicts. She knows Mila was bad fucking news, even if Darrel's heart, mind, and cock have lied to him. She has the sudden urge to tell him she's the only reason he's still alive—because she's reached a verdict. She's not killing him. She's sick of taking orders, of being under a man's thumb, whether he's a fat Mexican or a clean-cut Venice yuppie with a *Mayflower* name.

The pounding under the floor gets louder, so that Lola can no longer pretend not to hear it. She sticks out a hand to shake Darrel's, and he responds in kind. They've struck a truce, for now.

"Fuck!" It's a roar from the floor, a pissed-off male voice that shakes the wood as a fist thunders against it.

"How 'bout you take your brother now?" Darrel says.

Lola smiles. "He being a handful?"

"Motherfucker's just plain loud. I need quiet to play pool."

Darrel strides over to the patch of floor that's rumbling. When he lifts a board, Hector's head emerges like a demented jack-in-the-box. Dried blood crusts his lip, and he's sporting one black eye. Lola shoots a look at Darrel, who shrugs.

"He pulled a piece on my front porch."

Hector, you stupid fuck, Lola wants to say, but she'll save her punishment for later, when they're behind closed doors and she's had time to decide—with her mind, not her heart—what pain Hector should feel.

As Darrel unleashes Hector from his bonds, Lola sees the anger in her baby brother's eyes. But it's not directed at Darrel. Hector is looking right at her.

"Why didn't you come after Mom?"

"Don't need to talk about this here," Lola says. Again, she has the feeling of being a parent whose child is having a meltdown in a public place, sinking to the floor in a puddle of tantrum while Lola, the mother, begins the impossible task of gathering up a person going to pieces.

"Like hell we don't," Hector continues. His hurt has shifted to disrespect, and Lola can't have that, especially in enemy territory. To Darrel's credit, he looks away.

"Hector," Lola warns.

"Mom deserves better than you. This dude's been keeping her here, tied up like an animal."

Darrel starts to interject, but Lola holds up a hand. "He's full of shit. I know," she tells her rival before turning to her brother. "We're gonna go get in the car now."

"Don't talk to me like I'm a child."

"Then stop acting like one."

"You're the one can't forgive Mom. You're the one ignoring her and shit."

"Hector." A warning rings clear in Lola's voice. She hopes to whatever god created this world of hunger and suffering and tarnished children that Hector hears it.

Instead, Hector gets in her face. "I ain't gotta do shit you tell me. I'm done. I'm here to save Mom. And that's what I'm gonna do."

Hector lunges toward the table. He has grabbed Lola's blade and pulled it on Darrel before Lola can stop him. She curses this woman's body, its natural tendency to be slower and weaker than a man's, even when that man is acting like a child.

Still, she dives as fast as she can onto Hector's raised hand, her stomach missing the blade by a mere centimeter, and wrestles him to the ground from sheer will. A second later, she's on top of him, straddling his stomach. But Hector holds fast to the knife, and when Lola tries to wrench it from his hands, he spits in her face.

Lola feels her brother's saliva wet her cheek before she can absorb what's just happened. For Hector, there will be no going back from this, and it's like he knows it, because he stops fighting. They sit there for a second, Lola on top of Hector, Hector staring up at the ceiling. This is it.

Lola takes the blade, easy now, from Hector's limp fingers. The only weapon she can process right now is the spit on her face. She stands and faces Darrel, who has taken the opportunity to open a safe with more guns than Lola can count. Lola sees the extent of the slight Hector has just dealt her in the way Darrel opens and closes his mouth. Shocked.

Lola places her blade next to the near-empty tequila bottle on the table.

"We're going," Lola says to Darrel. She heads for the door, and she hears Hector's boots hitting hardwood. She's not facing him, but she knows he's standing up. The boots start walking, one, two, one, two, but they stop before speeding up to a run.

When Lola turns, she sees Hector, good and bad hands raised, ready to close over Darrel's throat, and Darrel bending toward his gun safe. She sees her puny blade on the table next to the tequila bottle. It takes Lola three steps to reach the table. By then, Darrel has his own hands on a gun, but Lola knows her blade won't be enough. Before Darrel can aim his gun at her brother, Lola smashes the tequila bottle on the table and shoves the toothed glass edges into Darrel's neck. Darrel falls against her, his mouth still opening and closing. He is all muscle, too heavy for her to pretend to hold up, so she lets him sink to the floor with a thunk.

Lola grapples for her phone, but by the time her shaking hands have pressed 911, Darrel is staring up at her with lifeless eyes.

"He dead?" Hector.

Lola can't answer. She knows Darrel is, in fact, dead, but she's wondering, as sweat springs from her pores in the Los Angeles cold, how Hector can't see it, too. When she sees that Hector is looking at her and not Darrel's body, Lola wonders why she's always the one who has to see the hard things.

"Shit," Hector says. "Shit. You saved me. Lola, you did this for me."

No shit, Lola thinks.

"This is my fault."

No shit, Lola thinks again.

"I gotta make it up to you. I gotta . . . what can I do?"

Stop fucking up, Lola thinks.

"We have to find Maria," Lola says aloud. She's done pretending to care for their mother. She's done protecting Hector and his feelings. She can even tell the difference between her sweat and his spit, even though they're mingled now, on her face.

"Think they're keeping her inside."

"Find her."

Hector seems relieved to have a task. He disappears back into the house, and Lola remembers that Darrel's mother is in there, maybe rinsing plates and glasses, re-covering food with aluminum foil. She doesn't seem the type to let the dishes wait until morning.

Is it morning? Lola wants to step into the yard, to see for sure, but she feels it's wrong to leave Darrel's body here alone. He needs his mother. Lola does not need hers.

When Hector returns, Maria is behind him, rubbing her eyes, a pale blue silk dressing gown over her drifting, ghostlike form. Lola thinks her mother looks like a spirit, something sent from above to haunt or soothe or both.

"Oh, my God," Maria says when she sees Darrel. "That's Lorraine's boy."

I know, Lola wants to say, but she doesn't like acknowledging that she's paying attention to what Maria's saying.

"You killed Lorraine's boy," Maria says, looking from her daughter to Lorraine's son.

"He was going to shoot Hector," Lola says.

"Because I went after him," Hector says.

"Why?" Maria asks her son. "Why would you do that?"

"Because he took you."

"Yes, but . . . they were so kind. They took care of me," Maria says, and Lola hears an accusation there even if Maria doesn't mean it. *They took care of me better than you two.* "They were my friends. Shame on you."

When Maria turns her back on Hector, her only champion, Lola sees the heartbreak on her baby brother's face. Part of her is glad he is seeing the consequences of his actions. Part of her wants to pull him close to her and say, *See. I'm the one who gives you love. Not her.*

"Hector. We're going to fix this," Lola says instead. "Go get the sleeping kid in the Sentra. Call him Sherman. That's his name. Tell him his boss is asking for him."

Hector nods and disappears again. Now it's just Lola and Maria standing over Darrel. Except Maria's not standing, she's kneeling, closing Darrel's lids over his dead eyes, bowing her head in prayer over someone's dead child.

"We have to tell her," Maria says. "We have to help her get some closure."

"We have to get out of here."

"He's her child."

"Just like you, gettin' hung up on someone else's child."

"Not the child. The child is dead," Maria says, summoning the sign of the cross from some deep Catholic well inside her. The sight of her addict pimp of a mother performing a blessing over Darrel's dead body makes Lola feel a surge that's equal parts impatience and guilt.

"You done yet?"

"Lola. You know better than this," Maria says, and Lola knows her mother is right. Goddamn her.

"What do you want, Maria?"

"We need to tell his mother. That's all."

It's the "that's all" that worries Lola. Maria is good at starting shit—a heroin addiction, for example. It's the stopping that her mother has never mastered.

"You're so worried, you tell her," Lola says, arms crossed, at a stalemate over Darrel's body.

"Okay," Maria says, lifting the edges of her gown so it doesn't collect man cave dirt from the concrete floor. Fuck.

Lola finds herself following Maria across the yard. She feels she is scurrying in a panic, trying to dart ahead of Maria, who is gliding, so slow, yet Lola can't seem to catch her.

"You stay out here," Maria says as she reaches the back door.

"Fuck no," Lola says. Although she doesn't think Maria would sell out her own children sober, Lola has learned the one constant about her mother. She is unpredictable.

From here, Lola can see Lorraine sitting at the kitchen table with a steaming mug. The image shifts something inside her. Lola wants to run to Lorraine, to confess her sin, to explain that it was in defense of her brother, and she wishes she'd killed Hector instead.

Lola has the door open and is striding toward Lorraine, who sets her mug on the table and stands.

"What is it?" Darrel's mother asks. She is looking right at Lola.

Then Lola feels a hand on her shoulder and a soothing whisper. "Lola. No." It's Maria, telling her daughter not to confess.

With her mother's touch, all the truth inside Lola falls somewhere deep in her stomach, where the bile and acid start to churn it to nothing. Fear of getting caught hasn't quashed her urge to confess to Lorraine. Lola's sudden silence is because Maria has reminded her she doesn't know how to tell a mother her child is dead.

Before Lola knows it, she has stepped aside to let her mother stand between her and Lorraine. Lola watches her mother take Darrel's mother's hand.

"Lorraine," Maria says, "it's Darrel."

It is a mother-to-mother language Maria is speaking now, because those two words are all she has to say for Lorraine to lurch toward the back door. Darrel's mother moves so fast it's like she's been stung scared by a bee. She knows her son is dead, and Maria knew she would know.

In an instant, Lola is after Darrel's mother, sprinting across the yard, wanting to get ahead so she can control the situation before Lorraine has to see it. But again she can't seem to reach the older woman. At least now Maria is trailing her daughter, meandering across the grass like she's got nowhere to be. Besides, Darrel is dead. There is no amount of damage control Lola can do that will make that okay.

By the time Lola arrives in the man cave, she finds Lorraine already standing still over her son's dead body. Lorraine looks up and sees Lola seeing her.

"I know who did this," Lorraine says.

Lola feels her heart seize up so tight with fear she can't imagine it's bigger than a walnut.

"Him," Lorraine continues.

It's only then Lola sees Sherman Moore, the dead-eyed corner boy, standing to her left. The deadly man boy, unaffected by the accusation, has his hands in his pockets, his feet shifting in a bored shuffle beneath him, when Lorraine jumps on him, pummeling his chest and asking him how could he.

"Let's go," Lola hears Maria's voice behind her, and it's only then Lola realizes her mother has saved her ass.

THIRTY

THE SENTENCING

With forty-eight hours to live, Lola lies in bed, curtains lowered so the morning sun frames the window in a dull glow. Darrel King is dead. Maria Vasquez protected her daughter, not over Darrel's dead body, but in the kitchen where she kept Lola from confessing everything to Lorraine. Garcia has taken Lucy to the park with Valentine so that Lola can rest. Alone in the dark, Lola can't sleep. Her mind won't sit still. She has passed Eldridge's loyalty test. He'll give her keys to the kingdom, show her the stash, she's in.

But the fat man . . . he will seek her out and make sure she dies a traitor's death.

Hector. Hector. Her brother's name rings loudest in her ears, because she knows what his punishment should be. She knew what it should have been as soon as he fucked up the drop. She knows now it must involve a blade and a tarp and soldiers gathered around, pinning down limbs while screams echo and blood spatters plastic. She is surprised to find that her largest objection to this plan now is letting her living room serve as a makeshift death chamber while a five-year-old sleeps down the hall.

Lola reaches a hand to her cheek. She scrubbed it with soap and scalding hot water when she got home, rubbing her skin to the point of rawness. Still, she feels Hector's disrespect there, a smear she can't erase.

Sleep impossible, Lola sticks her feet in slippers and pads to the kitchen. She puts the coffee on and cracks eggs in a skillet before she remembers she is supposed to meet Andrea this morning. Andrea. The connection between Eldridge and the corrupt system that seems to be protecting him. And in Eldridge's mind, Lola is an ally now, too.

She dumps the eggs in the trash and pulls on real shoes. If it's one of her last days on Earth, she will spend it at the park with Garcia, Lucy, and Valentine.

The air outside is new, with a bite of cold that shakes Lola out of her own private nightmare. Children with torn backpacks trudge out of front doors carrying house keys and family-sized bags of Doritos and two liters of Coke—lunch. The house keys are for later, when they return from summer school to the four empty walls and barred windows they call home. Parents gone. Working manual labor that hardens hands but not hearts. Now, years later, Lola longs for a childhood with Maria gone eighteen hours a day. Or does she, now that Maria kept Lola from confessing to Darrel's murder? It's the most maternal thing Maria has ever done for Lola, but it doesn't make Lola happy. It just makes her feel that something is off, like a tiny pebble in her shoe she can't find.

Last night, Lola had dropped Maria back in her apartment. The last she saw of her mother, the woman was turning a circle in her living room like she'd never seen the goddamn place before. Yet she was sober.

"Lola," Maria had said, and Lola had heard her, but she didn't want to give her mother a chance to fuck up now that she'd done good by her daughter. Lola had shut the door on her mother's voice calling her name. She hadn't thanked Maria for delivering the necessary news to Darrel's mother. Let that closing door be her mother's last memory of her daughter. Let her live with all the shit she's done to wreck Lola. Lola can only hope it hits Maria one day like a ton of bricks—the white powder kind—just how bad of a mother she was. But it won't, Lola knows, because that is not the way of the world.

Screaming, running children fill the playground at the park. The swing sets are rusted, the grass losing a battle with the weeds, and the children have learned early to dodge the used condoms that dot the grounds. Still, there is a wild happiness here.

Lola tries to pick out Lucy from the groups of children lumped together in masses of black hair. One group climbs the steps to the slide. Another cluster tries to push the merry-go-round that hasn't moved since before Lola was born. A third group has given up on the play structures completely and appears to be lifting and dropping grains of sand. Lola wants to yell at them to not eat the sand. She keeps quiet, though—she doesn't want to give them any ideas.

Lola sees a whir of spit-up gravel and flattened weeds under rubber tires, and the kid with the bike is standing in front of her, feet planted on earth, hands clutching handlebars.

"Hey," he says.

"Hey," she answers.

"Word's out."

"Don't know what you're talkin' about."

"What you did to Darrel King. His mama tellin' the cops it's one of his crew, but people here gonna know the real story. Don't worry—I won't let it get back to West Adams."

"Don't know what you're talkin' about," Lola repeats.

"Whatever," the kid says, and he's gone in another blaze of gravel and hurt feelings.

But he has given Lola a valuable piece of information. The word is out. It won't spread to West Adams. The neighborhoods are isolated, two worlds in one city. But here in Huntington Park, where she's been Garcia's girl for so long, her end is near. Unless she figures out how to fight a losing battle. She'll die whether she fights or doesn't fight. Even if she were to live through the week, she will have to live here, in Huntington Park, where people will begin to whisper that she killed Darrel King. It will only be a matter of time before Kim is banging on her door, demanding to know what the fuck Lola did to her brother.

Regardless of the path Lola takes, death or exposure, her days as a shadow leader are finished. Never has her fate seemed more certain, and the idea that she knows what's going to happen brings her peace. She can be herself.

Lola fires off a text to Andrea, asking to meet later in the day, and the woman writes back almost immediately—"K." Lola sends a follow-up text—"My hood?" Because what the fuck does it matter now if someone sees them? Another immediate response—"K." Lola wonders what would have happened if she'd responded to Darrel's stabbing as quickly as Andrea has responded to her texts. He might still be alive. He would still be alive. He wasn't stabbed in the heart. She could have dialed 911 faster. Lorraine's son could have been saved. Or maybe he couldn't. *It is worse,* Lola thinks, *to never know.*

Arriving at the park, she puts thoughts of Darrel aside to search for her family with hungry eyes.

She spots Kim first, not because she's wearing a halter top that shows a bare, toned midriff, not because her tits are spilling out of said halter top, and not because she seems to be missing three-quarters of her tight leather skirt. Most mothers at the park now are dressed the same, pushing their offspring on swings in hoochie gear and fuck-me pumps. They're single and looking for men they can snare and keep, upgrades from the men they snared and couldn't keep once a child appeared on the scene.

She spots Kim because she's with Garcia. Something about the way their heads are bent together, foreheads a hairbreadth from touching, tells her not to approach. She wonders for an instant if Garcia could be telling Kim he made a mistake three years ago, that he couldn't be with Kim because he had fallen for the woman who killed her brother. Lola wonders if Garcia is telling Kim the truth. Then she remembers she's a dead woman, and that it no longer matters. She can be the leader. She can die the leader. The thought is a revelation, and she finds herself floating above all this, the park, the adultery, the enclaves of Los Angeles the white power makes sure the immigrants can never leave.

Lola waits for the foreheads to touch, then the lips, then for Garcia to tell Kim in his breathless whisper that they should get out of here. Lola won't be able to hear it from this distance, but she'll know when he says it, because his mouth will go to Kim's ear, close enough to wet the lobe as he speaks. Then he will take her hand and pull her faster than she ever thought she could go in those hooker heels.

Instead, the foreheads break, and Garcia and Kim turn toward Lola, their two sets of eyes scanning two separate directions. These are not the eyes of cheating assholes afraid of being seen. These eyes are fucking terrified.

For the first time, Lola realizes that she never saw Lucy in the clumps of huddled children. The thought causes her feet to toe dirt, getting a running start as she sprints across the playground, dodging children, their laughs ringing sharp and mean in her ears.

She can't see anything but straight ahead of her—the slide, a line of children waiting on a scared little girl at the top to gather her courage. But it's not Lucy. Lola can't pry her eyes away from the frightened girl, looking down at the plunge she can't take. Does she hear the children behind her, taunting?

"Lola!" Garcia's voice startles her, and when she turns, her own forehead smacks into his chest. She feels the sweat that's soaked through his T-shirt against her skin. Why is he sweating in this morning chill?

Because something has happened to Lucy.

"Where is she?" Lola breathes in the salt of Garcia's shirt, the faint scent of his body odor comforting her. "Did someone take her? What did he look like?"

"No," Garcia says. "It's not like that."

"Then what?"

"Rosie," Garcia says, and Lola falls against him, wrapping her arms around his waist and squeezing. *What a fucking shame,* the thought flashes through Lola's mind tornado fast, Lola would rather it have been a pedophile, a temporary trauma. To suffer at your own mother's hand means all hope is lost.

Lola pounds her fists into Garcia's shirt, knowing he's not feeling any pain she's making for him. "You couldn't fight off that junkie bitch?"

"I could . . . I just . . . I ran to the store."

Lola pulls away from Garcia, her eyes on his, demanding an explanation. She told him not to leave Lucy alone. What is it with men, disobeying her cute little orders?

"I didn't leave her alone," Garcia answers her unspoken question. "Kim was watching her."

Lola needs to sit down. She walks over to a bench, but she isn't so foggy that she doesn't notice the biker kid motion for the three kids sitting there to make room for her. Someone thinks she's the shit. Still, once the biker kid has cleared the bench for her, Lola finds she can't sit. She needs to pace, her fingers at the roots of her hair, tugging at the nerves there so she knows she's not in a dream.

"I'm sorry," Garcia tries, but even he knows the words are going to fall flat.

"Tell me what happened," Lola says.

"I left to pick up some food. For you, too." As if that is any consolation. "Kim said she'd watch Lucy. And she did."

"Then how come Lucy isn't here?"

"'Cause Rosie stopped by. Sober. Told Kim she wanted to take Lucy shopping."

Lola snorts, and she hears an echo. Out of the corner of her eye, she spots the biker kid snorting too, calling equal bullshit on this story. She wonders if he's seen little Lucy on this playground with her junkie mother or just her mother's boyfriend, Mamacita's landlord's son. She wonders if this kid has put together how Rosie can afford her smack and help her own parents keep their business at the same time. He must have, if he can snort like that here.

Lola feels another flash of anger—the biker kid would have known better, and Garcia does not. Is it a natural leadership instinct, for the day to come when familiarity breeds contempt? When it is time to clean house? Lola thinks of the Bible, of Noah, God, and the flood, of everyone on Earth dead.

Lola wants a fresh start, too.

THIRTY-ONE

PLEA BARGAIN

The diner where Andrea agreed to meet is in Lola's neighborhood, ten blocks from Lola's house. Lola has come to Freddy's before with her crew, a seeming fifth wheel to Garcia, Hector, Jorge, and Marcos. She had stayed quiet while the men talked too loud. She had eaten migas while they told tales of conquests Lola knew were bullshit. Funny, how the diner patrons had seen the men as a threat. Lola wonders how talking the most and the loudest became the cue to the outside world that you were the leader.

The smell of fry grease coated with cinnamon sugar and mingled with sub-blue-collar sweat gobsmacks Lola as she enters Freddy's now. She closes her eyes and sucks it in, hungry for comfort starch and fat. Freddy's smells like what Lola's mother's kitchen should have. Lola sees the steady, dependable boyfriends her mother should have had lined up in a row at the counter, hands circling burgers or bringing coffee cups from saucer to mouth. They wear T-shirts yellowed with ancient sweat, badges of hard manual labor and honest work for shit money.

Lola has donned sunglasses, but they do nothing to disguise her from her neighbors. She wonders for a minute if she should have let Andrea take her to the Westside, but there was something biting in the air this morning, something besides her brazen realization that her game is up. This other something was nagging at her, telling her not to go far from home. Maybe because Rosie took Lucy. Maybe because Lola is sick to death of having to live in the shadows of the neighborhood she rules. Besides, being a shadow leader is no longer possible—she has outed herself to the cartel, to Eldridge, and apparently to the teenage boy on the bike. It is only a matter of time before the neighborhood knows, too. And if Andrea is playing for Eldridge's team, she will know everything Lola says to her at this meeting is bullshit.

But that is part of Lola's plan.

Her to-do list for her last two days of living was impossible to achieve even before Rosie abducted Lucy. Now, it is longer. But Lola has added an impossible feat: to live. She must live. She can't leave Lucy with Rosie—that's not happening, if she lives or if she dies. She's going to get Lucy back. She has Jorge and Marcos out scouring every back alley and crack house for any trace of Rosie or the little girl. Even when they find her, though, she can't go dying, because then she will have to leave Lucy with Garcia. Garcia, who leaves her with Kim, who fried meat in Lola's kitchen like she owned the damn place, moving from stove to utensil drawer, retrieving a spatula like she already knew where it was.

Lola must live. It's the one thing on her list she doesn't know how to accomplish.

Still, she can meet with Andrea. She can fix other people's lives here and now, even if she doesn't know what to do about her own.

Lola plucks two menus from the shelf and seats herself in the corner. She has arrived early because this is her turf. She is hosting this meeting. She is in control. If Andrea knows this, Lola will know for sure that Andrea is working with Eldridge, that he shared his intel with her. If she doesn't, maybe she's just another prosecutor building another impossible case against a drug trafficker. Still, Lola can use her.

Lola opens her menu, perusing each item in detail—huevos rancheros, empanadas, fried potatoes. Her stomach rumbles, then she remembers she's playing a part, and maybe that part shouldn't be so focused on food. She thinks so hard on how to silence her hunger that she doesn't see Andrea until the small woman is standing over her, clearing her throat.

"Hello," Andrea says, and Lola wants to stand and shake her hand, leader to leader, but instead she remains planted in the sticky smooth booth.

"Hey." Lola shrugs, and it pains her that she can't speak to this woman as an equal. It pains her to play the victim. "Got us menus."

"Thank you," Andrea says, her fingers toying with the laminated plastic as she sits across from Lola.

"Food's pretty good," Lola says. She will be surprised if Andrea touches anything in here, although the fact that she's opened her menu, the unidentified stickiness there not deterring her, is a good sign. Lola watches Andrea's eyes scan the menu with laser focus. Lola can tell it would not be a good idea to interrupt her, that the way Andrea has a meal in a restaurant with another person does not involve small talk until after she has decided on her order. Lola can also tell Andrea is not one of those people to ask her companion what's good. She will make her own decisions.

A waitress with pear curves and silver bangles in her ears arrives. "What will you have?" she asks, accent thick. At Freddy's, English is a fallback if Spanish doesn't fly.

"Migas," Lola says. "Nine one one spice."

The waitress turns to Andrea. "And for you, please?"

Lola waits for Andrea to ask for an iced tea, no sugar, and a plain tortilla. Instead, the prosecutor says, "I'll start with the fruit cup, extra chili powder on top. Then the huevos rancheros with avocado on the side. Flour tortilla instead of spinach."

The waitress nods, scratching at her pad and disappearing with a flip of her long black ponytail. Her ass swishes under her cheap cotton uniform—left cheek, right cheek, keeping time like a soldier on the march. The waitress turns each patron's head as she passes. Now would be a perfect time to pull out a gun and rob the place, catching everyone off guard. But Lola has never tried armed robbery—that was Carlos's thing. It seemed dishonest, letting others make the money, then taking it right out from under them.

But wasn't that what she was doing at the drop between Eldridge and Darrel? Robbing from the rich to give to the richer?

"How are you?" Andrea asks, leaning forward in a way that's so intimate, Lola thinks the woman might take her two hands in hers. Lola leaves her hands on the table, just to see if she will.

"How do you think I am?" Lola retorts. She must toe the delicate line between combative and damaged. She should have ordered pancakes, too—this damsel-in-distress shit is exhausting.

"Stupid question," Andrea says. "Has he come back, since the parking garage?"

"Course he has. He's my brother."

Lola's unexpected response causes Andrea to sit back. Lola understands—Andrea thought Hector was Lola's boyfriend, some banger fueled by unrequited lust, blood, and whatever drug he could afford that day. Lola had debated telling Andrea that was the case, but it would be easy enough for the prosecutor to catch Lola in that lie. And for reasons she can't name, Lola likes the idea of being honest with Andrea.

"Most domestic violence cases involve boyfriends, spouses . . ." Andrea says, trailing off. Lola has never known this sure-spoken woman to trail off. It must be a tactic. She wants Lola to fill the silence. She's getting her to talk even though she's assuming Lola doesn't want to.

"Yeah, well," Lola says, and when she removes her sunglasses, she has a fresh black eye. Hector had nothing to do with this one. Lola doled it out herself, in front of her vanity, after she'd gone through her normal steps to leave the house—brush teeth, wash face, moisturize, moisturize, moisturize, and give self black eye. The pain had felt good, setting her whole body ringing fire, forcing her to forget about Hector, about Lucy, about the torture awaiting her at the hands of the fat man.

To Andrea's credit, she doesn't flinch at the sight of Lola's black eye. Instead, she observes, "It looks fresh. Did he come after you today?"

Lola nods. "Found out I'd called you. Got pissed."

"Does he know we're meeting?"

"I told him I got scared, canceled."

"Did he believe you?"

Lola shrugs. "See when I get home."

"I don't think you should go home," Andrea says. She reaches into her purse, a Louis Vuitton monster of a bag, and plucks out a business card—the woman's a virtual library of them. What really amazes Lola is how Andrea keeps eye contact with her as she plucks the card from the depths of the bag. How does she know where the card is without looking? "This is a battered women's shelter."

Lola stifles a laugh at that word, *battered,* as if she's been dredged in milk and flour to be fried in a pan.

"The director, Corey, is expecting you."

Lola doesn't accept the card, not yet. That would be suspect. "And if I say no?"

"Your choice."

"What about . . . him?"

"I'll have Huntington Park PD pick him up within the hour."

"Yeah, but say he gets all that due process shit, goes to trial, makes a deal, whatever the fuck it is, how much time is he gonna do?"

"The maximum is—"

"First offense. He won't get the maximum." *Shit. Too smart.*

Andrea hesitates, then nods, something inside her breaking. She leans forward, closer to Lola, leveling with her. Finally, the prosecutor is talking to Lola as if they are equals . . . but Lola isn't sure that's what she wants, not yet. "Look, your brother can cut a deal. He'll do ninety days, maybe, then probation and some community service."

"What, like picking up trash on the side of the highway or some shit?"

"Yes," Andrea says.

"Not good enough," Lola says, pushing Andrea's hand and the card away from her.

Andrea sits back, and Lola thinks she's stumped the prosecutor. Then she sees the waitress marching her soldier ass cheeks over with their order. Andrea is sitting back to make room for her plates.

"Here is your food," the waitress says, and the words sound formal. Then she disappears, her ass once again turning heads like puppets connected on a single string.

Andrea digs in, starting with the hot food. Lola wants to eat—she sees the crisp triangles of tortillas glistening with just the right amount of oil in a pillow of fluffy scrambled eggs. But Lola can't eat, not playing this part.

"What if I know something . . . about something else?" Lola asks.

Andrea pauses to chew and swallow. She dabs at her lips with a signature Freddy's flimsy paper napkin.

"What something else?" Andrea asks at last. Her pause has muted Lola's courage. Her next word, the one she knows is for the best, she can't take back.

"Murder," Lola says.

The word doesn't shake Andrea. She stabs a grape with her fork and shoves it in her mouth, disappearing it in three chews.

"Whose murder?"

The question that really matters. It's fine if you kill the right person—a minority, preferably one with a criminal record, although that's not a necessity. Young black men are the easiest victims for getting a perp off with probation, a little community service, and a pee test every once in a while. Mexican men are next. And Lola can't leave prostitutes off the list law enforcement and prosecutors are willing to let die sans justice. Drug addicts. Damaged girls. Blue-collar immigrants who don't pay taxes because they fear deportation. The list of souls who don't matter is too long for Lola to bear.

The thought prods Lola to eat, to sustain, and she starts to shovel her own meal into her mouth. The grease and the cream and the crunch of the tortilla mingle against her cheek, soothing as a cold compress against an open wound.

"Darrel King," Lola says, and Andrea does sit back, for real this time, surprised, her mouth opening a little so Lola can see bits of egg against tongue. Then she closes it, and she is Andrea, fiery prosecutor with no flaws.

"Holy shit," Andrea breathes. She looks around, spotting the waitress refilling coffees and doling out smiles, all eyes on her. "Do you want to talk somewhere more private?"

Lola has already considered this option, and her verdict was simple—fuck it. It's time for her to step from the shadows, before someone forces her into the light.

This place, Freddy's, is in Lola's hood. Her people can get on the boat she ordered two by fucking two, or they can drown.

She doesn't even whisper as she replies, "No. This is fine." She takes another bite. Heaven. "Fuck, this shit's good."

Andrea notices the change in Lola's behavior—the eating, the posture, the cursing. The Lola in front of her is not a victim. She is pure perp, at home with blood and collateral damage and torturing loved ones to get to her.

Lola is ready to start calling the shots. She takes her last bite of migas, gulps her last coffee and juice, and sits back. "Ask me about Darrel."

Andrea doesn't move.

"You don't want to talk about Darrel because you know who wanted him dead."

Andrea's appetite must have disappeared. She pushes her plate away, toys with her fork. She doesn't know what question to ask next.

"Eldridge," Lola says. She signals to the nice-ass waitress to refill her coffee cup, but she keeps her eyes on Andrea. The woman's cheeks flush, and she reaches for her water glass. Lola hears the crunch of teeth on ice, breaking the tiny squares into shards.

"You're working with him."

Andrea looks up at the waitress, then to Lola—her eyes pleading with Lola.

"Don't worry. She doesn't give a shit. She's got honest work. Isn't that right?"

"Sí." The waitress smiles so that Andrea can see the woman has no idea what they're saying. Then she's gone.

"What do you want from me?" Andrea asks.

"I want you to make an arrest in the murders of Darrel King and his girl, Mila."

"I can't. I don't have a suspect."

"You don't have to link this shit to your boy," Lola says, annoyed that the ferocious prosecutor has crumbled right in front of her. "Keep Eldridge's name out of it. It was a gang thing. Killer was making a play for Darrel's territory. Done."

Andrea is quiet, her hands folded in front of her. Lola wants to poke her—*Come out and play. Come on. Let's make a deal.*

But Lola is beginning to see the scenario she hadn't pictured before this moment. Andrea is working with Eldridge, yeah. But they're not equals. Andrea fears him.

Shit.

Andrea unfolds her hands and speaks in a whisper. When she's uncertain, as she is now, she sounds like a little girl. "My educated guess would be that Mr. Waterston is under the impression you work for him now."

Lola has to think about her reply. "And what's your impression?"

"I think you work for yourself," Andrea says.

"Who's to say I'm not working for the enemy? Los Liones." Lola tries out the cartel name to gauge Andrea's reaction. The woman sits up straighter.

"If you work for . . . them, and they think your gang is involved in Darrel's death, you're in for a world of hurt."

"Unless Eldridge protects me."

"Why would he do that?"

"Who do you think the order to kill Darrel came from?"

Andrea sits back, and Lola feels betrayed. She had wanted to meet with a powerful woman, a woman who didn't have to run back and forth between a man and Lola to make assertions and strike deals.

"Here's what I think," Andrea says. "The cartel hired your little gang to fuck up that drop between Eldridge and Darrel. You did, but you really fucked up. There's no cash, the heroin disappears—"

"How is Sergeant Bubba?" Lola asks, and Andrea stops. It's all well and good to dance around drug lords and murder charges, but Lola has mentioned a dirty cop. That's Andrea's world, her side of the table.

"You don't understand."

"Cartel knows there's a dirty cop on Eldridge's payroll."

"How?" Andrea asks, her eyes alert, nervous.

"I told them."

"Told who?"

"Don't know his name. All I know is he's real fat. And he likes sushi."

The description has intrigued Andrea. "Where did you see him? Tijuana?"

"Tijuana? Nasty-ass town." This, though Lola has never been. "Nah, he was right here. Los Angeles."

Andrea signals the cheeky waitress and tosses some crisp twenties at her.

"Gracias, gracias," the waitress repeats, and the way she bows reminds Lola of the fat man and the sushi that stung the insides of her mouth it tasted so damn good.

Andrea is on her feet, ready to go, but she doesn't leave. "I'm sorry I can't arrest you for murder. I'm guessing you're counting on some kind of protection inside, while things cool down out here. But they won't cool down."

Andrea has misunderstood Lola. Still, she is not an ally, not yet, so Lola doesn't bother to correct her. It takes her three seconds to click from table to door, and then she is gone, leaving Lola at a booth, food finished, check paid, nothing left to do but await her fate.

THIRTY-TWO

SLICE

Outside Freddy's, Lola finds herself staring at the traffic. Even in the ghetto, people have jobs to get to, families to provide for, loved ones to cuddle, loved ones to beat. Everyone is in a hurry, except Lola. She has put some semblance of a plan in motion, but her game is chess. She has to wait for Andrea's next move to plot her own.

With nothing better to do, she walks in long, calm strides, catching a glimpse of her shadow. It fills the brick wall of the alley behind Freddy's. She is larger than life.

Bangers revving their lowriders' engines at a crosswalk stop their pissing contest to let her pass. She doesn't look, but she knows their eyes are on her. Like the waitress in Freddy's, she is turning heads, but it's not her ass doing the work. Is it possible, Lola thinks, that her whole neighborhood knows her power?

Yes. Ghetto gossip spreads faster than lice at a daycare, hopping from head to head, brain to brain, growing, changing, and morphing into the best narrative to trade over coffee or tequila or cocaine at the kitchen table.

And now that Andrea knows Lola's truth, it makes it real. She has made it onto a prosecutor's radar. The "good" people know she is bad.

A '90s model Geo Metro, bright green, pulls alongside her, and Lola knows Jorge will be behind the wheel.

"Yo, you dig my wheels?"

"They're the shittiest you've dug up in a while," Lola says. Next to Jorge, Marcos grunts, approving the insult.

"My dad's old. He got IBS. He ain't got time to steal the dope whips."

"He doesn't steal. He chops."

Marcos rolls his eyes. Lola, too.

"Look, whatever, man, we found her."

Lucy.

"Where?"

"At her mama's place."

Marcos shoves a slip of paper into Jorge's hand, and Jorge passes it to Lola. It is Rosie Amaro's address, heretofore unknown, as junkies don't tend to pay their rent long enough to leave a trail of residences on the Internet.

"You want a ride?" Jorge again.

But Lola is moving at a run, away from the shitty car and her faithful soldiers. This shit's personal. She finds herself on the apartment's doorstep before she knows where she's going. The doormat is tattered to shit, but Lola can still make out a faded chili pepper, red and green like Christmas, under her feet. She doesn't have a key, but when no one answers her knock, she tries the door. Unlocked.

Inside, the reek of rotting dairy overwhelms her—spoiled milk and queso baked bad in the sun. The flies prefer the rancid fry meat stewing in filth on the stove. Empty beer bottles line the kitchen counter like green glass soldiers. The same bottles, overturned, are scattered across the living room floor. The apartment is small, with a shoebox of a kitchen and a living room too full of broken-down furniture—a coffee table with a broken leg supported by old phone books, carpet peppered with brown stains, a sofa with coils poking out from ripped fabric.

The woman slumped on the sofa is rail thin and shaking. Her skin is brown. Her whole body doesn't look like it should be able to stand or breathe or eat or shit. She is unnatural. She should be dead.

Rosie Amaro musters the strength to raise her head and register Lola.

"Where's Lucy?"

Rosie cocks her head to one side, searching for an answer. She is too low to find any anger to direct at Lola. It's possible she doesn't even know who Lola is. The only thing Rosie knows right now is she needs a fix.

The man bursts through the apartment door in a whirlwind of wiry energy. He is young, younger than Lola, twenty-one or twenty-two, with a shaved head and lean muscles under a Polo shirt. He wears khaki pants. He is white. He does not belong here.

"I got it," he says, his voice trying to contain his excitement, like a child bringing home a good report card. He holds up a bindle, a little vial of white powder. Heroin.

Lola can tell her junkies apart—bad teeth and pockmarks for the tweakers, skeletons with popping veins and chicken-thin arms for the heroin addicts. This man, in his upper-middle-class uniform, is neither, and Lola can tell by looking that he has brought just enough smack to tide Rosie over for maybe half an hour.

He holds the drugs out to Rosie without asking for cash. She will pay him some other way.

Lola looks down at her clasped hands. She hadn't realized she'd assumed a prayer stance, because she doesn't want this to be what she thinks it is.

"Who are you?" the man asks, having registered her presence now that he's handed over the drugs.

"Don't worry about it," she says.

He straightens his spine and sputters, "You're in my girlfriend's house. I have a right to worry about it."

He has no idea how many rights he has. Lola can't help herself. She peeks out the front window, where the dirt chokes any sunlight that might have made its way into Rosie Amaro's apartment. An apple red car is rounding the corner, too far away for Lola to see its make, but it doesn't matter. It doesn't belong to the piece-of-shit pedophile in front of her. Then she sees it, parked among the Hondas and Nissans and Impalas. A brand-new Mercedes. No tinted windows. Not a ghetto dealer's prize, but a white boy's privilege. She has the plates memorized before she speaks.

"Your car. Your daddy give it to you?" Lola asks. Daddy is the Amaros' landlord. This man is a child rapist.

"At least I have a daddy," the young man sneers, and Lola barks a laugh.

"Got me there."

Rosie gives a half-assed cry from the sofa, but when nothing happens, she gets pissed enough to launch herself off the sofa coils. Rosie disappears behind one of the two doors off the living room, and when she returns, she's got Lucy by the elbow.

"Say hi," Rosie insists, as if she can't believe her daughter's rudeness to this privileged pedophile piece of shit. Lucy tries to hide her head in her mother's ripped jeans, but there are no soft edges on Rosie. There is no comfort there.

Somewhere inside Lola, her heart snaps.

But Lola can ignore a broken heart. For now. She pulls the knife she packed in the pocket of her cargo pants this morning. Unlike the knife she took to Darrel King's house, the one she's carrying today is big, too big for her pants, and she's lucky she never stood up with Andrea. She flicks open the blade, and it is long, with a serrated edge. The weight of it in her hands feels too much, but this is all too much, and she has to fix it.

The thought that she is about to make this right causes Lola's broken heart to leap up into her throat, but it's not nerves. It is what she imagines people mean when they say their heart soars. The thought pushes her forward, and she closes in on the young man.

He dangles the bindle like a cat toy. Rosie, that dumb junkie bitch, is about to take it, but Lola breaks up the party.

The man squeals, because Lola does not fuck around. She puts the blade to the bare, delicate skin of his pale throat.

Fucking kill him, a voice in her head screams truth. But Lola tells it to be quiet, if for no other reason than so she can hear him plead for his life.

"Please. Please don't kill me. I was just—"

Lola does not let him give an excuse. "Give me that bindle," she says.

The man hands over the bindle, and Lola hears a hiccup escape from skeleton Rosie as her would-be loot disappears in Lola's clenched fist. The sorrowful hiccup sends a shiver of pleasure up Lola's spine, greater than the pleasure she would feel if she sunk this blade into this sick fuck's dick. This man's a villain, sure, but a woman who pimps out her own daughter is a monster.

"Please," the man says again. "Let me go." He doesn't realize that he is closer to the front door than Lola. He has forgotten that he can run right back to his Mercedes and gun it out of the ghetto. He can leave this behind, but Lola and her blade have made him forget his entitlement.

"I got your plate number. I'm gonna find your name, where you live, your fucking credit score. You try this shit again, I will know," Lola tells him. "Do you understand?" The man can't move. He doesn't believe she is letting him go. "Nod if you understand."

Lola asked him to nod because the gesture forces him to move his skin against her blade. It doesn't cut him, but he thinks it will. She salivates at the terror in his eyes. She has to let him go now, to get to the real work, but he'll remember that feeling of her blade against his skin. It is as good as a leash, at least for a little while.

When she pulls the blade away, the young man runs as fast as he can to his Mercedes. The engine purrs, so calm in the face of his terror, and ferries him out of Lola's neighborhood.

Lola has flustered him with her baptism by knife. He'll be born again, wearing his leash no one can see. Maybe she's saved a few young girls from his violent sick thrusting until he starts to feel safe and picks up his habit again. When he does get the urge to kiddie rape, and he will get the urge, he will be some other hood's problem.

Rosie is a different story. She lives here. She belongs to Lola.

When Lola turns to her, the fierce promise on her lips is gone, and she gives the addict mother a peaceful smile. It is a smile that promises something besides violence, death, and justice. It is a smile that promises relief.

Lola holds up the bindle, so Rosie takes her eyes off Lola's face. The drugs are more important. "Got something for you, Rosie."

"Okay," Rosie says, their last encounter washed from her stupid leaking brain. Heroin has erased the image of Lola with the baseball bat, poised to crush Rosie's sick skull. Like her many mistakes, Rosie's memories don't linger. She will never learn.

"Just need a little favor first."

"Okay."

"Do you recognize me?" Lola asks.

"Yeah. Lola. Garcia's girl."

Lola smiles again. "That's right."

"You need a favor?" Rosie asks. "Just tell me. My girl works with women, too."

"Lucy," Lola says. "Your little girl's name is Lucy."

Rosie gives a vicious little laugh. "Right. You kept her. You didn't want to give her back to her momma. Why'd you want another woman's child, anyway? What'd you do to her?"

The implication bursts Lola open like a single drop of water exploding a whole pan of oil. She wants to rush Rosie, to feel the stringy ligaments of her neck squishing under Lola's small, mighty hands.

"No," Lucy's voice, quiet but firm, douses Lola's anger like a flood. Lola remembers God and Noah and wiping out the evil. Lucy has done all that, just now.

"Whatever," Rosie mutters, and even wanting her fix, wanting to pimp out her daughter to get it, Lola can tell Lucy has hurt Rosie's feelings because she likes Lola more than her own mother.

Time for the real flood.

Lola takes out the single sheet of paper she printed off the California Courts' website the day after they met Ms. Laura. It is form GC-211, the Nomination and Consent of a Guardian.

"You're going to sign this."

"Fuck I am," Rosie says and turns her ugly mean face toward the cushions.

Lola holds up the heroin, though, and it's like Rosie can smell it. She turns back.

"You got a pen?"

A decent mother would ask what the fuck she was signing. Not Rosie. Lola hands her a red ink pen from her pocket, and Rosie signs her name in neat cursive, with a heart over the "i," like a flirtatious schoolgirl. It's pathetic. Lola folds the paper in four neat squares and puts it in her pocket. In the corner of the room, Lucy exhales.

"That it?"

"One more thing."

"Okay." Rosie does not ask Lola what that one thing is. Even if Lola were to tell her, though, she doubts Rosie would object. She keeps her eyes on the prize powder.

Lola curls to the ground, back rounding as she comes up, graceful as a dancer. She shakes her black hair back over her shoulders, out of her face, and when she comes up, she shows Rosie the green glass bottle before she smashes it against the wall. Beer backwash wets the drywall, a remnant of someone else's too-good time. Lola thinks for a second of Darrel, of the improvised weapon she used on him. But this is different. She is not going to hurt Rosie.

Rosie doesn't have the energy to jump in surprise at the noise. Instead, her face screws up in confusion.

She doesn't know what's about to happen to her.

"Lucy," Lola says. "You have a television in your room?"

"Yes."

"Go back there and turn it up. As loud as it goes. Whatever you want to watch."

Lucy nods, as if Lola has given her an important task instead of a treat. Lucy's instincts are correct—her task is to not see what's about to happen.

Lucy skitters away, and as Lola edges toward Rosie, putting herself between mother and daughter, she holds up the fractured bottle, her hand on the neck. The blare of the television from Lucy's bedroom lets Lola know it's safe to continue.

"See this bottle?" she says to Rosie. "Just draw the edges across your skin. Like this."

Lola's words verge on the edge of breathless. Her tone plays and seduces as she turns her hand palm up and draws the teeth she broke into the green glass across the delicate skin that runs from her wrist to her elbow.

"Really?" Rosie asks. "You sure that's all you want?"

"This is what I want," Lola replies.

"And you'll give me . . . that?" Rosie licks her lips, eyes still on the bindle. Lola nods. "Okay, then," Rosie says. It's clear from her tone she thinks Lola's getting a bum deal.

Lucy's mother takes the bottle from Lola, turning her palm to the cottage cheese ceiling, and draws the sharp teeth across the mottled flesh of her wrist.

"Deeper," Lola says.

Rosie repeats the motion, pressing harder into the flesh, the green glass catching a reddened river of a track mark on its journey. She cries out.

"It's okay. It's okay," Lola says. "Just a little deeper. Then we're done."

Rosie obeys, and now the reddened river opens up, springing blood that's almost purple from beneath the skin's surface.

Lucy's mother looks to Lola, her eyes hopeful. Has she done enough? Lola smiles and steps toward her, taking Rosie's hopeful happy face in her hands.

"Thank you," Lola says. She rubs Rosie's cheek with a finger. It's a gentle caress, and Rosie nuzzles into Lola's hand, as Lucy has nuzzled into her shoulder, unused to comfort but eager to accept it.

"I did okay?" Rosie asks from Lola's palm.

"You did so good," Lola responds. "Now you just have to do the other."

Rosie pulls away from Lola, determined, and turns her other palm to the ceiling. In a matter of seconds, she has opened up the same purple fountain there, and Lola wonders if some of Rosie's blood pulsed past the wound on the first arm, escaping, only to be caught on the other.

Rosie gives one faded smile to Lola before she starts to sink to the floor, but Lola goes with her, a strong hand under the woman's neck. She lays her onto the shit-stained shag and whispers, "You did great."

"Thank you," Lucy's mother says.

Before Rosie breathes her last breath, Lola presses the bindle into her hand. Lola sees the smile spread across Rosie's face, her fix secured, as the last of her life escapes onto the scratchy carpet.

When Lola looks back, she sees Lucy, back turned, leaning against her bedroom door frame. Lola knows the girl saw nothing. She knows Lucy understood why Lola told her to turn up the television. Lucy understood that Lola wanted her to protect herself.

"It's okay, Lucy," Lola says. She walks to Lucy and kneels in front of her. Lucy buries her head in Lola's shoulder. When she looks up, she is beaming at Lola.

Her happiness will pass, Lola knows, and this event will mix in with the laundry list of traumas she's been through in her five years. Still, the buck has stopped here, with Lucy's dead mother. It's time for Lucy to have a childhood.

"Lucy," Lola says, "the things your mother made you do. You will never have to do them again."

Lucy gives Lola a solemn nod, believing her.

Lola gathers Lucy in her arms, and the little girl goes limp, relaxed, her tired bones no longer keeping her stiff and on guard. She doesn't need to watch her back when Lola's carrying her.

When Lola has made sure Lucy's head is buried in her shoulder so the little girl can't see her dead mother, flat bones leaking blood onto carpet, she starts out the door. The young man scum left it open in his hurry, and Lola, feeling the confidence of a true leader, hadn't bothered to shut it before she helped Rosie do what was right. No one in her hood would rat her out.

But it is not someone from her hood who has witnessed what just happened.

It is Andrea, holding her car keys, clicker under thumb, as if her ride is nearby and what she sees will only distract her for a moment. Lola watches the prosecutor's eyes go from body to glass bottle to bindle.

Lola remembers the apple red car rounding the corner. Andrea's red Audi.

"You following me?" Lola challenges. Instead of weakening her, having Lucy helpless on her shoulder has only added to her strength.

"Yes," Andrea says, and Lola nods acceptance. There's another pause, a stalemate, Lola thinks, until Andrea continues, "An addict commits suicide with a full bindle in her hand."

"She got those drugs from a man who was here before you. She didn't give him cash." Lola shifts Lucy on her hip so that Andrea can see her worn young face. "This is her daughter."

Lola does not have to spell it out for Andrea. She doesn't have to explain that the man wasn't a dealer, that he was a predator preying on an addict and her child to get his own illegal fix.

Andrea turns her back on Lola and Lucy. Lola can't say for sure how much she saw or didn't see. Lola hugs Lucy tighter, because she can't keep her promise to Lucy if she's in jail.

But Andrea doesn't leave. She enters the apartment, bypassing the rancid meat on the kitchen counter. She does a minimal amount of digging in the few bare cabinets before coming up with a greasy square of aluminum foil. She returns to Lucy's dead mother and bends, covering her own palm with the foil as she plucks the bindle from the dead woman's palm.

"Get this out of here," she tells Lola. "Without it, it's a suicide."

Lola nods as she takes the foil that looks like it once contained a burger. She sees drips of mustard and mayonnaise, forgotten wilts of iceberg lettuce and faded red tomatoes, now serving as insulation for the heroin bindle.

"Thanks," Lola says, then, "Guess you've been through some shit."

"Guess so," Andrea says.

Lola is smart enough to ask an immediate follow-up. "What do you want in return?"

"Help me get the fat man," Andrea says.

"And if I don't agree? You charge me in this"—Lola is about to say junkie, then remembers Lucy and corrects herself—"woman's murder."

"Doubt I'll have time."

"Why's that?"

"Because we'll both be dead."

Lucy presses her forehead so tight into Lola's neck, Lola can feel the glaze of sweat on the little girl's brow.

"Deal?" Andrea says, extending a hand to Lola.

"Deal," Lola says, her heart quickening as Andrea shakes her hand.

And just like that, Lola has an equal.

THIRTY-THREE

HIGH HORSE

"From scratch," Lola says, serving slices of chocolate cake on paper plates to the cooing older women of her neighborhood. They demur and deny, saying they shouldn't, too many calories. They tell Lola she should have their pieces. She is too skinny.

Lola is pleased with the way this impromptu end of summer barbecue has come together. It is the night after she helped Lucy's mother do the right thing. The evening air contains a bite of chill that wasn't present a week and a half ago, when El Coleccionista crashed the first party she and Garcia had hosted. Lola's world has shifted beneath her, and she wants all the people of the neighborhood, her people, together before she tries to conquer the two men who want her dead.

"Don't insult me," she says to the padded objecting women now. "Have some cake." It is not a request the way it would have been at the last barbecue.

The women obey, taking their slices off the tray Lola found somewhere in the depths of her kitchen cabinets. Now, looking at the metal, she notes the burnt crusts of dough stuck to the surface. It is not a tray, but a cookie sheet. Oh fucking well.

As the ladies sink their teeth into the rich chocolate concoction, Lola closes her eyes and enjoys their sighs of pleasure.

"Better than mine?" The woman's voice, equal parts anger and sadness, would once have quickened Lola's pulse.

Now, when Lola opens her eyes to find Kim standing in front of her, hands on hips and heeled foot tapping, she feels peace wash over her in a gentle wave. Garcia's ex is wearing too much makeup. Her mascara has run enough to let Lola know she's been crying. Lola wonders if the tears are because Kim has figured out Lola murdered her brother, or if they are the result of realizing Garcia knew the identity of Carlos's killer all along and never told her.

"Kim," Veronica says, stepping forward before Lola feels the need to speak. "Why don't you go on home?"

"It's okay," Lola says, placing a gentle hand on the older woman's shoulder and moving her aside. "I'll take care of this."

Veronica's silence tells Lola that's exactly what she's afraid of. Like everyone else here, Veronica now knows Lola is the true power behind the Crenshaw Six.

"Come with me," Lola says to Kim.

"Lola . . ." Veronica again, her tone as close to warning as she dares to get with Lola now.

The doughy ladies have stopped forking moist crumbs of chocolate cake to their mouths.

"I'm not going to hurt her," Lola says, drawing Kim closer to her. Veronica bristles like a scared porcupine at the sight of the two women standing shoulder to shoulder.

Halfway to the door, Garcia intercepts, grill tongs still in hand. "Hey. Kim. Where are you going? Stay out here. Have a beer."

"Start the burgers," Lola says to him. He retreats, and Lola sees Kim's head tilt in confusion—*How can he give up on me so quickly?*

Inside, Lola tells Kim to wait in the living room. It is empty here, all the guests wanting to know what's going on but not daring to come inside.

"You killed my brother," Kim says, anger and sadness being replaced by exhaustion.

"It's okay," Lola says again. "You're so tired. You can relax now."

When Lola returns from the bedroom, she finds Kim sinking into the foxhunting chair.

"Comfortable, isn't it?" Lola asks.

Kim nods.

"You want it?"

Kim looks up at Lola with questioning eyes. "What?"

"To set up house with Garcia."

"He told me not to come here. He told me you would hurt me."

If Garcia is painting Lola as the villain in this scenario, he has not told Kim the whole truth.

Lola steps toward Kim, feeling three times the other woman's height as she stands over her.

"I'm not going to hurt you," Lola says. "I'm going to save you."

Lola holds out the stack of bills she retrieved from the pile of dirty cash.

"Five thousand dollars," she tells Kim.

"You can't buy my silence."

"I don't need to. Because I already have his."

"His?"

"Garcia's."

"He just found out. There was evidence, he said, in the house, that he just found . . ."

"He was here. When it happened."

The realization knocks the wind out of Kim. Her shoulders slump. Her hands clasp and unclasp. She wails, and Veronica appears behind Lola.

"Lola?"

"One second."

Lola kneels at Kim's feet and whispers so they are the only two people who can hear.

"He knew all along. He betrayed you. Do what you want with me. I'll probably be dead by tomorrow. But take this money and get as far away from him as you can. He's a chickenshit. You're not."

Lola presses the cash into Kim's shaking hands. When Kim collapses onto Lola's shoulders in racking sobs, Lola finds her own arms encircling the broken woman and holding her tight.

"Veronica," Lola says finally. "Take Kim home, please."

Veronica nods her obedience and takes Kim by the hand.

When Lola rejoins her party, the neighbors' whispers turn to pretend laughs. People start to eat and drink again. Garcia grips the spatula in one hand and a beer in the other. When Lola gives him a nod that everything is okay, he is foolish enough to take her at face value.

Lola catches a glimpse of Lucy across the yard, trying to join in a game with some other neighborhood children. But the others form a line of little dark heads, blocking Lucy out of their fun, and right then Lola is determined that the plan she and Andrea hatched earlier over Rosie Amaro's dead body will work. She must live. She has to protect this little girl, and she has to shake all the shit out of her own little corner of this world.

Lola strides across the yard. A tangle of boys trips past Lola with the thin, fiery sparkler sticks in hand. They lead the way for her, and in a few steps she has arrived at the line of black-haired bitches barring Lucy from her first chance at a normal childhood.

"Yo," Lola says, and the line of long straight black hair turns. The girls are identical to Lola, despite their different features—round faces, skinny legs, crooked wicked smiles. "Let her play." Lola jerks a thumb at Lucy.

"No," one girl says, and Lola gathers from the way the girl draws herself up, tall and straight and unbending, that she is their leader. "You can't make us."

This queen bee is trouble, Lola thinks. She herself was never the queen bee in school. She kept to herself and her books and tried to do right by her little brother. If anyone bullied her, she didn't notice. She had other shit on her mind. But now, with Lucy here, safe, with no older man waiting in the wings to hurt her, Lola is realizing how mean other little girls can be.

"Is it true your mom's a whore?" The queen bee poses the question to Lucy. Queen Bee's future flashes through Lola's mind—straight Cs, eating disorder, high school pregnancy and shady abortion, fake nails and stinky cheap hairspray. Lola wishes she could share her mind with Lucy now, to let the little girl see the smallness of this particular queen.

Instead, as Lola fights the urge to go for the blade she always has in her pocket, Lucy says, "Yes."

The little girls exchange glances—they don't know what to do with Lucy's honesty. Even at five, their worlds already consist of twisted truths and ulterior motives, of overcomplication and the sobbing melodrama inherent in the telenovelas they watch with their mothers on cheap sofas. For once, Lola is happy to exist in a man's world, where everything is simple—*do my bidding or you're dead.*

"Oh," Queen Bee says. In profile, Lola sees the beginning of a puffy tummy over her jeans, and Lola takes secret delight in the realization even as the little bitch steps aside to let Lucy join their group. The row of identical black-haired heads bent in studious play absorbs Lucy seamlessly. Still, Lola thinks, is this the crowd she wants Lucy running with?

Then she remembers that Lucy just diffused the clique situation on her own. Where does the little girl's independence leave Lola?

Her eyes scan the party. She digs its cobalt sky backdrop, now that the sun has left the sky. She hears the low rumble of voices around her, the high-pitched second-long scream of a child in happy play. She sees Garcia turning meat on the grill again, even though everyone here already has full stomachs.

Over the past twenty-four hours, her interactions with her partner have been minimal. She tells him to pass the salt at dinner, she asks if he wants her to bring him his coffee in bed, she offers blow jobs and is both hurt and relieved when he refuses. Now she knows why—he has betrayed her. He has told Kim a version of the truth, one that vilifies her and absolves him.

Kim's confession has forced Lola to admit what she's been feeling for some time—that Lola is not sure Garcia belongs in her picture. Because what is her picture? It is not miniskirts and manicures and menial tasks and chocolate cake recipes. Lola can't be that woman Garcia seems to want, and, over the past two weeks, as the world has broken open to her and to the Crenshaw Six, his inability to see her as both his boss and his girlfriend has become a streak on what used to be the clean clear glass of their relationship.

It is lucky for him the plan she hatched with Andrea as Rosie Amaro started to rot under them will most likely get Lola killed.

As with the drop, the plan is simple. The fat man, Andrea told her, is not supposed to be on American soil, but since Lola has seen him, maybe she can wrangle him again. Andrea can call in the feds, she'll get credit for the arrest, the cartel will be disorganized and leaderless long enough for Lola to plant the Crenshaw Six flag in their own neighborhood. She'll be her own boss, Andrea has promised.

The only obstacle, if the fat man is stupid enough to fall for Lola's request for a meeting, is Eldridge. But that is Andrea's part of the equation. She has promised to share the location of his stash with Lola, but Lola had to promise her something in return.

"Hey." Her little brother's voice makes Lola jump.

When she turns, she finds Hector holding a pie piled high with browned meringue in perfect peaks.

"Brought something. From . . . her," he says, looking at his feet, which kick at tufts of sprouting grass. He even apologizes like a child, wordless and destroying her property. "I know it's weird, but she wanted to, and I didn't know how to tell her no."

In all the excitement of a plan hatched with another woman as smart as herself, Lola has forgotten, or tried to forget, Hector's disrespect.

"Thanks," Lola says, taking the pie. She shouldn't care that people are watching—this is her coming-out party, of sorts. Lola should smash Amani's perfect baked good in Hector's face. She hates that her brother turned on her, after she gave him so much. She raised him. She was his mother when their own mother couldn't be . . . but if she were his mother, really, wouldn't she have stayed strong and loved him even when he turned on her? But she is not his mother. And she doesn't have to be.

Lola puts the pie in the kitchen where no one will see it. She pulls out her cell and presses send on a text she drafted hours ago. When she looks up, Hector is there again. It's odd, seeing a man in her kitchen during the barbecue. This is women's territory, but Veronica and her friends are outside, gathered around a table and calling out to the children running with sparklers to slow down. Dinner is over. Food is forgotten.

"Want me to slice it?" Hector asks of the pie. Lola wonders if he came in here to make sure Amani's enemy pie would be enjoyed at the party, or if this strange question is his way of starting to make up with her.

"You should go outside," Lola says.

"I can help clean up," Hector offers, and the favor he seems to think he's doing, stooping to women's work, turns Lola to steel. She draws herself up, and, even though Hector has a good seven or eight inches on her, he takes a step back.

"You should go outside," she says.

"Don't much feel like a party," he replies.

Lola wants to tell him she didn't mean he should go outside to enjoy the party.

"Lola," Hector says, head hanging, eyes cast down to the browning linoleum Lola can't make sparkle, no matter how much she gets down on her hands and knees and scrubs. "I'm sorry."

There are the words, but he still can't look her in the eye.

"Go outside," she says. Hector understands now that it's an order, and the way he walks, taking each step carefully, as if he's afraid of stepping on a land mine, feels correct. He is not such a child that he hasn't realized there is no use talking to her anymore.

Lola looks down at the pie Hector brought, courtesy of a girlfriend Lola could not invite to her home. Except she could, because she's the boss. She could have welcomed Amani with a cold beer and a vise-grip arm around her shoulder as she introduced Hector's black girlfriend from Darrel King's territory to all the soldiers in her neighborhood. Because that's what these people are, Lola thinks, gazing at the makeshift court of her backyard, a small dusty brown-green square of her tiny kingdom. Tonight, all her soldiers have gathered, from the fat old gossips to the kid sadists with their sharp tongues and fiery sticks.

Standing at her kitchen window, watching them now, Lola feels a peace that has evaded her. All the people she cares about are here in her backyard, where she can protect them, if she chooses.

She will sacrifice her life for them, if necessary. But if the plan she has hatched with Andrea works, her community, her territory, will thrive.

But first Lola has to clean house.

She picks up the lemon meringue pie Amani baked, turning it all the way around to get one last look at its perfect meringue peaks. She hears a rustle in the backyard, a collective wave of anxiety in tiny gasps and shouts. She doesn't look up, not yet, because she has found only a single clean fork in her silverware drawer. She scoops a bite from the middle of the pie, fucking it up beyond repair, and lets the citrus sting her as it goes down. Goddamn, Hector's girl can bake. Lola wonders if Amani will stay with him, now that things are changing.

"Hands up. Let me see your hands." The white man shout echoes through the bright kitchen, and Lola squints into the dark.

She sees four figures in SWAT gear—boots, bulletproof vests, helmets. LAPD, not just Huntington Park. The men have dressed for war to come to a barbecue in her backyard. The thought both pisses her off and makes her swell with something akin to pride— she has the LAPD scared.

Lola watches the party crowd part into two lines. Women grab at their children, one snatching a little boy by the scruff of his neck, as if he's a cat she needs to save from drowning. The cops are the water. The cops are the flood.

Lola uses the small fork to dig the rest of the pie out of the disposable plate. Amani must have known better than to send glass here. She would never have gotten her dish back. Still, Amani's understanding of the situation irks Lola. Why not show a little faith? Why not send something more permanent?

Lola dumps the sugary tart concoction into the garbage disposal. When she flips the switch, she can still hear the SWAT commander's voice. It is a loud boom, a bomb that shakes the South Central ground.

"Everybody freeze."

Everybody does. Lola can see the narrowing of eyes, the hatred, the distrust as her people stand shoulder to shoulder, staring at their oppressors.

"You got a warrant?" Garcia steps forward. In the kitchen, Lola fights to stop an eye roll. She can't blame him, though. She didn't tell anyone the police were coming.

"We do, sir."

"You want to search the place, I gotta see it," Garcia insists. Lola wonders if he knows she's watching. Is he trying to impress her, playing ghetto lawyer?

"Better not be one of those folded-up pizza ads, neither," Jorge pipes up, and Lola knows he's about to launch into an anecdote, despite the shields and the weapons. "I saw it on TV once, how you cops do, waving around a plain piece of paper all folded up, saying it's a warrant, when it's really two-for-one pepperoni."

Behind Jorge, Marcos gives a half guffaw. Lola is proud of these two, staying true to themselves in the face of SWAT. The clown and the monster. Her soldiers.

"Show me the search warrant," Garcia says.

"We're not here to search your house, sir," the SWAT commander says, and Lola hears a questioning murmur shoot through the crowd.

She has disappeared the whole pie now, ground up and spit out in her garbage disposal. She tosses the foil pan into the trash, cramming it in with grease-stained paper plates sticky with forgotten food.

Party's over.

Lola grabs a hoodie to walk into the chill night air. She has her arms crossed over her chest, as if she's just wandered into the dark to gaze at the stars.

"Lola," Veronica says, and Lola hears the plea in the woman's voice. *Do something. Fix this. Make it right.*

Even as Garcia argues with the SWAT commander about rights and racial profiling, everyone looks to Lola. *Tell us what to do.*

"It's okay," she says, and her quiet voice overrules Garcia's and the SWAT commander's. Her people strain to hear her, and when they do, they relax. Lola nods to the SWAT commander—say your piece.

"Hector Vasquez," the man says.

"Aw, shit, man," Jorge says. "Hector didn't do nothing—"

Lola catches Jorge's eye. He shuts up and blends into the neighborhood crowd. Marcos follows him.

Hector looks to Lola—*Do something.* Lola stands still. *Step forward,* she thinks. *Step forward like a man.* When he doesn't, Lola gives him a nod that is equivalent to an order—*Step the fuck up.*

Hector does. "I'm Hector Vasquez," he says. Lola wishes he would stop looking at her like she's going to save him.

"You're under arrest for the murders of Darrel King and Mila Jamison," the SWAT commander booms. The man must know Darrel, must not have hated him, the way he says his name. Lola wonders how many calls SWAT took in Darrel's territory, if this man and Darrel were on a first-name basis. She herself has learned to cooperate with police in the case of a joint enemy. It's why they are here now.

Once the initial surprise has passed, everyone again looks to Lola.

Hector stares at her, how calm she is, and he knows she is the reason these men are here. Lola's heart swells with pride as Hector holds out his hands for the cuffs she as good as placed there.

THIRTY-FOUR

BEST-LAID PLANS

When Lola enters the gym, her ears fill with the sounds of blaring televisions, pop music with a thumping bass beat, and the grunts and moans of human effort. She passes a snack bar on her left. A woman tells the polo-shirted cashier to go light on the mayo. The cashier nods as if this is a normal request. Same goes for when the woman asks for a chocolate chip cookie and a diet soda, explaining she just got done spinning.

Lola gave Jorge and Marcos the day off. Tonight, they will be on call for her meeting with the fat man, but she knows they are both still reeling from Hector's arrest and the fact that Lola let it happen. Jorge will deal with his feelings about Lola's loyalty. He will accept her as he did last night, when he shut his mouth at a nod of her head. Then he will tell Marcos to feel the same, or, if Lola's sociopathic soldier can't feel, to at least obey Lola's orders. If she survives tonight, she will tell them both the truth.

Lola passes the spinning room—rows of bikes, men and women in tight spandex clipping spiked shoes into pedals. The instructor, a six-packed woman in sports bra and workout underwear, tells everyone it's time to get moving. She blasts Michael Jackson through the speakers, and for a second Lola regrets her own wardrobe choice—cutoff jean shorts rimmed with tattered threads and a tight tank with built-in bra. She found some sneakers, but she has no ankle socks. If she were wearing proper attire, would she be able to join the class unnoticed? She's getting some strange looks as she wanders the cold, blue-carpeted tundra of Mila's gym. But what the fuck does Lola know about working out? She doesn't understand the all-but-hallelujahs coming from the spin class, but she wants to. Is there another god present here that no one ever told her about, the god of self-worth and self-confidence and self-esteem?

Even so, a spin class would not be how she would spend what might be her last day on Earth. She is not here to work out. She is here to fulfill her part of the bargain she struck with Andrea. Andrea arrested Hector. Lola has to do her a favor in return.

After Lola and Andrea had struck a truce over Rosie Amaro's dead body, Andrea had confirmed Lola's suspicions. Yes, she is on Team Eldridge, but she is not an equal. She is a pawn. Eldridge knows something about Andrea's past. Lola doesn't know what that something is, but she does know Andrea was willing to stand over a dead junkie mother pimp Lola had just coaxed into killing herself and look the other way. Lola can imagine the something in Andrea's past, the shit she's seen, involves sex, drugs, and/or money. She can also imagine it's something her wealthy blue-blooded psychiatrist husband, Jack, does not know. Lola likes to imagine maybe Andrea had sex for money to put herself through law school. She finds that version of Andrea's past inspiring, but the story itself doesn't matter. Andrea has a secret. Eldridge knows it. As a result, the case Andrea is building against him borders on the verge of being able to make an arrest, without ever crossing that line. In return, Eldridge gives a portion of his drug profits to Andrea. She can use it however she sees fit—to fund her husband's clinic, for example. He's giving back to the community, even if that community is Malibu, where financial aid is a dirty word. Andrea told Lola that she uses her cut of Eldridge's cash to fund other drug clinics, too, some in the ghetto, some in the suburbs, but she didn't say how much, nor did she bother to explain why Eldridge felt the need to cut her in when he could just blackmail her. Maybe Eldridge is just a stand-up drug trafficker with prosecutors and dirty cops on the payroll.

Sergeant Bubba, Andrea had told her, is Eldridge's contingency plan, the cop who swoops in when a drop goes to shit. The night of the Crenshaw Six fuckup, Bubba was parked nearby, listening to the police scanner, ready to retrieve any product before it became evidence. Andrea didn't say whether he'd managed to get the heroin that night—in which case Eldridge is just plain greedy, wanting the cash, too—but she did say Bubba picked up Sadie and made her his own criminal informant so he could control any intel she might spill on Eldridge or Andrea or drugs or money.

"Excuse me," a woman's voice stops Lola now.

"Yeah? Yes?" Lola says, correcting herself. Mila's gym is not in West Adams. She drove the ten minutes on the 10 Freeway to Mid-Wilshire, where museums and tar pits flank this particular upscale chain gym. Lola should have pegged the suburban junkie for a snob. Darrel should have, too.

"I couldn't help noticing your calves," the woman says. She wears a breathable tank and black yoga pants. Her arms are lumps of muscle under stretched skin that's just starting to wrinkle at the crevices.

"What do you do?"

"Distribution," Lola says, thinking the woman is asking about her job.

"No, I mean, for exercise. Here."

Lola shrugs, waving her hand toward the bevy of cardio machines—treadmills, ellipticals, bikes.

"But it can't just be cardio. What do you do for strength?"

Damn good question, Lola thinks. Lola feels Lucy now for the first time since they've entered the gym. The little girl has been so quiet Lola has forgotten she's with her. Even if Lucy were talking, though, she has become such an extension of Lola that Lola sometimes forgets where she ends and Lucy begins. She's sure as shit not leaving the little girl with Garcia.

He's home now, and Lola wonders if Kim is there, too. Has she disregarded Lola's advice and her cash? Is Kim instead knocking on Lola's door, asking Garcia to commit to a meal she cooks? Lola wonders if they would cut the bullshit this time and go straight to bed, her bed, to twist into one wrong body that spreads its disease onto her sheets. At this point, though, what does it matter if Kim and Garcia get together? If her plan doesn't work tonight, she's dead anyway.

"Weights," Lola says, and it's true. Weights—Maria, Hector, Garcia, Carlos, Kim. Her soldiers. Her hood. Her burden. Her mother. Her albatross. She takes Lucy's hand and leaves the woman behind them.

After they've walked a few steps, Lucy asks, "Why are there so many women here?"

This question jabs at Lola, a little pinprick blade to the gut. Lola does not want to tell Lucy that women are batshit crazy, that they feel the need to deprive and suck in and exist on less and give more than men. *It is too early for that lesson,* Lola thinks, catching a glimpse of her and of Lucy in the mirrors that line every wall here. *You can't forget your appearance,* the mirrors seem to say. *You shouldn't.*

"Women hold themselves to higher standards," Lola says.

"Why?"

"Because women can do more than men." *God, if that isn't the truth,* Lola thinks.

"Where are we going?" Lucy asks.

"The locker room," Lola says. Her hand finds the key ring in the pocket of her cutoffs.

Lucy stares up at her with questioning eyes. She doesn't like the sound of any room with the word *lock* in its description. A cage? A trap?

"It's a place where you store your stuff while you work out." The boring explanation soothes Lucy—she doesn't understand the world of diet and fitness and eating disorders, but at least she knows Lola is not taking her someplace she won't be able to leave.

The locker room is a wave of women's bodies, naked, dressed, toweled, shaking, dimpled, taut, sagging, and firm. Blow-dryers fight both the music pumped over the speakers and the television tuned to the evening news—the daily Los Angeles hit-and-run, a surprise proposal, a mother drowning her child in the bathtub, a councilman embezzling funds, who wore it best. The noise blends and drowns out any original thought in Lola's head. The world of the upper-middle-class gym rat overwhelms her with its intensity, its constant movement, its to-the-minute scheduling.

This was Mila's world. Or the world Mila wanted for herself.

Lola fingers the keys again, taking them from her pocket this time. Before the barbecue, Lola had sent Jorge and Marcos back to the storage locker where they'd kept Mila's effects—her wallet, some gum, a stick of lip gloss she apparently couldn't do a drug drop without. There, they'd retrieved her keys, and Lola had counted Mila's life in the doors she could unlock. Darrel King's house. Darrel King's Escalade. Darrel King's mailbox. And a gym locker— number 23—at an upscale fitness center chain whose name even Lola recognized.

Lola sees the locker now. Beside it, a naked Asian woman who doesn't wax slings wet black hair over her head and crunches it between her fingers as she moves the blow-dryer up and down, up and down. Her ass, somewhere between fat and fit, sticks into the airspace reserved for Mila's locker. Lola doesn't know how to ask the naked woman to move her ass. She doesn't know locker-room etiquette. If she were in her hood, she would jut a hip bone into the soft pillow of flab, pretending not to know what she'd done, covering with a loud, cruel laugh that would tell the woman not to fuck with her. Here, with museums and culture and money on all sides, she can't do that.

"'Scuse me," Lola tries, but of course the woman can't hear over the buzz of the blow-dryer and the blare of bad news.

Lucy looks up at Lola—what next? Lola doesn't have an answer. Lucy backs away, and Lola wants to ask her what's got her freaked out. But when Lucy is a reasonable distance from the locker, she gets a running start and plunges toward the Asian woman, a rambunctious child acting out. The woman spooks and sidesteps as Lucy crashes into her bare thigh.

She looks up, her black eyes searching for this girl's mother, and she lights on Lola, arms crossed over her small chest, cutoff jeans sagging. Somehow, the Asian woman knows not to reprimand either Lola or Lucy.

"Sorry," Lola says with a shrug. The woman takes three steps back and covers herself with a towel. *What kind of armor is that?* Lola thinks, but Mila's locker beckons. It's time.

"Can I open it?" Lucy asks.

Lola nods and hands the little girl the key. She lifts Lucy under the shoulders, because Mila's locker is on the top row, and Lucy is too small to reach without Lola. The little girl fumbles with the key and the lock, trying to make them fit.

"Relax," Lola says, and Lucy does, shoulders sagging in Lola's arms. Then the key fits, the lock turns, and the locker is open.

Lola shifts Lucy to her hip, where she fits perfectly, perched on bone and sinking into Lola's waist. When Lola lifts Mila's workout clothes, ripe with dried sweat that has stiffened them to a cardboard consistency, she sees the gym bag. Black. Velcro. A perfect match for the bag Mila brought to the drop.

Except this one is not filled with paper.

Lola does not let Lucy see the cash. She only unzips the bag enough to peer at the green inside. She sees the rows and stacks, perfect as library shelves.

Lucy slips her hand into Lola's. Together, they exit the locker room, leaving behind the blow-dryers and the bad news. They pass the cardio machines and the skeleton women doing endless mindless reps of bicep curls and squats in front of the inescapable mirrors. *See your flaws. Fix your flaws.* They stride by the café where hungry ladies salivate at the turkey burgers and opt instead for salads with dressing on the side. Together, Lola and Lucy push open the glass doors of this training academy for trophy wives, a factory in its own right. Perhaps it's better to be raised in the ghetto, away from this sweatshop of a different color.

Lola has her own keys out now. She's clicking the Unlock button on the fob when a black car with tinted windows skids to an impolite stop, blocking Lola and Lucy from their vehicle.

"Run," Lola says to Lucy, and the little girl does. Parking lots are dangerous places, but so are tinted-window cartel cars.

Lola was not supposed to see the fat man again until the meeting they'd set for later tonight, the deadline he had set for her. Yet even though Lola has not seen him through the dark windows, she knows he is here, in the back of the car, waiting to surprise her.

"Hola, chica," a voice says somewhere behind her, then there's a black bag over her head. She sucks in air and gets fabric instead. They are stifling her, she thinks, as her body lands in the trunk of the car and, somewhere above her, light goes to dark.

THIRTY-FIVE

BEAUTIFUL

The fabric that lines the trunk scratches at Lola's bare legs like tiny claws. She rubs calf against calf, hoping to calm the itch, but it doesn't work. The man who staked out her house and beat the shit out of her in the parking lot of the sushi restaurant has duct-taped her wrists and ankles together. He is much taller than she thought, maybe six foot six, with high cheekbones and a symmetrical face lined with scars. Blades have written the story of a violent life on his skin.

He doesn't talk much that she can tell, although their two meetings haven't been of a social nature. He speaks English with a thick accent, one that makes her want to respond in Spanish. Something about their minimal exchanges makes her want to embrace Spanish as her mother tongue, although she has perfected English to fit into a world that doesn't want her.

The trunk is dark black and so stifling hot Lola has to suck at the milkshake thick air to breathe. She smells her own salty sweat in her coffinlike accommodations. She hears the purr of the expensive car as its tires spin over the pavement below her. She sees black, all around her, until her eyes adjust and she sees a lump at her feet. Someone must have removed the black bag from her head. She must have passed out. The lump doesn't move, so she wonders what it could be—heroin? No. The fat man wouldn't be caught traveling with his merchandise. Cash? No. Same reason.

Lola remembers the duffel bag and her hands go wild from wrist up, a blooming flower rooted at the wrong place. Where is the bag? Where is the money?

Then another thought intrudes—there is no one to find her. No one knows where she is. She has stopped sharing her hopes and dreams and deals with Garcia. Jorge and Marcos weren't scheduled to meet her until the fat man's fake deadline later tonight. Andrea knows where to meet her—she is the one who dictated the address of Eldridge's stash to Lola, from a pay phone in a shitty part of town where no one would recognize her. Andrea couldn't risk anyone discovering that she, an assistant district attorney, has known all along where Eldridge Waterston keeps his stash. Lola assumes the address Andrea gave her belongs to a warehouse. Lola doesn't know where else a drug lord keeps a stash large enough to supply their mutual sprawling city of citizens lacking impulse control, hooked on everything from drugs to booze to pills to sex to power and, of course, money.

Lola's army knows where to meet her, but they will be too late. The fat man using his hot muscle to toss Lola in a trunk was not part of the plan. By Lola's watch, she had a few more hours before he was to come calling for his assets or her ass.

The car stops, abrupt, like it's surprised to have found the place it's going.

Lola hears Spanish above her, some sort of dispute, probably something about to kill or not to kill. Actually, she's sure it's not a question of if they will kill her, but how. Slow or fast. Painful or unfeeling.

The lump at her feet begins to move, and Lola scrunches her bound ankles up close to her chest, an instinct to get away from this living thing she does not know. She realizes her feet are bare—they have taken her sneakers.

"Rmph," a little voice says. A dog? "Rmph." Again. More human this time, and when the trunk lifts with a hiss of compression, fluorescent light from somewhere to the car's left pours in, illuminating the lump at Lola's feet. Lucy. Mouth, wrists, and ankles duct-taped.

They must have run her down and trapped her, a little animal. Lola sees a bruise on the girl's face. She sees skinned knees that should have been from learning to roller-skate or bike, but instead come from a fat man's car chasing Lucy down until she was too exhausted to run anymore.

Lola hops out of the car, fighting mad, off balance from bound ankles as she charges the hot muscleman with her hard skull. She drives him back with her whole body. As bone meets six-pack, he gives a whooshed exhale. She has surprised him.

The fat man has made a mistake. He has not duct-taped her mouth. Maybe he wants to make it easier to cut out her tongue, but now, with Lucy black-eyed and skinned up in the trunk, Lola doesn't give a fuck.

"Big man, huh? Giving a little girl a black eye?" Lola speaks in a tumble of Spanish, the words rolling off her tongue like coming home.

Lola charges the hot guy again, and he lets her land another blow. When he buckles over her, his whisper tickles her ear. "That wasn't me."

The fat man. Fuck him. Andrea wants to arrest him, but their plan has already gone sideways.

Sideways. It's then Lola thinks to look to the left, her head hooked under the muscleman's arm. He lets her crane her neck toward the fluorescent light. She sees a beauty supply store, shelves of shampoo, nail polish remover, and hairspray stacked against the windows. It's massive, a long, low building, with only the front lit up. The back has no windows, no way to see what's inside. Lola glances at the number on the curb—4777. She remembers the number—it is the same one Andrea gave her over the pay phone.

In the front, Asian women in smocks wander here and there, talking among themselves, looking busy despite the place having no customers that Lola can see. Are these women Eldridge's employees? Does he traffic in humans as well, trading passage to America for a few years slaving in a beauty supply store, inventorying hair product and heroin?

The fat man must have had his muscleman remove the scrap of paper with the address from her pocket. There are several minutes Lola doesn't remember between the time the hood went over her head and the time she woke up in the trunk. One of these two ass-holes must have punched her, she realizes only now. She can take a punch. She's an adult. But Lucy . . . fuck. She had promised the little girl she wouldn't let anything happen to her. Now the cartel has her, and Lola imagines little girl limbs torn from a tiny torso. She bends farther over the muscleman's vise-grip arm and vomits on pavement.

The muscleman drops back, releasing her so she can be sick in some sort of privacy. The fat man chuckles.

"No stomach for beauty?" he asks her.

Lola wipes the back of her hand across her mouth, then rises up to look the fat man in the eye. "Hair product's a waste of fucking time." It's true. Most days Lola lets the sun bake her long black hair dry.

The muscleman pulls a matchbook from his pocket and lights a cigarette. Smoking. Nasty habit. Weak and unhealthy. If he were her man, she'd stop that shit.

Lola doesn't know why her mind insists on seeing this man, the man who beat her to an unconscious pulp only last week, as a friend. Is it because he made it a point to tell her he hadn't touched Lucy? At least he has a sense of right and wrong. Right is violence and payback and torture for an adult. Wrong is any of those things for children.

"You killed my best customer," the fat man says.

"And here we are. At your competitor's supply," Lola says. In Spanish, she is eloquent, a lady. In English, she's a banger with a couldn't-give-a-fuck lilt.

"You certainly have an odd way of accomplishing your goals."

"But I accomplish them."

The fat man can't argue with that. Lola can see the muscleman sucking on his cigarette, which he's perched between thumb and forefinger, then letting smoke rings go from his mouth. He sucks and purges, sucks and purges, as the fat man considers Lola.

"I didn't realize you had a little girl. That was a surprise. A welcome one," the fat man says as the muscleman's cigarette incinerates to ash.

Lola hocks up saliva and aims at the fat man. He doesn't see the spit coming. It is worse than a bullet.

Lola thinks she sees a quick corner-of-the-mouth smile from the muscleman, but when she sneaks a glance at him, his lips are a thin line. He saw Lucy in the street with Lola last week. He knew about the little girl, and he did not tell his boss.

Is he an ally? Can she win?

Lola's wrists start to fight against her bonds, and she longs for her blade, which of course they've taken. Struggling, Lola remembers Hector's spit on her own face. She wonders if the food in prison will keep him from losing too much weight. He is particular about his coffee, too. He would have appreciated that hipster coffee shop where she met Eldridge. Maybe if she'd included him more in the business. Then she remembers how her little brother couldn't stomach possible harm to one tiny tweaker, and she knows she is not the one who did wrong. Even her mother said so.

"You're dead," says the fat man, and his voice has become a growl. She has caused him to lose his cool, another mistake—for him.

Lucy whimpers from the trunk, and, in response, Lola's wrists wriggle free from their taped prison. She finds her right ankle with her left big toe. The muscleman has bound her so she can get free. Or maybe Lola's power comes from the little girl's sadness flowing into her, becoming strength that pulses through Lola like an electric current.

"You brought me here for a reason," Lola says. "Tell me what you want from me."

The fat man recovers, because here he is, letting his emotions get the better of him while the woman in front of him keeps it all business.

"Find our competitor's supply," the fat man says now.

Lola throws her arm back in a sweeping gesture that includes the beauty supply store's sick light and the dark windowless storage area behind it. "Here. This is it."

"We have to know for certain. Before we . . . acquire it."

"Gonna need more than the three of us to do that," Lola says. The observation annoys the fat man. She is backseat driving his operation. Still, she's right. She's strong and fast, but the amount of heroin she imagines Eldridge has in that back warehouse would break her and the muscleman. They would have maybe ten minutes before Eldridge would arrive to protect his pots of gold. Andrea has promised his presence here, regardless, although he's not due to show for at least another hour.

"Confirm the supply," the fat man orders. He's not speaking to his muscleman, because the Asian ladies, with their hands in their smock pockets and their chattering lips, must have been educated in the fine art of recognizing a cartel soldier. First clue—brown skin. Second clue—eyes alight with caliente Mexican passion, but these particular soldiers get off on violence. Third—silence. The fat man, their leader, doesn't abide by this rule, because he is the leader of the villains. He can't overpower anyone with his flabby arms and gut. He can't even outrun Lucy, Lola bets, and the picture of the little girl flying after the cartel leader who's not supposed to be on American soil makes Lola smile. She can see Lucy, arms and legs flailing, still learning to run, as the fat man waddle sprints slower than Lola walks. And now that he's giving Lola orders, despite the fact that she betrayed him, killing his best customer, pisses her off. What does she have to do to get men to stop telling her what to do?

"Okay," Lola says. She feels the muscleman's eyes on her as she turns toward Eldridge's store. He tosses his matchbook and ashy cigarette butt to the pavement. A smoker and a litterbug. He needs training. As he moves to cut her duct-taped wrists and ankles, Lola asks, "What about her?" She juts her chin toward Lucy. "Can she come with me?"

"We keep her. Collateral."

Lola thumps her bare foot on the pavement, scrunching up her feet and bringing up little pavement pebbles. They pierce the skin between her toes as she shakes her head. "She comes too."

"Or?"

"You see for yourself what's in there." This task is impossible for the fat man or his muscle. They know that. The fat man doesn't exchange a glance with his muscleman, though, because they are not partners. He is the boss. No one questions him. Lola can't help thinking his business might be faring better if he were open to some advice every now and again. She spoke to Garcia as an equal. He listened to her plans. When he pointed out flaws, he was careful. Still, he never let himself be her partner. Or was it her, thinking of her blade and that new tarp she needed to buy every time he did or didn't argue with her, that kept him at arm's length? Will there ever be anyone for her, she thinks, then hates her own weakness. She looks to the little girl in front of her and thinks, *There, she is the one for me.* "It'll look legit, me and her," Lola continues.

The fat man considers, but Lola knows he will say yes. She has made her case—she will look a lot less suspicious with her brown skin and caliente eyes if she has a child with her. He doesn't speak, just gives a curt nod, because he's jealous of her intellect. The muscleman pretends not to notice the headway she's made in escaping her bonds as he cuts loose her wrists and ankles.

Free now, Lola takes Lucy's hand, feeling a twinge of guilt that she's about to walk the girl into one of the city's largest heroin supplies. She hopes the move will turn Lucy off drugs, although stacks and stacks of neat white powder bricks, sugar walls on all sides, might have the opposite effect.

A bell rings to alert the Asian ladies to their entrance, and all heads turn toward Lola and Lucy. Lola takes stock of them—one with a Jackie O bob, another with braces and braids and a goofy greeting smile, a third with a sharp beauty that intimidates Lola because there is something ancient and royal in those matching high cheekbones.

"Yes?" the scary beautiful one says in English.

"I need some shampoo," Lola says.

"Are you licensed?"

"Huh?"

"Do you have cosmetology license?" the beautiful one says in haughty accented English. Her question strikes Lola as both harsh and seductive.

"Left it in my car," Lola says. "I'll go get it before we buy."

Lola wants to see the back room. She's not sure how to do that yet, so she walks Lucy up and down the aisles of expensive shampoo they don't stock at any ghetto bodega. The prices here are much higher than she would expect, although she guesses it doesn't matter, since this whole thing is nothing but a front. She wonders why Eldridge would choose something that probably does less cash business than a nail salon or a car wash. Beauticians most likely buy supplies in bulk, and surely it's a business expense that requires reporting to the IRS.

"Excuse me," Lola says to the goofy-braces girl, who's standing in front of her with a smile, feet planted hip width apart when Lola turns a corner. "She needs a restroom."

Goofy Braces nods and smiles in a way that makes Lola unsure she understood the request. She pads away in clogs that thump against the tile floor. Someone has polished it to a gleam, reminding Lola of New Horizons, Andrea's husband's facility, one of the many rehab facilities Andrea told Lola this place funds. Lola wonders if they have the same cleaning crew. Maybe not—this place reeks of chemicals, alcohol and acetone. That shit would not fly at rehab. There, the cleaning fluid smells of lavender-coated vinegar, natural cleansers that are easier on the delicate flower noses of recovering cokeheads and alcoholics.

To Lucy's credit, she does not dispute Lola's assertion that she needs a bathroom. Instead, she clasps Lola's hand in hers, as if she's the one leading the way. Lola likes the feeling of Lucy taking charge, though of course she can't allow that with Lucy as a habit. Lucy is her charge. Lola can take care of herself.

Goofy Braces nods at a chipped, gold-knobbed door at the back. The sign on it shows a blob of man next to a blob of woman. Unisex. How many men come here? Probably a suspicious amount, if these ladies are peddling more heroin than hair gel. Next to the restroom, Lola sees another door with a taped paper sign in neat block letters. It reads, EMPLOYEES ONLY. The back.

Goofy Braces bows—Japanese?—and disappears. Lola bets she wouldn't have gotten as lucky with the scary beautiful woman.

Lucy tugs at Lola's sleeve. "I do have to go," she says, knowing the bathroom is a ruse. Lola both admires and fears the girl's intuition. She doesn't like making Lucy an accomplice.

Lola swings open the door, discovering a tidy bathroom with a time-release air freshener glued to the wall over the toilet. A plastic flower arrangement stands next to the neat stack of paper towels on the sink. Lola starts to leave Lucy alone, but the little girl pulls her pants down and starts to sit on the toilet without a seat cover.

"Wait," Lola says, and something tugs in her chest because she knows Lucy doesn't know what a seat cover is. Lola yanks the thin paper sheet from the dispenser and places it on the toilet seat. Lucy sits, her face red at not knowing how to do one of the most basic of human activities. Lucy might not live to learn, and even if she does, Lola won't be around to teach her.

Lola's own face burns red fire now. She is pissed at the fat man outside and his littering hot muscle, the man Lola can only fantasize is an ally, ready to twist both her and Lucy into painful pretzels before shooting them in the head and dissolving their bones in lye so their loved ones can't identify them. But who are their loved ones? The Amaros, Lucy's grandparents, have yet to call to ask after her or their daughter. Garcia will be sorry but relieved. Jorge and Marcos will be late to the killing party. Lucy and Lola, the two of them together in this bathroom, are all they've got.

They have to survive tonight, and then they have to live.

THIRTY-SIX

THE DRAGON

The back room is long and low, with shelves stretching a length Lola can't see. Three bare bulbs, spaced equal distances apart, light each row in dim pockets. She spies cardboard boxes, shut with packing tape, stacked on each row of each shelf. She can't imagine how many bricks of heroin the back room is holding, but the thought of the number causes her to lick her lips. For a moment, she is a queen surveying her kingdom's product, the wealth and stores for the times of turmoil. Then she remembers this is Eldridge's stash she's staking out for the cartel. This shit is above her pay grade.

Lola looks to Lucy, who walks at her hip, mouth shut tight, eyes wide with the same hunger Lola feels. But Lucy's longing is for simpler things—love. Safety. Not to be pimped out to strange men before she even knows the proper names for her parts. Also pizza, because everyone likes pizza. Maybe Lola will order one for Lucy tonight. She hasn't thought about dinner, and maybe she shouldn't.

Will there be a tonight for her? Lola's not fool enough to think the fat man's going to let her live. She'll do her job—finding the stash—then he'll dispose of her. And of Lucy. It's that second part that doesn't fly.

Lola reaches for the pocket of her cutoffs, but of course there is no blade there. How is she supposed to cut through the tape on the boxes?

"Here," Lucy says, and when Lola looks over, Lucy is holding a box cutter.

"Jesus." Lola's breath whooshes. "Where did you get that?"

Lucy points to a workbench behind the door. Packing tape, cardboard, and shipping labels pepper the top.

"Are you okay?" Lucy asks.

"Yeah . . . yes," Lola says. She has to learn to watch her language around Lucy, the way Garcia did, not necessarily for cursing, but for proper, respectful grammar. "This is perfect. You saved us," Lola says, whispering truth. A box cutter. Holy shit. Is it enough to give them both life, this cheery yellow plastic-sheathed blade?

Lola jabs the sharp metal teeth against the tape of a box. She expects bricks beneath, maybe a little white powder on the tip when she pulls it back. Instead, there is white cream, a milky liquid. Lola sniffs it—rosemary and grapefruit, maybe. She has never heard of heroin cut with grapefruit and rosemary, although it's not a bad idea, to appeal to the purists, the wild-caughts and non-GMOs and organic cage-free types. Eldridge works the Westside—maybe he knows his customers. Except it's liquid. In a beauty supply store.

Lola lifts a bottle out of the box—the same bottle she's cut into. She reads the label—"Rosemary grapefruit daily conditioner for normal to dry hair. Leave-in." Lola dips two fingers into the bottle and comes out with more cream.

The trunk ride has messed up her hair, ratting several stray strands together. Lola slicks the cream against her matted hair. When she runs her fingers through it, the tangles have disappeared into straight, smooth lines.

Motherfucker. This isn't the stash. This back room isn't a front. She can forget pizza for dinner, or even a painless death for her and for Lucy.

"Lola?" The little girl must have seen the thoughts flashing across Lola's face, sweat springing from her pores as panic sets in. "What's wrong?"

"Nothing."

"Do you want that conditioner? Is that why we're here?"

"No. I thought . . . I was looking for something else."

"You mean the powder," Lucy says, and when Lola's chin springs up, sharp, to look at Lucy, the little girl is hanging her head, ashamed at her own smarts.

"What do you know about the powder?" Lola asks, keeping her voice even, not happy, not disappointed. Disappointment is worse than anger to a child. Of course, Maria had never been sober long enough to feel disappointment in Lola. Maria didn't feel anything but fucked up or wanting to be fucked up. How simple. How nice.

"I know it's worth a lot," Lucy says.

"Right. And you know you should stay away from it," Lola says, still even.

Lucy nods. "But we can't. Not here."

"There's no powder here."

"Not in this room," Lucy says.

Lola steps toward Lucy, trying to take in the little girl with her head hanging and her left and right sets of toes turned toward each other in un-self-conscious innocence. She tries to memorize her now, the sleek black part right down the middle of her hanging head, the thick eyebrows that will torment her as an adolescent trying to tame her changing body. If she gets that far.

"What do you mean?" Lola asks, her voice taking on a soothing tone as she lifts the girl's chin out of shame. Lucy looks up at her with solemn eyes.

"It's in the other room," Lucy says.

"What other room?"

Lucy points toward the front.

"How do you know that?"

Lucy hangs her head again, fighting the slight force of Lola's hand on her chin.

She removes a bottle of shampoo from behind her back, economy size, so large Lola can't believe she hasn't noticed it before.

"I was going to take it," Lucy confesses. "For you. But it was wrong."

"I get it. I do. And it was good of you. But you're right. Stealing

is wrong." Lola has never imagined herself preaching such a sancti-
monious black-and-white lesson. It makes her skin crawl now, right
versus wrong, good versus evil. All sides are interchangeable—east
becomes west depending on where you're standing.

"No. I mean the weight was wrong."

Lucy hands the bottle over to Lola, and she's right—the heft is
wrong for a bottle of liquid this size. Lola unscrews the top. The
powder is packed so tightly that it spills on the floor, dollars scattering across the concrete.

Holy shit, Lola wants to say. But she can't, because Lucy is here.

Lola takes Lucy by the hand, rushing her from the back room to
the front. When they scurry onto the gleaming tile, the scary beautiful one is waiting for them.

"I call him," the scary beautiful one says.

"Excuse me?" Lola says, what she imagines to be a polite smile
she's never had occasion to use pasted across her face.

"Mr. Waterston. I call him," the woman says, and Lola sees the
portable phone in her hand. But Lola is confused by her tenses—
does she mean she's already called him, or she's going to call him?
Either way, the woman's look is fierce, and Lola knows there's no
talking them out of this one.

"We want to buy this shampoo," Lola says, holding up the now-
sealed bottle Lucy was planning to pocket.

"No," the woman says. "I not listening."

Lola grabs another bottle from the shelf—dandruff shampoo.
She screws off the lid and, as the scary beautiful one gives off a
siren's wail that seems to shake the windows in their frames, dumps
the dandruff-white powder onto what used to be the clean floor.
Lola does the same with the next bottle and the next, until the
three Asian ladies surround her in a circle of screaming. Lola keeps
turning her body so she's always shielding Lucy, even though these
women have no weapons other than their shrill voices.

She hears the clanging of the bell on the door. The fat man
appears, panting and sweating through his tailored suit. Behind
him, the muscleman almost collides with his boss, who stops short
to bend over, hands on knees, and recover.

In the next second, the storage room door opens, and a pajama-clad Eldridge appears, Mandy beside him in plaid sleep pants and a gray tank top. *They have a baby,* Lola remembers. *They were probably trying to sleep.* They must have woken too abruptly to bother bringing muscle, because they appear to be alone.

"What's going on, Emily?" Eldridge says to the scary beautiful one.

"Eldridge," Mandy says, because she's had time to look at Lola, to look at the fat man, and to see the tall, tough man behind him. She knows this shit is real.

Eldridge zeroes in on the fat man, a light of recognition dancing in his WASP-blue eyes. Then he says, "Juan Gomez."

The muscleman stands up straighter. The fat man looks indignant. So that's the fat man's name, Lola thinks, used so sparingly it stings like a slap.

"And you are?" the fat man asks.

"Eldridge Waterston."

"Mandy Waterston."

To his credit, the fat man nods at them both.

"I thought there would only be one of you."

"We're a team," Eldridge says.

"You're married?"

The fat man looks from man to woman, confused at this feisty chestnut-haired, bump-nosed, would-be beauty with several years on her husband. In his country, in his position, a man does not marry an older woman. The muscleman has lit another cigarette, taking in the scene as he would on a sidewalk outside a bar—slow and lingering, amused, thankful their problems aren't his.

"You should be ashamed of yourselves," Juan Gomez says. He looks around the beauty supply store. "Acquiring your product from terrorists."

"There's a demand in this town for quality product. There are people with higher standards who don't buy from you because you cater to a different clientele."

"Quite well, in fact. We're merely a niche service," Eldridge follows up his wife's statement with some ass-kissing.

Again, Juan Gomez takes stock of the rows of product disguised as shampoo, and he says, "This does not look like a niche service."

"Our customers are not your customers is what we mean," Mandy tries.

"I don't understand."

Lola has had enough of these people tiptoeing around the race aspect. "She means they sell to white people."

"Yet you attempted to supply one of my largest customers with your product. A product you claim is too good for the ghetto," Juan Gomez says, and for a second, Lola is on his side, brown against white, even though she knows as soon as he's done with these two, he'll slit her throat at best.

"We were foolish. It won't happen again," Mandy says. Lola notices at the same time as Eldridge's wife that all the Asian women have disappeared. Lola wonders if she can do the same, but she is no longer a shadow leader. She has made herself matter, and now she can't escape.

"Give me the heroin your police officer stole, plus another two million in interest, and we have a deal."

Eldridge and Mandy look at each other. Lola wonders if one of them will cave first and give up Bubba, or if they will stay a team until their respective painful ends.

"We don't know where he took it," Eldridge says.

"You are his boss, and you don't know where he put your heroin?"

"We don't know. That's the truth," Mandy says, in a tone that lets Lola know it is. But isn't Bubba on their payroll? Didn't he swoop in when he heard the drop got fucked up to rescue the gym bag with its two million in product before anyone could log it into evidence? Isn't Bubba their contingency plan?

"Enough," the fat man says. "Tie them up."

The muscleman flicks his cigarette butt onto the clean floor, and Lola sees Mandy frown. Is she sad that he's marred her sparkling tile? The muscleman takes her first, and Lola watches with admiration as Mandy fights this losing battle, kicking her legs out from under her so that the muscleman is lifting her in the air by her wrists.

Eldridge lunges at the fat man, churning out expletives Lola has never heard any white man use. But the muscleman is on him in an instant, Mandy's wrists and ankles already bound, and he wrestles her husband to the tile in under ten seconds.

Together, Mandy and Eldridge yell and sob underneath their multimillions in heroin. They have no muscle of their own with them now. But Lola has Lucy here with her, watching. She can't just let this screaming couple across from her die. She's going to have to fight their battle for them.

Lola eyes the muscleman's discarded cigarette butt, seeing a tiny flicker of flame rising up from the ash. A baby dragon drawing its first breath.

In one quick movement, she swipes a bottle of nail polish remover from the shelf. Its packaging is clear, its contents liquid. The acetone slosh is not a front. It's the real thing, and it's flammable. To her, right now, this two-dollar economy-size bottle is worth more than all the heroin in this place. She starts for the cigarette butt, but when she turns, Lucy is holding it out to her in two open palms, as if she's letting a butterfly fly free.

Lola is too thankful for the little girl's worldliness to let the panic for Lucy's bright future fighting cartel leaders and drug kingpins overpower her relief.

Lola strikes flame to alcohol and casts the concoction atop the pile of heroin on the floor. The fire that sparks there shoots up, high as Eldridge is tall. The fat man jumps back, shouting his own curses at the muscleman in Spanish—*moron, death, pain, idiot, asshole.*

Lola uses the time his curses have bought her to take the box cutter to the duct tape around Mandy's wrists and ankles. The fat man is still cursing at the muscleman as she goes for Eldridge, pushing Lucy behind her every few seconds.

"Run," Lola tells Mandy as she moves on to Eldridge. Mandy doesn't move. She's not looking at her husband, though. It's Lucy she sees, a child surrounded by growing flames. Mandy reaches out a hand to the little girl. When Lucy looks to Lola for permission to go with this strange, kind, fierce woman, Lola nods. She knows somewhere deep in her gut that Mandy will not hurt her child. "There's a door in back," Lola says.

Mandy gives her husband one last look, then she and Lucy are gone, flames springing up behind them as the fire transitions from warmth and light to certain death, feeding on the air and the acetone, growing.

The fat man and the muscleman have started stocking their arms with beauty bottles—shampoo, conditioner, hairspray. They are pocketing as much of the stash as they can before it burns. The drugs take precedence, over her, over Lucy, over Eldridge. Lola still has to save him, though.

"Gotta get the fuck out," Lola says to Eldridge as she cuts his bonds.

"We have to take the product," Eldridge says. "We have to save it."

Lola jerks her finger toward the fat man and the muscleman. "Let them deal with that. You can take it back outside."

"No," Eldridge says, and he leaps from his broken bonds up toward the shelves, the thick, smoky air licking at his arms and face. He moves with a ferocity the fat man doesn't have, because this is his turf, these are his drugs, and if Lola doesn't stop him, he'll die defending them.

White men will do anything to protect their power, Lola thinks.

She has to get Eldridge out of here. Mandy saved Lucy. She has to return the favor.

Lola strides to Eldridge and sucks in just enough air to speak clearly. "If you don't come with me right now, I will slit your baby's throat." She wishes she weren't able to sound like she means it.

Eldridge believes it. He drops the bottle in his hands because he must have seen a capability in her she knows is there, somewhere deep down, a coldness that makes her Lola.

He follows her as she leads the way through the gray, choking air to the back.

As they emerge into the fresh night and Eldridge makes a run for it, away from his drugs and away from her, it is not relief Lola feels, but self-hatred for being able to so easily convince Eldridge she would take an innocent life.

THIRTY-SEVEN

SHOOT UP

The alley behind the fiery beauty supply store is dark, but the orange glow of the flames behind her illuminates a path for Lola. She is running alone, arms pumping, legs springing off pavement. She is out of breath. She sucks in air but gets smoke instead, then has to stop to cough up what doesn't belong. She doesn't know where Eldridge went, but she got him out alive. That is what matters.

They took the same back exit Mandy and Lucy must have taken, but she doesn't see them now. If the Asian women escaped—as she's assuming they did, having no dog in a battle over white powder—she doesn't see any sign of them.

She sees headlights at the alley's opening ahead. A street. Cars. Help. It's only now Lola remembers she's not wearing any shoes. No wonder the Asian ladies were suspect. Something has pierced the tough hide of her sole, and when she bends to examine her foot, she finds a triangle shard of glass, green glass, the same color as Andrea's eyes.

Where the fuck is the prosecutor with the cops?

The plan never included Lola setting fire to what she thought was Eldridge's stash. Still, she figures it's a nice touch for Andrea to put in the case file against the fat man. He'll take the blame when the LAPD arrests him. No one has to know Lola was there. She can remain a shadow leader, if not in her own neighborhood, to the cops and prosecutors who are supposed to practice right and quash wrong.

She reaches the end of the alley, limp-running with the shard stuck in her sole. The street is a main thoroughfare, peppered with fast-food drive-throughs and dollar stores, both treat Meccas for the poor and oppressed. She waves her arms above her head, and she must look like a true battered woman—shoeless, bleeding, and streaked with the remnants of a building angry flame. *Is there ash on her cheek?* she thinks, and when she checks with a finger, the tip comes back smudged black.

A shitty pickup truck pulls over. The back holds gardening tools—a rake, a shovel, hedge trimmers. Lola knows it will be a brown man behind the wheel, wearing a short-sleeved collared shirt stained yellow under the arms.

"Can I have a ride?" Lola asks in Spanish. He nods, too tired from his backbreaking work to ask questions whose answers he thinks he can tell by her appearance. Angry man beats woman to shit, she runs away, a pure victim. But it is dangerous to judge people by their appearance.

"Where?" he asks.

"I need to find my . . . daughter," she says. "She's here. Somewhere."

If the landscaper notices the flames licking the black sky a block over, he doesn't say anything. Instead, he turns his wheel to the right, circling back, and Lola keeps her eyes peeled for Lucy and Mandy.

It is easy to find them. One more turn, one more gleam of headlights, and Lola catches sight of the duo, ducking behind a Dumpster in another alley, one over from the beauty supply store's back entrance. To Lola's relief, Mandy is holding the little girl close, stroking her hair and speaking something soft in her ear. Lucy is safe. For now.

Lola feels the landscaper's eyes on her.

"You see them?" he asks, and she catches the lick of tongue

against lip. It is a hungry gesture, a gesture of wanting, and it cautions her. *Don't judge people by their appearance.*

"No," she says, shaking her head.

It's a long few seconds as he lets the truck idle in the alley. Lola prays to someone that Lucy and Mandy don't see her sitting in this passenger's seat and spring from their hiding place to greet her. Finally, the landscaper puts his foot to the gas and guns it out of the alley.

"Where are we going?" Lola asks, though she knows now she's misjudged him and the situation.

The landscaper doesn't answer as he swings another right and parks next to the town car whose trunk Lola knows all too well. Of course the fat man has more than one muscleman, although this guy doesn't seem to be muscle. She looks back to the shovel and the buckets. No, she thinks, this man isn't muscle. He is cleanup. He is the one who will make sure no one ever finds her body.

"Fuck," she says, under her breath, she thinks, but the cleanup man cracks a smile.

"Kind of music you like?" he asks in Spanish.

"What?"

"I take requests. Sometimes more than one. In case it takes a while."

It dawns on Lola that he's referring to her death. His simple, sick kindness—offering to play her out—touches somewhere deep, making it seem like this, her impending death, is the way it should be. But that can't be. Lola has never considered herself a good person, but she knows the evil in her is less than the evil in others.

She thinks of Lucy crouching beside the Dumpster, Eldridge's business-savvy wife with her. Lucy is with a role model. They are safe. That matters.

The passenger's-side door opens, and the muscleman appears beside her. He takes her by the arm, but his touch is gentle. The tenderness sends a shiver of fright through Lola's body. She can barely limp across the pavement, the sole of her foot aching where the glass has made its home.

Lola wonders what death they have planned for her. How many songs will it last? How much will it hurt? Lola doesn't want music she likes. She doesn't want the pain to ruin her love for her favorite songs, upbeat pop music Garcia can't stand. When she cranks it in the car, he scrunches up his nose and asks when noise started passing for music. She calls him an old man. He says sure, but he's her old man. Lola wonders if he and Kim were arguing over the radio when Garcia, distracted, slammed into a semi and she lost their baby. Or was he distracted by the thought of Lola shooting Kim's brother between the eyes only a few days before, of wanting to tell Kim but not being able to, having sworn his loyalty to Lola.

Her thoughts shift back to the present, and it's a relief, her death a puzzle with a definitive answer. She will never know if Garcia loves Kim more than he ever loved her, or if he just got tired of carrying the secret of Carlos's murder. It is a complicated question. Death is simple—stabbing, shooting, hanging. The cartel has two vehicles—the cleanup guy's pickup and the fat man's town car. They could draw and halve her, although she doesn't know if the cartel considers only pulling someone apart in two pieces cheating. Probably doesn't take as long, either, ripping a human body along the dotted line of the torso, leaving limbs attached to upper and lower halves.

The beauty supply store burns behind the fat man as he gets out of the car. Lola spots the duffel bag, her duffel bag, there—two million in cash. She has the box cutter in her pocket. She could . . . But she is tired. Lucy is safe with a Westside woman who can take care of her better than Lola. She remembers Ms. Laura and the kindergarten and thinks how the conversation would have gone differently if Mandy had been there instead of Lola.

"It's time," the fat man says.

"Shooting, stabbing, drawing and halving," Lola says, and she laughs, her head lolling back as she gets on her knees without being asked. She's accepting her fate.

The fat man doesn't know what to do with Lola's willingness to die. He seems to have had some kind of speech prepared, but she has surprised him. He's going to take the heroin he could get. He has his two million in cash in the car. Soon he will have a dead Lola. He can start fresh.

Lola has flooded his earth with fire, cleaning house like God did with Noah, but she will not survive the test. Her own scorched earth is about to burn her dead.

Will it be fire? Lola hadn't considered that. She can use the box cutter, if the pain gets too much, but they can tell people about the little second-generation Mexican who thought she could run with the big boys, the one they watched cook and writhe as her skin sizzled like a rotisserie chicken.

The fat man nods to the muscleman, and he disappears into the town car as Lola waits with Juan Gomez in awkward silence.

"Are you married?" Lola asks the fat man.

"What?"

"Do you have a wife?"

"Yes."

"Do you love her?"

"Yes. Very much," the fat man says.

"That's nice," Lola says. The fat man looks at her in a way that tells her he expects her to continue, to make some sort of plea for her life. She realizes he must like that part, the begging and pleading, the power it gives him. But she is withholding this pleasure from him. For a second she considers it, what the hell, why not make his life a little better. But she is tired, and her foot is throbbing, and she wants to get this over with.

The muscleman emerges from the town car, and she sees it, how she will die.

"No," she breathes.

The fat man's eyes light up with her show of fear, for it is fear she feels now, her heart pumping fast again instead of preparing for a permanent sleep.

"We did our research," he says in a rehearsed tone that lets Lola know he has practiced in front of a mirror. "An addict for a mother. But you always abstained."

The muscleman holds a syringe, a tourniquet, and several bindles of powder.

"No," Lola says, but it's more a quiet mouthing, since her throat and lips have gone dry. She tries to stand, but the muscleman pushes her down. His movement is mechanical, and he can't look her in the eye. He . . . feels bad? *Then stand up,* she wants to tell him, *help me.* She feels his boot on her back, pressing her belly into pavement, and she squirms, wriggling her neck so she can strain her face toward his. She lets the muscleman see her plea. To her surprise, he leans close, an invitation for her to speak her case privately. "Stab . . . me," she says, and her hand retrieves the box cutter from her pocket. The muscleman looks at the weapon, then shakes his head.

"This will not be so painful," he says in accented English, too soft for the fat man to hear. "It could be it will feel good."

He is wrong. But he doesn't take the box cutter away, until the fat man pads over, his shoes making no noise as they cross the pavement. The cartel leader snatches the box cutter from Lola's hands. Behind him, fire springs up, higher and higher, and from here, on her knees, it looks like the flames might lick the moon, so far up and quiet in the sky.

Lola is going to die, with the moon peaceful up there, looking down on her.

"Tie her," the fat man orders.

Lola feels the rubber of the tourniquet tightening on her arm until it shuts off the blood flow. She sees a fat blue vein popping from her skin, clamoring for a chance at the drug. She sees the needle drawing up the black tar, magically liquid now.

Somewhere in the distance, she hears sirens. The fire department. The police. Maybe both. But she can tell from the low wail that they are too far to save her.

"Well," the fat man says, his tone urging the muscleman to get on with it. He stands close to the muscleman, all fat and bull, yet he could not do what the muscleman is doing. He couldn't beat the shit out of Lola in a strip mall parking lot. He can't inject her with her worst nightmare next to a burning beauty supply store. He has someone to do that for him.

The thought angers Lola. She sees the tarp again, Hector begging for mercy, but in her kingdom it is Lola who wields the knife herself, against Hector, against Darrel King. She is the invisible blade that stabbed Hector in the back by sending him to prison.

She has no respect for the fat man. But she has no blade.

The pain of the tourniquet subsides, and Lola feels throbbing from her bare foot.

The muscleman's fingers turn her vein toward him. The tip of the needle touches Lola's skin, and she is surprised to feel a tingle of pleasure at the sting. For a second, she wants to surrender. Has she ever felt bliss like the kind black tar will give her?

"What are you waiting for?" the fat man says in Spanish.

"How do we know it will kill her?" the muscleman asks.

The fat man is quiet, first in surprise that the muscleman has talked back, then in anger. "If it doesn't, we will find another way. But it will. It is in her blood, to die this way."

In her blood. In her blood.

Lola curls away from the muscleman, writhing into the fetal position, going back to when Maria gave birth to her, a curling, squirming ball of innocence. She lets out a wail that sends both men stepping back, scared.

Her hands close on the triangle of glass in her foot. She feels the blood of her palms springing forth as she rips the shard from her sole.

She jumps up, faces the fat man, and plunges the glass into the folds of his neck.

She feels the shard sink through layers of fat and gristle to open up the artery that starts to leak his life's blood.

The fat man looks into Lola's eyes, and she sees his pupils light up in the fire-lit dark. "You," he says, as if he recognizes her for the first time. Then he crumples to the pavement, where the pebbled concrete starts to soak up his blood.

Lola hears a low whistle behind her. It's the cleanup man, whom she's forgotten. When she turns, she sees him surveying the fat man's body, then looking to his supplies, calculating this unexpected job. He is a hired gun, chained by fear of the cartel. Is the muscleman the same?

When Lola turns to him, she finds him lighting another cigarette. The sirens are getting louder. These men aren't going to kill her.

"Run," she says, the order she has had to give so much lately.

"And him?" the cleanup man asks.

"I'll take care of it," Lola says.

The muscleman is about to put out his cigarette and throw the butt on the ground.

"No," Lola says. "Don't leave your shit here."

The muscleman nods thanks. Then he gets in the passenger's seat of the cleanup guy's truck, and they are gone.

Lola has just enough time to grab the duffel bag of cash from the fat man's town car and stash it in a Dumpster one alley over. When she starts back toward the death scene, she sees cop cars and fire trucks peeling in, hoses and guns out.

She sees Andrea emerge from an unmarked sedan. Sergeant Bubba gets out of the passenger's seat. Andrea looks to the dead fat man on the ground, and even from this distance, Lola sees the flash of anger in her green eyes. Andrea looks around, searching for Lola, who steps out from behind the Dumpster in her bare feet and cutoffs. Andrea makes an excuse to Sergeant Bubba, who must have come here to disappear the inevitable score that Lola didn't have time to get from the town car. Mandy and Eldridge were telling the truth, she realizes now. They don't know what Bubba did with the heroin he rescued from the drop, because he's not on their payroll. He's on Andrea's.

"I was supposed to arrest him. He was supposed to live," Andrea says, jerking a thumb toward the fat man.

"Oops," Lola says.

THIRTY-EIGHT

NEW HORIZONS

Lola's knees smart at the contact with the hard brown linoleum of Maria's kitchen. It's been two days since the fat man ordered her on the ground and shot up with black tar, but still her knees ache with the memory of the pebbles grinding against bone.

"You don't have to do that," Maria objects from her post in the living room. Lola can only see the back of her head, black-gray hair centered on the sofa—how does she do that, pick the exact middle ground to watch her game shows and telenovelas? The television is too loud, and Lola hears a man confessing his undying love for a woman. She doesn't need to see the woman to know she is sobbing.

"Your floor gets dirty," Lola says.

"It's stained."

Lola can't argue with that. She turns to Maria just long enough to see Lucy sitting on the beige carpet, her dollhouse in front of her.

Mandy, the owner of record of the beauty supply store, had returned Lucy to Lola when she showed up on the scene, demanding that the police stop their investigation and tell her exactly how her building caught fire. In the wake of Mandy's overwhelming demands, the police had neglected to notice Lola and Lucy walking away from the scene, hand in hand, as the warehouse burned bright behind them.

Now, Lucy is holding two dolls, a woman and a child. For a second, the little girl just stares at the dolls. Then, she places the woman's arms around the child. Lola is so proud she wants to jump off Maria's kitchen floor and squeeze Lucy tight. But she doesn't.

Instead, Lucy peers back at Lola and asks, "Am I doing it right?"

"Yeah," is all Lola can say without choking on the lump in her throat. "You're doing it right."

Lucy turns back to the dolls and their house.

"See, that's Marco, and he's in love with Lucinda. Lucinda . . . that's like your name, isn't it?" Maria says, her tone that of a teacher imparting an important lesson. Lola takes comfort in her mother's consistent cluelessness. It would never occur to Maria that someone would be able to tune out a telenovela.

Lola knows without looking that Lucy is nodding out of politeness. Still, the little girl is smart enough not to trust Maria with her words. Not yet. She'll have to earn that.

"Men can be convincing, when they want," Maria says.

"Maria," Lola calls, a warning. Lola is fine with leaving Lucy in the same room with Maria when she is here, but she will never forget the day she came home from school to find Maria on the sofa, Hector beside her, the tinfoil and powder and spoon on the coffee table.

"Sorry," Maria says now. She's so good at apologizing for the shit that doesn't matter.

Lola had told her mother it looked like Hector would serve some time for Darrel's murder. Instead of railing at Lola for letting her brother take the fall for something she had done, Maria had nodded and said, "That sounds right."

Lola had wanted to push it, but Maria made it so she didn't have to.

"You did what you had to do because your brother made you."

Substitute "mother" for "brother" in that sentence and Maria could have explained her daughter's whole fucking life.

Now, Lola continues the futile, painful, sadistic scrubbing of stained tile. The kitchen has begun to fill with the scent of baking, bubbling queso and mole. Why does she do this? Because she is a daughter, and daughters take care of their mothers. Also, she doesn't want to go home.

She tried, the first night, going home to Garcia, but the fat white men on their foxhunting chair felt foreign to her. Garcia had washed all the dishes and put them in their proper places. The bed was made, the sheets clean. Maybe Garcia meant the clean house to be a comfort to her, a nice gesture, but Lola looked at it as a cover-up. She knows she can't go back there, so she stayed here, under the same roof with her mother and Lucy, last night. It was an odd night, with Lola making up the sofa for her and Lucy, but Maria insisting they take the bed. Maria sang Lucy a bedtime song and told her a bedtime story about princesses, with the caveat that Lucy should not strive to be a princess, because what did they really do once they had snagged a man? Lola had wondered when her mother got wise to the fact that men saved nothing and no one. Maria had hugged Lola good night, and Lola had let her, thinking of her mother telling Lorraine that her son, Darrel, was dead, of delivering bad news, mother to mother, when Lola just wanted to run. Right before Lola was going to shut out the bedroom light, Maria had padded in with some antibiotic cream for Lola's scabbed knees. She had dropped it on the table next to Lola with no questions, no how did you skin your knees, just left it there in case it could help. Lola had shut out the lights and pulled a sleeping Lucy close against her as she shed some silent tears in the dark, because Lola had understood why she had come here, to Maria's, if only for a few days.

It is because she has always been her mother's daughter with the straight-line mouth, trying to do the right thing in the wrong way.

Lola works for herself now. Jorge and Marcos are still her soldiers. They showed up at the fat man's death scene in time to whisk Lola away in their newfound Prius. Jorge had talked the whole ride home about reducing the gang's carbon footprint, and Lola found his loyal talk of the future so soothing she had fallen asleep on Marcos's shoulder. They will change their name to the Crenshaw Four, which Lola has convinced herself has a nice ring to it. She has dropped Carlos from the count because she doesn't fucking feel like including people who don't deserve her respect. She will not leave Hector out of her count. He is her brother. He went to prison with his hands up in surrender because she willed it.

Andrea, the true queenpin, didn't get to arrest the fat man, her competition, to try him, but who was she kidding? Feds would have been on a wanted cartel head like flies on rancid, rotting meat. Sure, the cartel might send another man, another leader and this one won't be fat, maybe, or maybe he will. Lola saved Eldridge's life. She doesn't know if she will ever see him or Mandy again, but Lola will love the woman forever for covering Lucy's body with her own so no one would see the little girl, curled up between those Dumpsters.

Now, the knock at the door brings Lola to her feet in a surprised instant. Maria starts up, but Lola stops her.

"I'll get it."

Lola opens the door on Sergeant Bubba. He's sipping a smoothie from a Jamba Juice cup, every inch the New Age Westside LAPD officer.

"Yeah?" Lola says.

"How's your day going, Ms. Vasquez?" he asks.

"Fuckin' great, pig," Lola says. They are dancing, cop talking to criminal, role-playing like they're actually all good or all evil.

"Pretty language for a lady."

"Fuck you." Lola says it loud, so Maria's neighbors can hear her. She doesn't want anyone seeing her being polite to a cop, but she also doesn't care for Sergeant Bubba. He's corrupt, and unlike her, he should know better.

"Wouldn't be talking like that to me, if I were you."

"Why's that?"

"She knows you burned that place to the ground." Sergeant Bubba plants a scrap of paper in Lola's hand. "You have a nice day," he says.

Lola uncurls the scrap of paper and finds a Westside address and a time. Tonight.

It is from Andrea. Andrea, whose stash Lola sent up in smoke, whose front man she almost let burn to death trying to save a warehouse of heroin, whose cartel whale she stabbed through the neck and watched bleed out in under a minute.

Andrea is the head of it all. She imports the drugs, manipulates the system so there's always a front person, a kingpin she'll never prosecute. If Andrea is smart, and she is, she's cleaning up drug addicts and drug money at her husband's rehab facility. She's creating drug addicts and curing them, and she's making and laundering a shit ton of money.

Fuck.

"Who was that?"

"Cop."

"What?" Maria's arms go to Lucy, pulling her close. It's the protection instinct prevalent in this neighborhood, where cops are the villains. Lola used to want to think differently, but now, why bother?

"No big deal," Lola says. She doesn't know what to do. If she goes tonight, she's working for Andrea. But she doesn't want to work for someone else, not even this woman she can't help respecting. Still, Lola knows the Crenshaw Four are no match for Andrea.

She needs to rebuild her own army.

There's another knock. Maybe Sergeant Bubba needs directions. This time, Maria doesn't move. She keeps Lucy close as Lola walks back to the door with a sigh.

"What?"

But when she swings it open, she finds the cartel's muscleman, clearing his throat, as if he, like his dead boss, has prepared a speech. It takes Lola a second to realize the cleanup man is standing next to him, smaller, no less intimidating.

Lola steps out of her mother's home, shutting the door behind her. If they're here to kill her, she might as well not make it easy.

She moves closer to them, her face against the muscleman's. "You better get the fuck out of here and sit your ass on a plane to Mexico." Her Spanish is fast and rounded and beautiful.

"No," the muscleman says.

"You're not fucking killing me on my mother's doorstep. Assholes," Lola says, sweeping her eyes over the cleanup man so he has his own chance to be insulted. But it doesn't shake him. He just stands there, his hands clasped behind his back.

Lola starts back in the house. She's got knives inside. She's going to go out swinging.

"We're not here for that," the muscleman says, and Lola stops. She should never have turned her back to them, she thinks. She waits for the knife to land somewhere between her ribs, but it doesn't.

When she turns to face them, their heads are bowed. To her.

"We want to work for you."

The statement takes a second to get into Lola's brain, and when it does, she's telling them no. "Look, I got this crazy prosecutor bitch on my back already."

"We know," the muscleman says.

"Let us help," the cleanup man says.

It is his plea, simple and kind, that makes Lola's head bow back. A nod. A promise. The beginning of a new army. A new horizon. And Lola can change her gang's name back to the Crenshaw Six.

When she shuts the door on her new soldiers, she doesn't fear the scrap of paper, the assumption she will show. She can fight back, even if it won't be easy. Climbing never is. It's the falling that's fast and painless.

"Who was that? Are you in some kind of trouble, Lola?" Maria has come over to the door, keeping her voice down so Lucy can't hear. She's continuing to behave like a mother.

"I can take care of myself, Mom." Lola sighs, a beleaguered daughter.

Lola sees the smile playing at Maria's lips. "You called me Mom," Maria says.

"Yeah," Lola says, as if she meant to all along.

Maria tosses a look back to Lucy and speaks to the little girl like she's following the telenovela blaring on the screen instead of playing with her dollhouse. "That woman's had so much work done. There is nothing wrong with aging gracefully, Lucinda. Remember that." Then Maria turns back to Lola. "What can I do to help?"

Lola pauses before she starts to hand her mother the scrub

brush, but Maria grabs for it with eager, wrinkling hands. Her mother is getting old. Her mother is losing time to make amends.

Lola walks into the living room and sits on the floor with Lucy and her dollhouse. "Can I play, too?"

"Sure," Lucy says.

"You like your dollhouse?"

"It's the best," Lucy says.

"Oh, yeah?"

"I can make the dolls stand up or sit down. I can make them happy or sad."

"Yeah," Lola says. "You can."

And they play together, Lola and Lucy, as behind them, Maria scrubs linoleum that will never get clean.

ACKNOWLEDGMENTS

My sincere thanks to Sonya Roth, who spoke to me about the ins and outs of the Los Angeles District Attorney's office and specifics relating to the drug trade here. To Simone Shay, a prosecutor who's never met me, but whom I got to see in action while serving jury duty at the Van Nuys courthouse. To Yahira "Flakiss" Garcia, whose music inspired me and helped me keep going with this book.

To Nathan Roberson, my editor, who took a chance on me and has grown this book by leaps and bounds. To Eve Attermann, my book agent, who is my constant champion. To Blake Fronstin, my television agent, who is the best at what he does and might get around to reading this one day. To Oly Obst and Devon Bratton, my managers. Oly, thank you for being a wealth of knowledge and encouragement. Devon, thank you for your everlasting patience and for holding my hand through every draft of everything I've ever written. To Denise Thé and Amanda Segel, two of the best writers and people I know, thank you for your constant support and teaching me how to get through anything with grace.

To Veronica Gomez and Lucy Valdizon, who made the writing of this book possible. To Lauren Rawlins, for always being on my side. To my mother-in-law, Tobi Ruth Love, who always likes what I write and lets me know I am loved, and my father-in-law, Jay Love, the best Pop-Pop around. To my dad, Michael Scrivner, who taught me to always keep my guard up and to always empathize. To my mother, Georgene Scrivner, who embodies strength, kindness, and love. You both gave me every opportunity—you gave me everything, actually. I love you.

To David, my husband, my partner, and to Leah, our fierce girl. Thank you.